THE SLEEPLESS

THE
SLEEPLESS

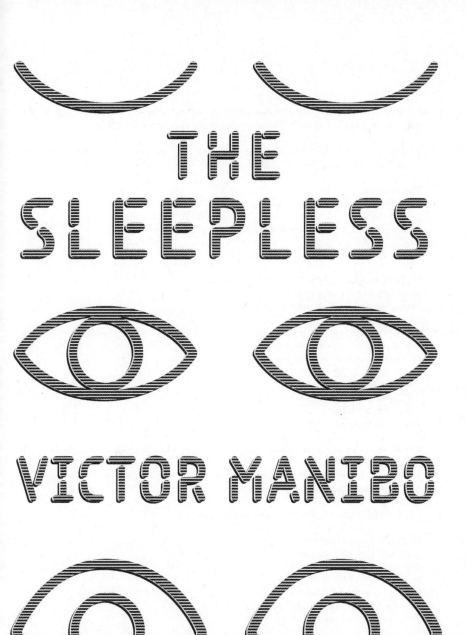

VICTOR MANIBO

The Sleepless
Copyright © 2022 by Victor Manibo

First published in North America by Erewhon Books, LLC, in 2022.

Edited by Sarah T. Guan

"Lorca & Jimenez: Selected Poems" by Robert Bly
Copyright © 1973, 1997 by Robert Bly
Reprinted by permission of Beacon Press, Boston

Erewhon Books
2 W. 29th Street, Suite 3S
New York, NY 10001
www.erewhonbooks.com

Erewhon books are available at special discounts when purchased in bulk for premiums and sales promotions as well as for fundraising or educational use. Special editions or book excerpts can also be created to specification. For details, send an email to specialmarkets@workman.com.

Library of Congress Control Number: 2022937055

ISBN 978-1-64566-046-0 (hardcover)
ISBN 978-1-64566-049-1 (ebook)

Cover design by Dana Li
Interior design by Cassandra Farrin
Lens by Adrien Coquet from NounProject.com
Author photo by Sean Collishaw

Printed in the United States of America

First US Edition: August 2022
10 9 8 7 6 5 4 3 2 1

To my father, Nelson,
who taught me how to love books,
and who would have loved this one.

Nobody is sleeping in the sky. Nobody, nobody.
Nobody is sleeping.
If someone does close his eyes,
a whip, boys, a whip!
Let there be a landscape of open eyes
and bitter wounds on fire.
No one is sleeping in this world. No one, no one.
I have said it before.
No one is sleeping.

    —"City That Does Not Sleep," Federico García Lorca

THE
SLEEPLESS

Part

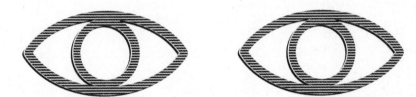

One

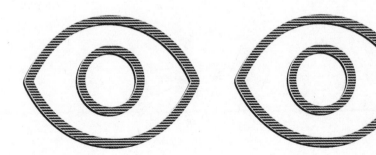

01.

Wednesday, 07/08/2043, 06:56 PM

In the last dream I ever had, I was eating a big, bloody hunk of steak. The details are hazy now: crisp white linens and a side of roasted potatoes, wood paneling, other faceless people at my table, and not much else. I don't recall the specific cut of meat, but it was definitely not a filet mignon; it was more like a porterhouse. The steak occupied the entire plate and threatened to spill over its border. I cut through the slab with a serrated knife, and, though I've had amazing steaks before, I have never felt anything as visceral as the frustration I felt when, before I could finish my plate, I woke up.

Dreams. It's been so blissful since I stopped having them, but lately, against my nature, they've been surfacing in my mind.

That last one in particular keeps coming back. To exorcise these thoughts, I've decided the best way was to act it out in real life: I've added cooking to my mile-long list of hobbies. I think I've finally mastered the perfect porterhouse. Or, I should say, porterhouse cooked just the way I like it. Medium-rare, with the right amount of sear. It took eight tries, meticulous timing, and calibrated heat on both sides, not to mention hours of instructional videos and tons of new kitchen supplies that I didn't yet own. My apartment has become a nightly test kitchen for steaks, but I got there eventually.

I admire the slab as it sizzles in the cast-iron pan. The timer counts down, and the stove promptly lowers the heat. The oven chimes as the roasted potatoes are done, and I move the spuds into the pan, gingerly placing each one in the right place and at the right angle. A sprig of rosemary across the top, and a dash of finishing salt, and it's ready for its close-up.

I take several pictures with the kitchen counter's top-view camera, scroll through the shots as they're beamed onto my visor, and then pick out the one that looks best. I post it on my news feed, no caption necessary. After I do, holo-ads materialize before my eyes: one for a set of Japanese steak knives, one for a Midtown chophouse, and a third for a ceramic barbecue grill. I pause on this last one, and wonder if there's enough space on the deck. Maybe after I have it redone. I wave the ads away with a flick of a finger, and they vanish.

I move the steak onto the carving board. A blood red jus seeps from its sinews. The firmness, the aroma, the right balance of browning and char—I nailed it.

After I've given the meat time to rest, I make one slice. One bite. It approaches, but does not quite reach, the sumptuousness of the steak in my last dream ever. As I did with the other failed attempts, I chuck the rest of the thing down the disposal.

The threat looms of another long night needing to be filled.

In the beginning, it was easy enough. I occupied myself by watching dozens of classic films that I'd always been meaning to watch. A lot of the movies I liked were adaptations, so I also read the source material. That's when I seriously moved on to books, and around the time I devised my lists.

I made goal lists and doggedly finished every item. I saw every Oscar Best Picture movie, finished every Pulitzer-winning novel. All of Hitchcock's films, Henry James's books, the entirety of *The Decline and Fall*. Then there were TV shows, podcasts, and of course, video games. So many video games.

I was consuming so much that, after only a few months, I felt psychically bloated. My brain tired of all the media, and my lists felt like drudgery, like I had been masochistically giving myself unnecessary homework. That's when I started to optimize my time by learning new skills.

I've progressively grown the number of languages I can speak, and recently completed Arabic II through a VR exchange program. I've mastered lockpicking, non-digital locks at least. I garden, if the box of soil I have up on the roof deck can count as one. I've learned how to write Gothic calligraphy and how to read Braille. How to weld, metalsmith, woodwork, build furniture with my own hands. How to play the violin, the double bass, the harmonica. How to knit and sew. How to juggle. How to finish a Rubik's cube with one hand tied behind my back. How to cook steaks.

And then there's poker. Talk about optimizing. Now I can fill my nights and make some scratch too. It's how I can afford this apartment, as well as all the toys and gear that I've accumulated for my less lucrative diversions. I'm quite good at it—I've had a lot of time to practice—though my online buddies keep teasing me about my tell, an alleged eye twitch when I've got a bad hand. I'm pretty sure that's jealousy talking, and even if I did have a tell, it hasn't stopped me yet from taking their money.

At some point in the past year, especially as the weather grew warmer, I felt the need to harness my extra time outdoors. At the turn of spring, I started running. I used my freed-up weekends to learn surfing and to train for dragon boat racing. I already have a blue belt in taekwondo, and as soon as I find a 24-hour dojo, I'm doing karate next. I've practiced all types of yoga, from Ashtanga to Vinyasa. I fence, I box, and once in a while, I get roped into a late-night game of pickup basketball with other folks in the building.

If for no other reason than this, I could never leave New York. Half the city's already Sleepless, or at least a convincing facsimile. Everyone's up at all hours, and up for doing any damn thing. No activity is too esoteric, no interest too specific. If I wanted to learn sailing, there are outfits all along the Hudson that can teach me. If I wanted to learn how to make chow fun from scratch, I know an eighty-year-old woman out in Flushing who gives private lessons. And if I wanted to join a grief support group for recently-dumped left-handed Asian male media professionals in their early thirties, I'm sure I could find one somewhere downtown.

As I wipe up the steak splatter on the counter, the buzzer beeps. I check the time. It's too early for the delivery to arrive. And in any case, we agreed that it had to be auto-couriered. Can't be too safe. Not with this package. I play the scenarios in my head, and I'm beginning to fume with anger as I approach the door.

I check the screen and am both relieved and petrified at the sight. Hannah.

For a second I think about not answering, but I can't help myself. I comb my hair with my grease-splattered fingers before opening the door.

"Are you alright? You look surprised," she says with no preliminaries.

"Well, this is a bit unexpected," I say, leaning in for a hug that she limply accepts.

I leave the door wide open and move aside. Her feet shuffle, and I subconsciously mimic her, doing the out-of-step dance of two people unsure of their footing. She wants to come in, but she decides to stay in the hallway instead.

Even as she restrains herself from entering, her attention has already wandered into the den. She peeks surreptitiously, no doubt judging the state of disarray. The pile of jackets on the couch, the empty takeout containers, the stacks of boxes still unpacked. The contents of my life that haven't quite reached their destinations: kitchen, bedroom, bath, storage.

I try to look unbothered. I would have cleaned if I had known she was dropping by, but the mess is also nothing she hasn't seen before.

A couple of times since I moved out of our Chelsea apartment, Hannah and I have slipped into our old habits. Nights that start with an errant message and a crosstown trip, ending in a guilt-ridden, awkward goodbye. There's always a twinge of regret the morning after, but one not strong enough to deter us from backsliding. She initiated, the last time.

It's been a while since—maybe a couple of months? I wait for her to decide. She doesn't meet my eyes.

"You might as well come in," I finally say, sliding an arm around her waist. "You've come all this way."

She flinches away from me. Slow enough to convey hesitation, but quick enough to show resolve. "I'm just here for the passport. Do you have it?"

For a second I think she's making up some thin excuse to drop by unannounced. She's not the type to forget things, and I myself have used the whole "I left something here" routine before. I have no idea what she's talking about, and it must show on my face, because instantly she rolls her eyes.

"Of course you forgot. Classic Jamie."

"I'm so sorry, I'm in the middle of this huge assignment and it's been crazy, and I . . ."

"Totally forgot about it. Yeah, I've heard this before."

I hold back the explanations. Work has been the standard scapegoat for my personal failures, and Hannah deserves better than the stock answer.

"Did we agree on Wednesday?" I ask. "I could have sworn . . ."

"Look, I really need it ASAP. I told you my flight's in a week."

"Yes, I remember now," I say, still not quite remembering. "I still need to look for it, but I'll get on that tonight."

"That's what you said last time."

"I promise. I'll do it right this second, just as soon as I—"

"Stop making promises and just do it."

The push and pull and pushback has a comforting familiarity. Our patterns are so intractable, hardened by the last five years into grooves in our language, our glances, in the way we touch each other. The way we keep reverting to each other. We're not together, not anymore, and though each of us sometimes forgets that, I've quit trying to figure out whatever this is.

"I'll be back tomorrow night," she warns. "You better have it ready."

She walks away, not waiting for me to respond.

❁

Thursday, 07/09/2043, 12:04 AM

The parcel drone beckons me onto the balcony, its red light blinking against the backdrop of the midnight cityscape. I rush out to meet it, assaulted by the whir of its propellers straining against the weight of its package. When I give it the all-clear, the drone sets down its delivery: a sturdy black box encased in a net of packing rope. A combination lock holds its lid shut.

The drone disengages and as soon as it flies out of my way, back into the cloudless sky, I drag the parcel into the apartment and slam the door shut behind me. I tear into the netting and, finding it too tight, I run to the kitchen to grab a knife. I slice through the cords then untangle the knots, fingers trembling, before finally pressing in the key code. The hiss and click are music to my ears. I then lift the lid as one does a treasure chest.

I'd searched and begged and dissembled and deceived, traded favors and secrets to get my hands on this. A thick stack of papers, maybe two reams' worth, each page printed with dates and names and figures and codes. I'd been at this a while, but there's still nothing as satisfying as holding a smoking gun in your hand.

For months, my energy's been focused on the July installment of *The Simon Parrish Files*, C+P Media's premier investigative news program. The episode will have been the culmination of hours upon hours of work, and when it airs on all the news feeds at month's end, it'll reveal a long-buried scheme involving Mason Dwyer, junior US senator from Minnesota, and how he funded his campaign with secret donations from anti-Sleepless hate groups.

Sleepless or not, I can't help but hate the guy. Dwyer first ran in 2036, around the time that the fear against hyperinsomniacs was at its peak. The election cycle fanned the flames, and the regulation of Sleepless persons was a platform issue on both sides of the aisle. At first, Dwyer didn't have a strong stance either way; he understood how deeply divided his purple state was. But by the time he ran for reelection, he was whistling a different tune: feeling the winds of change, he made pro-Sleepless legislation the centerpiece of his re-election campaign. Now the two-time junior senator—a former Marine reserve with dashing good looks and a picture-perfect middle American family—is rumored to be one of the frontrunners for the Republican primary in 2044.

As it turns out, the '36 Dwyer campaign got most of its spending money from the Senate Freedom Fund, a super PAC with unlimited funds from mostly anonymous donors. I say mostly because they're still required to keep a record of who's giving what, but the names are almost always holding companies with their own holding companies. A nesting doll of campaign corruption.

If you don't look too hard, you might miss the shell companies, the fictive entities through which organizations contribute to senate campaigns without having to report donor names. Organizations like the Alliance Defending Normalcy and Vanguards of Vigilance, which are still at the forefront of persecuting Sleepless persons. They advocate for the stringent monitoring of the Sleepless, and push for Sleepless discrimination in housing, the workplace, all spheres of social and political life. Those details alone would have been bad enough for Dwyer, but these groups also encouraged, funded, and sanctioned hate crimes. People died.

So you can imagine what kind of damage our piece could do to the good senator.

My boss Simon has been developing the Dwyer story for months, and since he has an entire team of dedicated professionals at his disposal, he delegated some pieces of the larger puzzle. As one of his assistant producers, my job has been to follow the money. I needed proof tying the Vanguards of Vigilance to the Freedom Fund super PAC and to Dwyer.

I spent hours of sifting through bank records, stock purchase agreements, capital investment receipts, from dozens of companies. The payoff from pulling on that thread is my source, an investment banker favored by less-than-savory organizations.

I can't say that the source has the purest intentions, but at least they're reliable. The sheafs of paper I hold in my hands prove it. The funds movements are all in here; I only need to assemble the data, separate wheat from chaff. My source previously gave me backdoor access to the firm's digital records, and if that were enough, my job would be done in an hour at most. But I can't sneak into their mainframe for extended periods of time, and besides, everything needs to be on paper. Simon wants the data quadruple-checked, and I very well can't have Simon himself hacking into an investment bank just so he can review what I've found. It's already a minor miracle I even got hard copies. So yeah, I gotta do this old-school. Pen and paper and marker and highlighter and stickie notes and flags. Good thing I've got an entire night with nothing to do.

✾

Thursday, 07/09/2043, 03:22 AM

I'm on hour three of poring through the Vanguards of Vigilance records when I hear a loud crash coming from the hallway outside my apartment. I go and check, and find that a luggage cart has tipped sideways, spilling its load of end tables and ottomans and throw pillows onto the carpeted floor. A thin old man with a full head of curly gray hair scratches his head in exasperation. I step out barefoot and in lounge pants, and offer to give him a hand.

"Moving in?" I ask as I lift the upright cart from its side. A beeping sound issues from its motor, and the wheels lock into place.

"Yes. I'm 9G," he replies, pointing behind him.

"Welcome to the building. I recently moved here myself."

"Where from?"

"Locally. Used to live downtown."

"Yeah? Me too. NYC, born and raised," he says. "They told me moving at this hour was fine. I hope the racket didn't wake you."

"Not at all. No chance of that in this building," I assure him. *Pretty much all the tenants here at the Everbright are Sleepless,* I almost add, but if he's heard of the building's history, then it's probably the reason he's moving here to begin with. I reposition his small furniture, balancing them on the platform of the robotic cart. An elevator dings open and another cart rolls by to join us, carrying an assortment of potted palms.

"What happened to the freight elevator?" I ask. "Movers usually go in through a separate back hallway."

"The men we hired are downstairs figuring it out. Apparently some bums broke the locks trying to get in through the service entrance," he explains. "That doesn't happen a lot around here, does it?"

I wonder what would be more comforting to him—reinforcing this rumor he heard, or explaining that it's most likely anti-Sleepless vandalism. He's a born-and-raised New Yorker, which means he's seen it all, but I don't know his experience with being Sleepless. Maybe he's used to light property damage and crude graffiti. Maybe he's used to delivery folks scurrying away after dropping off goods to his door. Maybe he's used to living in a building that gets groundless noise complaints almost every other day. Maybe he's all right with added security protocols and the higher building maintenance fees that come with them.

"Nah, homeless folks don't do that. I'm sure that's not what happened." I leave the last part open for his imagination.

He gives the luggage cart a firm tug once we load the last of the furniture. The motor remains unresponsive, though the wheels are no longer braked. I offer to guide the cart along with him, and he thanks me effusively.

We slowly inch toward the far end of the wide hallway typical of the Everbright Apartments. If I squint, I can still see the former hospital building's old bones. The corridors that used to lead into different wards, the open entryways that once featured swinging double doors. Tasteful sconces have replaced the industrial light fixtures, but the carpeting and its minimalist lines remind me of the linoleum floors, the multicolored directional tape that one uses to navigate a hospital. As I lose myself in these thoughts, the luggage cart I'm steering starts to feel like a gurney.

"I was a patient here once," the old man says as though reading my mind. "Decades ago, before they closed it down. Nothing serious, just a bum knee. Never thought I'd be back to actually live here."

"The developers did a great job fixing up the building and repackaging it," I reply.

"Yes, I don't think anyone even remembers this was a quarantine site."

It's subtle, but the message is delivered with the old man's downcast glance. The stealth is not necessary, not here, but I understand the impulse. I've had to deploy the coded words and read the clandestine cues, balancing the need to protect myself and the desire to know.

"Did you recently become Sleepless?" I ask without ceremony or hesitation.

"Around New Year's," he replies, with some vigor. That takes me aback, though not in a bad way. Less than a year Sleepless. He's in for a journey. I'm only half a year ahead of him, and I'm still figuring it all out.

"You don't see that very often anymore," I say. "A new case, I mean."

He nods, smiling. "My own doctor was surprised; so was I. Had to get third, fourth, fifth opinions. Everyone keeps saying the Sleepless are a dying breed, but here I am bucking the trend."

"Dying" is a bit of an overstatement. I'd describe us more like an increasingly rare find. There aren't as many new incidences of Sleeplessness as there once were, which, depending who you ask, could be a good or bad thing.

"That's why I moved," he continues. "My old lease was up, and I've always thought this place was fascinating. All that history . . . and now, what's come out from all that."

"The community's great too. Someone from the tenant's association will catch you up on everything, and they also informally double as a counseling service for the newly Sleepless, if you ever need a hand."

Behind us the elevator dings again. Two burly men in overalls emerge, struggling to extract a mattress from the cramped space.

"Oh, you still have a bed. Me too," I add. "Most tenants don't anymore. Waste of space, they say."

"It's mostly for the missus. She's not like us."

The last bit rankles me, but I try to be generous. He is probably still learning how to talk about it, and the proper rules of etiquette shift with every passing day.

"Well, I'm sure she'll feel welcome here nonetheless."

With their brisk pace, the movers catch up to us as we reach our destination. The men take over in assisting their client, and I hand the cart off to them. I tell the old man to ring me at 9A if he ever needs anything. Just then, his wife arrives on our floor. She's about his age, though not nearly as fragile. A woolen scarf hangs around her neck, an odd choice in this weather. She approaches us cautiously, her arms balancing a crate full of purple tropical orchids.

"Making friends already?" she asks. "Try not to talk the young man's ear off, Ron."

"Honestly, I've been doing most of the talking," I reply. "Can I help you with that?"

My offer hangs in the air without acknowledgment. She surveys me from head to toe, unspoken questions written on her face. I try not to take offense. This is all new to her, as much as it is to him.

"We'll manage. But thank you," she says, punctuated with a cloying smile. Ron gives me a slight bow in gratitude, and, I'd like to think, solidarity. He then unburdens his wife of the crate and she clings to him, her arm around his shoulder, while I'm left watching them march down the hall into their new home.

As I reenter my apartment, an unexpected heaviness comes upon me. I linger in my foyer and gaze upon the open door of my own bedroom, its king-size bed falling into disuse. After all these months, it still smelled new. Even though I have no need for one, not for sleep at least, I bought it when I moved out of our old apartment. I guess I got one to maintain a sense of normalcy. Looking at it now, it just seems like a waste.

The futility of all that space, that remnant of a life I couldn't leave behind.

I head to the kitchen and pour myself a shot of Bourbon. As I knock it back, my eye is drawn to Hannah's passport card laying on the counter. Maybe when she comes back tomorrow, things will be different. Easier. Not back to where things were—she's made it clear there's no chance of that—but at least without disappointed looks or soul-deep sighs of frustration. No sense of me having failed her yet again.

The first one doesn't ease the weight pressing down on my chest, and I pour myself another shot. Still nothing. I should get back to work, but my mind's too muddled right now. I need a break, a way to exorcise distractions out of my system. Maybe a total sensory overload will do the trick.

I put on my full-body suit and scroll through the milieu options on my ReVRie: Swiss Ski Chalet, Hammock by a Private Beach, Mossy Cottage in a Highland Glen. None of them entice me, not even my go-to, Desert Campfire at Night.

I decide to load China Shop instead.

Within seconds I am standing in the center of a porcelain emporium, wall-to-wall shelves of jars, vases, dragon statues and potbellied

Buddhas. Through plate-glass windows, the rendered milieu mimics Chinatown in the 1920s. My avatar stands by the entrance. I don't need to look at myself to know that I'm decked out in a white tank and braces, with a newsboy cap covering my head. The system default.

By my side is a long rack of cudgels of all shapes and sorts. Golf clubs, two-by-fours, a lead pipe. There's even a bullwhip. I vacillate between the Louisville slugger and the crowbar, but then the battle-axe catches my eye. I pick it up, feeling its heft in the haptics of my gloves. Suit pressure on my forearms further heightens the sensation. I make a couple of tentative swings in the air, and the weapon loudly swishes with each one.

I raise the axe over my head. My palms are sweaty and I use both hands to grip the haft. With might, I bring it down on the nearest display case. Everything breaks in a booming crash. The dragons shatter into jagged shards; money toads and lucky cats crumble under the weight of my weapon's double blades. I sweep it across the next rack and then the next, clearing each shelf like it's my mission. Every clink and crack is rendered in precise, almost symphonic, audio. Slivers of jade and ceramic fly all around me, flung into sharp projectiles that instantly vaporize as they touch my avatar body. Soon enough, the entire store is leveled and I am the only thing standing amid the wreckage.

Before my physical momentum wanes, I quickly reload the milieu. Even though I've run this program many times over, there's a newness to every fracture and every splinter. The objects return to how they were with each reload, but I get to break them differently every time. Endless replayability. I ramp up the Fragility setting to Highly Brittle, and take another first swing.

I clear and restart three times, switching out my weapon to nunchucks this go around. Once the latest round is done, I check the clock.

It hasn't even been an hour.

Time still hasn't passed, not in any meaningful way. There's still so much of it to kill.

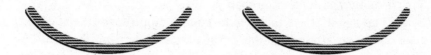

02.

I'm the first to arrive on our side of the floor. The C+P Media head-quarters is quiet, though the overnight folks are surely deep at work downstairs. The rest of the news division doesn't roll in until around ten, if they come in at all. Closer to the weekend, the staff work on the field or remotely from home, so the quiet isn't too odd.

I head to my office, almost skipping in anticipation. First thing when he comes in, I'll show Simon what I got from my source. He's been waiting for this lead to pan out, and finally I can show him that my instincts were right. The source had exactly what we needed, and this package, along with the internal reports Simon got from his own whistleblower, is more than enough to bury Dwyer.

I drop off my bag at my desk, barely willing to let the documents leave my sight, and head to the break room to get a coffee. One of the perks working for C+P is the company's understanding that the staff can only function when caffeinated, and they're willing to pay for it, even with coffee prices being sky high.

On my way back, I pass by the hall that leads to Simon's corner office. Through the clear glass walls, I catch a glimpse of Simon slumped facedown on his desk. His brambly head of black hair is turned away from me, looking out onto the floor-to-ceiling windows. Pulled another all-nighter, probably.

As I approach, I see that a wine glass is tipped over the stack of papers strewn around his desk. The carpet, pilly from foot traffic, now sports a soggy sunburst pattern of maroon. I knock tentatively at the closed door, but get no response. I walk in to take a closer look.

The spill has seeped under the left side of his face, which lays flat against the clear surface of the desk. A crimson halo frames his lifeless profile, mouth agape. His eyes are turned to a hazy view of midtown Manhattan.

I yell out his name, and then step around to shake his shoulder. He is motionless. I feel for a pulse by his jugular but it doesn't stir. His neck is tight and forms a deep ridge where the muscles have stiffened.

Panicked, I dash out of his office and cry out for help. No one answers. My instincts tell me to run, but my body has not quite caught up with my head. I stand in the hallway, frozen. The quiet is stifling. Soon enough, I gather my wits enough to slide on my earcuff and voice-command 911. The AI voice talks me through the few details I incoherently relay.

As I wait for help to arrive, I dial Elliott.

"Boss is dead," I say, trembling. "He's dead, I just found him in his office."

"What the fuck? How?"

"I don't know, he's lying there and I . . ."

"Call 911. I'm a block away."

I close my eyes and inhale. The sight of Simon's dead body is already seared in my head. It pulls at me, impels me to come closer. I hear his voice from deep within me, a faint echo of an oft-used directive.

Why the fuck are you just standing there? Do something.

I draw my visor from my jacket pocket. I place the lightweight glass-and-steel band over my eyes, its probes pressing up against my temples. My vision is filled with my default layers, icons for accessing calls, messages, and most critically at this moment, the record function. Instantly, the display tells me that it's synced to my earcuffs and that its sensors are primed to detect my hand gestures. I shake my hands to confirm and, once convinced that the device is detecting my fingers' fine muscle control, I press the red icon hovering on the left side of my field of view.

Recording.

With a deep breath, I step back into Simon's office.

The bottle of red, the wine-logged papers, the sideways glass—I make sure the visor captures all the details. Simon's body, the rolled-up sleeves and stringy hair, the look of death in his eyes. A top-view of the table.

Teetering on the edge of his desk, right by the wine bottle, is a clear pill tube. Empty, with its cap off and right next to where it lay. The cap's a pale avocado green in the light. Its underside has some sort of emoji logo. An eight-point star? Fuck. This was an OD. Party drug, if I had to guess.

I reach for the pill tube but stop myself. Best not to contaminate the scene. I inch closer and take a sniff. All I pick up is the burnt acridity of the merlot. I whisper this observation to myself, for the recording. I stretch out the fingers of my left hand and then the visor display zooms in, capturing every aspect of the pill tube and its green cap in full 5x magnification.

With sideways and vertical swishes of my fingers, I dial up video resolution and audio sensitivity. I start tiptoeing around Simon's desk, careful not to move his body any more than I already have. On the right side of his desk lay his tablet. His left cheek rests inches away from the screen. He was working when it happened?

A scrap of yellow paper is tucked under the tablet. I pick up his stylus and nudge the tablet ever so slightly. A phone number, written in Simon's angular handwriting. Again I zoom in, and the visor picks up the numbers, copies it into a sidebar. I ask the device to run a quick directory search.

No record found.

I scan the couch against the far wall. Simon's suit jacket, his backpack, main compartment slightly open. Without touching, I peer in, aiming my zoom at the bag's contents, but it's too dark. Flicking my fingers turns the brightness up, but nothing short of sticking a flashlight in there will help, and I don't want to move anything.

Sirens blare. I make my way back toward the doorway, and get a wide-angle shot, panning from left to right. I speed past the vid screens along the long wall of the room. Each of them is tuned to a news channel, all on mute. Then, I rush over to another corner and do another sweep, recording every inch of the room as it is. Finally I go behind Simon's desk and record from his point of view.

As I finish my final shot, I hear footsteps approach from outside the office. I crane my neck out. It's Elliott, rushing down the hall, sweat dripping from his brow. I take off my visor and slip it back into my jacket, hoping he's too upset to notice what I'd been doing.

"Motherfucker," he says when he gets to the doorway. He runs past me, straight toward Simon, like I'm not there. I step in and try to shield him from the scene.

"Don't touch anything. I think he might have OD'd."

His hands hold his head steady, fingers running through the waves of his auburn hair. He begins to tremble and heave. Then he falls to his knees, collapsing against the trash bin in the corner by Simon's desk. His body convulses, and the air fills with the vinegary odor of vomit. I kneel on the floor next to him and stroke his back.

"What do you mean? OD'd on what?" Elliott asks, wiping his mouth with his sleeve. He stays on the floor and crawls to lean back against a wall, hugging the trash bin with one arm.

I leave the floor, then slide Simon's stylus gently into the opening of the pill tube on the desk. I lift it and slowly set it back down.

Elliott tries to get up but stumbles. I lunge to catch him, and he clings to my neck. He smells of pineapple and puke. He cries, and though I feel the need to, the tears don't come at all.

Moments later, the beat cops arrive, three of them in all. Young ones sent to respond in case it's some sort of prank. Once they see the quite-real body, they ask us to clear out of the immediate vicinity: Simon's office, the offices next to it and across the hall, the cubicles that formed an aisle in between. It's early enough in the day, and most of C+P is remote on Thursdays and Fridays, so crowd control is minimal. One of the uniformed officers gets a statement from me, taking notes in her handheld while also recording me on her visor. The other two stand guard and radio for the next cavalcade.

The detectives come next, wearing their boxy suits and their surly expressions. They talk to their underlings, survey the scene, then interview me. Again with the visors and the handhelds, they ask questions I'd only just answered ten minutes ago. Then it's the medical examiner's team. Same questions, same answers. One of them's wearing what looks like a hazmat suit, but none of them touch the body at all. No one has, in fact. They just stand around there. Have to wait for the crime scene photographer first, says the guy in the hazmat. The photographer arrives, and she asks me to do the whole spiel again. Same question, same answers. Life slowly seeps out of me with every repetition, but maybe that's a good thing. Better to be numb right now. The woman takes her photos, runs a visor capture of every angle, much like I had before the entire floor ended up looking like the pit of an NYPD precinct. After she's done, more hazmats arrive, with a body bag and a stretcher. They all confer about the details they've gathered so far, but that doesn't spare me more questions. Was the body like this when you found it? Has it been moved? The sight of the black tarp bag, the reduction of Simon to a body, the claustrophobic sight of men in hazmat suits and masks and goggles—they almost make me vomit. Still, I manage to reply coherently. Yes, it was; no, it hasn't.

A crowd has gathered at this point, the first wave of staffers in for the day. They've amassed beyond the perimeter formed by lines of police tape. As my questioning ends, the hazmats begin to lift Simon from his seat. His head hangs to one side, red wine dripping from his hair. Gasps and a loud shriek issue from the onlookers as Simon is placed into the body bag, but already I've fled to the nearest bathroom, spilling my guts out into a porcelain sink.

❂

By noon, everyone's gathered in the C+P amphitheater two floors down. We use the half-moon auditorium for talks and presentations, and other public-facing events. Its stage has been graced by a president or two, but today there's a lone podium where company CEO Maxwell Cartwright is expected to brief the staff. Of course, this is a building full of news folk and everyone already knows exactly what happened. The gist of it at least. Simon Parrish is dead.

The last person who needs to be here is me. I could well break the news in more detail than Maxwell can, and I'm surprised no one from the higher-ups have gotten a hold of me yet. Surprised, but grateful. They can get their story from the detectives. I'm all tapped out for the day.

I'm only here to see what the plan is for moving forward, if there is one. The entire company is agitated, and they need some assurance that things will be all right. In my experience, things won't be. It's nice to hear someone say it just the same.

"Hey there. I heard what happened," says Mia Stuart, one of the news division's lead factcheckers, as I enter through one of the side doors near the back of the theater. I'd hoped to avoid any interaction, but that was futile. She reaches out and pats my arm reassuringly. I flinch before catching myself and try to make up for it with a cursory "thank you."

"How are you feeling?" she asks.

"I'll be all right." I disengage quickly, heading to the back row. As I do, I survey the hall, which is almost at capacity. Many of the faces are familiar, though my knowledge of them is mostly through vid screens for remote meetings. Now they're all here, in person, come to gawk and gape. Pay their respects too, I'm sure.

Shannon Carrera, our DC bureau chief, is in the front row, next to some field reporters who never set foot in the New York offices. Next to her is João Oliveira, our international conflict correspondent who's in the city to accept a Peabody for covering the regime transition in Nicaragua. After Simon with his two Pulitzers, Oliveira's the most decorated journalist in here.

When I find a seat in the back row, I zip up my hoodie and cover my head. The conversations are intense and rapid-fire, and every now and then I get snatches of dialogue. The same and usual questions, and mostly the same answer. "I don't know." Above the chatter, I hear the booming voice of Gregg Goldin, C+P's chief financial correspondent, resident fiscal and social conservative, and host of *The Goldin Hour*. His normally smug face now bears a dismal frown in faux-sympathy. He and Simon have butted head many times over the years, and it's hard to believe he's as dejected as he looks.

The international bureau chiefs are waiting on standby via holo-presence, and despite their distance from the scene, they seem just as downtrodden and anxious as everyone in the hall. Liang Li Fang, Beijing bureau chief, has called in from the Asia headquarters, even though it's past midnight where she is. She's another one whom Simon's had a rancorous relationship with; at the last all-company conference, Simon criticized the bureau's cozy relationship with the oligarchs they're supposed to be covering.

We've all gathered here for Simon, and so it's tough for me to divorce these people from his view of them. I suppose it's always been hard for me to assess others without Simon's voice in my head subconsciously dictating my opinions. And the more I look around, each time my sights land on a colleague, a subordinate, an equal of his, all I remember is how Simon treated them. Which is, not very well.

The amphitheater suddenly feels smaller. It's no longer a gathering hall of top journalists and media professionals. It's now just a room of people, all of whom came to confirm that the rumors of Simon's death are not exaggerated. In my mind I see Simon's lifeless body, and I imagine what all these people are truly feeling, trying to parse the subtext in their apparent shock and grief.

Just then, a hand lands on my shoulder, jolting me. Elliott leans over and whispers in my ear. "I heard some folks are heading to the corner bar for a round. You wanna ditch this and come with?"

"I do wanna leave," I say. "But I think I'd rather head home."

"You don't look too good. Maybe it'll help to talk it out a little?" he said. "Or not talk, whatever. But I think you should be with people."

Talking means I'll have to describe what happened all over again. Whoever's coming to the bar will surely ask what I found, when it happened, how it felt. I wouldn't want to relive all of that for an audience, but beneath Elliott's casual tone is a desperate insistence. He needs the company more than I do.

"All right, but let's go somewhere else," I reply. "And just us two."

"I know the perfect place," he says. "And it happens to be right in your neighborhood."

03.

Thursday, 07/09/2043, 1:32 PM

A workday afternoon at Rheingold Hall looks no different from the weekend. The long oak tables are always filled with patrons, drinking their beers from massive steins, underneath the exposed beams of a vaulted ceiling. Some folks are dressed in power suits, sneaking in a drink or two for their lunch hour, while some look like they've come to unwind from a long day, exhaustion lining their faces. A few look as though they've spent their entire day here at the biergarten. Rheingold represented a couple of the perks from the Sleepless pandemic: 24-hour venues and the loosening of social codes against day drinking.

The unctuous scent of bratwurst wafts from the outdoor grills into a covered pavilion, greeting customers as they enter. Elliott and I are promptly welcomed by the host, an elderly blonde woman who knows Elliott by name. Without asking, she leads us down the hall's main aisle, to his usual booth. Servers and bartenders give him a friendly nod as we pass.

"How often do you come here?" I ask.

"Often enough," he replies as we settle into the booth. His swanky new apartment in Murray Hill is nine stops and a transfer away, but clearly that hasn't stopped him from becoming a regular. Meanwhile, the place is a five-minute walk from my apartment and yet I haven't stepped foot in here since I moved.

A server comes by with salt-encrusted pretzels, warm and glistening in a wicker basket. Another arrives with two steins of an amber lager. Before I could tell them that they got the wrong table, Elliott stops me; this is something he expected.

Down the aisle from us, dozens of people sit side by side on long wooden benches, sipping their beers and gorging on their sausages and slaw. Their spirits are high, yet the scene fails to lift my mood. Neither does it Elliott's.

"To Simon," he says, wearily lifting his mug. He tries to say more, but the words catch in his throat. I toast with him, and we both take a sip in silence. Our booth is a solemn bubble amid the verve of the beer hall.

"I don't know whether this was a good idea," I say after a long pause.

"Being with your people should make things easier, right?" he asks, resigned.

Everyone in here is a stranger to me, but I could see what he meant. Rheingold is more than a beer hall; it's a de facto social club for the Sleepless, and the sense of community comes standard. It helps that the place has been in the neighborhood for years, well before the old hospital got converted into the Everbright's luxury apartments. Back then the biergarten was smaller, a tiny old lodge where the locals went to drown their sorrows. When Mount Sinai got designated as a Sleepless quarantine site, Rheingold became the way station for families of the Sleepless, where they somberly waited for visitation hours or release days. As the Sleepless population grew, so did Rheingold's coffers. Now the biergarten is the size of a cathedral, with its rows of communal tables, bandstands and meeting rooms.

Soon, a pimply-faced kid walks up to our booth. He looks too young to be in this place. He slides next to Elliott and hangs an arm around him. "I thought I saw you back here."

"Jamie, this is Fred," Elliott says, trying to muster some enthusiasm. I shoot Elliott a look. I'm not in the mood for new company. "He works here."

"You good, my man? You're looking a bit bleak."

"I'm as good as ever," Elliott replies. That's as noncommittal as it gets, I suppose. Here's hoping the kid will get the hint and leave us be.

"Are they taking care of you?" Fred asks as he leans over to see who's at the bar. He signals to the bartender, twirling his finger to ask for another round at our table. "My second shift ended a while ago, but my band's playing later. You guys should stick around."

"What, do you live here now?" Elliott asks.

"Might as well. Could do a lot worse."

"Don't you get sick of being here?" I ask, finally joining the conversation.

"Better than being at my shitty apartment with four shitty roommates," he replies. "Meanwhile, all my friends are here." He gives Elliott a wink.

"Oh, so you're finally paying rent," Elliott teases. "I remember when you first came to the city, no place to go, going from gig after gig, keeping your clothes at a storage locker, and showering at the public gym."

"It was a solid plan," Fred says, laughing. "I didn't need my own place, or a kitchen, or a bed. I could work my three shifts, save some money, and then worry about everything else later."

It's a journey many Sleepless folks have made. After travel restrictions were lifted, they moved to major city centers, like many others before them, to make money. It also helped that cities like New York tended to be more supportive of newly-Sleepless people than wherever they came from. Once here, they'd do the gauntlet— job #1, #2, #3, the only breaks being a quick shower, a bite to eat (one of four or five meals), or a pint with friends before everyone moves on to the next gig.

A server brings us three steins and I feel the pressure to rush through the one I'm still nursing. Fred chats with the server a while, trading stories about their back-to-back shifts. I realize for the first time that this place does not have any BarVenders or DumWaiters at all, none of the mechanical waitstaff typical of other joints. The grills on the backyard are not automated either. A couple of pit masters are dripping in sweat as they stoke the coals and wield their implements over an open flame.

A commotion stills the lively air as a team of security guards lift a drunk patron by his arms and drag him out the beer hall. The man, with his disheveled hair and untucked shirttail, is completely passed out. I'm reminded of Simon from earlier this morning, the way he looked as he lay lifeless. Elliott's grave expression tells me he's thinking the same. We stare at each other, reminded and rebuked of why we were there to begin with.

"Do they need help?" I say, attempting to dispatch Fred.

"We've got more than enough security around here," Fred says. "Too much, if you ask me. I mean, we don't get as much trouble as we used to. Obviously we can't throw out people who aren't Sleepless, but they don't bother to come anyway. Even when they do, they play nice." Elliott and I say nothing, and Fred takes this as a cue to keep rambling. "This place only needs one or two bouncers, really. We don't need to keep an eye out for the normals. Mostly we just need to deal with our own folks getting too shit-faced."

Finally, I kick Elliott under the table.

"Hey, buddy, Jamie and I have some business to discuss. Can we catch up later after your set?"

"Sure thing. I gotta bounce anyway," Fred says. He moves on to another table, intruding into a group of tipsy twenty-somethings. Elliott and I finish our first steins and move on to our second round, clinking again in Simon's honor.

✺

"Simon Parrish, 44, newsman and half of C+P Global Media, is survived by his wife Rita, and two children, Rakesh and Niketa," I tell Elliott as I polish off a warm pretzel. "That's how I'd start the obit." Then I'd recount Simon's greatest hits: every scummy politician taken down, every scathing op-ed against the feds, every media startup absorbed into the burgeoning empire that he built from nothing. "The piece would then circle back to his humble upbringing, to the meteoric rise of C+P, and then culminate in a paean to old-school new-media journalism."

"An apotheosis sounds about right," Elliott says. It's an apt word choice, knowing how people viewed Simon like a god. "Kinda boring though."

My private version of an obituary would probably be a bit more personal. I muse on Elliott's challenge, then reply. "We could start with an anecdote, go all eulogy-like. Humanize him a bit."

"That's a tall order," he replies, earning a knowing nod from me.

"Okay, so I'd likely start out with the story of my final stage interview for C+P."

Elliott leans back and crosses his arms, daring me to dazzle him with my offering. He and I joined the company at about the same time, and he knows what that process was like, but I start telling him the story just the same.

Simon Parrish and Maxwell Cartwright were involved in the hiring process for every one of their employees. This was back when C+P was still a fledgling news outfit, not the multi-platform behemoth it's become. They made a visually interesting pair. Maxwell, the Southern dandy, and Simon, the South Asian gruff. Maxwell with his three-piece suit and Simon with his rolled-up sleeves and loosened tie. Their demeanors conveniently matched their outfits. Simon was closer to my age, and about fifteen years younger than Maxwell, their age gap further magnified by his boyish features in contrast with Maxwell's weathered face.

Rumor was that the final interview was mostly a formality, but I still came in ready to spar. I did extensive research. Simon looked like me and had the early professional trajectory that tracked mine: the scrappy young brown boy with big hopes and an even bigger hunger to get his hands dirty. I figured that might play well. If anything, it gave me a boost of confidence going in. But seeing Simon in that conference room—wearing clothes that I would wear, carrying himself in the way I would, having the career that I'd always dreamed of—made me feel something more: a connection that I wanted to be mutual. I wanted the job, but more than that, I wanted him to like me.

Maxwell led the meeting while Simon hung back, absorbed with reading my résumé and watching video clips of my portfolio on his tablet. He made some marks with his stylus, but was very still otherwise. I fielded Maxwell's questions and tried to build rapport, but found that I hadn't quite caught Simon's attention at all. Twenty minutes had passed, and he had yet to utter a single word.

Finally, Maxwell turned to him and asked if he had anything to add. Simon's face had the look of an automaton that had been booted up to consciousness. He put down his tablet and reached over to a stack of papers and then looked up at me. That's when I realized he had been reading something else the entire time. He probably didn't even notice I was there.

"Jaime Vega. Barely out of j-school."

"Yes, sir," I said, immediately regretting the "sir."

"So which is it? My assistant used the Spanish pronunciation."

"Most people call me Jamie, but either one's fine, really, sir." God damn it, I couldn't help myself.

An eyebrow rose. "Are we your first choice?"

"No," I reply with confidence, to Simon's dismay, until I added, "I didn't apply elsewhere, so you could say C+P is my *only* choice."

Simon cocked his head aside, his lips pulled into a taut line. He gave me a once-over, unimpressed but not hostile, the kind of look you'd give an interviewee who tells you a line you've heard one too many times. He then shrugged toward Maxwell before turning back to his tablet.

His manner made me feel like my answers didn't matter either way. Worse, he made me feel as though he had caught me in a lie, even though in that moment, I had been telling the truth. C+P was my only choice, and I would have wanted nothing more than to work for him. Yet it wasn't about the truth. He could see right through my eagerness to impress. My desperation. That's what soured him toward me, or so I thought.

Of course, I still got the job, much to my complete shock. When I think back to that interview, I remember how I felt, how he made me feel, and how it's formed the foundation of everything else that followed between Simon and me. Since that first day, I'd been hopelessly trying to earn his approval. Lord knows if I ever truly got it.

"That's what you start out with?" Elliott asks bemused. "Obits don't tend to make the deceased look like a jerk."

"I'm going chronological, okay? And maybe I have my own set of journalistic standards for imaginary obits of people I know."

"Knew."

"Right."

I've had enough death in my life to know that the real eulogies happened not in church, or at temple, or before an open grave. They happened on the long car rides home from the funeral, or the hushed corners of the family kitchen after the reception. Now I've learned that they too could happen in a crowded, open-air bier-garten in the middle of the afternoon.

✿

Above the entire length of the Rheingold's bar, stretching spans and rising all the way up to the ceiling, is a mural. Vibrant in color-shifting hues, the painting tells the yet-short but nonetheless tumultuous story of hyperinsomnia. From one end, right by the entrance, there is depicted the early days. Fences and barbed wires, faces turned in abject horror. A viewer's eyes are pulled along the rest of the picture, which then progresses into symbolic representations for science and world harmony. Men and women in gleaming white lab coats, dignitaries shaking hands and signing agreements with a quill. By the edge of this section is a small rendering of a protest march, a passing acknowledgment to the equality movements. The latter section, the one closest to our booth, is the most vibrant and most specific of all. Lifelike faces and bodies, some actual Sleepless people, shown in various states of success. Athletes being lavished with medals, performers being showered with laurels.

It's meant to be inspiring. A more uplifting *Guernica*, a *Garden of Sleepless Delights*. There's no arguing the benefits of Sleeplessness with this canvas of marvels towering above you. How many more artists flourished during the pandemic and after? Didn't the extra time afford people more money, more freedom to pursue their creative endeavors? Literature, film, the visual and performing arts, all blossomed despite the uncertainty and fears and chaos. People had time to write their novels, practice violin, take a game design and coding class, make the commute to an all-night ballet studio on the other end of the city. People had money to support the arts. To buy and consume them in record numbers. Paintings, books, plays, photographs and sculptures and holos and games. People can debate the net effect of Sleeplessness all they want, but this renaissance is an unalloyed good.

As though a sober reminder, below the mural hangs a long plaque. Across the top, in elegant script, the words "In Honor of Those We Have Lost." A four-column list follows, a roll call of folks who died from hate crimes against the Sleepless. The names are burnished in bronze, etched in metal lest we all forget. The inscriptions have aged and darkened at the top half of the list, during the years where the greatest number of Sleepless had fallen. In the bottom for the current year, the space is empty.

When the pandemic hit ten years ago, governments panicked. Humanity reverted to their old ways, responding just as they had throughout all of history. Whenever there existed something new, inexplicable, or plain different, their instinct was to fear and vilify it. So they treated hyperinsomnia as a threat, and hyperinsomniacs as a menace.

Each country went into strict quarantine. Borders were closed the world over. In the worst cases and worst places, the Sleepless were detained. For public health and safety, as justified by various governments. Here in the US, they started a national registry of hyperinsomniacs. There were also rumors that the feds performed involuntary scientific procedures on the quarantined, but these were never verified.

Though it's only been a little over a decade, those days feel so long ago now. The borders are open once again, the quarantine centers are shuttered, and the registry has been completely expunged. The world's more like the final section of the mural than the first. Yet the plaque still hangs there, its blank spaces waiting to be filled.

"Do you think Simon was Sleepless too?" Elliott asks when he sees where I'm looking.

"I don't think so. Though if he were, he'd definitely keep it to himself," I say.

"He knows that we are though," Elliott says.

This surprises me. Simon firmly erected a barrier between his personal and professional lives. Unless it impacted how we did our jobs, he didn't care to share details of his life, and neither did he encourage us to share ours. That's partly why Elliott and I previously agreed that it was better to keep our Sleepless status under wraps at work. Better to have our increased productivity appear to come from natural drive rather than as a product of a disease.

"At least I suspect he knew," he continues. "Because of my mom."

"Oh."

I only met Laura Nahm once, a couple of years back, before the osteosarcoma diagnosis. When the cancer became aggressive and she required intensive chemo, Elliott started shuttling back and forth to live with her in Philadelphia. The Eastern Seaboard maglevs ran all night, and the hour-long trip didn't bother him, he said. He always tried to get home before his mother fell asleep, but he often failed, given our long work hours.

"I thought about asking him for a better schedule, to do more remote work, but I didn't want to let Simon know that she was sick," he says. He values his career too much to risk any perception of weakness or divided attention. "But he somehow found out anyway."

After frantic weeks of juggling doctors' visits and post-production all-nighters, Elliott got an email from Simon. A new shift schedule. Elliott wouldn't be on call on weekends anymore, he'd be allowed remote work full-time, and on the rare occasion that he'd have to be on site, his workdays would end at seven, no exceptions. Closing out the email, Simon referred Elliott to an old friend, some rockstar oncologist at Sloan-Kettering. Simon had already made a consult appointment on Laura's behalf. Finally, attached to the email was a fund transfer confirmation from C+P Media, several thousand dollars into Elliott's account for "moving and other personal expenses."

"Wow. You never told me any of that," I say.

"I didn't want you to think he was giving me special treatment."

"I wouldn't have. I knew how things were with your mom. I'd help too if I could."

"And you have. All those nights covering for me," Elliott replies. "Don't think I've forgotten. I owe you. You and Simon both."

It feels unfair to share that credit. I may have carried some of Elliott's workload, but Simon did that too, on top of paying for expenses and getting Laura access to the best medical care. She probably wouldn't be in remission now if it weren't for Simon's contacts at Sloan-Kettering.

All this talk made me think of what I owed Simon. The skills I never would've learned from anyone else, the relationships I never would have built. He molded me. And just as he's helped Elliott's personal life, he's saved my hide once or twice too.

"I wish I'd seen it coming," I say after a while.

"Stop. That isn't helpful."

"Seriously though, do you think it was suicide? Simon's got a family, he's on top of his game . . ."

"I'm going to stop you right there," Elliott replies, firmly. "We don't know anything yet and I'd rather not think about it until we know more. It's best that you do the same."

I should know better than to wonder why someone would kill themselves. That kind of question is only going to drive me insane in the search. It almost did, not too long ago. But being in this situation again, I can't help but think that there was something I could have done. Something I missed. There must have been. Or maybe I'm missing something now. *What if . . .*

"It doesn't feel right, is all. If things were different and Simon were here, he'd tell us to pursue that instinct. 'Follow your nose,' he always said."

"I hate when you get like this," he says.

"I'm only like this because he made me this way."

"Jamie, I think your eagerness to make sense of his death is less about Simon's influence and more about deep personal baggage. No offense."

He's not entirely right, but debating the point means addressing the aforementioned baggage, and it's been too long of a day to get into that, on top of everything else.

The afternoon passes. More beers arrive, and the drinking helps. It's apparent that Elliott and I are ending the day insensate in a drunken stupor. I miss being able to sleep things off. Now, if something devastating happens, the only coping mechanism I have is blacking out. As the hours drag, the ponderous silences grow longer. Elliott proves to be the ideal companion in grief. He doesn't speak to fill the quiet, and he doesn't ask too many questions. When he speaks, it feels more than anything like he is trying to get me sorted out. He is taking care of me, and it seems that's his way of taking care of himself too.

04.

Thursday, 07/09/2043, 08:39 PM

When I get home from the biergarten, after some necessary sobering up, I suit up and download my visor recording. It took time for me to feel comfortable leaving Elliott in his sorrows, but I'd been itching to review the file all afternoon. Toward the end, when our conversation grew repetitive, I found myself half-listening, half-thinking about the scene in Simon's office.

The system takes a minute to render everything from a flat visor recording into a full VR environment. Waiting gives me a moment to steel myself before being re-exposed to Simon's dead body. I shut my eyes and breathe-count backwards from ten, my finger trembling when I finally press play.

My apartment fades away before my eyes, and the field of view brightens. The sunlight makes me squint as my eyes adjust to being in broad daylight from the darkness of my living room. Instantly, I am transported back to this morning.

I am standing inside Simon's office.

I walk closer and look down at the red wine dripping from his desk. The sight triggers the smell of the wine, my own sense memory becoming more heightened as I view the visor recording. The experience is potent, and it's as though I'm not just recalling but reliving. This must be what perfect memory feels like—too real, leaving no room for the forgiving erosion of forgetting. I slow the video playback, to cue my brain that what's before my eyes is not actually happening. That also allows me to make closer observations.

The wine bottle is toward the center of the desk, near Simon's head. The glass is tipped out toward the front, inches away from his left hand. He is wearing a gold wedding band. The soaked papers are court transcripts from a story we worked on months ago.

The pill tube is sideways beside this stack of papers, clear and cylindrical. My arm reaches across Simon's desk, toward his right side, and I pick up his stylus. It barely fits, but I manage to slide it into the vial. I slowly lift it up to my face.

I pause the recording and zoom in. The plastic bottle occupies my entire field of vision, but the video gives me no detail, except that the tube is empty.

I scrub to rewind, going back to the cap that lay next to it. A light green screw cap, logo on the underside. A red and yellow starburst emoji, with a black A in the center. Cartoony looking, the type of thing dealers like to use to brand their contraband. I capture the image and run a search, without much hope that it'll turn anything up. It's too generic.

I scrub forward. I am once again setting the pill tube back down on the exact spot from where I lifted it. I am walking beside Simon's desk, then behind his body. The video forces me to look at Simon's corpse. I am standing on his right side, with a full view of his lifeless face. Both his eyes are open, bloodshot. His mouth is slightly agape. The slower playback lingers on his body, and I feel like I have somehow desecrated him by my presence.

I follow Simon's line of vision, away from his body, toward the quiet Manhattan morning. The sky is cloudless, a portent of yet another sweltering day. I pause and zoom in on the window.

I notice the two corners on the lower edge of the glass are smudged. The marks are almost invisible, and I zoom in further to get a better look. On full magnification, I see multiple fingerprint marks dragging up into thin, tapered streaks.

As though someone tried to slide the pane upward to open it.

I take a snapshot of the prints, then I rewind the playback to take a snapshot of Simon's left hand. I run a comparison. The system matches the prints.

Simon tried to slide the window open. Why? He couldn't have . . . could he? The echo pain from an old wound overcomes me, pressing on my chest. I need a second to collect myself.

I resume playback, and my vision returns to Simon. His right hand sits on top of his tablet, balled up in a fist. My hand reaches for the stylus again, and uses it to slide the yellow scrap of paper under the tablet. 4046589102. I hear myself saying, "Phone number search." The recording flashes, *No record found.*

I ask the system to run a full online algorithm search—bank accounts, international numbers, basic number ciphers, whatever those numbers could possibly be. This is going to take a while.

Then I am back around the right side of Simon's desk, facing the door. Next to me is an entire wall of screens, all on mute. There is a news item on the Brazilian energy crisis, and the rubber factory strikes in Java. I am walking toward the door, and when I reach a full view of the room, I begin a sweep of the place. As the video pans from left to right, I slow down the playback even further. I magnify every sector of my field of vision, searching for anything out of place. Magnify, revert, magnify, revert, over and over, but nothing stands out.

The clip ends and I fling away my visor in frustration. I had hoped to get more about the vial, or that green cap, that starburst logo, but the video gave me nothing more than what I already knew from memory.

The only leads so far are the weird numbers from his desk and the fingerprints on the window. Neither are enough to support what my gut tells me: this was no suicide.

Yet I remind myself to be patient. Leads take time to bear fruit. Those numbers could be something. The fingerprints might clarify another detail yet undiscovered. Still, it's hard to ignore what I didn't find—any signs of foul play. Right now it's hard to separate signal from noise, but against my so-called instincts, everything on this video tells me that Simon killed himself.

Maybe I should be looking at this from another angle. Not the how, but the why. A reason anyone would want him dead. Simon's a powerful man, a difficult man, a man who made enemies for righteous reasons, but enemies just the same. How many episodes of *The Simon Parrish Files* have ended in the disgrace of politicians, the indictment of industry titans, the shuttering of corrupt organizations? The list is long, but I'll start with what's at hand: Senator Mason Dwyer, Simon's latest target.

I grab my tablet and connect to the C+P servers. Once in, I pull up a list of all the employees of C+P's news division, and run a conflicts check on all of them. When the program asks, I tell it to find any strong-to-moderate connections to the Senator, his family, the companies he owns. Ties to the anti-Sleepless hate groups too. For good measure, I instruct the algorithm to include all other parameters from the last time our team ran this background check six weeks ago. Right around the time I secured my source.

As I watch the progress bar and its protracted crawl, the doubts begin to surface. We'd done this check before and came up empty. No links to anyone at C+P with this story at all. Probably a low chance I'll turn up something now. Also, there are easier ways to get to Simon *outside* the C+P building. The motives may be there, but the means don't make sense yet, not for powerful men who have special ops forces at their disposal. Still, this is my best bet, and I'll dig through the Dwyer story all over again, all night if I have to.

05.

Friday, 07/18/2043, 01:27 AM

I've hit a wall with the Dwyer lead. After four hours, all the data have started to bleed together into a puddle of incomprehension. The Parrish team hadn't left an angle unexplored, and neither did I. Yet there's something else I'm missing, and I won't find it by combing through another interview transcript or call log.

I send off a message on the encrypted line. *911.* A tad dramatic, but the moment requires it. I need reinforcements—reliable outside information—plus, I need to warn my source. Better for them to hear it from me that a key player has turned up dead.

Dead.

That was just yesterday morning, wasn't it? Hours of grunt work had given my mind a respite from the after-images of Simon's pale face, but the tremor in my fingers tells me that the distraction hasn't been enough to smooth me out. Seems like I need reinforcements in more ways than one.

I grab my jacket and head out, summoning a robocab to meet me in my building's lobby.

The Sleepless have various ways of dialing everything down to zero. Meditation is standard, and a ReVRie session is reliable. Since everyone does everything in their suits anyway, it's an easy switch from v-meets to movies to games to a stretch of VR downtime. Sitting still isn't for everyone though, especially hyperinsomnia-grade meditation, which can last hours. There's also medication: licit, illicit, alcoholic. Booze won't do; I need my wits about me, and I think I'll lay off the narcotics, considering.

Everyone has their preference, and I typically enjoy the full panoply. I portion off my late-night hours between making some money at the poker tables, tending to the hobby du jour, and a mix of VR milieu relaxation, meditating, and getting a Bourbon buzz. The routine's usually enough to reenergize me for another round of the daily grind.

Tonight though, I need a nice, long REST.

In due time the cab reaches the inland edge of Sunset Park and announces my destination: a squat building of white limestone, its curved edges outlined in purple neon. The rest of the neighborhood is dead silent, and none of the other establishments have any lights on.

I walk up to a signless door so nondescript it blends into the wall. I swipe my member card over the handle, wait for a chime, and then head inside.

Dim purple light that fills the length of a narrow hallway. I make my way down, squinting toward the end, which opens up to a brighter, yet still softly-lit anteroom. Behind a high counter, a man wearing a white frock waits for me with a smile.

"Welcome back, Mr. Vega. Will you be having your usual?"

Not quite Elliott's biergarten, but I have my own haunts too.

Something about sensory deprivation calms the Sleepless mind better than other coping mechanisms. It had been out of vogue for decades, dismissed as new-age bullshit, but then the pandemic happened, and the use of Restricted Environmental Stimuli Therapy resurged. Detractors claim it's nothing more than a spa treatment, but devotees—myself included—swear by it.

The receptionist leads me into a changing lounge, provides me with my necessaries. He returns after enough time has passed for me to strip and shower, then leads me to my appointed chamber.

The black tiled room has only one thing inside it: the pod. An oblong pool with an upper hatch, fully agape and made of polished steel. A massive silver clam, and just as briny. A faint ring of purple light shows me the way, and I step inside. I descend into the tingly warmth of waist-deep saltwater, and when I reach the center of the pool, I lean back and lie on the water's surface.

The pressure lifts me, floats me up away from the bottom, stops me from sinking. My skin is slick from the water and the humid air, and it's impossible to tell which part of me is above or below the water line.

"Close," I command, and the clamshell obeys. The hatch descends, sealing me shut. The ring of light dims until I am entombed in total darkness.

I close my eyes, though it's no different from having them peeled. In here, there is no sight nor sound, save for my breath. The world falls away, and all that remain are me and the void.

❀

When I was nine, my Auntie Sara and her son Paolo moved in to live with me and my family. She was going through a divorce, and they needed a place to stay for a few months. Maybe it was the way Mom sprang the news on me and my brother Charlie, but I recall being very wary about the change, chiefly because I had never met either of them before in my life.

That wariness transformed into resentment when Dad moved my new bed to the basement, where my aunt would be sleeping. It had only been a month since I got upgraded to a full-size bed, and now I was losing it again. Dad took out of storage the old double decker that Charlie and I shared until recently, and said that I would have to bunk with Paolo, who was the same age as me.

Charlie and I have never been particularly close, but especially not back then; he was six when I was nine, and at that age, it may as well have been a three-decade gap. I didn't have very many friends either, not close ones anyway. Whatever bonds I had with the kids from school felt tenuous; we'd all forget each other as we left the schoolyard at the end of the day, only to need reacquainting the next morning. That all changed with Paolo's arrival.

The new sleeping arrangements coerced Paolo and me into spending every waking second together. From the moment we rolled off of those bunk beds in the morning, until I climbed up the rickety steel ladder at night, it was him and me. He transferred to my school, attended my classes, sat at my lunch table. My parents also tasked me with easing him into his new life, which meant that I needed to do everything with him.

The forced camaraderie worked, as it tends to with kids. Paolo and I quickly discovered how we liked the same games, the same music, the same classes. He got along well with the handful of friends that I had at school. He made me laugh, and I made him comfortable, I suppose. Soon enough, we had become each other's best friend.

The more time we spent together, the more I saw that he was an all-arounder. He got good grades, did after school extracurriculars, and helped around the house too. When I felt lazy, he did my chores for me behind the grownups' backs. I did the same for him too, but in sum I'd probably gotten more out of the deal. It didn't take long for me to realize that he was more than a cousin and a friend, he was someone I looked up to.

The school year flew by, and two weeks into summer vacation, Auntie Sara announced over dinner that she and Paolo were moving to Missouri. She was a veterinarian, and she'd gotten a job assisting with the acclimation of recently loaned exotic mammals at the Springfield Zoo. The gig sounded great (I was going through my biology nerd phase at the time), but I was inconsolable. Paolo was too. Auntie Sara promised us both that she and Paolo would come back to visit every holiday and every summer. Though I had no reason to, except childish stubbornness and catastrophizing, I didn't believe a single word she said. I thought that was the end, that I would never see Paolo again.

✿

Memories are more vivid in the dark of the immersion pod. Not necessarily more accurate, but stripped down. Unfiltered. I should have known Paolo would invade my thoughts. On some level he's been intruding onto my subconscious ever since I saw Simon this morning. In my need to find a respite from the questions, I've again turned to the one thing I always go back to. Is this better though, wallowing in this other loss instead?

The warm water splashes as I extend my arms and uncurl my fingers. My head hasn't dipped underwater, and yet I taste the salt on my tongue.

I try to silence my mind. I do a mental scan of my body, starting from the top of my head, inching down to the other end. I feel the weight of my hair, tension in my nape, every sinew of my neck muscles. I appraise each part of my body, focusing on the limited sensations that I have access to, that of touch. The thoughts quieten, and I start to feel lighter again.

There is a soothing simplicity about being in this pod. This is why I keep coming back. Here, I can easily imagine I'm adrift in starless space without a care in the world. I can imagine I'm a fetus, an embryo. Pre-thought. Pre-life. Or, post-death. This must be what that feels like. I don't know which of these is the worst, or if they are any different at all. The dark is the dark is the dark.

❁

Paolo and his mom did end up visiting us the following summer, and every summer after that, except on the occasional year when we were the ones who visited them in Springfield. The rest of the year, he and I spent a ton of time online. Gaming mostly, but also shooting the breeze in VR meetspaces, griping about school and swapping stories of schoolboy crushes. We had our own private universe. We started to call each other brother.

At the start of senior year, Paolo and I agreed to apply to Columbia for college. I'd go to their journalism school, while he would major in economics. Of course, we also dreamed up a fancy bachelor pad in the Village, as though we would be able to afford it. Still, that collective goal (and Paolo's constant nagging) motivated the astronomical jump in my GPA and my SAT scores. In the end, I got in, and got a full ride too. So did he on both counts, but that had never been in doubt.

After graduation, we celebrated by taking a month-long trip through the Grand Canyon. For weeks, Paolo and I hiked trails, climbed cliffs, and camped in the desert, enduring the blistering days and savoring the star-filled nights. We missed greasy food and strong cocktails, and we barely showered, but we had the time of our lives. Every breathtaking vista, every fiery sunrise, made us feel like the world lay right before us, ready for the taking.

Soon after we got back, Paolo and I moved into a small apartment in Harlem. It wasn't quite the bachelor pad we dreamed of, but it was cheap for a high-rise suite with a partial view of the Hudson, and right on MLK and Amsterdam Avenue too. Close enough to school, but not entrenched in the Columbia neighborhood of Morningside Heights. Being the homebody, I enjoyed the space and the view more than he did. He enjoyed the convenience of being able to shuttle between home and classes and multiple internships and parties and the occasional hookup here and there. He'd always been a hard worker, and super smart too, so it was no surprise that despite his packed schedule, he graduated at the top of his class.

As for me, I made it out of j-school all right. I got solid grades and plum internships, mostly out of sheer luck. I had a number of options for jobs all over the country, mostly on the West Coast, but Paolo wouldn't hear it.

"You have to stay in New York," he insisted. "Why would you leave the center of the goddamn universe?" Just got his diploma and already he was beginning to sound like your typical high-finance guy.

In keeping with that image, he bought a luxury condo in Greenpoint with his massive signing bonus from the investment bank he joined right after school. "High ceilings, wrap-around terrace, river view, just the way you like it. The other bedroom's yours." It only took one look at the place and I knew I was staying.

We stuck together through horrible jobs, through grad school, through the worst of the pandemic and the rush of our mid-twenties. Those seven years in Greenpoint saw me start my career, join Simon's team, and meet Hannah. Meanwhile, Paolo did what he did best. He hustled. He amassed untold sums of wealth, almost got engaged, found and kicked a cocaine habit, buried his estranged father. It was then, too, that he became Sleepless.

When he contracted it five years ago, Paolo was already ahead of the curve with his views on Sleeplessness. Back then, a hyperinsomnia diagnosis still carried a stigma. People weren't assaulted as often as before, but the discrimination remained. Paolo faced it all with reckless aplomb, as though his change in status were merely a change of clothes. He lived fearlessly and, true to form, he embraced the advantages of his new life. He worked nonstop, and always harder than any other Sleepless person at his firm, with more than enough time to spare for family, friends, and the occasional lover.

People in Paolo's orbit reacted positively to the change, a microcosm of the wider cultural shift that was already underway. The more they knew about his Sleeplessness and saw how he excelled in all spheres of his life, the more they warmed up to him, and to the idea that maybe being Sleepless wasn't so bad after all.

I thought so too. I admired how he chased his goals and celebrated his successes, and if I'm being honest, I envied him too.

Everything ended on March 9, 2041. It was a Saturday, and I had spent the week with Hannah and her moms in Seattle but I had to cut my vacation short. Simon called me back into town to go over edits, and being a junior member of his team at the time, I did not want to disappoint. I took the earliest shuttle out and landed at JFK around seven that morning.

Well before I got into our apartment, I was ready to crash from the potent combination of a vegan red wine hangover and a crack-of-dawn transcontinental flight. I shuffled down our foyer, dragging my luggage behind me, barely standing. Tired and bloodshot, my eyes hadn't fully adjusted to the light.

That's when I saw him.

The sky burned with a warm amber glow, casting him in a golden aura. It all felt like a dream, Paolo a hazy vision of a bird about to launch in flight. He sat on the ledge of our living room casement window, looking out onto the view of the East River. Paolo straddled the barrier unsteadily, one leg over the sill. Arms outstretched as if to brace himself, he held the frame of the wide-open window.

It took me a while to collect myself, and when I do, I scream.

"Fuck! What are you doing?"

He turned his head to see me. "You're—not supposed to be here."

His face, streaked with tears and sweat, contorted in anguish. His right hand let go of the window frame to wipe his face dry, and my heart lurched out of my chest. He then turned his back from me, as though in shame.

He howled. The sound was feral and almost subhuman, coming from that place inside of all of us that few ever reach into.

"All right, look at me. Let me help you down," I said, holding down the panic in my voice. I inched toward him, and despite my outward calm, my eyes raced to find a safe way to pull him back. A sleeve, an arm, anything to grab on to.

"Paolo, please, we have to be very careful . . ." I came closer, repeating words over and over as calmly as I could. Be still. Don't move. I'm coming. I'm here. All to no avail. His leg stayed over the edge, his hands on the window frame, his sight on the sky brightening over the river.

"Hey, remember that trip we took to the Grand Canyon?" he said through sobs. "That was a good time."

"Of course, I remember . . . Please come back in, Paolo, please . . ."

Tears streamed down my face. I reached out to him, my hand trembling as it gently landed on his shoulder. He gazed down onto the freeway, twelve stories below. Finally, he turned around to face me.

"Thank you, brother. For everything. I'm sorry."

✱

The days that followed were filled with an endless series of questions. The whys and what ifs. The same ones that are always raised when a life ends this way. What did I miss, what could I have done. How did it come to this, how could I have failed.

In time, everyone stopped asking. Acceptance came with the knowledge that there are no answers, or at least no answers that would bring Paolo back. That there were no answers that could ease the pain. That there was solace in knowing how full Paolo's life has been, cut short as it was.

That solace never came to me, and the questions hounded me long after he died. I scoured our entire apartment for a note, a final message, a farewell. I found nothing. I talked to everyone that knew him. Family, friends, casual acquaintances. I interviewed his colleagues, his clients, his doctors and his drug dealer; the medical examiner, the cops who responded to the scene, the lead detective who ruled it a suicide. I traced the events of that day, and the days and weeks and months before. I built a timeline; charts were drawn, spreadsheets made. I downloaded every shred of data from all of his devices, the ones I had access to anyway. I studied them for signs, divining the tea leaves of his digital life. Did that work email mean something? Did that text? Is that a scowl in his last selfie? Why did he post that update? Everything I found led to more questions, increasingly granular, increasingly extraneous to any cause or reason. Yet I pursued those questions with rigor, knowing full well that they were nothing more than minutiae. I kept searching and asking and chasing down leads and almost-clues. I drove myself to madness.

I got some answers, if you could call them that: details about where Paolo had been the day before, what he'd had for dinner and with whom. The last party he attended, the last deals that he closed for his job. The peaks and valleys of his bank accounts, his stock portfolio. That he had a will, that he didn't have any known enemies, that sort of thing.

I got facts. Empty, lifeless facts. None of which led me closer to the truth.

The deeper I went, the more I reached the limits of my skills, and I began to sense the futility in my quest. In the end, all I learned was how a narrative can calcify around a death, not unlike the sculpting of a statue in someone's honor. How in the absence of tidy answers, the people left behind tend to weave a patchwork of explanations to let themselves grieve more easily.

Paolo was a workaholic, some said. Never knew how to have fun. Others said he had too much pressure at work and no life outside of it. Or, it was probably undiagnosed depression. Worse, it was probably the hyperinsomnia; all that time can make someone crack. He dated too much, had empty relationships. He was lonely, he was loveless, he was heartbroken.

I knew Paolo best. We'd spent most of our lives together, and maybe that was why no one asked me what I thought. Out of respect or propriety, no one shared with me their conjectures or solicited mine. If someone had asked me though, pressed me for an explanation, I would have told them what I gleaned from all that time I spent looking for one. Paolo wasn't lonely or deprived of pleasure or release, and it certainly wasn't depression or Sleeplessness that did him in. It was the way he lived his life.

Ever since we were kids, Paolo had always been a striver. He always had goals, and he had plans to achieve them; for the most part, he did. But he never had a purpose larger than the relentless pursuit of more, of the "better than this." Was that too much to expect of a young man in his prime? Maybe. But work was all he knew, and he gave it his all. Even though he didn't know what for. So he strived and he toiled, but a spinning top can only spin so long. Eventually, the momentum runs out, or the ground becomes unstable, or the equilibrium shifts such that the interference of the slightest force can send it careening away. I still can't say that one specific factor drove Paolo to do what he did. It may have been everything all at once. But there's one thing I know for sure.

It was the hustle that killed him.

✸

Has it been an hour? It's impossible to tell. Maybe I relived all those years again and a decade has passed, and everything has changed. Or nothing has. Again, I don't know which is worse.

Time, I ask aloud. Eighty-six minutes, the void answers.

For the last two years, there's been this pit inside of me, much like the pit I am floating in. I've been trying to find its metes and bounds in an attempt to fill it, smooth it over. Yet it is both formless and unknowable. All I know of it is this feeling I now have: that it has grown larger with Simon's death, and that I, inevitably, shall fall to its bottom.

I lower my legs to reach the floor of the pod. For a split second, I fear that there isn't one, and I flail my arms to sink. My entire body tingles as blood rushes to my extremities. Then I open my eyes and ask for the light.

06.

Friday, 07/10/2043, 06:07 AM

Sun's up and another day begins, at least for everyone else. I run through my routine and queue up my morning espresso before heading to the shower. Just then, a voice message comes in through the bathroom's mirror display.

It's Maxwell Cartwright's assistant, already working at an hour ungodly to most people. She says I've been given the day off to recover, and a few days more, if I require it. I detect a hint of maudlin concern at her mention of "recovery" and remind myself that no, Portia is not alluding to my history. She'd only been hired recently and so she couldn't have known about my quite public meltdown two years ago.

"Thanks, I do need an extra day," I voice-reply. It was completely out of character for Cartwright—he's never been big on mental health days—but I'm not one to question it. Portia quickly responds that C+P will have grief counselors on retainer by Monday, and I should consider taking advantage of them. The surprises keep coming. Next thing you know, there'll be wellness seminars and self-care workshops, possibly a speaker series on mindfulness or work-life integration. Correctives, and ineffectual ones at that.

Beneath ghostly images of the back-and forth notifications, I catch my reflection. I wave off the digital display and lean in closer to the mirror. Tufts of black hair matted by sweat, eyes bloodshot from failing to administer my eye drops yet again.

I strip and turn to the full-length mirror. I take myself in, head to toe. I look like shit, but a year of no sleep hasn't ravaged me as I feared. Despite being repeatedly assured by all the medical literature, I still had this notion that I would waste away because of being Sleepless. That I'd be undernourished despite consuming more food, wither away despite more activity. Irrational, I know. The Sleepless have the same physiology as everyone else. We're not more or less prone to any known diseases. Our muscles get tired the same amount despite increased use, and we are not faster or stronger or smarter. We can still get drunk, black out when we overdo it, faint when our blood sugar dips too low, get disoriented when we're knocked on the head. And no sooner or later than average, we still die. Like everyone else, if we don't abuse our bodies, we have a good chance of living to see our eightieth birthday. Overall, there are no biological differences. All we get is more waking hours.

As with every other fear I had, my health fears dissipated as I kept myself busy, filling my hours and thinking about how I'd fill my hours. All those hobbies helped too—rowing, running, jiu jitsu, dance. Aside from passing time, it had the bonus of giving me more strength, endurance and muscle definition. I'm fitter now than before I became Sleepless, I'd say. Except for the last twenty-four hours.

Since finding Simon, I feel like I've aged a decade in a day. In this early morning glow, I look it too. My frame seems leaner than it was only yesterday; my cheeks look sunken, and my pallor is the brown-gray of frozen mud. The REST session was supposed to revitalize me, but it only made me feel worse, and the outside's starting to reflect the inside. It's going to take more than a shower and caffeine to make me look halfway human.

Blood flow. That's what I need.

I start doing jumping jacks, slowly at first. In my nakedness, I am reminded of the Vitruvian man, which as a child I thought was an illustration of proper jumping-jack technique. When the mirror display tells me my heartrate's up, I quicken to a more frenetic pace.

Sweat drips down my temples and splatters around me in a drizzle of salty mist. I go faster and faster still, because I'm not feeling better yet. I gotta push harder. Five full minutes should get my color back, make me look less pallid.

I think it's working, it looks like it's working, but I have to keep going, just a little bit longer.

❀

Friday, 07/10/2043, 08:30 AM

Barges and tugboats crisscross with the ferries that traverse the East River. The sun beats down and casts a blinding reflection on the water. I bear the lack of shade and settle onto my park bench. Behind me, a high steel fence separates the riverside path from the neighborhood dog run. The yapping of toy dogs provides the upper register of a cacophony that includes ferry horns, joggers, and the rumbling of the subway as it goes over the bridge.

Her blush pink jacket is the first thing I see from across the way. It's heavy for this weather, but the lady must have her Chanel. Her head of white hair is wound high in a bouffant, and her face is obscured by dark, round spectacles. Designer visors, not like the wide, translucent band of tech across everyone's faces. In one hand she holds a brushed gunmetal walking stick. With the other she leads an Afghan Hound so regal, it must be a prizewinner.

I avert my eyes and wait. It's not until I get a whiff of ylang ylang that I swipe my visor on. I'm not connecting to her, not on a call that can be tapped or traced. I expect she's doing the same.

"Lovely weather we're having," I say, acting as though I'm on a vidcall.

"Go ahead and socialize, Moritz," she says to her dog. It's hard to hear her with her back turned to me, but I suppose that's the point. We were never supposed to meet at all, and especially not so soon after delivering the package.

"This better be fucking good." She enunciates each word with disdain.

"You heard what happened?"

"It's all over the news."

"Wanted to warn you," I say. "I'm not sure it's a suicide. I think it may have been staged to look like one."

"Why?"

"Call it a hunch. The man made a lot of enemies doing what we do."

A pause. Her bangles clink, and I imagine her shifting in her seat, crossing her arms. She clears her throat. "You think it has to do with our recent endeavor?"

"You haven't told anyone, have you?"

"This is the reason you came here, isn't it?" She says it sweetly, and I know she's pissed. "I'm at greater risk than you, mister. I'm not stupid. Besides, I need Dwyer out so that my own pony wins the race."

She's right on all counts. I needed to understand how exposed Simon was. That meant making sure that she hadn't exposed him. But I truly did want to warn her too. I owe her at least that. She's stuck her neck out for this Dwyer story, and for all the precautions we've taken, there's still a chance that things lead back to her. Then her investment firm is ruined. Worse, she could end up like Simon.

"Maybe you should spike the story," she says, more as a command than a suggestion. "Find another way to get at Dwyer."

"I'm gonna see this through. I have to," I say. "It's what Simon would've wanted."

"If your guesswork is right," she replies, words drawn out, "It's also what got him killed."

I can't tell if she's trying to get a rise out of me. She would have succeeded, too, if I didn't worry about being seen or heard. "I'm doing some digging, but no real threat has come up. Not yet anyway. That's why I'm here. For what it's worth, it might be nothing. Still, can't be too careful."

"Assuming this is what you think it is," she says, "What makes you think it has to do with our project? I'm sure the man made enemies in other ways."

"Yes, I'll look into others too." The list of Simon's enemies, nascent only in my mind for the moment, is long. "But recency dictates that I start with Dwyer."

"I have experience with things like this, you know," she says. "Almost always, the threat comes from inside the house. The same holds here."

"How do you figure?"

"Look at where he died. Why there?" she replies. "A sniper bullet as he left the building would have been easier."

I've been hyper-focused on the how and the why that I'd neglected to notice the where. C+P is Simon's castle, where he is safest, or at least where he would feel most secure. And to have his death appear to be a suicide, that implies closeness too. Someone would have to be close to orchestrate the scene.

"The incentives may have come from outside. It may be the Senator," she continues. "But the hand that dealt the blow is quite certainly closer than you think."

"No one at C+P would," I say. "He built that place. He's beloved."

"Everyone seems that way until they're stabbed in the back."

Nearly everyone who worked with Simon can be described as driven, ambitious, persistent. Lethal and treacherous are not words that come to mind, but given the right motive and under the right circumstances, that same ambition can turn dangerous. Only yesterday the C+P amphitheater held the entire staff all in one place, and I'd wondered how they truly felt about Simon. Now I run through those names and faces again. Cartwright, Carrera, Liang, Oliveira, Goldin . . . not to mention Cleo Johnson, assistant news chief and Simon's tenacious second-in-command.

The woman might have a point.

"You say you've dealt with this before," I say after a while. "What did you do?"

"I cleaned house." She huffs, proud. "But then again, what do I know? It might be a suicide. Not everything is a conspiracy."

"When you're a hammer . . ."

"In case you're right though, I think I'll be spending the next month on a remote private island. Perhaps in the South Pacific." She calls her Afghan Hound with a high-pitched whistle. "Goodbye, Jamie Vega. *Don't* call me sometime."

07.

As soon as I return home from downtown, I decide to call Hannah. If her routine hasn't changed, then she should have time to come by after her swim and on the way to the lab before her first stretch of meetings. She's always been a morning person, just like I am.

Was.

I guess I can't be an anything person anymore.

The line keeps ringing. She doesn't pick up. I skip voicemail and text her. *Got the passport. You can pick it up this AM if you're free.*

She replies instantly. *Be there in thirty.*

Ten months since and the doubts are still there, each time her path crosses mine. How would things have changed if I had told her? Maybe she'd still be with me, instead of coldly avoiding my calls. The other option's equally true, and maybe she'd have ended things regardless, but at least I wouldn't have to hold on to my secret.

All might have been easier if I'd already been Sleepless when we first met, but she and I both still slept five years ago, at that penthouse party in the Upper West Side. Elliott brought me along (it was his college buddy's thirtieth), and I eagerly played the role of guest of a guest.

Within minutes of arriving, I lost Elliott in the crowd of well-dressed revelers. Adrift and alone, I slunk away to one of the penthouse's automated bars, ready to plant myself in a corner and enjoy the free booze. That's when I first saw her. The button nose, the flaxen hair, the steely composure that somehow exuded warmth.

Coupe in hand, I watched as Hannah chatted with a man who stood close enough to her that his black suit appeared to blend in seamlessly with her dress. The two of them looked to form a two-headed black hole in the otherwise glittering scene. Then, she smiled my way. At me or past me, I couldn't tell. I peered into my glass and pretended not to see.

After a beat, I stole a sidelong glance and, without my meaning to, our eyes locked. She shot me a plaintive look. Maybe the man was not her date at all. I gulped down my whiskey sour and began my approach.

Before I could reach her, she leaned into the man, whispered in his ear, and gave him a light peck on the cheek. She slithered past him and toward me, meeting me halfway.

"Looked like you needed a rescue back there," I said, trying to be cool.

"What, from him?"

"Well, you were looking at me, and you seemed—"

"I was timing you. Wondering how long it would take for you to walk over. Four minutes, by the way."

After we did our introductions, she took my arm and steered me to the opposite corner of the room, away from the not-boyfriend. We ambled toward another bar, where automated spigots dispensed cocktails on demand. She got herself a refill, and so did I.

"Tell me something about yourself, Jamie," she said, like a challenge.

"Such as?"

She taps her chin with her finger, exaggerating thought. I'm instantly smitten. "Tell me something you're bad at. That'll be a nice change of pace from the last guy. Try not to impress me."

"Oh, I'm a horrible liar . . ."

"All the better. Like I said, I don't want to be impressed."

"No, that's it. My flaw. I'm bad at lying. No matter how hard I try, you'd just see right through me."

❁

Hannah's mothers are crunchy granola types from the Pacific Northwest. One is an arborist for the Crater Lake National Park, and the other is a designer for a sustainable fabrics manufacturer. Together they raised a materials engineer specializing in biohybrid nanopolymers, which I suppose was completely predictable. Also predictable, though entirely less impressive, was her parents' distaste toward the Sleepless.

Hannah's moms are staunch conservationists, and in the aftermath of the pandemic, they joined the Global Balance Network, one of many environmental groups that formed in response to hyperinsomnia. These groups aim to safeguard ecological sustainability in the face of what is effectively a population boom. Some groups advocate for a cure, while others have resorted to crueler means, but their rationale is the same: Sleepless people spend a third more time awake, and thus as much extra time impacting the planet. All those extra hours mean more eating, drinking, breathing, traveling, consuming, producing and polluting. The GBN believes that such increased impact had to be "balanced" somehow, through lobbying, public advocacy, and resource management. Sounds reasonable enough on paper, and so thought Hannah's parents.

Out of all the people who have something bad to say about us, the environmentalists seem the sanest. It helps that they have science on their side. Yet even back when Hannah and I were together I knew, too, how some of these groups operate from a place of fear. I only had to trust that Hannah and her mothers did not. Of course, all I'd heard from Hannah's parents were things said in polite company, and I never got to confirm the depth of their commitment to the GBN cause.

Despite being a conscientious consumer herself, Hannah never bought into the GBN. Indeed, she'd sometimes get into arguments with her moms about the subtle bigotry of the group's underpinnings. That didn't mean she was completely spotless.

A few months before I became Sleepless, Hannah was up for a promotion at the lab. Her biggest rival was a junior colleague, a hyperinsomniac who made it a point to wear that identity proudly. They both had impeccable credentials, and controlling for other factors, only two things set them apart: Hannah had been working at the lab for longer, and she was not Sleepless.

She lost the promotion. In the days that followed, she railed about it nonstop, decrying the bias against her and "normal" people. She used the word "freak" once or twice. I let her go on, knowing how hard she'd worked for that lead researcher post, how exhausted she'd been, scrounging for funding for her projects.

She caught on though, once she calmed down. She told me how she regretted her tantrum, and apologized to me as though I could absolve her. I couldn't, and I didn't hang it over her head either. After all, this kind of othering was a typical enough refrain.

In the beginning, it was because hyperinsomniacs were different and inscrutable (and potentially contagious), on top of the fact that the increased activity threatened to ravage the planet. Ten years in, those fears have mostly been borne out, with the climate worsening, energy reserves depleting, and agricultural land degrading at record rates.

On top of that, the Sleepless have gotten what to many seem like unfair advantages. This was where Hannah was coming from. Companies hire more Sleepless employees; after all, they work longer hours and they don't sleep on the job. Sleepless folks also got more shifts at work, or more time-intensive, more critical, more valued assignments. They didn't get bogged down by the limits of the ten-hour workday, and so they got paid more, and they climbed the ladder more quickly.

As these things tend to go, the resentment got directed at the individuals. After all, the more time a person has, the more labor that can be extracted from them. That made the Sleepless more valuable to the system. No one ever placed the blame on the corporations that exploited these extra hours and restructured the economy to favor a workforce that didn't sleep.

Hannah's outbursts mimicked what many had already been saying, so I didn't read too much into it at the time. Once her anger passed, she never made any stray remarks about the Sleepless ever again. I told myself it was a one-off, and when I eventually became Sleepless myself, I assured myself that her feelings for me would never change.

Yet I couldn't help but worry that her mothers had an outsize influence on her regarding the subject of Sleeplessness. The possibility always nagged at me, and some days I still tell myself that that's why I kept it from Hannah. The coward in me wanted to shift the blame to her and her family. As though they forced me to keep secrets, to lie.

When I became Sleepless, Hannah and I had already moved in together, and for the most part, we kept the same hours. That had to change, so for the first few nights of my hyperinsomnia, I told her I was working on a major assignment and needed to stay up late. I still went to bed at some point, in case she woke up in the middle of the night and wondered where I was. Then I would just lie awake, hands behind my head, staring at the ceiling. I'd spend silent hours lying beside her, thinking about the day that was or the day ahead, dreaming awake.

After a few weeks of this, I spent less and less time in bed. I made sure not to wake her with whatever I had decided to do till sunup, but that was difficult given the acoustics in the apartment. Mostly I read on the tablet, which I could easily explain as work in case she awoke. I don't know how I managed to keep it up.

"Why haven't you been coming to bed?" she asked one time over breakfast, apropos of nothing. She didn't even ask *if* I'd been coming to bed.

"What are you talking about?"

"You haven't been sleeping," she replies, aloof. "Is everything okay?"

"Yeah, it's just this new story we're working on. The research has been keeping me up late."

"What's it about?"

"New geoengineering proposals from the governor. Pretty heady stuff."

"So that's it?" she asks. "Nothing else is going on?"

"Nothing's going on."

I'd managed to convince myself that I simply needed time to be ready. That I upheld the lie out of fear of change, and with enough time, I'd be able to tell her everything. See, I'd been lying to myself too. I knew the truth. More than the fact that I had become Sleepless, I would also have to tell her *how* I became Sleepless. How I'd put both of us at risk, and how telling her would put us at even greater risk. I knew deep down that no amount of time could possibly prepare me for that conversation.

That night, I went to bed at the same time as her. I did so all the other nights that followed, and I kept that up until the end. I would wrap myself around her, listen to her breathing. Like the rocking of a cradle, the undulation of her chest under my arm calmed me, and I would intertwine my legs with hers, lying awake, pretending to sleep.

❁

"You look nice," I tease as I open the door. She's wearing a pantsuit and a sleek blazer. Not a departure from her usual ensemble but too dressy for the university. She only stares at me blankly in response.

"Lemme grab it, one sec." I dash to the breakfast counter, expecting her to stay by the doorway like last time. Instead she steps in, hovering tentatively by the foyer. She surveys the place, her eyes landing on the few remaining moving boxes that, a year later, I still have yet to unpack. Is that regret I see on her face, or is it pity?

"Here it is," I say as I flourish the passport card. She snaps it out of my fingers and slides it in her inside jacket pocket. "Remind me where you're going again?"

"I have a conference in Berlin next week."

I sense that this is code for something else. I've sensed it since the first time she mentioned it, omitting any details about the trip. We've gotten good at picking these things up, but I don't press her on it. "Sounds good. Coffee?"

"No, thanks. I should go."

"Simon died yesterday," I blurt out as she turns to leave. "I found his body."

Hannah stops in her tracks. Without preamble, I tell her what happened. How I came to work early and thought he was sleeping.

How I called 911, dealt with the paramedics, the cops. She comes closer to me, hands lifted tentatively, not knowing where to land. Finally, she leans forward and hugs me.

"I'm sorry," Hannah says. "I know how much he means to you."

I could read into those words ungenerously, but the gloom in Hannah's eyes tell me she bears no malice. Still, her concern is unexpected. She respected and maybe even admired Simon, but she never liked him. I daresay she hated him, or at least hated the way he'd been a priority in my life, often more than she was.

And what did Simon mean to me? I learned more from him than I did in college, grad school, and all my other jobs combined. He was my mentor, and though he bristled when I used this term in the presence of others, it was a role he assumed in earnest. Yet whatever I've learned from him came with a steep cost that he never flinched at extracting. He pushed me to my limits, and I gave him my all, as often as I could. First, because I was simply happy to have a job, and with the great Simon Parrish! Then, because I wanted to be like him. And then, after Hannah, I gave Simon my all because he was all I had left.

And now I've lost that too.

Hannah sits with me in silence, holding both my hands in hers. Then, for the first time since yesterday, my tears begin to fall.

She leans for a half-hug, and I detect a tremble of hesitation in her arm. I suddenly feel guilty. Here I am, almost a year later, still asking more of her. I wipe my eyes dry.

"You probably have to go," I say.

"It's all right. I have time."

"I need to go to work anyway," I lie. "Today's going to be crazy."

Hannah lingers by the doorway, waiting to see if I'll change my mind. She knows I want her to stay, but she wants me to say it. Not out of spite, but because she wants to hear those words. That I choose her over work, that she might finally be a priority rather than an afterthought. In our years together, we've grown attuned to the gravity of each other's needs and desires. But things are different now, and so instead we ignore what we both know to be true, and she leaves without saying another word.

08.

Friday, 07/10/2043, 12:37 PM

Veronica is late per usual. It's a habit I've learned to appreciate, as it gives me some quiet time before I'm swept away by her frenzied energy. As I cradle my mug of black Peruvian coffee, the heat on my fingertips is translated into a more sublime warmth within me. The aroma is intoxicating. Heady notes of nut and smoke fill the air around me, transporting me to lush mountains with its slight, lingering hint of wildflower. The first sip is just as moving. The smoky bitterness rests on my tongue like a luxurious quilt on a cold winter's night. It's these sensations, not the sourcing or the artisanal craftsmanship, that makes each cup worth the twenty bucks I pay almost every day to get. I wait for my friend, savoring every rich, expensive drop.

Our usual La Defense location is in the grungier side of Williamsburg, a converted chapel of some indeterminate Christian denomination. With its high ceilings and elongated layout, it looks like a veritable temple to coffee. On what was the raised platform for an altar is now a white tile wall lined with vid screens.

La Defense is one of the few true coffeehouses still in existence. Many of the formerly ubiquitous chains shuttered their stores during the global coffee crisis, when, in the late '20s, the land area suitable for coffee farming shrank by half due to rising global temperatures. Couple that with overconsumption, and it was inevitable that the nonstop growth in demand would soon suck the plantations dry.

As the climate and market forces laid waste to the fuel of the service economy, science kept itself busy finding a solution. Not one that reverses the planet's march into a heat death, but one that fills the coffee demand when crops are nowhere to be grown. The solution was synthetic caffeine.

By the turn of the decade, the whole world was drinking fake coffee, which, to be honest, sometimes tasted better than the real thing. And it was a lot cheaper too. We would all pay extra down the line, but no one knew at the time.

Following the hyperinsomnia pandemic in the early '30s, CDC researchers found that consumption of synthetic caffeine had a minor correlation to a defect in serotonin processing in humans. Other independent studies also found that synthetic caffeine had adverse interactions with environmental factors, particularly lithium, low doses of which are introduced in most water supplies. The confluence of all these things led to the conventional wisdom that synthetic caffeine caused hyperinsomnia. It's not conclusive by any measure, but it's the closest to a cause that anyone's ever come up with.

Personally, I think everyone longed for an easy answer, and we were only too eager to accept the first one that sounded good enough. No one has sufficiently explained how synthetic caffeine can alter fundamental brain functions, or how the condition has spread to parts of the world that don't consume coffee in large quantities. Toxic contamination doesn't work that way. But when you're dealing with a global pandemic, overcorrection is easy. Maybe even necessary.

It was no surprise then that, three years into the pandemic, world governments came together to ban the manufacture, production, use and sale of synthetic coffee. Under the auspices of the UN, a multilateral treaty was signed by all member states, imposing a worldwide synthetic caffeine embargo, complete with harsh criminal and economic sanctions for both private actors and states who failed to enforce the treaty within their own borders. Within days of the treaty ratification, synthetics stockpiles were confiscated and destroyed. Armed skirmishes blew up weekly between unscrupulous agri-tech companies and government enforcers. Those eventually died down, and the embargo became another fact of life in the advent of hyperinsomnia.

Because of the ban, the price of real coffee reached heights even more astronomical than before. Sometimes I feel half my paycheck goes to my coffee budget, but it's worth it. And yes, I would trek to another borough for a decent cup.

La Defense refused to serve synthetics well before the coffee crisis, a testament to their belief in an unadulterated coffee experience and a bit of brilliant marketing. Their untainted status has earned them a rabid band of regulars, including Veronica and me. We're both Sleepless, and though we don't need it to stay awake, coffee isn't a habit most Sleepless are willing to break. Also, the coffeehouse still employs humans. It adds to the retro vibe, plus we get a break from dealing with yet another disembodied head floating on a screen. I'm not even miffed by the inconvenience of having to walk up to the counter, which had been fashioned into food service functionality from waist-high marble choir stalls.

Pews have been spaced and fitted with tables and stools on which people of all stripes congregate. Every morning, the entire place gets colonized by freelancers and creative types working their second or third gig. Some are Sleepless, some are not, but everyone looks the same when they're wired on espresso: dark bags under red eyes, shaky fingers sliding across tablets. Veronica arrives in such a state at my table. Another cup of coffee might not be the best idea.

"Would you like to take a trip with me?" she asks.

"Uh-oh."

"What?"

"Need I remind you of the Saint Kitts fiasco?" I say.

She smiles, feigning ignorance for our last vacation, the one that ended in a diplomatic incident. I stare her down, and she breaks within seconds.

"It was one night in jail!" she replies.

She conveniently omits what came before it: the drunken night at the beach club, her quite public canoodling with someone who turned out to be the Governor-General's eighteen-year-old daughter, and the ensuing car chase across the island in order to evade her bodyguards. All three of us were lucky that I was sober enough not to crash our convertible, luckier still that Veronica and I got off with only a fine and a slap on the wrist.

"The embassy had to intervene, my dear."

"Whatever, we didn't die," she says. "Besides, what I'm thinking is closer to home. No risk of needing a consul to bail us out."

She doesn't let me respond, pushing her tablet toward me and turning the holoprojector on. Before us materializes a scaled-down, tabletop ghost of a sprawling metropolis in the bottom of a lush valley.

"You've heard of Wakefield, yeah?"

Sure, I've heard of it. A soulless new city with the too-on-the-nose name. All the amenities, none of the personality. The Sleepless talked about Wakefield, Maine, like some sort of promised land. A technological marvel, a neo-cultural ground zero, a place where anything was possible. In little less than a decade, it has become the country's fastest-growing city, both in terms of population and income, thanks to the Sleepless. Despite its well-deserved moniker, New York has been outpaced by Wakefield in the sheer number of Sleepless people within its city limits. No matter: my city still has way more reasons for its inhabitants to stay up.

"Why would I ever want to go there?" I ask.

"Wakefield has the biggest and oldest Sleepless cluster in the world. The entire city is basically a massive Sleepless commune! It's only about an hour north by train. All-night bars and theaters and all our people . . ." she trails off. Next to the city hologram, ads pop up announcing a sale on maglev tickets and cheap hotel deals. "We could make a weekend out of it."

"Sounds fun," I reply with sarcasm.

"Come on, I reaaaally wanna go. You're my numero uno travel buddy. And you know I can't take Torian. She won't enjoy it as much as you." What she really means is that she herself wouldn't enjoy it if she took her normie girlfriend.

"I don't think I should be taking any trips right about now."

She pouts, but then finally picks up on my mood. "All right, what the fuck is up with you?"

"Simon died. I found his body when I came to work yesterday."

"Oh, my god! Why didn't you tell me?" she gasped. "What happened?"

"Suicide," I say without batting a lash. The word feels wrong as it leaves my lips.

Veronica falls silent, and I give her the broad strokes. She listens intently, and it's not only because she's held rapt by the details. She's watching how I am. She attempts to form words, but clearly needs more time to process my news. When I finish, she gives me a tight hug.

"All right, we need to take your mind off of this," she says. "If only for the afternoon."

This is exactly what I came for, and Veronica delivers as usual. "What do you have in mind?" I ask, finishing the rest of my coffee in one big swig.

❁

Her girlfriend's VR suit fits me perfectly. Convenient, as we somehow always end up at their place on the East Side. Veronica's been known to grace my Astoria apartment with her presence, but as with many Manhattanites, she's stricken by a mild case of borough snobbery.

Their apartment is an unmitigated disaster zone. Devices and wires all over, clothes on the floor, half-eaten scraps of food in unexpected corners. I should be used to it by now, but my jaw drops upon entry. Veronica gives me a listless shrug.

"How's Torian, by the way?" I ask, pushing away an empty pizza box with my foot to clear a path.

"I think I'm wearing her out. She hasn't said anything; she's good to me like that," she replies. "But I feel her being tired. And her tiredness is making me tired."

"What do you mean?"

"She's very low energy. More than usual."

"Maybe you should be a bit more patient with her," I say. "It can be hard to keep up with you."

She takes it well, despite the teasing. I've always thought that To-rian's a bit too reserved, but that grounded energy is a good coun-terbalance for Veronica. I keep reminding her of this, but by now I know when she's trying to wind things down. It never seemed to matter what kind of person she was with—guy, girl, nonbinary, or anyone else along the spectrum; younger or older; Sleepless or normie—by the three-month mark, Veronica always found a reason to bolt. In the aftermath, I'd always be there as shoulder to cry on (and she always did cry, even when she was the one doing the leav-ing). I can tell she's going to need me again soon.

"The thing is, she's not getting tired keeping up with me—she's getting tired of me."

"Is that why you want to go on this getaway to Wakefield?"

"What? No," she says. She's already forgotten the trip she planned only moments ago. "I just think it'll be a fun adventure."

"Everyone gets stuck in a rut. You two just need to spend more time together."

Her sole reply is a look of disgust. Yes, the advice was hokey, but I can hardly be blamed from dispensing what I've learned from my own failed relationship.

Though Torian's the domestic type, I'm tempted to suggest that they should go out more. Veronica is at her best when she's out and about, in conversations lubricated by alcohol, where she can be open, excited, alive. Before I can say more, she loads up a movie, one that she picked sans discussion: a period romance from the '80s fea-turing a time-traveling playwright. Not my first choice, but I'm in no mood to bicker.

Given how Veronica and I first met, I suppose it was unavoidable that our friendship would have relationship therapy as a main fea-ture. Hannah had dumped me only a couple of months prior, and on one of my late-night, post-breakup jaunts, I found myself at this French bistro in Midtown. One of those narrow nooks tucked away in a side street between the loud avenues. I'd been drowning my heartache with a flight of red wines, trying to endure another inter-minable night, when Veronica walked in from the cold. She sashayed around the bistro as a regular would, bantering with the wait staff, the bartender, the other patrons who seemed to know her from the neighborhood. She halted her step by my table and gave me a quizzical look, like a queen spotting a new face in her court. Emboldened by Côtes du Rhône, I gestured to the chair next to me and asked her to join me.

In less time than it took to finish her glass of red, Veronica told me that she was Sleepless. I was surprised and thrilled; I had never before met one in the wild. (I'm not counting Elliott, who's an exception on several levels.) Veronica came out with it without fanfare or buildup, the same way she told me about the rest of her life, like where she's from (Baja California, born and raised) or what she did for a living (character designer for a hybrid RTS/RPG game I'd never heard of).

Immediately after she revealed that she was Sleepless, I told her I was too. Over more flights of wine, I then told her all the details of my Sleepless life. We discussed how we each filled our time, and commiserated over the stretches of boredom alternating with late-night mania. All the things I never got to share with Hannah.

"Is that why you broke up, because she's different?" Veronica said the word without judgment, but it felt pointed just the same. It gave me an odd feeling; I was so used to seeing myself as the one who's different, not because I was Sleepless, but because of how I became Sleepless.

"She doesn't know," I reply. I polished off a glass of wine and hoped to end it at that. Yet Veronica kept staring at me, and the discomfort compelled me to go on. "I couldn't tell her because then it would be this real thing that's happening to me that she isn't part of, but that she has to put up with." Close enough to the truth, in vino veritas, and all that.

"There's nothing to 'put up with.' It's not a burden," she argues.

"There are things that I can't tell her."

"That's life, my man. You can't share everything with any one person, Sleepless or not. You gotta keep some things for yourself. It's actually healthy."

We talked some more about being Sleepless, mostly at my urging. She told me how, before she became Sleepless, she never liked sleep. She only slept because she needed to. "And I've always been kind of an insomniac," she said. "Though I didn't really think about being Sleepless until I became one."

"And what was that like?"

"When it happened? I was scared at first. I now had this permanent, life-altering thing. My life, my relationships, my work, my body, everything was going to change. But the more I thought about it, the more I welcomed it. I saw the potential in our extra time. It's a gift. Realizing that transformed the way I want to live my life."

"And how's that?"

"Unafraid."

That's where this all began, this platonic ideal of a platonic friendship. Veronica became my new Hannah, without the romance and the sex. I became her partner in between partners. A constant presence in her life, one of the few whom she's let stick around for longer than a couple of months. Though that night at the bistro was not too long ago in normal people time, to us, with all the long days and longer nights we've spent together since, it feels like ages.

✺

"Something doesn't feel right about Simon's death," I tell Veronica over the end credits. The film was fine; I'd seen it ages ago and though I found myself appreciating it in a new light, my attention had been divided.

"Of course it doesn't," she replies, indulging me. "An untimely death never feels right."

"I mean, a suicide though? I simply can't imagine him taking his own life."

She shifts in her seat, realizing how the conversation has turned. "Well, that's what the cops said, right? You don't agree?"

"Can't quite put a finger on it, but there's something off," I reply. "I think it could be foul play made to look like a suicide."

Veronica narrows her gaze. "I know where you're going with this, Jamie. And it's not anywhere good."

"I visor-capped the scene," I say, ignoring the look on her face. "I got everything on video before 911 got there."

"Now why the hell would you do that?"

"I don't know, journalistic instincts? It's what Simon would have done."

"Your instinct was to treat it like a damn news story? This is someone you know, Jamie."

"Exactly. I know Simon. I worked with the guy for three years. Sixty-hour work weeks. And it doesn't make sense to me. From the very second I saw him dead, my gut told me it's not a suicide. That's why I hit record. I wanted to come back to it and work it out."

"What is there to work out?" she says with incredulity. "This is shock, mi amor. Have you meditated? Called your therapist?"

"It's not shock, and I'm fine," I reply, stressing the last word.

"These are not the words of someone who is fine! And no one would expect you to be fine, given everything with Paolo."

"This has nothing to do with him. It's completely different. Simon had a family, and he never let the 24/7 news cycle dictate how he lived. He's nothing like Paolo at all. He had also no reason to kill himself; if there was something, I would have seen it coming. You'd think I know better by now. I would have known."

"Listen to yourself. This isn't healthy," she says firmly. "I need you to call Dr. Cassis. Today."

I already know what the doctor will say: This is denial. This is me rejecting the idea that lightning strikes twice. The idea that yet another person in my life has taken his own. Still, I relent.

"All right, I will." I almost mean it.

I rest my head on her shoulder and try to quiet my mind. I let comfort wash over me, but the moment is soon interrupted by a message from Elliott.

"You're needed at C+P. The cops are here. They're saying it's suicide."

09.

Friday, 07/10/2043, 03:25 PM

Simon was mercurial, but his unpredictability was always in response to external events. Many things tortured him about the world we live in; that was precisely what made him a good newsman. It drove him to fight, not to fall into despair. And as for his home life, I've met his wife and kids, and they were a stabilizing force in his life. There was a lot of love there. That he would leave all that behind is unimaginable.

I abruptly call Elliott back. "What's going on?"

"The detectives are back, talking to Maxwell. From what I've heard, they're going with the overwork angle. High-pressure job, lots of demands from all sides, everyone counting on him, and he couldn't handle it anymore. Some signs of erratic behavior too, flareups and such, though if you ask me, that's just Simon being Simon."

"Absolutely. Simon's been at this for ages. If anything, he's better under pressure."

"Well, the lead detective seems convinced otherwise. Said he only needs a couple more routine interviews and he's about ready to close the case up."

"Bullshit," I snap. "It's only been twenty-four hours! How are they so sure? Did the cops find something? Like a note, some sort of hard evidence?"

Elliott lowers his voice. "Anyway, the cops are coming back first thing Monday to talk to you and me. Maxwell needs you to come in ASAP, so Legal can brief you before the interview. Something about external communications plans."

I understand the need for damage control. I've managed to avoid the news feeds so far, but I can imagine how wild the frenzy and speculation must be. Media insiders must be having a field day. But getting briefed by C+P's legal team before meeting with cops isn't standard. And if there's anything I hate as much as talking to cops, it's talking to lawyers.

"That's shady as fuck," I say, hackles raised. "What's Maxwell trying to do? Coordinate stories, shape the narrative? I suppose someone's gotta make sure nothing shakes up the buyout offer."

"It's for our protection," Elliott replies, his disbelief evident. "Make sure nothing gets pinned on us."

"Right, I'm sure C+P's doing this for *our* sake."

✺

Maxwell Cartwright's office occupies the floor's other corner, and though his Midtown view is indistinguishable from Simon's, that's where the similarities stop. Whereas Simon's office teems with piles of papers and boxes in disarray, Maxwell's is pristine. Next to his screen wall and tech accoutrement, he has ornate display cases filled with mementos from his travels around the globe. Stone artifacts, jade carvings, a couple of portrait miniatures of medieval royals. In a corner of the room there stands what looks to be an antique cannon. The place looks like a museum, a curated space of refined taste, one that fits the man who inhabits it. Always in his three-piece suit, Maxwell's the most composed and well-manicured person I know.

Today appears to be a rare exception. He is scribbling furiously on his tablet when I arrive. His brow is damp, his Windsor knot is loose, his neck exposed. It's clear he's anxious after his interview with the cops. I barely know the man's tells, but he's showing the classic ones.

"My apologies for having you back in here on such short notice," he says with his Georgia drawl. "And after I gave you the day off too. Off to see our legal eagles?"

"Soon enough. Thought I'd drop by here first," I answer. "Check in, see how you were doing."

"Why, that's very considerate. I appreciate that." I notice he doesn't answer the question. The dead air hangs like a raincloud, and Maxwell is the first to break. He waves me in to take a seat and commands the door to close behind me. "Since you're here . . . I wanted to ask you about something. It's about Simon."

"How can I help?"

"You see, Simon and I, we built this place together, and it's a marvel how far we've come, but we had grown too busy for each other." Maxwell's regret is both palpable and familiar. "You've spent more time with him than most, and, well, I suppose you might be able to tell me. What was he like, the last few days?"

I hate this question. Hate that I'm being asked it, and even more so what it implies. What possible answer could explain what happened? What kind of insight into Simon's mental state would ease his grief? I don't resent Maxwell for asking; it's what people do in the face of inexplicable loss. It's what I'd ask too, in his place, and it's what everyone asked me after Paolo died. Then, as now, I have the same response.

"He seemed fine, no different than usual."

Maxwell nods slowly, and his eyes convey both disappointment and yearning. The questions are drawn on his face. *Why did he do it? How could he?* I'm asking them too, and for his sake and mine, I wish I had answers.

"And how are you doing, son?" he asks after some time.

"I'm hanging in there."

"That's the most we can do, isn't it? Hang in there." Maxwell sighs. "This place would be nothing without Simon and now that he's gone . . . It'll be hard moving forward."

I don't doubt it. Cartwright and Parrish aren't just names on a shingle. It's a deep and abiding friendship that stretched decades. Together they co-founded *The Daybreak Dispatch* during the new media boom, and with a series of mergers, acquisitions, and strate-

gic partnerships, they transformed their online-only news aggrega-
tor into one of the country's leading media outlets.

As their empire grew in complexity and stature, Maxwell took
the management reins as co-CEO and president of the C+P
Board. Meanwhile, Simon was the Board chairman, and as co-
CEO, he handled the day-to-day top-level steering of the ship.
Still, Simon never seemed comfortable with executive life, and
the only role that he truly relished was that of editor-in-chief of
C+P's News Division.

"Between the two of us, he's always been the better journalist," he
says conspiratorially. "Especially the last few years. I don't remember the last time I worked on a piece myself. I suppose I should
thank my lucky stars the company has folks like you."

"Thank you. The newsroom's shaken, but we're a tough bunch."

"That you are," he replies. "And you're in good hands too. Cleo
Johnson's more than capable of taking over the News Division in the
interim. Not that it'll stop her, but she'll have a lot of horse manure
to deal with in the next few days."

"Yes, I've been checking on the feeds," I say, adding a sharp in-
take of breath, readying myself for the ramp-up. "We're getting
wall-to-wall coverage . . ."

"Nearly all of it untrue," he adds, with displeasure.

I shake my head. "It's disgraceful, really. Vultures, all of them."

"Vultures blowing hot air, making a scandal out of a tragedy."

"Not just a scandal—a circus," I add, indignant. After a beat, I arrive at the point. "Can't be good for the Zephyrus buyout bid."

Maxwell winces at this, but a split-second is all it takes for him to
catch himself and turn that wince into a smile. He's seen what I've
done, and he's weighing how to respond. He recovers quickly. "Generous as it is, their offer to buy C+P is just that. An offer, one that
we're not particularly pouncing to accept."

That's nice to hear, but my bullshit detector goes off. The C+P
Board might not be fully on board, but I know through the
grapevine that Maxwell's the lead proponent for selling out. The
company's not struggling, not by any measure that matters to corporate behemoths in search of new quarry. To wit, our stock value's
continuously increased in the last eight quarters, and is only pro-

jected to keep rising. C+P is at the top of its game, so it's curious that anyone would even consider selling the company, especially one of its founders.

"Zephyrus hasn't pulled out, given everything?" I ask.

"Tragic as this is," Maxwell says bluntly, "I'm afraid there's no tragedy large enough to deter their appetite."

I nod knowingly. We're talking about the company that lobbied to declassify the Everglades as a National Park and then bought all that land for a pittance, no more than six months after Hurricane Jacinta ravaged the entire tip of Florida.

Though their brand has become synonymous with international logistics, with Zephyrus's exclusive dominion over the new Arctic shipping lanes, the company's burgeoning portfolio grows larger by the day. They're also in commercial rail, renewable energy, consumer goods, agriculture, and pharmaceuticals.

Lately, they've set their sights on tech and telecommunications, snapping up device manufacturers, software developers, data storage solutions, and most of all, content providers. Media outfits of all kinds, from children's programming to sports networks and of course, news media. C+P is one of many, and they've bid on the biggest names in the last few years, often with success.

Everyone has seen how those news outlets were transformed after their holding companies got acquired. More than the loss of jobs, the staff feared that C+P would lose its soul. It's a fear I know Simon shared too.

"So is the Board still voting on their offer on the twentieth?" I ask. "Shouldn't you postpone, at least for a while?"

"And why would we do that?" he asks.

"Out of respect for Simon? He wasn't exactly wild about the offer . . . "

This was never a secret, and Maxwell reacts nonchalantly. Simon never liked it whenever anyone tried to buy out C+P Media, and there have been many offers before. He and Maxwell have built an attractive target, one that has entertained proposals from megacorporations, international news agencies, and the occasional Middle Eastern crown prince. Simon rejected them all, of course; he never risked losing ownership, and especially losing the News Division's independence. And though the Zephyrus offer is billions over the others he'd fielded, Zephyrus also asked for that journalistic independence in exchange. I'm surprised Simon didn't outright tell them to fuck off.

"To the contrary," Maxwell says. "Simon had come around to the proposal quite recently. He was no longer as hostile as he was at first, especially after Zephyrus sweetened the offer with some concessions."

"What kind of concessions?"

"Mostly financial in nature," he replies. "Share prices and asset valuations in terms more favorable than their initial approach. Simon, as you well know, had concerns about operations too; he wanted to keep key employees and maintain a high level of independence. With some wrangling, Zephyrus buckled. There will still be a lot of changes, especially as pertains to organizational structure, but Simon got most of what he asked for."

Sounds like the company is dead-set on acquiring us, if they're budging that much. Yet Maxwell said *most* of Simon's demands were met. Not *all*. A crucial distinction.

"What kind of changes?" I ask.

"Ah, you know I can't divulge specifics," he grins. I had to try. "But those who are privy to the details are quite excited. Zephyrus has grand plans for us."

"That's comforting." My sarcasm seems lost on him. "So Simon was going to vote yes?"

"With the deal as it stands? Yes." Maxwell leans toward me and lowers his head. "Look, I understand where these questions are coming from, Jamie. Truly, I do. Let me be the first to assure you that there's no cause for alarm. No one is losing their jobs, and C+P is not going to change. The last corporate restructuring we've had was before your time, but Simon and I have always taken care of the employees. That'll still be the case, even though he's gone. Especially so."

"I'll hold you to that," I say with some deference, though job security is the farthest thing from my mind. Of course a major corporate deal is a stressor, one that the cops have probably identified as a cause of Simon's apparent suicide. But a multibillion-dollar deal is also a motive. If Simon stood in the way of the offer, or indeed if Maxwell is to be believed and Simon had come to support it in the end, the Zephyrus bid would be an excellent reason for anyone to want someone dead.

❁

At the helm of the control room, Cleo Johnson paces back and forth, arms crossed. She whispers into her comms, calmly but sharply directing the mixers in the pit below. Before them is the two-story curved wall showing myriad holograph screens. Some feeds are from C+P's own in-house, remote and virtual studios, live and recorded broadcasts shot from different angles. Most of the feeds are those of our competitors, all of them running stories on the death of Simon Parrish. Elliott and I hesitate to interrupt her, not when she's in the zone.

"How'd your briefing go?" she asks, without turning to face us.

"Not as painful as we thought. Stick to the talking points *or else.* That sort of thing," Elliott replies. The legal team was thorough about the guidelines and consequences, but neither he nor I are in the mood to rehash it any further.

"You know I fucking hate all of that, too, but it's gotta be done. Now we can focus on fixing this mess Simon's left behind," she says. "Things are going to be hard around here for a while, and we all need to be topflight. You boys ready for what's ahead?"

"Of course," Elliott says.

Cleo eyes the cockpit, sends more instructions to the crew below, who instantly do as she says. Screens light up, change, shift, and reassemble, cameras focus and refocus, on-screen anchors do her bidding. No way does she appear uneasy slipping into her new role. In a newsroom full of strong and talented personalities, Cleo's been the only one who truly matched Simon's skill, not to mention his temperament.

Up until yesterday, she was executive editor and Simon's second-in-command, but she'd been running the C+P News just as much as he had. The two of them worked in lockstep, sharing the same journalistic values and doing things the same headstrong way. It was no surprise that he'd been grooming her to take over his role someday, leaving her to manage the day-to-day tedium while he focused on *The Simon Parrish Files* and spent more time with his family.

Unofficially, she'd been the news chief for months. As of twenty-four hours ago, she's the first Black woman to officially hold the title, both within C+P and in any of the Big Five news corps.

"Everyone's powering through," she continues, eyeing the mixers hard at work on the controls. "But I know they've got questions. Worries. You two probably most of all."

"Sure we do," Elliott replies. "As I'm sure you do too."

Cleo shrugs. "I'm too swamped to be worried. Things need doing." She recognizes the coldness in her tone and corrects herself. "Today did have its down time, and yes, the questions crept in. It's hard keeping them at bay."

"Totally understandable," I say, hoping we'd move on, to no avail.

"I stayed up all night racking my brain thinking, Why? What was weighing on him so much that he had to take his own life?" Cleo says it sharply, rhetorically, but her face shows a searching desperation. I don't know how to respond; neither does Elliott. Finding no answers, she continues.

"I've known the man fifteen years, worked next to him for most of that, and I got nothing. All I know is we would do well to meet with that grief counselor," she says, setting her sights back onto the cockpit. "It might not seem that way now, but violence of this nature can affect us in subtle and unknown ways."

"Violence?" I ask.

"Simon took his life in such a public way, and he knew that we would all see it. We may never find out what was going on in his mind, what state he was in, why he did what he did . . . but this much is clear: he wanted us to see. To bear witness. That's intentional and painful and deeply fucked up."

The bitterness in her voice leaves a similar taste on my tongue. I can't say I blame her. Part of me believes that her history with Simon should have entailed a more generous reading of his intentions, but the other part believes that that history justifies the pain that she clearly needs to release.

I empathize, but mostly I'm disappointed. I've talked to three seasoned journalists, and all of them are all too willing to believe the possibility that Simon killed himself. I knew Elliott would insist on keeping an open mind, and I've now learned that Maxwell has competing concerns, but if anyone would share my doubts, I expected it to be Cleo. She'd be the one to disbelieve suicide, the one who'd raise a stink about how improbable the cops' theory is. As it turns out, her hurt might be clouding her otherwise razor-sharp judgment.

"Can't come at a worse time too, with Zephyrus and all," she says after a while.

"The offer's still on?" Elliott asks.

"Yes. And the Board of Director's poised to accept it on the twentieth." Cleo pinches the bridge of her nose. "We've got ten days, and without Simon to block the vote, we're all fucked."

I knew Maxwell had been embellishing when he said that the staff was excited about the buyout bid, and unless Cleo's mistaken, he'd also been embellishing about Simon backing the deal. The question is, why?

Before I can ask more questions, Cleo raises a finger to stop me and barks into her comms, telling an on-air field reporter to stick to the goddamn prompter. When she's done, she takes off her earcuffs and visor, then asks her assistants to clear the helm. She voice-commands for soundproofing as the door closes.

"Anyway. The reason I called you over here," she starts. "You both have done a tremendous job, and I mean that independent of Simon," she says. "I gotta pick up a lot of slack now that he's gone, but so do the two of you. As interim news chief I'm not looking to make any changes, especially since we have a structure that works great. So what I'm thinking is, for the time being, you two will be co-EPs of *The Simon Parrish Files*. How does that sound?"

I knew a lot of changes would be coming, but I didn't think they'd come so fast. For one, I didn't foresee that this day would end with Elliott and me running the show. Picking and pursuing our own stories top to bottom, start to finish. Helping people, informing the public, making the world pay attention to issues that are neglected or hidden from view. We get to do all that. To top it off, we get to carry on Simon's legacy.

I mouth the words, but Elliott beats me to it. "Yes. We'd be honored."

"Fantastic. We'll have to find a new anchor, of course, and re-name the show after the appropriate time has passed, but you two would still be running our premiere investigative news show," she says.

"Cleo, I can't tell you what this means to me," I reply. "To us. We won't let you down."

"You sure as fuck better not," she warns. "We can talk next steps after this police business is over, but I'm thinking for the July episode we'll do a Simon Parrish retrospective. The best stories of his career."

"Wait—what about the piece on Senator Dwyer?" I ask. Elliott nods in agreement. "We've got more than enough time to polish the episode by month's end."

"I don't think it's the right move for now," Cleo replies. "Maybe for August."

"But we already have that story in the can, and we can't have two retrospectives back-to-back," Elliott counters, referring to our next episode, a deep dive on the UN synthetics embargo on the occasion of its ten-year anniversary. "Besides, this Dwyer story is time-sen-sitive. Please don't tell me I had to do all those interviews with the American Health Research Council for nothing."

"And shouldn't we have a special edition specifically devoted to Simon?" I ask her. "He deserves more than a regular episode of his own show."

"I'm not saying no. I'm saying not now," she replies. "The Re-publican primaries are months away, and those secret donations happened ages ago. Plus, those anti-Sleepless groups are mostly powerless now. Half of those groups have shuttered."

"Yes, but while we wait, Dwyer gets more traction by the day," Elliott says.

"The public's going to care just as much two months from now. You can try and sink Dwyer's career then."

"But what if—"

"And quite honestly," Cleo snaps, "I don't know that we can take this Dwyer story to the finish line without Simon."

Seconds ago she was all praises, but now we can't hack it? There's something else going on here. "We can handle it," I say, less certain of it than I sound. "We already got everything we need. If we don't do this story soon, Dwyer and the super PAC and everyone else involved will have time to cover their tracks. They might already know we're on to them."

"And not for nothing, it would be a shame if Simon's last assignment ends in failure," Elliott adds. "Come on, Cleo. If there's ever a time that we can do him proud, this story is it."

"Look, we don't have to finalize this now, but—" I add, but Cleo cuts me off.

"It's pretty final from where I'm standing, but sure, we can talk it out some more. On Monday." Her displeasure drips from every word. She picks up her devices and starts slipping them on again. "Honestly, all I wanted was to give you two a bit of good news— Lord knows we all fucking need it. So don't make me regret this."

Elliott and I take our cue and leave the control room seething. We've both worked so hard on the Dwyer story, the prospect that it would go up in flames is enough to dull our excitement at being promoted.

"So much for being an EP," Elliott says. "Something tells me our new roles are gonna be pretty symbolic."

"Not if we have something to do about it."

"She's feeling a lot of feelings, and she's got a lot going on," he replies. "Simon dying, the buyout, taking over the News Division . . . let's hope she's no longer on edge after the weekend."

Something tells me Cleo's got more than those things in mind. She's adamant about delaying Simon's last assignment; it's as if she wants it spiked it completely. It sure as hell feels like there's more to this than a programming schedule. Between Maxwell's revelations and her decision on the Dwyer story, plus the unusual ease with which they both accept that this is a suicide, I'm beginning to believe my source is right. The call is coming from inside the house.

10.

Friday, 07/10/2043, 09:48 PM

RachelK, 225 feet away. TheOneAliNYC, 40 feet away. JustNicholas, 904 feet away, hosting and not traveling. Pass. I need someone to come to me. JordanB, 0 feet away, probably in the same building, though surely I would've seen them around? Browsing through profiles is a good waste of time in itself, but after a while, the pictures start to look the same, so I make my choice with minimal vetting. Vespertine32 is nearby and has a well-lit headshot. Cute, quick, and easy. I initiate a conversation.

The preliminaries tend to be tedious. What are you into, what are your limits, how do you like it. Laying down the ground rules is critical, and I'm not one to rush through these things, but at the moment, all I ask is if he's good to go. His response has the type of crudeness that both repulsed and excited me. To close the deal, he sends over a cock shot. I send him my address.

I've been cycling through my options since Thursday and none of them have got me centered, not like they used to. I've had booze, done meditation, did VR milieus, and even taken a dip at the immersion pod, but I'm still not dialed back down to zero. Time to try

some human connection. Random hookups often leave me dissatis-
fied or disassociating, but it's the only thing I haven't tried, and I
badly need to mellow out from the one-two punch of Simon's death
and Hannah showing up at my door twice in one week.

The guy arrives a little bit late, a little bit high, and little bit
shorter than advertised. His handshake is firm but clammy, and he
moves into a half-hug. He smells of sweat and the bar around the
corner. From what I can tell through my own whiskey-induced
haze, the man is at least forty, not thirty-two. The scruff along his
jaw has patches of gray. Not as fresh-faced as in his photos, but
more rugged, distinguished.

"Nice place you got here. Lots of toys." He lets out a low whistle,
broadly gesturing at the tech scattered around the living room. He
grabs my forearm and pulls me closer, steering me into the couch.
Our faces verge on touching, then he leans in for a kiss. I pull away
and lead him straight to my room.

"You know, I've always thought you're cute," he says, then continues before I can ask. "I've seen you around the neighborhood. At
the biergarten . . . "

He doesn't seem worried about giving off a stalker vibe, and I'm
too turned on to care. "It's a fun place," I reply shortly.

"You're Sleepless, yeah?"

I nod, trying to blow past the remark. Some advertise that sort
of thing on their profiles, the same way they use descriptors like
"dog lover" or "ultramarathoner," words to set themselves apart
from the gallery of head- and torso-shots. I don't do that. Used to
be that identifying as Sleepless got you autoblocked. You might
have gotten a slur or two, and though the current algorithms try
to stamp that down, some still get through. But overall, times are
a-changin'. Now, the greater risk is that folks will turn out to be
Sleepless chasers.

"I am too." He has a devilish grin on his face.

This surprises me. Usually, the fetishists are not Sleepless themselves. They're normies looking for a taste of something different,
expecting some sort of freak show, or worse, thinking the sex would
be somehow better. (And no, being Sleepless does not make one better at it. I checked.) The worst are those who think that we'd be a

certain way in bed—more driven and intense, or maybe more meditative and deliberate. It's never one thing with the chasers, though they always tend to say the same thing: you're *special*. I've met enough of them to know how to dissociate and go through the motions. Once or twice, I may have exploited my status to pull a hottie into bed. I get through it just fine, but never without the morning-after sense of unease at being objectified.

Of course it's ignorant, and if you look deep enough, it's bigotry. If you press them (something I've learned is never worth the conversation), they'll argue that it's no more than a preference, and really, doesn't it in fact prove that they're pro-Sleepless? This is why I'm always caught off guard when one of our own has the same predilection. You'd think we'd know better.

"Wow. An *actual* bedroom," he says when we get to the doorway. "It's like a hotel in here. Matching nightstands, a duvet . . . one, two—four pillows. What's the thread count on your sheets?" he teases.

A lot of Sleepless folks get a studio. Without the need for bed space, they get to save a lot on rent. I guess I could too, but I'd rather have the space than save money. Plus, some of us still like to have sex on a mattress, and being Sleepless doesn't preclude lying down for a rest. Before she moved in with Torian, Veronica kept a bed, though she used it as kind of an open shelf for her art projects. As for Elliott, the rare times he needs to lie down, he does it in his home hyperbaric chamber.

"You should feel the sheets against your skin," I reply, deflecting from the small talk. I pull him into the room and shove him closer to the bed.

"Easy, rider. There's no rush. I got all night. And so do you."

Yes, you're Sleepless, I get it. And a chaser too, but I venture forth.

I take off my ratty T-shirt. He gazes at me, taking me in before pulling me closer. He then undoes the knot in my sweatpants and pulls them down. When he drops to his knees, I lift his shirt over his head and throw it aside.

I feel his warm breath on my skin. He waits until I look down at him. When our eyes meet, he takes me in his mouth. I don't know if it's the whiskey, or the last couple of days, or the skill with which this stranger works his tongue, but I buckle and I fall back, bliss-filled, into my pristine, luxury hotel-quality bed.

❀

In 2032, when the UN declared hyperinsomnia a global pandemic, no one yet understood where it came from and how it spread. All that the world's best doctors knew at first was that people weren't sleeping anymore. It all happened so quickly: cases were documented in all parts of the world—Europe, Australia, sub-Saharan and Northern Africa, South Asia.

In a matter of weeks, a good 10 percent of the world was Sleepless. 850 million people.

The world plunged into widespread and unrelenting hysteria. As a disease, history had never witnessed an outbreak with symptoms so unusual and infection occurring so randomly. Governments acted swiftly and harshly, imposing quarantines and segregation, and tamping down on any and all feared causes or vectors.

A few months after hyperinsomnia had been classified as a pandemic, the CDC and the WHO came out with two bits of good news. First, they ruled out airborne transmission. Scientists were still trying to determine how it spread, but knowing it wasn't in the air allayed a lot of fears. The strictest quarantine laws started to ease up then, much to everyone's relief. Second, they announced that hyperinsomnia did not have any short-term adverse effects. Their doctors said that the Sleepless were physiologically and psychologically no different from everyone else. They said their life expectancy, physical and mental attributes, their personalities, were entirely unchanged after becoming infected.

They're just like us. There is no cause for alarm.

A year later, the UN declassified hyperinsomnia as a pandemic. Can't call it that if it's not transmissible. Months of nonstop research identified no vectors for the condition. It's not airborne, nor does it spread through contact or fluid exchange. Nor is it heritable. No children have acquired it from their parents, and, with rare exceptions, it never develops in children under twelve.

Without a means of prediction and prevention, scientific efforts focused on the cure. We might not yet know how it gets you, but we'll be ready to fix you when it does.

Health tech companies scrambled too, building on existing research on sleep aids. They figured they could try and replicate sleep, but none of the early drugs reversed the effects of hyperinsomnia permanently. As the quest for a cure dragged on, society molded itself to accommodate the Sleepless population—24/7 hubs, three-shift workdays, bedroomless apartments, and of course, the latest in ReVRie and meditation technology. The world adapted.

Attitudes changed too. Sleep-status discrimination dropped sharply as Sleepless people became more valued as laborers and consumers. They started gaining some social and literal capital, and soon it seemed their ascendancy was all but assured. No one had given up on a cure, but at that point, everyone decided it was not the highest priority.

The most recent sea change happened three years ago, when the spread of hyperinsomnia began to slow down. At that time, the Sleepless population has grown from 850 million to 2.275 billion—an increase from 10 percent of the population to about 25 percent of the world's nine billion souls.

From 2032 to 2040, more people were becoming Sleepless than were being born. In those first eight years, hyperinsomnia incidence steadily grew by about 150 million new cases a year. But beginning in 2040, the Sleepless population peaked at 25 percent of the total population, and the ratio has hovered there ever since. That was the year that the number of new hyperinsomnia cases dropped in proportion to both the world's birth rate and the Sleepless death rate.

Initially there were fears that the Sleepless were dying off, and speculation flew about unforeseen side effects and shorter life spans, the sort of rumors that persisted in the early days of the pandemic. But by then the world had gotten slightly better at gathering and assessing data about the Sleepless, and the scientific community quickly laid those rumors to rest: the Sleepless were not dying off prematurely. There simply were fewer and fewer new cases; proportionally, more people were being born than becoming Sleepless. They also stressed that Sleepless folk were dying at the same pace as they had before, the same pace that non-hyperinsomniacs did.

With the incidence rate slowing and the replacement rate stabilized, people began to call 2040 the Plateau Year. The year that the Sleepless held steady.

As with every new answer about Sleeplessness, new questions came. The world knew what was going on with the incidence rate, but didn't know why it happened. To this day, the world's top researchers still cannot explain the Plateau. They don't know why there are fewer new cases, and they don't know if the replacement rate will drop further in the future.

Given that we still don't know what exactly caused the pandemic, or how hyperinsomnia is caught, we of course are no closer to knowing why the Plateau came about. The prevailing theory mainly attributes the Plateau to the effectiveness of the synthetic caffeine embargo. The lithium embargo is also cited as a contributing factor, as is the decline in coffee consumption worldwide.

The Plateau exasperated tech and pharma corporations that catered to the Sleepless population: the content providers, the consumer electronics manufacturers, the Sleepless health and wellness industrial complex. In general, shareholders demand unrestrained growth, and none were as demanding as the shareholders of companies that placed large bets on a Sleepless boom. A stable replacement rate meant that sales plateaued too, but instead of folding, they doubled down like a poker player on a long upswing. Maybe the Plateau was temporary, a blip, and if it was, then they had to keep going. At the same time, in many parts of the world, folks wanted to become Sleepless. Fear and loathing predominated during the onset of the pandemic, but eight years in, attitudes changed. People began to wish that they could catch the disease somehow. To meet this demand and shore up their bottom lines, corporations started research and development of artificially-induced hyperinsomnia. They raced to find a drug or a procedure that could turn someone Sleepless.

Back then, the global embargo treaty didn't prohibit the use of synthetic caffeine for research purposes, in the hopes that private and public institutes would find answers to hyperinsomnia's unresolved questions. Tech and pharma corps used the treaty's "scientific and medical exception" provisions to avoid government regulation of their R&D efforts, despite knowing that the exception was never intended for artificial hyperinsomnia. Indeed, the embargo was intended specifically to prevent the further spread of hyperinsomnia, natural or otherwise.

As soon as the UN got wind of what was going on, they gathered world leaders and passed an amendment to the treaty, banning synthetic caffeine for any and all purposes. "These corporations are playing with fire," the UN Secretary-General said. "We don't want another pandemic on our hands." Almost overnight, materials stockpiles were destroyed, and component parts and machinery were designated as contraband. They also added new international sanctions specifically targeting the development of artificial hyperinsomnia anywhere in the world. Those sanctions, both criminal and civil, had been adapted into the local laws of every member country, to varying degrees of severity, but all uniformly harsh. In the US, a mere conspiracy to trade in hyperinsomnia contraband is classified as a Class A felony and public health threat; given a zealous prosecutor, it might even get charged as a terrorist act.

My part in this history started about a year ago, when I became Sleepless myself. One of the rare, new post-Plateau cases. *Special.* I got what most people nowadays wish for: more time awake. More time to make money, be productive, follow your dreams. None of the downsides and all the perks. What nobody talks about is the best perk of all, at least for me: being Sleepless also means being dreamless. No more dreams, no more unexpected trips into the subconscious, no more dark dives into the past.

Can't have nightmares if you can't sleep.

✺

"I lost you back there," he says after a long silence. Laszlo (he finally shared his real name) lies naked beside me, running his finger in the folds of my ear.

"Nah, I was with you all the way," I reply languidly, my eyes fixed on the ceiling.

"What were you thinking about?"

"I wasn't thinking, I was feeling. And what I was feeling was good." As much as my mind had been flickering between here and now and the past, Laszlo made me forget all my worries, including the last few days and the mess that I'd been working to unravel. The sex was even good enough to make me forget that he's a chaser who I'd nonetheless let into my bed. Worse, it made me give him the benefit of the doubt. Maybe he just wants to connect with another Sleepless person; maybe it's no more insidious than that. Maybe a fervid desire for people like oneself should be enough, and the unexamined reason behind the desire shouldn't matter.

He sits up and pulls his vape pen from his jean jacket on the floor. He takes a long drag. Cannabis perfumes the air. He turns to me and offers the pen. I shake my head.

"So, what do you do?" he asks. I'd hoped we wouldn't have to do post-coital small talk, but here we are.

"Insurance adjuster." That usually grinds things to a halt. I don't bother asking him back, but that doesn't stop him.

"I'm a data miner. Yep, glued to a screen all day every day. It's good money though, especially with the offshore clients. I work for one of those ad analytics companies, VoluMetric? Heard of it? It's around the corner from here, actually. That shiny new building right by the Rheingold."

"Cool."

He studies my impassive face, dejected. He takes another drag, then gets up and starts dressing. "You know, it's actually good you messaged back when you did," he says as he turns to leave. "My break was almost over, I thought I wouldn't get any bites."

"You're going back to work?"

"Fourth shift. Gotta keep hustlin'."

I make a half-hearted offer to walk him to the elevator, but he declines. "We should do this again sometime," he says, and I know he means it. "You're a special guy, Jamie."

There's that word again. My skin crawls. I knew I should have sent him packing the moment I pegged him as a chaser.

"Oh yeah? How?" My tone has an edge to it, but he's doesn't sense it.

"I don't know, just . . . different." He says it tenderly, authentically, and it grates on my ear.

Different. If only he knew how.

Laszlo leans over the bed and holds my chin up. He kisses me on the lips, and he's lucky I let him. "Call me."

I nod, knowing full well that I won't.

When the front door clicks shut, I fall back onto the bed, tired but satisfied. I close my eyes and meditate. Deep breaths begin to bring me to a place of restful calm. The scent of sweat and sex and the faint note of marijuana informs my consciousness that pleasure was had, here, in this bed. It should make me feel better. This is the closest I've come to relief in the last forty-eight hours. I do feel better, I tell myself, in vain. Deep down, all I truly feel is shame.

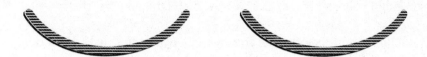

11.

After Paolo, Elliott was the next Sleepless person I knew. I guess I should have seen it coming, that night at the diner out by the Hudson Yards. He and I were out on assignment by the Midtown Tunnel, which had suffered structural damage only a decade after its reconstruction. Team Parrish was working a corruption angle. Apparently the subcontractor had cut some corners, and vibration tests indicated tensile stress cracks in the tunnel's concrete lining. Catastrophic water seepage was likely within a year. Without major rehabilitation, the newest and shiniest of Manhattan's arteries could collapse on itself.

Simon asked me to run point, and Elliott was backing me up. We had nonstop interviews with engineers, who demoed for us their latest sensor arrays. It was well past midnight when we realized we hadn't had a bite to eat all day.

From outside, Nighthawks looked to be in the throes of a midday rush. Upon entry, we were greeted with clattering trays, clinking glasses, and the aroma of bacon grease and fresh bread. The diner teemed with Sleepless patrons on their early fourth meals. The bar stools were all occupied by freelancers furiously typing away at their laptops. Their bulky headsets blocked the noise from a nearby group of college kids, drunk, rowdy and clamoring for their loaded nachos.

Elliott and I took the last free booth, a two-seater tucked in a corner near the bathroom. At least it was by a window, looking out on the skyline of Weehawken. In the next booth, a group of Francophone tourists huddled over a tablet, planning out the rest of their night. From what I gathered, the plan was to walk south through the city, stopping at dive bars and other points of interest along the way, ending at the tip of Manhattan for sunrise photos of the submerged Old Battery Park.

At this hour, any other New York diner would have maybe two or three patrons, at least one of whom might be a homeless person nursing a cup of lukewarm tea, waiting for daylight when the streets were a bit safer. There might be a couple on a late-night tryst, or a maglev worker coming off her shift. There definitely wouldn't be a book club meeting, like the one currently going strong at a long table by the window.

Amid the din, a sole backpacker was asleep one table over, slumped with her head resting on folded arms. She stood out against the energy of the diner, which was too lively for a weeknight and too loud for an out-of-the way joint right on the edge of the island. She was the only one in that diner who looked normal to me.

At the time, I remember thinking that this must be what it was like to be Sleepless in a sleeping world. Largely unremarkable until set apart by contrast. No wonder they congregated at this place, this tiny little bubble where they could be with people like them. A place where, for once, they didn't stand out.

The backpacker didn't stir at the beeping of a DumWaiter holocrate as it passed next to her, nor at the voice of the ethereal server that apparated to take my order. The sight of her was contagious, and I started nodding off as well. Elliott slammed his hand at the table, which jolted me. I flipped him the bird.

"So, do you remember that story we did about the biopunks?" he asked.

"Yeah, what about it?"

"They called me again, said they got something huge."

I mustered a tired eyeroll. A while back, Team Parrish did an hour-long episode about a fringe group within the transhumanist community called the Genomages. Mostly made up of early-twenties libertarians with too much time, money and brainpower, their members fervently believed in unfettered science. Their anti-establishment, anti-regulatory ethos opposed the FDA, the CDC, OSHA, and any other acronym that symbolized the government's attempts at shackling free thought.

In prior years, the group's scientific work, if one could call it that, focused on biomodification. All their efforts were directed toward finding ways to exercise total dominion over one's body. Pre-pandemic, the Genomages claimed to develop neural interfaces, electromechanical implants, biosyncing augments, and other "secret projects" that veered into the illegal. Then as now, biomodification was heavily regulated, and most forms of bio-hacking—gene editing, molecular cloning, anything approaching eugenics—were outright banned. Yet collectives such as the Genomages still persisted, and indeed grew more defiant the harder the establishment came down on them.

In truth, they're mostly harmless. Every now and then, one of their cohort grabs public attention by announcing some earth-shattering biohack that turns out to be an empty promise. One of their latest stunts involved the use of octopus genes to create color-changing tattoo ink.

"I met with their leader," Elliott continued. "The guy claims they've developed artificial hyperinsomnia."

"Yeah, right. They've been saying that for years. Those biopunks just want attention so they can get crowdfunding money."

"They have proof," Elliott said with a smug grin.

"Or so they say. How many times have we gotten this line from them?"

When the pandemic hit, the Genomages were the loudest advocates for free and open hyperinsomnia research. For a while, it seemed that they had turned a new leaf and truly wanted to do good: in their modest way, they at least appeared to work toward discovering the origin of the disease and developing a cure. But as time marched on and more people saw the upsides of being Sleepless, they seemed to have returned to their old biohacking ways.

"They're all bark," I said. "If they were anywhere close to it, the feds would be all over them."

"I don't know, man . . . what they had seemed pretty solid."

"What, you've seen it?"

He gave me a knowing look then shifted his glance away. Between him and me, Elliott had always been the bigger skeptic. But not this time. Not only had he met with the Genomages, he actually seemed convinced. And I knew it wasn't because he had reason to believe that their claim was legit. It was because he wanted to believe.

"Think about it, the actual choice to be Sleepless," he continued. "Wouldn't you do it?"

"Not me."

"Are you telling me if you had the choice, you wouldn't want to be Sleepless?"

"What would that choice even look like?"

"It's the choice between more or less time, and the answer is pretty obvious."

Elliott and I had had this conversation several times before, and I knew where he stood. He'd always viewed the Sleepless as the lucky victims of a cosmic accident, and he dreamed about what he would do if he were one of them. And so with this dubious claim from the Genomages, he again rhapsodized about the possibilities, the scenarios that he played out in his mind, the fantasies from old conversations rehashed.

Inevitably he'd start going on about his superpower theory. "Hyperinsomnia is as close as we've gotten to a real-world superhuman ability," he used to say. Not like flight or invincibility or precognition, but in the same way that being a billionaire is a superpower—it gives you access, opportunities that others don't have. There's an obvious allure to it, one not lost on a dreamer like Elliott.

"I can do whatever I want, whenever," he said. "I don't have to wait to retire to do anything. I don't have to wait until the weekend . . ."

"You still need money."

". . . I can have two or three jobs and make tons of money. I can work at C+P by day, then get another job, maybe something that pays a bit more, and still have time to spare. I can be a masked vigilante at night . . ." Here his tone became mildly playful, but still grave enough to tell me he was at least half serious.

"You can't be Batman."

"He trained for years with some ninjas. I can do that in a month, easy!"

"It's illegal. Plus, you can't become a billionaire from just working two jobs, plus . . ."

"You can be my Alfred." I raised my eyebrow. "Fine, you can be Robin."

"That's only slightly better."

"Jamie, you could quite literally do whatever you want. Change yourself. Change the world. All anything ever takes is time."

"I've heard this all before," I replied. "Hell, I've seen it. The Sleepless sure as hell make a lot more money. They get to do more with their lives, I guess. But is that enough? I don't know. What I do know is I wouldn't want to mess with my body like that. Especially not with stupid Genomage tech."

Elliott looked at me with an aching insistence, but beneath that willfulness was also resignation. He knew how I felt about these fantasies of his. I'd dismissed him enough times, and just like those other times, he'd give me the same pained look he always made, the one that he tried to conceal with a haughty certitude in his ideas.

This time was different though. I didn't know it then, and had no way of knowing, but he was trying to tell me something. I didn't know how much I had let him down until the next day.

❀

While Elliott and I were in the thick of post-production on the Hudson Yards piece, Simon dropped by the editing suite, wanting to redo his tracks. He said his voiceovers sounded overwrought. I assured him that he sounded fine, and so did the editors who were about ready to wrap things up, but Elliott offered to redo it if it'd calm his doubts.

"Great, always could rely on you, Elliott." Simon said. "But don't you have a train to catch?"

"I should be all right to stick around a while longer," Elliott replied.

"Go be with your mother—that's an order," Simon said. "Jamie's got it covered, yeah?" I was more than happy to help a friend out, but it had also been a long day, one that now promised to last even longer. The editors and I exchanged weary sighs.

Before he left, Elliott pulled me aside with a grave look on his face. "About last night, I didn't quite get to my point. Call you on the ride down?"

I was still in the middle of scut work when he called. I wearily excused myself from the editing bay and took the call at my desk. Elliott asked me to turn on video, something he rarely does.

"I want you to let me finish before saying anything," he started. On screen he looked pale, and his camera was shaking, and not because of the train's motion. "A week ago, I took Levantanil. It's an artificial hyperinsomnia drug developed by the Genomage guys, and—and I haven't slept since. What I'm saying is—Jamie, I'm Sleepless."

"The fuck? How?"

A thousand thoughts raced through my head. Not only was he telling me that he was Sleepless, but that he's also committed biohacking of the highest order.

"My coke guy, Kingsley, he's biohacked. Nothing serious, just an exo-suit and I suspect some gene edits. Anyway, a few months ago, he started slinging Levantanil. I was intrigued, had a lot of questions, so he reconnected me with the Genomages, who were all too willing to talk. At first I thought it's all bullshit, they're just trying to grab headlines, whatever. But I saw what they have, Jamie. Their lab, their research, all of it. It's real, and it works. They've been selling in Joburg and Kyoto for months now."

"This is impossible."

"No, it's not. The science was always there, waiting to be done. The money was there too. Ban or no ban, it was only a matter of time. So I dug some more, did my due diligence. If this was all an elaborate scam, at least I'd have a huge story on my hands."

"Elliott, this is insane . . ." Words sputtered out of me in an incoherent cascade. There's a reason biohacking is outlawed, especially biohacks related to hyperinsomnia. This isn't something that we should reproduce, let alone unleash at will. There are still a lot of unanswered questions: how it came about, how it's transmitted, how it can be cured. Not everyone wants it, no matter how good the Sleepless seem to have it now. Whatever the upsides, no one should be messing with the most potent pathogen humanity's ever seen, not when there's still so much about it left unknown.

"And you know how thorough I am," he continued, oblivious. "I double-, triple-checked their reports, consulted with doctors, scientists, anyone I could talk to who'd comment off the record. Everything I learned told me one thing: there's no difference between turning Sleepless naturally and popping a pill to become one."

"So you just did it? You fucked with your brain because it's just like the real thing?"

"I gave this a lot of thought. Months. There was an incredibly low probability of a bad reaction. The Genomages pre-screen everyone for it, and I was in the clear. And there's no risk of reversion. All their testing showed that Levantanil works permanently."

"All that talk about what you and I would do if we were Sleepless —that was just us daydreaming," I replied, my voice raised. "You didn't have to carry through and take a risk so fucking stupid!"

"It's a calculated risk, and it will pay off," he said, keeping his cool. Though his words were measured, I could tell he was resisting the urge to yell back at me. A vein on his temple throbbed like it was about to burst.

"You don't need to worry," he continued. "Remember how you once said that if I became Sleepless, you'd be happy for me? Well, here we are."

"This is not what I fucking meant. I never thought you'd biohack yourself. How do you expect me to be happy about that?"

"The result is the same, Jamie. Only the method differed."

"And what if you get caught?" I asked. "Are you willing to go to prison for this? And what about side effects? What if this pill kills you?" The worst-case scenarios flashed before my eyes, and I spat them all out as fast as I could imagine them.

"Levantanil has no side effects," he said. "Just like hyperinsomnia."

"You don't fucking know that," I replied.

"I'm not going to die. Not yet, not for a long time, and definitely not because of this," he said. "I'll live a long and healthy life, with more waking moments to do what I want. Even if there are risks, shouldn't that be worth it?"

"Fuck no."

Elliott sighed and lifted his head. A smile cut across his face even as his eyes began to well up. He was steeling himself, being patient with me. I knew I wasn't saying the things that he wanted to hear. I searched his face and though I found pain, I also saw relief.

"You're the first person I told." His voice cracked as he pushed out the words. "Do you know why? Because you're the only one who'll understand."

"Well, I don't."

"You do. It might not feel like it right now, but you know why I did this," he said. His next words would stay with me for a very long time. "You know because you would have done the same thing."

12.

03/2042

After Elliott told me about the biohacking, I stopped returning his messages. I came in to work at erratic hours to avoid any interaction, steered clear of him when we were both in the building. But he and I spent too much time together. That absence of a few days felt like weeks, and the longer that went on, the more I felt a void in my life. Hannah helped, but my relationship with her was different. She occupied a different space, as did Elliott, and as did Paolo, who I had lost not even a year ago. When I think about it in those terms, I suppose Elliott assumed the role that Paolo played in my life, and with him taking this strange pill, I found myself on the verge of another devastating loss.

"What the fuck is this?" Simon yelled, flinging his tablet onto the clutter of his desk. He'd finished reviewing the final edit of our Hudson Yards piece, and called both of us in for a grilling. "I've seen you do a lot better than this steaming pile."

"We still have time to fix it," Elliott replied, saving me from responding even though I was the lead on this assignment. "Just tell us what you want changed, and we'll rush it for tomorrow in the a.m.

We'll pull an all-nighter if we have to."

"This is fucking amateur hour," Simon replied, seething. "I don't even know where to fucking start."

Truth be told, neither did I. The story was solid. We'd gotten the material we needed, talked to the right people. We had receipts. The piece didn't have a smoking gun that would lead to an indictment, but it was enough to raise questions in the right quarters. Besides, hadn't Simon seen the rough cut himself? Now he was just nitpicking.

With a sideways glance, Elliott prompted me to answer, but I was also waiting for him to speak since he'd already started. Neither of us wanted to be in the line of fire. Simon's comments hung in the air, without a response, and the pause was too long to bear.

"What the hell is going on with you two?" Simon yelled. "Someone answer me before I sack you both."

"Nothing," I said. "Yes, I agree, it's substandard work, I see that now. But we do have time to make changes. We'll head back out to the yards right now if you want us to."

"What I want is for you two . . ." Simon started, before getting interrupted by a call. He walked out of his office with his earcuff in place, motioning for us to stay like one does with their dogs.

That meeting was the longest Elliott and I shared the same space since he'd told me about Levantanil. He looked my way, eyes bloodshot, and I wondered if it was because of all the work stress or because of the change he'd been going through.

"Jamie, I know you're hurt, and I'm sorry," he said quietly. "But this was a decision I had to make for myself. I know that this is probably scary for you, but I'm kind of scared too."

"Then you shouldn't have fucking done it," I replied.

"I never got to tell you my reason," he said. "It's not all those things I wanted to do, not the stupid Batman superhero vigilante crap we've been joking about. I did it for my mom. I'm losing her, Jamie, and she's well worth the risk."

Guilt overwhelmed me. With all this talk of hyperinsomnia and biohacking, I had lost sight of what truly mattered to him. His real reason for wanting to be Sleepless. He didn't do it for money, or opportunities, or so he could live a fuller, longer life, whatever that means. He had a reason that was far more profound and more valid than what other Sleepless-wannabes have. And because of my own selfish fears, I'd completely missed it.

"I'm not saying I'm scared," I said. "But I'm not not-scared. What's going to happen if it all goes to shit?"

"I know you, Jamie. You don't back down from fear," he replied. "You don't run away from the action, you rush toward it. If the worst is coming, wouldn't you want to stop it from happening?"

His words brought me back to the year before, to the time when the worst had happened and I failed to stop it. There I was again, given another chance to save someone I care about. I couldn't possibly say no. I gazed into Elliott's reddened eyes, and following a sharp breath, I nodded.

Simon soon marched back into his office with a spring in his step and a boom in his voice. "Where were we? Ah yes, you two shat the bed and were about to get sacked. Now tell me precisely why I shouldn't do that."

❁

Though I still had some reservations, I began to be involved with every step of Elliott's journey into the world of the Sleepless. Back then, as now, we had been putting in long hours at work every single day. That placed me in the best position to observe any adverse changes.

For a naturally Sleepless person, full onset takes about three weeks. The body craves sleep less and less until it doesn't anymore. For Elliott, that period took about a month. He was sluggish for the first couple of weeks and fended off the fatigue with uppers, which seemed like a bad idea because he also acted a bit manic at the time. Mania's not a symptom of hyperinsomnia; Elliott was simply too excited to become Sleepless.

I observed him closely during those weeks. I interrogated him about his doctor's visits, his schedule, his emotional state. I reminded him about his eye drops. I made nonstop visor recordings of him, which we reviewed together, me more closely than he ever did. If anything was amiss about his health and mental state, I would catch it.

The endeavor reminded me of how I was in the weeks after Paolo died. How I studied every memory I had of him, searching for clues, cracks in the façade. Every irregularity felt outsize, and often I wondered to myself, was that it? Was that the sign? There I was, doing that again, that infinite parsing, the close scrutiny of every movement. The only difference this time was, if something bad were to happen to Elliott, I'd be there to prevent it.

I wanted to make sure he was the same Elliott as before, and in all ways, he was. He sure seemed happier, even after the initial post-change high. A lot of it had to do with his mother. He got to spend more time with Laura, never needing to stress about train schedules and his growing workload. He also started making money on the side, going to casinos while his mother slept through the night.

Elliott seemed happier at work too. He took on more assignments, did double shifts. Simon loved this new and improved hyperproductive version of him. As for me, Elliott covered my ass as much as he could, doing more than his fair share of the copious work Simon dumped on both of us. He spent a lot more time doing background on our pieces, putting in extra hours here and there.

"You've been a great help with all this," he told me once. "Me doing more work for you is just payback."

"Well, helping you now is just payback for all your help when Paolo died."

Elliott had been a real comfort during the darkest days of my grief. Not only did he pick up the slack for me at C+P, he took care of me, relieving my family and Hannah, who suddenly found themselves saddled with a depressive. After I had to check in at the facility, he made sure that I eased back into work without missing a beat. He continued to cultivate my contacts in my absence, returned messages and calls on my behalf. He wrapped up all my pending assignments, and even quelled workplace rumors about my condition. His name appeared on the New Dawn facility visitor logbook as often as Hannah's did. I owed him much, and it was a debt that I was more than happy to repay.

"Seems like we're gonna keep paying each other back 'til eternity," he said.

"Except you have more time than I do."

I suppose it was amusing, the two of us alternating in the role of carer. Though I have to admit, what I did for him back then wasn't a purely selfless undertaking. Sure, I wanted him to be well, to be the Sleepless person he always wanted to be. Yet I also did it for myself. I wanted to see how Levantanil changed a man because I was curious, driven by an unspoken yearning to take the pill myself.

13.

06/2042

It took Elliott about three months after he turned before he started aggressively recruiting me. By then, a post-midnight snack at Nighthawks had become our staple way of closing out long work nights. I'd have a whiskey double to smooth my edge out and get me ready for bed, while he scarfed down his second dinner of the day. He usually ordered a coffee with his meal. Although it was pricey and the caffeine literally did nothing for him anymore, he liked the taste of it. Some nights I almost ordered a coffee too. My energy couldn't keep up with his, and being around a bunch of Sleepless folks only made me more tired and cranky.

"You might be in a better mood if you got some food in you," Elliott said as he usually did when feeling self-conscious about eating alone. Since turning Sleepless, he'd become more meticulous about his calorie consumption and energy expenditure, making sure he didn't eat more than what his body needed to run 24/7. But being newly Sleepless, he still often forgot that we have disparate calorie needs.

"I don't have the same metabolism as you do," I reminded him. "I don't need fuel if I'm just going to sleep right after."

"Sleeping still requires energy."

"Not as much as being completely awake."

"And you can always hit the gym if you start gaining some weight."

"With what time?" I asked. "I can barely keep up with everything else."

"Well, you know what can fix that . . . ?" he asked devilishly. Elliott alluded to Levantanil every so often, testing the waters of my approval. I generally dismissed him with a hand wave and he'd leave it at that, but as the months passed, he grew more determined.

Card counting. That was his first attempt at a real pitch. He told me how it works and how, with enough training and practice, he'd made enough money at the blackjack tables to attract the unwanted attentions of pit bosses up and down the coast. He shuttled out to Boston or Atlantic City most nights, then headed straight to work the next morning with thousands more in his bank account.

"That explains the new VR rig," I said. Pre-transition, he never would have splurged on such a setup, not with his mother's medical bills.

"What can I say, I had a string of good luck."

"By definition, card counting isn't a matter of luck," I reply. "Can't you be like other hyperinsomniacs and keep your head down? Get a second job or something?"

I gestured toward the row of tablet jockeys on their usual spots at the diner counter, their zombified faces underlit by the glow of their screens. One of them actually worked at C+P. Maeve, an assistant from Finance. I gave her a wave and though she returned it, she pretended not to see Elliott. The two of them weren't out at work, and whenever they saw each other at Nighthawks, they'd act like complete strangers.

"What's wrong with doing a bit of freelance?" I said.

"Besides the miserable pay and assignments?"

"Didn't think you even had the math skills for card counting."

"Look, I only want to set myself up a little more comfortably, build a decent nest egg." He started to sound apologetic. "I promise I'm only using my superpower for good."

"It's not a superpower."

"Money's the best superpower. Time is money. And being Sleepless means more time. That's what Levantanil can give you. That's what it gave me." Elliott didn't bother to lower his voice at the mention of the drug. To the contrary, he seemed to grow more excited as he went.

"Do the math, Jamie. Hours by days by years, that's twenty-five to thirty more years. All this time, humans haven't been able to tap into those years because of sleep. Now we can. It's the best kind of life extension, because it's not at the end when you're old and weak. It's when you still have your energy and your wits about you. Three full decades at the peak of your life."

"That's a good way of thinking about it," I said. Life extension. Wasn't that what most human pursuits were about? Longevity, leaving a legacy. Immortality. A life not cut short. Wanting those things feels so natural, so human, that it was becoming impossible to deny that I wanted them too.

"Plus, the pill has no downsides. You've seen it yourself, with all your notes and recordings. You know there's no reason to worry."

"I'm not worried." At least not as much as I was at first. All my fears had dissipated as I saw Elliott become what he'd set out to be. All I saw now were the upsides. The extra money he made, the extra time he got to spend with his mom, the headway he'd made at work. His persistence grated sometimes, but I knew he only wanted me to have what he had. To be where he was.

"You and I talked about this way before we knew about Levantanil," he said. "What you'd do with that extra time, all the places you'd go, the things you'd learn. You liked the idea of being Sleepless as much as I did. Honestly, if I didn't know how you felt about it, I probably wouldn't have found the guts to do it."

"What do I have to do with it?" I asked defensively.

"We've always wanted the same things, and your validation, unstated as it was, motivated me to do it. Take it as a compliment. Or a thank you."

I didn't feel like I'd earned his gratitude, nor did I want it. I never would have encouraged him to biohack himself, implicitly or otherwise. Quite the opposite, I would have stopped him if he told me. Yet looking at him now, seeing what fruit his decision had borne, I wondered if stopping him would have been the right call.

"You're welcome," I said, half-sarcastically.

Something about the way I said it must have told Elliott that he was about to win me over. He knew I was close to saying yes, and he knew exactly what I needed to get there.

"How's grief counseling?" he asked in the lull of the conversation.

"It's just regular therapy now, and it's going all right. Dr. Cassis has been really helpful."

"And how long 'til it's over?"

"The mandatory part? The court order already ended, so it's all been voluntary since April. You know this."

"But you still haven't been sleeping well."

"Mostly because you keep wanting to hang," I reply. "After midnight, might I add."

"Are you still having those dreams?"

"What dreams?"

"You know what dreams."

I'd first told him about them during his visits at New Dawn, told him how my mind forces me to relive that day every time I go to sleep. How real it feels each time—the cold doorknob, the weight of my luggage in my hand, the warm saffron light of the early morning as it streams into the old Greenpoint apartment. The shadow cast on the floor, Paolo's dark outline on the marble tile. Then a blink, an unobscured window. The sweat on my brow as I look down onto the sidewalk, the splatter of black-red, the splayed limbs.

I'd also told Elliott about the subtle variations, how sometimes in these nightmares I'm too late and don't get to see Paolo until he's dead on the pavement, or sometimes we get into a heated argument instead of the teary, panic-filled exchange of our last conversation. Sometimes, too, I end up grabbing Paolo by the waist, wresting him from the window frame, but we instead both plunge to our deaths. In none of these variations does Paolo survive. In the worst of them, I am the one to push him off the edge.

"They're not as bad as they used to be," I lied. Often, the nightmare visions came in short snatches, and sometimes I'd get the full playback of the movie in my subconscious, but they still came nightly. Each morning I still woke up with cold sweats, heart racing, panting and drained of all energy. That was on a good day. Elliott reminding me about Paolo was an effective, if cheap, tactic. It wouldn't have worked, except that the nightmares had gotten worse as of late.

"So they haven't stopped," he replied.

"The therapy's helping."

"Sure it is. And the meds?"

"Those too."

I'd tried them all. Sleep medication, every sort of knockout pill, drinking myself into a stupor. Dr. Cassis didn't like that last one, but he had yet to find something that worked. The weekly sessions helped somewhat, and I tended to sleep better on the nights following a visit, but "better" was relative, a moving target. It mostly meant that I didn't wake up screaming, sobbing uncontrollably, or both.

A hush passed over us, and despite the clamor of the diner, I could hear my own breathing.

Elliott took a sip of his coffee.

"Right. Well then. I'm sure you'll be fine."

He spoke with the certainty of a man who knows that he's won.

The next day, I told him to make the call.

✦

Elliott briefed me about the process, though a rundown wasn't necessary. I had been there through his transition and done my own research. What I needed to know was who we were dealing with. Whether they could be trusted. Ten to fifteen years in prison was a long stretch, and that was on the low end of the sentencing range.

"You can trust Kingsley," Elliott said. "He's indie. He moves product for the Genomages, grows their customer base, but that's it. He's only in it for the money, and if the feds ever come knocking, he's not gonna snitch on us."

Every dealer would say that, and I had no reason to believe it. Of course I pressed Elliott on it, but his insistence and my desperation won over. Eventually I accepted this assurance on blind faith in my friend. "So how do we do this?"

"He'll set you up with a doctor who works with the Genomages. It'll be like a routine checkup. Results will be ready in a couple of days. Once you're cleared, Kingsley will need the first 45 in crypto. The rest on delivery. It's steep, but you'll earn that back in no time."

It dawned on me that I was days away from attaining the promise of Sleeplessness. The money, the time, the freedom that everyone Sleepless kept touting. The surface advantages of eight extra hours. Ninety grand was nothing compared to what I'd get in exchange.

"Thanks for fronting me the money, by the way."

Elliott waved me off. "Eh, I know you're good for it. And I know where you live."

"We're sure there's no trail? It's a lot of money to be moving around, and if the Genomages are selling a lot of this, they'll raise some flags."

"They know what they're doing. Kyoto and Johannesburg have been operational for months. And we haven't heard of any major international incidents, have we?"

"True," I say. "Why those cities, by the way?"

"Kyoto's pretty obvious, the demand's high. No more karoshi." Death by overwork. "Joburg, I'm unclear about. Might have something to do with their local connections."

So assured, I began planning logistics. I wanted to be home when I took the pill, but I needed Hannah to be away. Luckily, she had a work conference in Austin coming up, one that required in-person face time and a few nights' stay. As soon as she booked her flight, I booked Kingsley.

The man worked quick. He got the call on a Monday, scheduled my medical screening by Wednesday, and by Friday, he was at our apartment door ready to close the deal. He made a striking first impression, this hulk of a man in a black leather overcoat. In the low light of my kitchen counter, I made out his XFrame rig, the sleek platinum exoskeleton wrapped around his torso, shoulders and upper arms. Underneath the metal scaffolding was pure muscle, close to zero body fat.

Despite this showing, he put me at ease. My bullshit detector never went off on him either. Sure, he was this total stranger selling me contraband pharmaceuticals, but when he said "trust me," I truly felt that I could. It might have been his vibe, though frankly, I'd been dying to take the pill, so most of my inhibitions had disappeared by then, and the few that remained I readily ignored.

For one, my fears about health risks had been allayed since I witnessed Elliott's change. The risk of prison still weighed on me, but Kingsley had that air about him, like he was a principled, honorable man. Yes, he's a drug dealer, but he'd never turn me in if things went south.

The risk to my family did give me pause, but a little bit of self-deception helped with that. I managed to convince myself that the guilt of lying about Levantanil would be bearable, as long as I remained completely open to them about my Sleeplessness.

The only fear I had left was Hannah. What would she do if she found out I was Sleepless? Would she understand? Would her family, the dyed-in-the-wool hippie environmentalists who decried the rise of the Sleepless as the new era of rampant consumerism? I might survive losing esteem in their eyes, but what if Hannah felt the same? And what about the biohacking? Unlike with my family, I was unable to persuade myself that a half-truth would be enough. I couldn't lie to her forever, could I?

Kingsley held out his hand, and on his palm lay the pill that would change everything. I found myself staring at it, awed by the power it took to compress all those hours into a bolus the size of a fingernail. All that time. Time enough for anything. To live and love, to work or rest, if and when I wanted to. Time enough to make my dreams come alive, and to pursue new ones. Time to not dream at all. Surely Hannah would understand.

Time to say goodbye to my nightmares.

I took the pill, swallowed, then chased it down with a shot of single malt.

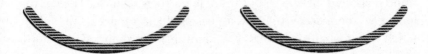

14.

In my line of business, skepticism is the bare minimum. That I have in spades, and more too: a deep-seated personal wound that I'll spend my life atoning for, an aching urge to please someone whose esteem I always craved and will never gain, and a propensity for suspicion borne out of my own need to keep a terrible secret. Do all those things make me good at what I do? No doubt.

I've been going over the conversations I've had and my observations of the C+P staff in the last couple days, and I've found that not a single person has raised the specter of murder. I seem to be the only one unwilling to believe that Simon's death was a suicide.

To my skeptic's mind, this atmosphere of ready acceptance casts everyone under the shadow of doubt. Not just Maxwell or Cleo, who clearly have something to hide, but all of C+P, anyone who had access to Simon. No one's made any hushed comments, no crude yet half-meant insinuations. No one's playing devil's advocate in a newsroom full of showoffs too ready to come to the devil's defense.

I recognize that this casts me apart, alone. No matter. I'll get to the bottom of this by myself.

At C+P Tower, security hasn't tightened despite the events of Wednesday night. At the very least I had assumed there'd be an additional credentials check, but there is no such obstacle. The guards don't give me a second glance as I pass the scanners in the lobby, which is unusual given that I'm coming in off-hours following a gruesome death.

It's like they don't know how reporters can be.

The reception desk on our floor, typically occupied on weekend mornings, is unattended. I get off the elevator and try to look casual. Yeah, I'm here on a Saturday morning, what of it? People work weekends, holidays, through late nights or weather disasters; mostly remote, but it still wouldn't be odd for anyone to be on the newsroom floor right now. What's odd is how completely empty the place is. Folks are probably trying to avoid the stench of death.

Works for me.

I march down the main hallway, eager to revisit the scene. If I'm lucky, those windows won't have been wiped clean yet, and Simon's notes won't have been bagged for evidence. There's a good chance of that, if the cops think it's a suicide. Less likely, those notes might have something about the buyout deal or the Senator Dwyer story, something to shed light on what Simon had been thinking in his last days.

The glass wall of his office, usually clear, has been set to translucent. I can only make out the blurs of where his desk and his couch and chairs are. Two bands of yellow NYPD tape cordon off the length of the wall, with two more bands of tape criss-crossing over the office door, but I've never let police tape stop me before. As for the surveillance cameras, well, it's not like I can't come up with a ton of valid-sounding reasons for going into Simon's office.

I slide my visor on, crouch beneath the yellow tape, and push the door open. The lights turn on as I step in, and I see that the scene's unchanged from Wednesday. With quick finger gestures, I start recording.

The dried wine still stained the desk, the papers still lay there dried and wrinkled. No one's been brought in for cleanup, and that gives me a thrill. One, that could mean that the cops have asked to preserve it as a crime scene after all. Two, that means I get the chance to find what I'm looking for. I approach Simon's seat but before I reach it, a familiar voice breaks the silence.

"Aren't you supposed to be on leave?"

I turn and find Anders by the doorway, a stack of folders under each arm.

"I thought Maxwell gave the team a few days bereavement?" he continues. "Of course, that's only for the higher ups. Apparently, us assistants don't get the privilege of grief."

"I—left some records here, after, you know, and I really need them to finish up the Dwyer piece."

"Right, the Dwyer piece." He raises an eyebrow and turns to leave. He's not convinced, so I tail him to his desk, on which sit stacks of boxes. He dumps the folders into one of them.

"Yeah, I finally got those stock sale receipts that I've been trying to chase down. But of course I forgot all about it when I came in here Wednesday."

"Of course you do."

"I need to keep myself busy, to get my mind off things."

"Oh, I'm sure you can do better by means of diversion." He winks.

The casual flirtation catches me off guard. It's been a while since Anders and I were flirty, let alone friendly. We dated for a few months post-Hannah, and it honestly seemed like a good idea at the time, notwithstanding HR's disapproval of office romances. We had always liked each other as coworkers, and we were plenty similar. We read the same books, and had a mutual intellectual attraction that matched the physical, which on my end was easy to see. Blonde, freckle-faced and blue-eyed, with a wry smile. He flashes one now, and I take it as an opportunity. With him here, I'd be hard-pressed to find a chance to snoop around Simon's office, but there may yet be a way that this morning doesn't go to waste.

"I've always found that the best distraction is work, don't you?" I reply, sheepish.

"I understand," he says. "You're EP now. You gotta step up."

"You heard about that? Yeah, kind of surreal, on top of everything else going on."

How'd he find out about it so soon? I put a pin on that question and follow a different line. "I don't know if I should be totally happy though. Cleo seems determined to delay the episode on Senator Dwyer."

"I see."

"Do you know anything about that?"

"Maybe it's not ready. Or maybe Simon thought it wasn't ready," Anders replies. "Pity though, that exposé would have made an excellent grace note for his career."

"That piece was ready," I say, ignoring the sentiment. "I'd lined up my source and my proof. Elliott found a lot of stuff too. The entire team's done the legwork."

"Ask Cleo, I guess." He shrugs, distracted by the mess before him. "Meanwhile, as you all get your leaves and promotions and whatnot, I gotta work all weekend. Someone needs to make sure nothing falls through the cracks during the *transition*."

He shudders at the word, and guilt comes over me. I hadn't even stopped to ask him how he was doing. There he is left with cleanup, job likely in jeopardy, and here I am yammering about my promotion.

"Hey, you want to grab a coffee downstairs?" I finally ask.

"Only if you're buying."

We pick a secluded table at the indoor courtyard of the C+P lobby, one shaded by towering Douglas firs. The smell and the temperature control make the atrium feel wintry, despite the ninety-five-degree day on the other side of the building's double-pane glass walls.

"How are you holding up with all this?" I ask, when he returns with our coffees.

"It's been rough," he begins, cradling his mug with both hands. "It's been a wild ride between sadness, shock and worry. Today it's mostly the last one."

"About your job? Cleo's not making any changes, she told me herself."

"I hope you're right. Though she can't really make any guarantees, can she? Things at C+P have been in flux well before this."

"You mean with the Zephyrus bid?" I ask.

"Yes. And let's face it, my value to the company lasts only as long as Simon. With him gone, and new bosses coming in . . . I probably shouldn't wait until I'm fired and start looking for a new job now."

"If you need me to talk to Cleo, make sure the higher ups find something for you . . ."

"Thanks, Jamie. That means a lot to me."

"Anytime," I say, giving him a reassuring pat on the forearm. I already feel dirty for what I'm about to do. "Speaking of Zephyrus, do you really think it'll happen?"

"Now that Simon's not here to stop it? Hell yes."

"I thought he'd cozied up to the idea," I reply. "Maxwell said that Zephyrus made major concessions to gain support from him. They didn't just throw more money at him; they agreed to demands about real things that Simon cared about, like employee retention and editorial control."

"I'll believe that when I see it," he replies. "And that's probably what Simon was thinking too. He might have trusted Maxwell, but he never trusted the Zephyrus folks, not for a single second."

That's Cleo and Anders both saying Simon opposed the buyout, despite Maxwell telling me otherwise. Does he know more than they do? I can see him trying to convince me that the deal's got employee support, but Simon backing it? That's a tough sell.

"It's not just Simon though," I say, then lower my voice. "Maxwell told me a lot of the staff's excited about the change, but I don't think that's true at all."

"Whatever he's smoking, I want some," Anders replies. "*No one* wants it to happen. Not the support staff, not the reporters, not even middle management. And it's not because of the potential layoffs, though that's a major part of it. No one wants Zephyrus to turn C+P Media into its corporate propaganda network."

It's a little alarmist, but not far outside the realm of possibility. "They've been trying to acquire some smaller media companies too," I reply.

He nods. "And everybody knows it. They can see what Zephyrus is trying to do. So there's no way the deal has employee support. I bet the C-suite folks can't wait for their payout though."

"Do you think that's why Simon, you know . . ." I ask hesitantly. "Because he thought he would lose the vote?"

"Could be. The vote's gonna be close. I hear it may even be a tie," he replies. "I can see how that would burden him."

"Him more than anyone else."

"He'd been agitated the past couple of weeks," Anders continues. "He hadn't been returning calls, and he'd often leave the building for hours without telling me about it. Used to be he couldn't even grab a sandwich without having me do it for him."

Working so close with Simon, I should have noticed the same. Yet I don't recall him being burdened or erratic, and he'd never brought up the Zephyrus buyout with me.

"You think this was all about the takeover?" I ask.

"I've been asking myself that since Thursday."

"If he was acting shifty and erratic . . . a drug habit could explain that, including the pill tube I saw on his desk. Whatever Simon took, he had to have gotten it somewhere."

"Is that what you think happened?" he asks.

No, I think it's murder, but of course I don't tell him that. "What do *you* think happened?"

"Pretty much the same. He'd been doing drugs, he's about to lose C+P, and that's how he checked out," he says, with some sadness.

If Anders had told me this two days ago, I would have been more disappointed. He's always had a sharp eye and even sharper instincts. Turns out he's another one quick to buy into the suicide theory. Why can't anyone see what I readily do?

"It's just so sudden," he continues. "Hindsight's 20/20, but I guess there were signs. He carried the weight of the entire world on his shoulders. Never settled for second best. Always had to have his way, whatever the cost. That's enough to break someone."

"That's what made him great though."

"Very true," he replies.

"He wanted to do good, even though his ways weren't always the best."

"Hah! Don't I know it," Anders says with a wry laugh. "Did I tell you what happened the last time I saw him?"

I shake my head, prompt him to keep going. He sweeps his hair back away from his face, an attempt to dam an oncoming swell of tears.

"Well, he'd been screaming at me all day, stressing out about a 'missing video file.'" Anders rolls his eyes, does mocking air quotes. "Some old recording of his commencement address at NYU. I don't know why he needed it, but I knew he was stressed about something else. He was just trying to find a reason to be pissed at me."

I nod, recalling how often the HooverBots come into Simon's office to clean up the shards of stoneware from all the coffee mugs he'd hurled at the wall. Sometimes for no apparent reason and never at anyone in particular, though Anders was always the closest. It's a minor miracle that he never got hit by shrapnel.

"Anyway, I spent all day looking for this one vid file that he says he saved in some folder somewhere but now he couldn't find it and somehow it's my fault. By six or so, I still hadn't found it and he called me a fucking idiot and said I was fired. One of his fake-out terminations that he retracts the next morning."

I laugh, which seems inappropriate, but I couldn't help it. How many times has Simon threatened to fire me, only to call me back to work the next morning like nothing happened? No bad blood, but no apologies either.

Anders continues to recount that night and I try to relate, but my mind is fixed on one thought—Anders may have been the last person to see Simon alive. More than that, he and Simon ended on the worst of terms between an employee and his superior. That moves Anders to the top of my list.

"He was like a bad boyfriend," he says.

"To all of us," I say, mustering empathy. "But to you most of all. I don't know how you let it go on for so long."

Finally unable to control himself, Anders tears up. "'Don't you ever step foot in my building again.' That's the last thing he ever said to me. *Yelled* at me. And I told him to go to fuck himself. I can't help but think that—"

"Don't do that to yourself," I cut him off, reaching to hold his hand. The tears come harder, steadily washing my suspicion away. "I know how guilt and blame can mess someone up. I've been there. It'll be hard, but don't dwell on it. Remember the good times instead. Those are the moments that matter."

I allow him his grief and let him weep in silence. Before long, Anders wipes his face dry. "Perhaps you're right," he says. "The good times were many, regardless of what his last words were."

"Hell, I don't even remember his last words to me," I reply in agreement.

A deep sadness suddenly overcomes me upon this realization, the inverse of blissful ignorance. Our last conversation was indeed the last, and I didn't even know it, not until this very moment. Our last words to each other were probably *I'm outta here, good night, see you tomorrow*, or something pedestrian. It feels wrong. Final moments should be momentous, have some weight and meaning. Instead I'm left with something mundane and forgettable.

As I watch him contemplate his grief, I begin to convince myself that he couldn't have done it. Sure, he fits the bill of the disgruntled employee with a clear motive for retribution, but had he been involved, he wouldn't have told me that he and Simon had a huge fight the same night Simon died.

"He said something nice about you once. I think it was the only time he ever did," he jokes after a while. "He said, 'Jamie's as naïve as a schoolboy, but he's gonna rock the world one day.'"

As far as compliments go, it's not great. Still, it manages to coax a tear in my eye.

❂

Saturday, 07/11/2043, 5:48 PM

Securing connection to noorJ . . .
   Encrypting . . .
   Gateway open.
   "Hello, Jamie. How goes the journalisming?"

That cool southern California cadence is a welcome sound to my ears. Noor doesn't always pick up, which thankfully is the only way he's ever unreliable. I start up video, and soon enough he's on screen with his greasy long hair and ratty grindcore shirt.

I get straight to it. "Need you for a job. Nothing too complicated, but there might be eyes watching."

"And it's something your factcheckers and infosec teams can't handle?"

"They might be the ones watching."

Noor raises a pierced eyebrow. "What type of trouble are you about to get into now?"

He knows it's the type of trouble that I can't do on my own. Something that can't be traced back to me, something I'd pay good money for. Already he's tallying up an invoice in his mind. On principle, I never pay for stories or access, but scut work and leads on leads . . . that's all fair game.

"I got a new boss, need to make sure she's clean." I pause for questions, but none come. Noor's eyes dart around, and I know he's started working his magic. "We've been working on this story, and she seems real interested that it doesn't get out."

"What's the hitch?"

"It's a chaotic time at C+P," I reply. "Someone died, the cops are on it. But with all the craziness, people will be distracted. You might get what you need without anyone noticing. And with your skills, it'll be a breeze."

Noor tsks, draws a breath in. His eyes aren't on me, still distracted on another screen. "Thanks, but I prefer my compliments in the form of crypto. And you still owe me from last time. Is that why I haven't seen you lately? You're not trying to avoid me, are you?"

Totally forgot about that, but that's maybe for the best. I was on a losing streak the last time I played him. A string of shitty hands one after another. "No, it's just been crazy at work, like I said. C'mon. You know I'm good for it. Plus, I've let you slide too, if memory serves. I'm not the only one who's had bad nights at the poker tables."

"Fine. So you need dirt on your new boss?"

"I'm hoping there isn't any."

"Cleopatra Johnson," he reads off-screen.

"That was fast." I reply, impressed.

"Quite a looker. Rockstar résumé, too. Odd lunch habits though. Cauliflower tacos three times this week, really?"

A fund transfer request pops up on my screen's sidebar. This is going to hurt. I press pay.

Noor grins. "All right, what exactly do you want to find?"

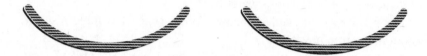

15.

It's starting to feel like I've been telling the story of Simon for three days straight, so I decide to cancel all my weekend plans. I need to be away from human contact. My scheduler sends everyone on the calendar a standard "I'm sorry, too swamped" email with a reschedule request. Immediately, I get a ping back.

"You're not missing brunch, mister," Mom's voice message says. My parents are atheists, but they were both raised Catholic, and so like any other Filipino Catholics, their homes held Sundays sacred. For their folks, it was sacred because of church. For mine, it was because of these weekly brunches.

"I need to catch up on . . . work stuff," I tell her with an affected whine. "Huge deadline."

"On a Sunday? Tsk, tsk. Don't tell me you don't have four measly hours to spare for your family."

I shouldn't have told them I'm Sleepless. Too late now.

Burdened with the guilt they so lovingly inculcated in me, I jump on the next express maglev down to Cape May, bringing the afore-mentioned work stuff with me: sheafs of highlighted pages from the

Vanguards of Vigilance documents, notes of my data summaries. Regardless of what Noor finds about Cleo, this story still needs to be ready soon. On the seat next to me, I plop down a tote full of greens from my rooftop garden. The plants are holding up well despite the summer heat, and I have more than I can keep up with in my cooking. In particular, the basil and rosemary are overgrown and in need of serious pruning.

An Audi waits for me at the Cape May train station when I arrive. It's a new one, shiny and champagne gold. Looks like Dad got another upgrade. I hop in, and soon after the car pulls away from the carport, his face comes up on the dash screen.

"It smells so good in here, look," Dad says, panning the camera toward the grill. Quartered thighs of chicken inasal sizzle in smoke. I could almost smell the lemongrass. I give him cursory nods and tell him I can't wait get there.

It isn't a complete lie. Despite my ill-humor and my desire to be alone for the day, a small part of me wants to be there, going through this weekly routine, regaining a sense of normalcy after everything that's happened.

The brunch thing had been Lolo's idea—my dad's dad. He had this fear that the family that he painstakingly brought over from Manila would become too "American." Detached, lacking the requisite warmth. He'd sermonize about this at length, as though familial closeness was unique to being Filipino, or at least foreign to being American.

Meanwhile, I saw that all families are the same. They're as close as each one allows every other one to be.

When my lolo died, Dad started hosting the brunches at our home. At first this meant having the whole extended family over after church, for those who still went. I didn't, stopped going in high school, but I was there for every meal.

I liked having guests over. They were a facile way of changing a subject or evading a response. Asking an uncle about work gave me at least fifteen minutes of spaced-out nodding between bites. A follow-up question about children bought me another ten. As soon as someone brought up any aches and pains, I knew I didn't have to talk until dessert.

But the attrition rate was high. People begged off as birthdays, vacations and divorces got in the way. Some cousins didn't bother responding to the invites at all. Soon enough, it was just the four of us every Sunday.

When I arrive, Mom greets me at the door with a hug and a kiss. She is wearing a house dress and again, as with every Sunday brunch, I feel overdressed in my jacket, button-downs and lace-ups. I hand her my offering, the fruits of my rooftop labor.

"You can put the greens in the fridge," she says after a cursory inspection. When I do, I'm greeted by a bunch of wilted arugula, still in the plastic bag I brought it in last weekend. I often wonder why I bother keeping up the gesture; they never seem invested in my gardening (or any of my hobbies for that matter). I take the soggy bag out of the fridge, chuck it into the bin, and wash the fresh batch that I brought with me.

"You know, you could use these on the salads."

"We're having a macaroni salad, anak," she replies. "Those won't do."

I grab the bottle of vodka on the way out to the deck.

My brother Charlie arrives as I'm fixing myself a stiff martini. He apologizes for his lateness though my folks don't seem to notice. He then regales us about his latest project, a new sundome complex in Dallas. He'd been appointed as the lead architect of what is essentially another office park with giant solar lamps. A colony for unsleeping worker bees.

"That's a bit . . . different from what you usually do," Mom says, verbalizing what I'm thinking too. Charlie gravitates toward more conceptual projects. He'd passed on designing corporate headquarters in favor of smaller developments that gave him more artistic license.

"Well, they wanted to bring in someone who'll steer them away from '30s style neobrutalism, so I said yes," he says with a smirk. Ever the art snob. I suppose this is what happens when one is a painting savant. Charlie was doing watercolors at three, and oils when he was just eight. He had "a real gift," or so said the pretentious private art tutor our folks hired to teach him.

"They're investing billions on the site, and giving me full creative license," he continued. "And I think it's about time there was a sundome that didn't look like a moonbase from old movies."

"Congratulations, anak. Project lead. We know you'll do great," Dad says.

"By the way, how are things with Greta?" I ask. "We haven't seen her in a while. She still working crazy hours?"

"Can't we get through a meal without you being a jerk?" Charlie replies, stabbing a carrot with his fork.

"Jamie, come on. You know they've broken up," Mom says.

"What? When?"

"A couple weeks ago." Charlie says. "I told you all about it last Sunday. How she sent a vid message and all that. It was devastating." Oh. That explains her absence today.

"Huh. Well, I . . . it's hard to keep up," I say, which it is. They've had such a tumultuous run, "on-again, off-again" is an understatement. Sure, he may have told me just last week, but Charlie can't expect me to remember every development, every spat. Not even the ones that he claims are devastating. "You can't really blame me, can you? There's always something with you two."

"Nice, Jamie. That's exactly what I want to hear." He slams his cutlery on his plate, and a glob of salad dressing splatters his shirt.

"Look, I'm sorry that . . ."

"Jamie, please," Dad says in that tone he uses to end conversations.

Charlie excuses himself from the table and heads to the bar. By the time he returns, Dad has already managed to steer the conversation toward his new home renovation project. Mom nags me to clear out my section of the garage, like I promised in the spring.

In time, after discussing the finer points of Dad's arguments with the contractor, they get to me. There are no partners to ask about, no one since Hannah (whom they adored), so they ask me about work.

"Simon died," I announce, punctuating it with a swig of my martini. Everyone falls silent. The only sound was the crackling of the coals as they burned out on the grill. "The cops say it's suicide."

"Fuck," Charlie says, stunned. Mom is the first to offer sympathy. Dad asks how it happened. I tell them the broad strokes but spare them the detail of me finding the body.

"Were you close?" Dad asks.

"Well, we worked together ten-plus hours every day for the past three years, so yeah." It comes out a lot blunter than intended, so I course-correct. "He was tough, but I learned a lot from him."

"Did he have a family?" Mom asks. I tell them about Simon's wife and kids, which raises more questions. Soon enough it feels like I'm relating Simon's entire biography. I rarely talk about him with my family, and their interest in him is uncharacteristic, and feels inauthentic. I signal my discomfort with truncated answers.

"Was he Sleepless?" Dad asks after a while.

"I don't see what that has to do with anything," I say.

"I'm just asking. It's a high-stress job, and you work these long hours . . ."

I should have known they'd get to the Sleepless question soon enough. I steel myself and shore up some grace. After all, they of all people would have cause to connect hyperinsomnia with suicide. And though I've dissuaded them so many times before, I get how the association is hard to sever.

"Simon didn't take his own life." I pause, then add, "Because of Sleeplessness. He wasn't even Sleepless, not that it's any of our business."

"You're right, it's not," Dad replies, almost as an apology. He never says one though. "What I was trying to get at was you. How are you doing through all this? It must be difficult."

My fingers clench around my silverware, and I mentally start counting down from ten, breathing slower as I do. I know where this is going next.

"It is difficult." .

"We hear news like this and of course we worry," he continues. "We want to make sure you're okay."

"I am."

"Especially given the circumstances," Mom says. "The last time didn't go so well. We're concerned, that's all."

The last time, as though death casually occurs around me on a regular basis. *Didn't go so well*, as though voluntary commitment to a mental health facility is just me having a bad day. At some point, we'll all have to learn how to talk about Paolo's death without elision or euphemism. A direct conversation about what happened to him, and how it's affected all of us. We'll have to reckon with what we could have done to save him. What I could have done. Maybe then, when we finally speak plainly, my cousin will cease to be a cautionary tale, the constant reminder of their fears for me. The avatar of my failure.

Today's not that day.

I can't say they haven't gotten better, but it's been like this since I came out to them last Christmas, over a meal much like this one. The four of us gathered over a familiar Noche Buena spread: the honey-glazed ham, the caldereta, the platters of grilled pork belly and morcon, the red, round queso de bola. Around that time, I'd been living under a cloud of nihilistic despair. Hannah had left me only a few months prior, and the pain hit me harder during the holidays. By the time Noche Buena came around, I'd decided I needed some relief, one that I thought I could get from a sense of release, from coming out.

My mother would be the worst of them, I anticipated. There might not be the gnashing of teeth and rending of garments, but she'd be distressed when I deliver the news. I remember how worried she was when she found out about Paolo, and I imagined that she'd be a whole lot worse now that it had happened to her own son. First, she'd be in denial about it, then frightfully apoplectic: fearful for me, yes, but also for what others might say. She herself was not devout, but she regularly socialized with the aunties who ran the catechism classes over at St. Ignatius. I could imagine their message threads, their murmurings over vidcalls. *It's unnatural, against God's plan. The scriptures say that Jesus himself slept, and were we not made in his image?* My mother didn't subscribe to these views, but under the circumstances, I could see her parroting these words. I looked up the parish website and breathed a huge sigh of relief when I found that the church didn't have an anti-Sleepless league.

Dad would be calmer about the news, but not much easier to handle. I'd expected that he would bring up Paolo, who he'd always treated as his own son, and as he did when his nephew became Sleepless, he'd ask a million questions. He would want to know how

I became Sleepless, the symptoms I experienced, how I felt in the days before and the days since. He'd ask for possible triggers, as though he himself could find a common cause that has still eluded science. He would couch all of this in terms of concern, maybe mention some articles based on unsettled research, about how certain hyperinsomniacs suffer certain physical or mental defects. I'd manage to brush that off, but I worried that he'd suggest that Sleepless people were predisposed to self-harm.

Because of course that's what it would all be about. The way Paolo died. This was not a concern when Paolo turned Sleepless, but now, each of Dad's questions would be designed to parse the similarities between him and me. It didn't help that Paolo and I were like brothers, that sometimes I felt closer to him than I ever did to Charlie. Behind all the questions was the ultimate one: was I likely to take my own life too?

Best case, Dad would keep it open-ended, say that it's a new and evolving disease and we don't know what could happen in the long term, so we have to look out for those afflicted. It's much the same as his current views, and though I never had cause to doubt his genuine concern, I know it's based on the idea that the Sleepless have to be guarded, or guarded against.

Charlie, I knew I would be able to rely on. He and I might not have had the smoothest relationship, but he always backed me up when I needed him. He'd field Dad's questions, ease Mom's doubts, shoot down irrational speculation.

Midnight passed, and the four of us clinked our glasses for Christmas. We stuffed ourselves with meats and cheeses, and copious amounts of rice. The conversation flowed easily throughout the meal. After the desserts were laid out, the coconut pandan salad and fruitcake, I told them my story, or at least as close a version to the truth as I could manage.

Telling my family about Levantanil would have been too complicated, and I knew that for them to ever feel at ease with this change, I'd have to leave that out. Also, I'd never want to risk turning them into accessories-after-the-fact to a highly illegal biohacking transaction. Most of all (if I'm being completely honest), I didn't want to risk any of them spilling the secret and getting me caught. None of them would survive being responsible for an indiscretion that sent me to prison.

So as with Hannah and Veronica before them, I lied. I told them about a doctor's visit that never truly happened. Grounding the story in a clinic with a medical professional (instead of a shady drug deal in my apartment) would set a reassuring scene. I told them that I went to the clinic complaining of fatigue, restlessness, and interrupted sleep that grew more frequent by the night. The doctor screened me for various ailments, and when she ruled out every other possible cause, she gave me the diagnosis.

There was a long pause. Mom had her hand over her mouth, and Dad's fulsome brows knitted in confusion. I then proceeded to explain what hyperinsomnia is, spouting off the FAQs from the CDC site that I had memorized. I must have talked nonstop for ten minutes. After a while, Charlie finally spoke up.

"This doesn't change anything," he said reassuringly.

"It doesn't," I add. "I'm as healthy as I was before the diagnosis. I'm still the same old Jamie."

Mom got up to give me a hug and kiss me on the forehead. Dad leaned over to pat my shoulder. They never asked when I got it or what the transition was like for me. In fact there were no questions at all, none of the ones that I had thought Dad would ask and that I had prepared answers for. No mentions, too, of human nature or God's plan, no discussion of how others view this condition, or how anyone outside my family would view me as a newly-Sleepless person. Most of all, though I could read recollection in their faces, no one spoke a word about Paolo. All they had for me were expressions of support and love.

To be sure, it didn't end there, and educating them has been an ongoing process for the past six months. They vaguely understand the science, but they've got the jargon down; they don't use words that have rightly been designated as slurs. I've gotten more militant about it, correcting them more swiftly and maybe a bit more harshly. I've also banned my folks from getting news from right-wing outlets and their pundits, many of whom are either religious zealots advocating for some sort of "purge" or bigoted concern trolls pushing for registration and regulation. I've even asked them to break ties with some distant aunts and uncles, Filipino doctors and nurses who still cling to Filipino ways of dealing with the Sleepless. That is, treating us like mental patients.

For the most part, my family's learned a lot since I came out to them. They listen, they are patient with me and themselves. They even do their own research. They still mess up sometimes though. When I'm tired or in a daze, Mom slips into some form of forgetful denial and calls me *puyatin*, as though my languor would be fixed if I just got a full eight hours. Dad sometimes talks in hushed tones about their Sleepless neighbors. And, as with today's brunch, they'd hear about suicide and speculate. *Is he Sleepless? Maybe it's related.*

Like I said—it's a process.

"First Paulito, and now this. I'm so sorry, anak," Dad says as he clears his plate. Mom shoots him a look, one that says, *Let's just move on.* She thinks I don't see her, but I do.

"Well, Paolo was a while ago. Things are different now. Jamie's in therapy, and he knows to take care of himself." Charlie says. I don't deserve the save, not after how I fumbled responding to the news of his breakup. I mouth "thanks" in his direction, and he winks back at me.

"Jamie's gonna be fine. Isn't that right?"

"Yes," I say. "No need to worry about me."

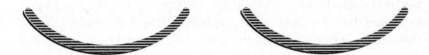

16.

Monday, 07/13/2043, 9:35 AM

I step into the C+P building filled with trepidation. It's the first full workday since, and I'm dreading having to rehash everything about Simon's death. I can see it now: the concerned stares from coworkers, the hollow pleasantries that I'm sure to receive. On our floor, a handful of staffers are already in, and well before I reach my destination, I'm assaulted with two knowing nods, two how're-you-holding-ups and one particularly mawkish I'm-here-for-you. I return their courtesy as best I can, and at the same time, I try to get a feel for their motives. How sincere was that greeting, how heartfelt was that sigh? Could they have wanted Simon dead? Results inconclusive. All I get is more frustration.

To top it off, I need to speak to the cops. Again.

From outside the conference room, I see the detective who's brought me in for yet another interview. This one's new; I don't remember him from Thursday morning. He's not low-level either, judging from the slicked back hair, the form-fitting suit, the age drawn in the lines of his face.

"Nathan Tetro, Homicide," he says as I walk in, extending a

handshake. "I just have a few questions for you."

Tetro gestures for me to take a seat as he fumbles around the control panel. He turns up the glass wall opacity and the room darkens, then does the same for the windows. The walls, the windows, the sixteen empty seats and the detective's linebacker frame all feel oppressive.

"I understand that you were the one who found Mr. Parrish on the morning of the ninth," he calmly starts. He slides into the power seat at the head of the table and leans in. I find some comfort in seeing through his intimidation tactics. "Why don't you walk me through what happened that day? Let's start from when you left your apartment."

I told him essentially what I had already told the first responders. "I left my place at around 6:30 a.m. and walked in at 7. I took a cab, driverless. No one was in the office, and I walked directly to my desk. I always start my day with coffee, so the break room was my next stop after dropping off my bag and turning my terminal on. When I was heading back to my desk, I caught sight of Simon's office. I saw him on his desk and thought he'd done another all-nighter. Then I saw that a wine glass had tipped over on the left side of his desk, and that prompted me to go in."

"Why?" the detective interrupts.

"I didn't want Simon to have any of his files ruined."

"What happened to the coffee you had?"

This takes a second to register. "Oh, I must've set it down somewhere, I don't remember exactly."

"Did Mr. Parrish do that a lot, spend the night in his office?" he continues.

"Sometimes, every few weeks or so. More if we're nearing a deadline."

"When was the last time he did?"

"I don't remember."

"Was he on deadline last week?"

"No. What does it matter?" I ask.

"From what I've heard, Mr. Parrish was a workaholic, and for that kind of guy, the worst stressors always come from work," the detective explains with surprising candor. "Would you say that he was particularly stressed lately, more than ordinary?"

"Stress is part of the job," I say. "But no, it hasn't been more stressful lately."

Tetro sucks in air between his teeth, bracing as though he already knows my answer. "What story was he working on so late at night?"

"You know I can't tell you," I reply, blunting my denial with a diffident grin. Even if it weren't confidential, it's irrelevant. Working on the Dwyer story didn't stress Simon out more than usual, least as far as I could tell.

He lets the point go, but I can tell I'm wearing out his patience. "I hear someone's trying to buy the company. That give him any trouble at all?"

I wanted to correct him, say that's not what's going on, not yet anyway. But the legal team was very specific about what we're allowed to say about the Zephyrus bid, which is not a lot. Not worth helping this cop if it meant breaking an NDA.

"I don't know anything about that," I say. "You'll have to ask the folks involved in the deal."

"Believe me, I've tried. All I've gotten is runaround after runaround," he says, unsurprised at my response. He turns to his tablet, then asks another question as though reading from a script. "Do you know if he had any particular stressors outside of work? Money problems, troubles at home?"

"No, I don't think so. But if he did, he probably wouldn't have told me. Simon liked to keep his private life private."

"Any other possible stressors? Health issues, maybe?"

I flash him another grin and before I could answer, the detective mimics me in exaggeration. "Yes, I know, 'that's confidential.'"

I nod, signaling him to move on. The only thing I know about Simon's health is that he's in therapy. Same as me, and same as 90 percent of the city. And I wouldn't have even known that if Simon hadn't pushed me to seek help, at that time of my life when I needed it most. Again, not a detail relevant to this investigation anyhow. Not when this cop should be looking at this case as a murder.

"Has he said or done anything in the past that could indicate suicidal thoughts?" I shake my head, and he continues. "Any dark thoughts, depressed mood . . . anything that might point to what would lead him to take his own life?"

"No."

He doesn't proceed, only lets the silence hang over us.

"Look, I don't know, okay?" I say. "I'm not a mind reader."

"No need to get testy," he replies in a monotone. "I'm trying to see where his head was at, that's all."

You and everybody else. These last few days I've had no refuge from those questions, the morbid speculation, the invitations to delve into Simon's mental state. Each interaction has this black hole, its pull so strong and its presence so massive, sucking all the air and life out, until the only thing left is *Why?*

I catch myself soon enough and try to keep a level head. "Wish I knew, Detective. I really wish I knew."

Tetro leans back, puts his hand behind his head. "Let's try a different tack. Did he have problems with anyone at work? Any tense interactions in the last few days?"

"What do you mean?"

"Arguments, shouting matches and the like."

"Why, do you think someone had it in for Simon?" I ask.

"It's a standard question, nothing more." He scribbles something down on his tablet. "Did he have enemies? People who wished him ill?"

"Of course he did."

In the past couple of days, I've assembled quite a long list of names from the Senate Freedom Fund and their shady donors, from Senator Dwyer's office, plus all their relatives and known associates, each of whom might have reason to hate Simon. And that's just from his latest assignment. In his twenty-year career, Simon has rightfully gained the ire of more politicians, capitalists and celebrities than you can count.

"Is that the angle you're looking at?" I ask. "Do you no longer consider this case a suicide?"

"No angle. Like I said, these are all standard questions."

"Do you have any suspects?"

Tetro chuckles. "You don't quit, do you? 'Suspect' isn't a word we just throw around. Not for this kind of case."

"So you still think it's a suicide," I say, less to the detective than to myself. Here I thought he'd at least validate what my gut tells me. Turns out he and I might not be on the same page, after all. "You know, I noticed some paraphernalia on his desk when I found him. A pill tube. He took something, didn't he? That's the cause of death?"

"I'm the one asking the questions here."

"Sorry, force of habit," I say, faux-humble. "Maybe we can help each other out. You give me something, and I might be able to give you something in return."

"Have you been holding out on me, Mr. Vega?" he asks, a challenge. "You know, some people might call that obstruction."

"Please, Detective. Off the record. I just . . . I need to know," I say haltingly, trying to gain his sympathy. "Simon meant a lot to me. I'm trying to understand how this all happened, for my own peace of mind."

"And I'm sorry for your loss," he replies, not unaffected. "But it's an ongoing investigation. Only way we'll get to the bottom of this is if you cooperate. You do your part and I'll do mine."

"All right," I say, setting aside my own questions for now. "What else would you like to know?"

"What's the last thing you and Mr. Parrish talked about?"

I think back to that night, and to my conversation with Anders. Final words with Simon, and I'm drawing a blank. "Can't recall exactly, it might have been something about this story we're working on. Nothing substantial."

"No long, drawn out conversations or anything like that on Wednesday night?"

"No, I don't think so. Just goodbye and goodnight, probably."

Tetro stares me down for a beat. He then reaches for his tablet, flicks it over and turns it toward me.

"Courtesy of C+P's own surveillance cameras."

He presses play on a four-screen recording of the long hallway right outside Simon's office, shot from different angles. No audio. He scrubs forward past 8 p.m., and I see a blurry outline of Maxwell Cartwright leaving Simon's office. He's going deeper inside the building, toward the opposite end of the floor where his own office was located.

Shortly after, I enter the frames from the end of the hallway that terminates near my office. I walk past Simon's office and the out of the screen. I don't even turn my head to look in. The shut door and all the walls are transparent but from the angle of the cameras, one couldn't see much of the interior, just the edge of his desk, and the rightmost edge of the shelves behind it.

Tetro scrubs forward, and I reenter the frame at 8:34 p.m.. I knock at Simon's door then go into the office, and shut the door behind me.

He fast-forwards again, and there is no activity for a few minutes. No other people walking past, the hallways completely empty. The door remains shut.

I walk out of the office at 8:48.

If I were outside of myself watching this conversation unfold, this would be about the time when I would yell at myself to ask for a lawyer.

"You were in there for a long time. What did the two of you talk about?"

I'm too stunned to hear his questions. "This is untampered? You checked?"

The detective nods. "Definitely not a deepfake."

"What about the rest of the video?"

"Before you, there was Maxwell Cartwright, who you just saw," Tetro replies. "And before him, there were Cleo Johnson, Anders Wolff, and Elliott Nahm. But you were the last, Mr. Vega. There was no one else until the next morning. Until you, again."

"I left the building earlier than that," I say, unsure.

"Well, C+P's dragging their feet giving us the employee entry-exit data, but sure, if you think you got something that disproves this, by all means, tell me about it."

He waits for me to answer, and I scramble to think about Wednesday night. What time did I leave exactly? I pull out my handheld and go through my calendar.

Meanwhile, Tetro takes out a 3D projector from his bag and sets it at the center of the table. He taps away at the tablet and a holographic rendering illuminates the room. Save for some grayed-out sections uncaught by the cameras, the recording materializes the scene out of thin air, showing a miniature version of me going in and out of Simon's office. He plays this on a slow loop as he proceeds with his questions.

"Time of death is estimated to be between 21:00 to 22:00, July ninth," he says, tired of waiting for a response. "You were the last one to see the victim, and the only one to see him around that window. Now I'll ask again—what did you and Simon Parrish talk about?"

"Like I said, work assignments and stuff. Nothing remarkable."

"Did he seem agitated or tired, or did he seem in any way as though he was about to harm himself?"

"No, I don't think so," I say. "I don't remember."

"That's four."

"Four what?" I ask, lost.

"Four times you said you don't remember."

"What, do you want me to guess?"

"I want you to answer me," he says, teeth bared.

"I am answering," I say, raising my voice. "What did you expect, Detective? I just found a dead man, someone really important to me. I'm not exactly in steel-trap condition."

"You're sharp enough to be evasive," he accuses.

"I have no reason to be. I'm telling you what I know."

"Ordinarily, I'd have audio to help you remember," he says in a way that suggests helping me isn't at all a priority. "But this entire building is flooded with bug blockers. Each room is a damn Faraday cage, including the victim's. No in-room cameras either. You folks really like your privacy. You got anything to hide?"

"Privacy helps us do our job better."

"Well, it's not helping me with mine," he replies. "That's why we gotta help each other." His intonation tries to be chummy, but the detective can't feign empathy. I take his lead anyway and de-escalate. I can't have him thinking I'm stonewalling, any more than he already does.

"I truly don't remember what Simon and I talked about," I reply. "But I'm happy to help you with all your questions. What else would you like to know?"

He considers this, and then asks, "How would you describe your relationship with Mr. Parrish?"

"We had a great working relationship," I say. I explain how Simon was beloved by everyone, including myself. He was firm but fair. More than my boss, he was my mentor. I tell him all the times he's helped me grow, but out of respect I leave out his bursts of anger and his expectation of near-total devotion to the job. "He made me a better reporter, a better person. I owe him everything I have."

"Would you consider yourself friends?"

"I'd like to think so," I say uneasily. "As much of a friend as you can have in this industry."

"The night he died, he had two wine glasses out. That wasn't for you?" Tetro asks. Two glasses. How could I have missed that? It sounds like a lie, and I could review my visor recording again to be sure, but I remember only one wine glass in that office.

"No, it wasn't for me," I reply.

"You sound pretty sure."

"Simon knows I never drink at work. He's asked enough times and I've said no enough times that he'd long stopped asking."

"Was he already drinking when you came into his office?"

"I don't recall." He shoots me another cautionary stare, but I insist. "Look, Simon drinks when he's working late, which is a lot of nights," I add. "If he were drinking on Wednesday, it wouldn't have struck me as unusual."

Tetro grunts, then reaches for his holoprojector. He shuts it down, stows it away together with his tablet. For a second, I'm sure that he's about to place me in handcuffs and drag me to the precinct. All he does is grab his phone. "I just sent my card to your work email. Call me if you remember anything."

"Wait, that's it?" I ask in confused protest. I haven't gotten what I need from him yet. "What happened to helping each other out? Who else have you talked to?"

"Everyone he worked with, people who saw him that night, close associates, the usual," he replies. "They're all praises."

"Maxwell said you're ready to close the case out. Is that true?"

"Yes. Almost. Just need to cross a couple more T's." He rises from his seat and extends his hand. I meet it, and his grip feels a lot firmer than when we first shook. "But if anything new comes to mind, anything at all, you be sure to let me know, all right?"

17.

As soon as I step out of the conference room, Elliott swoops in and paces down the hall alongside me. He asks what happened with the detective and I give him a quick rundown. Just the basics, none of the conjecture. I don't need him adding to my anxiety right now. When I'm done, he tells me about his session with the detective, earlier this morning. Their conversation sounded like it was briefer, covering the usual ground. Was Simon acting odd lately, etcetera? I tell Elliott that I got the same questions and gave the same responses.

"That's odd though. Somehow I thought he'd ask a lot more from you, seeing as you found the corpse," he says. I bristle at the word. Tetro did ask a lot more, but I think it's better not to worry Elliott. Last thing I need is him getting on my case, telling me to quit it with my conspiracy theories.

"What's weird is apparently I was the last person Simon saw." Not Elliott, not Anders. Me. "Tetro got it from surveillance."

"You're the last person he talked to *and* the first person who found him?"

"Yeah," I reply, with a hint of dread. "Wednesday night, do you remember what time I left the building?"

"Not particularly. Why do you ask?"

"Detective Tetro said I left at nine-ish, but I'm sure I wasn't here that late," I reply.

"You left way before I did. Why does any of this matter?" Elliott, honed by years of experience, studies my expression; he can tell something's weighing on me. Then comes that familiar look of concern.

"Jamie, don't do this. Remember what you learned from Paolo. There's nothing you could have done. There's no use thinking about reasons, or assigning guilt or blame."

I wish it were about that; it might be easier to think that I could have saved Simon. If I thought he'd killed himself, that's probably where my headspace would be. But that's not why I'm asking these questions. I need to know if the detective thinks this is a murder, just as I do. I especially need to know if being the last person Simon saw makes me their prime suspect.

"It's not that, I swear. I'm just trying to understand what happened," I tell him. "The video shows that Simon and I talked shortly before he died, and for the life of me I don't remember what we talked about."

"Yeah, I know. You told me at the biergarten," Elliott says, still concerned. "It was probably some dumb work thing. Do you remember what you had on the docket that night?"

"Yeah, prep work for a data packet from my source," I say, memories from that night slowly returning to me.

"See, there you go. Already it's coming back to you. Be patient with yourself. You'll remember better once the shock subsides." He slaps my back encouragingly. "Well, how about this? Hit me with more questions, let's try and jog that noggin of yours."

Before I can ask him another, I'm stopped dead in my tracks. Down the hallway, I see Simon's office, which even from afar looks a lot different than it did just two days ago. The police tape has been taken down. The glass wall is no longer frosted, and through it I see that the place has been emptied out. Fuck.

I hurry down the hall and slip my visor on as I go in. The name plate on the door is the only vestige that Simon Parrish used to inhabit the space. Gone are his clear resin desk and ergonomic chair, his books and his terminals, the plaques and diplomas on the shelves behind his chair, side by side with photos of his wife and children and dogs. The video wall's eight interactive screens and holo-projector are gone; all that's left are rectangular shadows on a wide expanse pockmarked with outlets for data cables. Most important, gone are the stacks of paper and towers of boxes that lined his desk and chairs and the far wall opposite his desk, on either side of the spare couch on which he sometimes slept.

"What are you doing?" Elliott says from behind me, but I barely hear him. I'm overwhelmed by the strong smell of bleach. The carpet has been scrubbed, professionally I'd guess. Even the wine stain is gone. There isn't a stray staple or paper clip on the floor.

I pace toward the corner window that Simon used to peer out of. They're clear. They were translucent on the morning he died, weren't they? I remember looking out the window, the view hazy. I should check my visor video again just in case. I find the dial near the sill and turn it once. The windows go completely dark. I do it again and the panes turn frosted, and then clear. I crouch down to where Simon's fingerprints should be, but they're not there anymore, wiped clean just like every square inch of this room.

Elliott peers over my shoulder to see what I'm up to, and I nudge him away. I run my hands along the sides of the window, checking the bolts on the edges of the windowpanes. All bolts are intact. Thick steel rods show through a slight gap between the frames, which means the window can't be moved or opened at all.

"Jamie, what is going on?" Elliott says with alarm.

"What happened here? Where's everything?" I say, finally turning to him.

"The cops came by yesterday to process the scene again," he says. "Yessir, they're calling it a 'crime scene.'"

I would have loved to have known that before going in to see the detective.

"It was a whole big to-do," he continues. "Rita Parrish stormed in here to make sure nothing of value gets taken." By that, she presumably meant family mementos; Simon never kept anything of intrinsic value in the office. "Maxwell and the folks from Legal came too, to secure anything confidential."

"But the fucking cops took everything," I snap, unable to hold my frustration. I didn't know what I was expecting to find in here, but whatever I could have, I sure wouldn't find it now.

"Nah. The cleanup happened *after* the cops did their sweep. Once the NYPD finished bagging and tagging, C+P crews came in and cleared the place. Docs, devices, data storage, etcetera. Those lawyers, man. They sure know what they're doing."

I recall what my source told me. When there's a threat in her company, she cleans house. This is quite literally what happened here. Was this Maxwell's doing?

"You were here yesterday?" I ask. "How do you know all this?"

"Assistants," he replies. "They hear everything, and boy, do they talk."

I've come to expect dismissiveness or indifference, maybe even relief, from many at C+P. After all, Simon didn't play well with others. But I didn't expect the same from Elliott. His archness throughout our conversation piqued me, and I found myself pacing around the room to avoid him.

"Look at this place," I say, seething. "It's hasn't even been a fucking week."

"They're just things. What does it matter?"

"Everything matters. Simon is dead, and you're acting like it's nothing."

"Fuck you. I'm hurting too, you dick."

"Do you think this is a suicide?" I ask, getting to the point that I didn't know I had until then.

"Yes—no, I don't know." Elliott withers under my glare, then finally surrenders. "Maybe not. If the cops are asking you all those questions, then maybe it's not a suicide."

That's the most I've gotten by way of validation from anyone, and it's not nearly enough. "It's not, Elliott. I'm sure of that, now more than ever."

"Look, man, you know I have your back, always. I'll help you remember, I'll talk you through your grieving process, whatever you need. God knows we've been here before, and I'm happy to do it again," he replies long-windedly, readying his proviso. "But I'm not going to encourage whatever this is you've got going on."

We both take a breath, and in the tense silence an unspoken apology passes between us. We've argued enough to know when our tempers are misdirected, and we know how to recover from them quick.

"I was hoping to find something," I say, as calm as I can. "Anything to make sense of this. And before you give me all that Paolo talk again, it's not about that."

"Then tell me what it's about."

Where do I start? I want to find out what Simon and I talked about on Wednesday, right before he died. I want to know why he told Maxwell he backed the merger, why he then told Cleo the complete opposite. Why he really fired Anders. Why Cleo's acting shady. I want to decipher those fingerprints on the window. I want to know what was in that empty vial. I want to get a hold of Simon's notes, his tablet, his calendar, his schedule, his logs, anything that will answer all of these questions. Most of all I want to know if I'm right. That despite everything that tells me otherwise, this is not a suicide.

All I offer Elliott in response is a weighty silence.

❁

"What's going on?" Cleo walks into Simon's now-empty office, uncertain. Her manner acknowledges the tension in the room but she chooses not to address it. "How'd the cop calls go?"

Elliott and I both shrug noncommittally, give grunts and murmurs of displeasure. She tilts her head, expecting a bit more, but neither of us feel like being forthcoming after our last conversation with her.

"Anyway, this might not be the best time," she begins, "But since you're both here, I wanted to let you know that we've let go of someone from Team Parrish. Anders Wolff."

"What the hell?" Elliott asks. "When?"

"We let him go this morning, though he's known since last week."

"I'm sure this is a bit of a misunderstanding," I say, suppressing my alarm. "He was just here on Saturday, sorting Simon's files."

"Yes, we let him clear his things quietly over the weekend." Cleo replies. "We would've terminated him sooner if we'd known, but things got lost in the confusion."

"Known what?" Elliott asks.

"That Simon fired him on Wednesday."

I roll my eyes. "Simon does that. He didn't mean it. He never does." Elliott nods in agreement. He'd been faked out with termination too, as many times as anyone else who worked for Simon.

"This isn't one of those times," Cleo replies with a knowing sigh. She walks toward one of the empty niches by Simon's window and rests herself against it. "These past few months, Simon had been concerned that there was a leak in the company, specifically within the news division."

Elliott and I turn to each other, and he's first to ask. "What kind of leak?"

"He wasn't entirely forthcoming about it. I don't know if you've noticed, but lately Simon had been holding everything close to the vest," she says. "All he told the executive committee was that he noticed data files disappearing, and that confidential information was landing in the wrong hands."

"What kind of information?" I ask.

"All sorts of things. His whereabouts, stories he'd been working on, people he'd been talking to. He never specified any further, since he didn't know who to trust."

That's a funny word coming from her. Up until a few days ago, I thought I could trust Cleo. Now she's fired an integral part of Team Parrish, and soon after deciding to delay the Dwyer piece. Something tells me that it's equally possible Simon didn't trust her either, or that she might not be telling us the whole story. Maybe both.

"And where was this information going?" I ask. "Does it have anything to do with Dwyer?"

"I don't know. He didn't want to tell me too many details 'for my own good,' he said. But I have my suspicions." There's acid in her voice, and instantly we know what she means.

"The buyout. Zephyrus."

She nods. Mention of the Dwyer story didn't make her flinch at all, and I wonder if steering our attention toward Zephyrus is a slick misdirect.

"But all of that is public information. What is there to leak?" Elliott asks.

"Unfortunately, Simon never got a chance to tell us any of that," she replies. "All he knows—as far as he's told me—is that someone from his own news division is acting against the company's interests. Against him."

"We're sure of this?" Elliott asks.

"*We* are not sure of this, but Simon was. He sent HR a series of emails on Wednesday night, and he was adamant. Turns out he and Anders got into a verbal altercation about confidential documents being sent to outside entities, and Simon claimed that they were sent from Anders' terminal. When Anders denied this, Simon fired him. HR was supposed to revoke his credentials that day, but like I said, things got chaotic by Thursday morning."

Did Anders play me? All that talk about grief and missing Simon, that whole bonding session we had, had it all been a lie? And if he'd been lying about that, what else has he been lying about?

Cleo continues. "Listen, I'm also shocked and saddened by all this. Anders has been with us for years, and I like the guy. But the executive committee is taking Simon's emails seriously even though his allegations weren't fully substantiated. Part of it was also about wanting to honor Simon's final wishes, even if it meant giving Anders a huge severance check so he doesn't sue."

"This is why we need a union," Elliott mutters under his breath.

"I'm going to pretend I didn't hear that," Cleo replies.

"I can't believe it," he says. "We all trusted him." Elliott turns to me, but I can't bring myself to say anything in agreement. Anders lied to me. About what he and Simon fought over, about him being a mole. About him being caught and getting fired for real. About having reason upon reason to want Simon dead.

He better have answers for me when I find him.

18.

Hardwick's is nestled deep within a block-size waterfront building overlooking the Red Hook neighborhood. The post-industrial facade has a rolling gate, over which a cast-iron sign bears the bar's name, though a tattered tarp running down the side wall announces the structure as the site of a food bank.

A steady stream of men empties into a graffitied door unmanned by a bouncer. I observe the line from across the street. Footsteps skitter in the alley behind me. I turn to look but no one is there, and I get the paranoid sense of being watched. Might as well head in.

Despite the run-down nature of the rest of Carroll Gardens around it, the Hardwick's interior might as well have been in Midtown. Chameleon walls morphed into varied neon shades to the beat of the immersive sphero-sound system. The guys are well-dressed, well-coiffed, and for some, well-oiled. On the main stage, a drag queen holo is singing the remix of a turn-of-the-century bop about life after love. An array of the latest BarVenders stand around a circular bar, which is exactly where I expected to find him.

"You're a hard man to pin down, Anders."

He regards me as he would a stranger, giving me the once over before turning away again. It's a very different Anders from the one only two days ago. Not stressed or burdened by loss, but aloof, self-assured. Like he's hot shit. He's dressed like it too, arms and chest bared under a slick vest, no shirt underneath.

"It couldn't have been that hard, seeing as you're here," he replies. "What's this about, Jamie?"

"You lied to me."

"Which part?" He smirks. A buff, pony-tailed man waves at Anders from the other side of the bar. He waves back, mouths something in reply.

"All of it," I say, gritting my teeth. "That Simon fired you, for serious, that your argument on Wednesday night wasn't about some silly video file. That you were leaking confidential fucking information."

He finally meets my gaze, his steel blue eyes made colder by neon lights overhead.

"Who are you working for?" I ask.

"I'm not the mole, Jamie."

"Then why did you lie to me?"

"Because I don't know if *you* are."

Anders takes a long swig of his drink, a blood-orange concoction garnished with a sprig of herbs. When he's done, he slams the glass down onto brushed-chrome bar top. "I gave everything to that company, to that man. For weeks I thought he was just being paranoid, but when Simon reported the data breaches to the tech team, who do you think they suspected first? To top it all, Simon tells them that he suspects me. Fucking asshole."

"I'm not the mole, Anders. *You* were the one telling me all sorts of things—about Simon and the buyout offer, the Board votes being tight, the details of his final day. That was all you. Or were those lies too?"

"I was trying to draw you out, see if you were the mole." Anders laughs as he says this, and the sound shatters my pride. There I was Saturday morning, thinking I was being sly, pumping him for information. All the while, he was playing me. He even cried, the bastard.

"Simon suspected me, and I needed to know who this mole was, if there even is one," he continues. "And with you snooping around his office, I thought, well . . ."

"Of course, accusing someone else happens to clear your name. How altruistic."

"I have to. More so now," he replies. "Disgruntled employee fired for cause the night he died? Not a good look."

"You think it might be foul play."

Anders shrugs lazily. "Maybe Simon's paranoia has rubbed off on me."

He's not the only one. "And you think the mole killed him," I reply.

"If he was—and I'm not saying he was, but if he was murdered —I think the killer's whoever saw Simon last."

Anders holds my gaze. He couldn't have known about the surveillance video, since he wouldn't be privy to that information after getting fired. He couldn't have seen me that night either; Tetro said he left C+P well before I went into Simon's office. Still, his expression has a knowing conviction that sends a chill down my spine.

"There's only two things I know for sure," he continues. "Simon was trying to find a mole within C+P, and then he ends up dead. Allegedly. Is it connected? Who knows. Why do you care, anyway?"

If he turns out to be the mole, I will regret this, but right now my instinct tells me I need to be vulnerable. It's the only way I'll get him to open up. I take the risk. "I care because I was the last person who saw Simon that night. The last person in that room with him. And the cops are starting to suspect murder."

He sets his drink down slowly, cocking his head to assess me. "Damn. How are you not sitting in a jail cell right now?"

"Same as you, I guess. Not enough evidence. At least not yet."

"So now we come to it," Anders says after a pause. "You didn't come here just to confront me. What do you need?"

"I'm trying to get ahead of this, in case it goes to shit," I reply. "The cops are asking all these questions about Simon's relationships, looking through surveillance videos. If they start investigating this as a murder, whose door do you think they'll knock on first?"

"Yours." Anders gives a wicked smile.

"Or the disgruntled employee fired for cause. So you can see how we're in the same boat."

"Perhaps. What do you propose to do about it?"

"I'm looking into this leak," I reply. "Whoever's getting info on C+P seemed to be targeting Simon specifically."

"I'm not entirely sure this leak or mole or whatever even exists," he says flourishing his hand dismissively. "Like I said, Simon's been on edge, paranoid."

"But if it's murder, it could clear both of us to find out who the mole is."

"I've told the cops all I know, which is close to nothing. Besides, they've collected his documents, they have server access. I'm sure our legal department has told them about the data breaches too. What else is there?"

"Simon kept a lot of things under wraps. There's gotta be something the cops didn't get their hands on," I say. "And I know you know things that don't leave a paper trail."

"That may be true," he says, clearly pleased with himself, "But why would I tell you what I know?"

"You may have been playing me the last time we talked, but I could tell it wasn't all lies," I say. "You cared about Simon, and you still care about C+P and the work we do. Otherwise you wouldn't be trying to find this mole. Well, I care about all those things too, and between you and me, I'm the one who's still in C+P. If you tell me what you know, I can get us the answers we seek."

He narrows his gaze, keeps me waiting. Finally, he produces a cartridge from his vest pocket. "Bump?"

I shake my head. He sticks the cartridge into his inner bicep and it gives off a sharp hiss.

The music picks up and before long, the patrons converge onto the dance floor. Without my noticing, the bar's gotten packed since I came in. The same drag queen holo starts singing a remix of another one of her hits, this one about time travel. Anders pulls me toward the crowd. I try to shake him off but he holds on to my forearm, sending a clear message: I'd have to dance for his intel. I slacken and let him lead me.

"Simon's been talking to someone," he says in between bass beats.

"Who?"

"Isidra Thorpe."

I haven't heard that name in years. Sid Thorpe was one of Simon's former producers. She was his right hand, his Cleo before Cleo. Our tenures never overlapped at C+P, but Sid's reputation preceded her. Everyone either admired her or feared her.

"What's the connection?" I ask, begrudgingly two-stepping along to the beat.

"You tell me. He had all these late-night calls, ones he kept off the call logs," he replies. "But he can't keep anything from me, not when he's yelling and I'm literally right across the hall."

"How often did they talk? And what about?"

Anders turns away, entangling himself in a knot of strange limbs. He glances at me like an afterthought and I shoot back a pleading look. He always did say I have pretty, puppy-dog eyes. He extricates himself from the fray and comes closer.

"Happened three or four times, maybe?" he finally replies. "Not all yelling, and no idea what they were talking about, either."

"Are they having an affair?"

"Nope, not that." He's withholding something, I can tell by the glint in his eye.

"What do you think it is then?"

"Well, what do we know about Isidra Thorpe?"

I never did find out what exactly happened to Sid Thorpe after she left C+P, but last I heard she landed at the upper echelons of the OEF, the Open Eyes Federation. A Sleepless interest group that might be more connected to Simon and C+P than I thought.

Anders grins, seeing the realization dawn on me. "Might be something, yes?"

"Definitely. Do you think you could get me—"

Before I could ask for more, he places a finger over my lips.

"That's it. That's all I know." My shirt gets dampened with his sweat when he leans into my ear. "Now, we have fun, yeah?"

Anders moves in closer and spins me around. I let him and the music charm me into motion. From behind me, he holds my biceps and grinds against me. I sway along to the beat, matching his rhythm. His fingers begin to make their way under my shirt, and his breath warms my neck. I find myself leaning into it, into him, until I finally turn to face him and lean into a kiss.

19.

Tuesday, 07/14/2043, 1:15 AM

When LaGuardia was decommissioned for being a coastal flood risk, real estate developers swooped in to exploit what little land area was usable. Barriers were erected, and the airport gates and terminals got converted into one sprawling shopping mall. The hangars were turned into events spaces: Hangar 4 is now Fly-Boys, an anti-grav stadium, and on the opposite side at Hangar 6 is an installation art museum currently staging a Kara Walker retrospective.

Hangar 5, our destination for the night, is now Arcadia. The trendy new playground of the party set.

Veronica's been begging me to check out Arcadia since it opened last month, and I've always said no. I'd sooner gargle thumb tacks than party with college kids, I kept telling her with variations on the form of torture, so of course she was skeptical when I called to extend a last-minute invite. She was only too happy that I'd finally said yes, so she didn't sense I had an ulterior motive.

When our robocab pulls up to the club, the back of the line is long enough to snake all the way to the next hangar. As if that isn't bad enough, it's clear that Veronica and I are on the far end of the age range of the people in line. All the kids are decked out in club wear, very avant-garde and au courant. I suddenly feel awkward in my black wraparound jacket and jeans. At least Veronica's little black dress looks timeless.

The queue moves forward anesthetically. At this rate, we won't get through the door for another hour. Veronica pulls me back when she sees me drift off onto the sidewalk, eyeing the robocabs that cruise past.

"No backing out now," she warns.

"This was my idea, remember?"

"Well, you looked like you were about to make a run for it," she replies.

In truth, I was searching for a familiar face. Suicide or not, there was that empty pill tube on Simon's desk, and not the pharmacy kind. They don't usually label their pharmaceuticals with starburst emojis. So if I want to prove what happened either way, I'll have to know whether Simon did drugs, and how he got access to them.

I've always suspected that he did, uppers most likely. There's a reason why seeing the vial didn't faze me, but it's not the type of thing I had reason to confirm, until now. Now, I need to know if he used and what, how he got it, if he might have had a bad batch, and find out, too, what he'd been like the last time he bought. And the person who can answer all those questions should be in the club right about now.

As soon as we pass the security threshold, I'm assaulted by neu-techno beats. The air pulsates with a force that sweeps me into a throng of well-dressed, manic revelers. From my vantage point, the dance floor looks as wide as a city block, with archipelagos formed by bars, plush couches, and gogo pedestals amid a sea of partygoers. Everyone has their visors on, some with a headset and forearm panels. Some are already wearing their hap-suits, slick and gleaming in the floodlights, goggles resting atop their heads.

Above us, a second-level dance floor-slash-viewing platform wraps around the perimeter, bounded by a catwalk that looks down onto the main dance floor. People line the rail as they would on an observation deck, tinkering with their wrist panels and scanning the crowd. And then there's a third level, a narrow open deck also encircling the main floor from above.

"The entire top floor is all VR lounges," Veronica yells over the sound when she sees where I'm looking. The level is lined with rooms of made of glass. Cubic bubbles that house people in full VR gear, partying in a world within a world. Some of the cubes are completely dark and opaque. "We can move our way up there later. For now—drinks!"

We venture deeper into the frenzy, Veronica wrapping her hand around my arm and shepherding me to a bar. I slide into the only empty stool and put my visor on. It tells me no contacts are nearby. I select another option and from the corner of my eye, I see "Friends of Friends." A handful of partiers glow with a yellow outline, the light flickering as they are intermittently obscured by the crowd's movement. The sensory overload suddenly bears down on me, and a stabbing pain hits the back of my eyes. The thumping of the bass line makes things worse. Rubbing my temples, I lean into the bar and enunciate into the BarVender comm. "Whiskey sour, please. Bulleit." A frothy coupe ascends from a hatch on the bartop. Veronica hands it over to me, and I take in one long gulp. She shakes her head.

"Long day?" she asks. It's a running joke; it only ever feels like there's one day.

Truth is, I need the liquid courage for what's next. That would take a long explanation though. "You could say that."

"Tell me about it." She says it both in commiseration and as an opening.

"Had a drink with Anders tonight," I start, and already she's rolling her eyes. She doesn't mind him, but she's got very strong opinions on my dalliances. "And I probably shouldn't have."

"Hannah drops in on you one night, then a few days later, you're seeing Anders? That's a rebound pattern, if I ever saw one."

"It's not like that." The kiss and the sexual tension notwithstanding. I'd probably be more honest if I could tell her the full story, but she has made it clear where she stands. If I tell her I'm still playing all these spy games, she'll never let me hear the end of it. Same reason why I can't tell her why I agreed to come to Arcadia tonight. "We were just commiserating about Simon."

Her demeanor shifts, softens. Nothing brings a conversation to a halt quite like a dead person. I assume she's content to leave it at that, but then she asks, "So why do you think you shouldn't have gone out with him?"

"I think he might still be into me."

"I say this with all the love in the world," Veronica replies, holding my chin in her hand. "But you are a complete and utter mess. Once and for all, go deal with your unresolved issues with Hannah, and until then, leave that poor man—or anyone else for that matter—alone."

If only things were that easy. She takes in a deep breath for more, but before she can continue chiding me, my visor pings me.

On the surface, Kingsley blends in with the crowd, though I'm sure no one else in here is as combat-ready. No weapons are allowed in Arcadia, and though his XFrame technically isn't a weapon, he keeps it low-key. Tonight, it's hidden under the bulk of a Kevlar dress shirt and fur-lined robe. More ostentatious than what I've seen him wear before, but look where we are.

"What's new, buddy?" I greet as he approaches. We do the half-shake, half-hug, back-tap greeting.

"J-man." he says not bothering to raise his voice against the music. "How's it flowin'?"

"Been a long time."

"Didn't I see you at the Black Party last month?" he asks.

"That was a wild one, yeah. Can't say I saw you though."

"Yeah, you did. I hooked you up with some pretty potent party favors."

"Well, that's probably why I don't remember."

Kingsley and I have transacted a couple times more after that fateful first meeting a year ago, but only for the usual party fare. Not the smartest idea to keep going back to him, but once you've pulled off a Class A felony with someone, you tend to trust them. You don't usually have a choice.

From secondhand info, I've since learned that Kingsley's the go-to for many at C+P, and not a few of them from Team Parrish itself. The initial shock of discovery wore off when he assured me that he's kept Levantanil on the lowest of the down-low. Via referral through

Genomages only, and no one else at work has gotten it except for Elliott and me. All I have in common with the rest of the C+P staff are a dealer and a need for speed, blow, pep pills, and whatever else can keep us going when caffeine and ambition aren't enough.

I gotta know if Simon's one of Kingsley's clients too. And if he isn't, well, then that gets me a step closer to finding whoever laced his wine with poison.

Veronica slides next to me, head cocked to one side. I give her a quick shake of the head. No, Kingsley's not another one of my rebounds. She understands the signal. The two of them swap looks, then smiles, then names. It's loud in here, but my audio hookup with Veronica clues me in to their awkward flirtation.

I seize upon a pause in the conversation and pull Kingsley away. "Thanks for meeting on such short notice."

He waves it off. He then gives me an appraising look, and I realize that he's scanning me for bugs, checking if I'm on record. I step back from him. "C'mon, man. It's like you don't know me."

"Trust but verify," he chuckles.

I make a show of scanning him too, turning my head up and down. "It's only fair."

He puts his palms up in exaggerated submission. When he's satisfied, Kingsley sends a secure feed to my visor. "Alright, pick your poison."

My left field of view gets filled with a display of familiar narcotics, both for Sleepless and normals. He's got the hits, the new releases, and some obscure stuff too. As the popups scroll, Kingsley gives me his spiel, talking up his wares in the same breathless way suburban moms talk up their kids. His tone gets more excited as he gets to the last on his list.

"And for you, I saved the best one for last. They're calling it A-Pop."

The pill tube materializes, and my heart drops. It's the same clear cylinder and the same pale green cap as the one in Simon's office. Only this one is filled by a row of gelcaps of the same green color, spherical globs gleaming like caviar made of absinthe.

This is it. This is how Simon died. Right before my eyes.

I'm too stunned for words, and Kingsley keeps going. "All the kids love it, especially the Sleepless. It's a trippy knockout for everyone else, but for the likes of you, it's the closest you'll get to real sleep."

"I've heard that one before," I reply in a monotone, trying to collect myself. Every now and then, dealers and pharma corps boast of some new product that's "the closest thing to Sleep." With no exception, they're all either frauds or weak facsimiles.

"This one's different. Believe me, you ain't had anything like this."

"Sure, I'll give it a shot."

A funds transfer request pops up on my screen. With a finger flick I pay him off. The price is steep, usually is for the hot new commodity, but I would've paid anything to get my hands on that pill tube.

"Right on," Kingsley replies. "Lemme do my rounds, you go and have fun. I'll ping you in a few."

He walks back to fade into the crowd, but not before he gives Veronica, watching from behind me, a playful wink. She waves goodbye, biting her lower lip.

"He's cute," she says when I return to the bar. "And by the way, don't think I didn't notice. If I'd known you were looking to buy . . ."

"It's not like that," I reply, a tad abruptly.

"Okaaay. No need to be weird about it," she says, then changes gear. "Wanna head upstairs? I got some friends in Cube 4D who say it's getting wild in there."

She doesn't allow me a chance to say yes, and next thing I know we're headed back to coat check to pick up our suit-cases. Soon enough we're in the third-level changing area, a long, tile-wall room lined with lockers and shower stalls on either side, a sink island in the center. There's some activity, people shuffling in and out, but it's a lot quieter in here.

I find an empty stall at the back of the room, walking past party-goers disrobing their elaborate outfits to put on their VR suits. Some of them have couture duds, full-body hap-suits emblazoned with designer logos, quite unlike my standard issue gray and navy with racing stripes along the side. I take mine out of its carrying case and hold it up against the light of the changing stall, disappointed.

I begin to undress, peeling off my jacket. Then, the tinny clink of glass hitting tile catches my ear. The thing landed next to my boot and at first I think my eyes are playing tricks on me, or my visor is. I crouch down and take a closer look. Right there on the cold floor, is a thin, transparent pill tube with a pale green cap.

It's empty.

I look under the dividers to see where it came from, but the stalls next to mine were both unoccupied. My mind is rebelling against the idea but there's no other explanation. This thing fell out of my jacket.

Still in disbelief, I slowly reach for the vial, my doubt is dispelled only when I hold it between my fingers. I unscrew the cap, then take a whiff. Nothing. A sense of déjà vu hits me. I turn the cap over, and there I see the red and yellow starburst, with a black A in the middle.

Instantly, I think back to Simon's office. I've watched that visor video enough times to know for sure that I left the vial in that room. The cops found it too. This isn't the same one. It can't be.

I clutch the vial and dash out of the changing room, back into the noise and frenzy of the club.

✺

I run out to the second-floor railing and find a vantage point to scan the crowd below. I activate the "Recents" overlay, searching the tangled soup of sweaty, dancing bodies. A blue outline highlights the bar area where I last saw Kingsley, and I find that he's still there, but barely. He's walking toward the exit.

I rush down the stairs but people impede my every step. I stumble through the dance floor, squeezing my way through. Pushing out the crowd only got me shoved in return. I yell at them to get the fuck out of my way, but no one hears me through the chaos.

I begin to feel dizzy from the strobing lights, the frantic rhythm, the whiskey sour I downed too quickly, and the adrenaline coursing through my body. I keep pushing and shoving and reaching for the exit, but Kingsley's outline fades fainter and farther with each second, until it disappears as I am swallowed by the crowd.

When I finally reach the exit and pass through the Arcadia's doors, the bright lights of the hangar's floodlights shock my system. The parking lot is still packed, and a line still looped around the building. Disoriented, I turn my head in all directions, hoping I haven't completely lost him.

Through the queue, his blue outline reappears on my visor screen. He's standing by a darkened corner, palming something off to a coed with a glittery mohawk. I dash toward them.

"Hey, man, you gotta give me time to go for a run . . . didn't I say I'd ping you?" Kingsley chuckles as I approach. The party girl skitters away with her purchase.

"Do you know anything about this?" I show him the pill tube.

He tries to get a hold of it, but I snatch it away. "Who'd you get that from?"

"I was hoping you could tell me."

"Look, this here's my turf, and if someone else is creeping in on it, I'd wanna know."

"So you didn't slip me this?" I ask.

"Slip you? Man, you're not my type," he replies. It almost seemed friendly, if not for the venom in his tone. "And you know I'm not in the habit of giving freebies."

"Who else has a line on these?"

"There's only a couple of us in the entire city that has the connect. These parts, it's all me," he says. "You wanna tell me what's going on?"

"That's what I'm trying to find out. It was in my jacket pocket and thought it came from you," I reply, hoping some forthrightness encourages the same from him. Even as I say the words, I know they sound absurd. Kingsley's squint tells me he's thinking the same. "I don't know how it got there."

"Don't know either, but I'm mighty interested to know how," he says with a scowl.

"Look, if I got this from another guy, why would I ask you and risk pissing you off?"

A pause. We've both made good points—it makes no sense for this vial to come from Kingsley; I'd have no reason to lie to him about how I got it—and so find ourselves at an impasse. After a moment's thought, Kingsley replies.

"Man, fuck it. Don't know where that's from, and I don't fucking care anymore."

He walks away, and I place a hand on his arm. This halts his step. He shrugs my hand off, annoyed. "Imma get you your stuff, don't worry."

"There's another thing—I need some information on someone."

Now he's both annoyed and confused. "What kind of information?"

"Just humor me for a sec. I've given you good business, haven't I?" Seriously, the amount of crypto I've wired this guy over the past year should be enough to pry his mouth loose. "Nothing specific, just a lead."

There's an implicit bond between every dealer and their client. One built from assurances of discretion and repeat business. Depending on what's traded, it's also built on shared risk, the need to avoid mutually assured destruction. It doesn't get any riskier than biohacking, and given what he's sold me, I'd like to think Kingsley and I have a stronger bond than most.

He gives me a stern look. Not a no, a maybe. I take my opening. I pull up Simon's image on my visor and share it onto his.

"Have you ever sold A-Pop to this guy?" I ask. "Yes or no, that's all I need. One word."

Kingsley takes a deep breath, staring into Simon's official C+P headshot. I can't tell if that's confusion or recognition written on his face. After a pause he turns to me and says sternly, "Man, you know I can't tell you. That's bad for business. What would my clients say?"

"This guy won't get into any trouble, trust me." Given that he's lying in the morgue.

"And how would you like it if someone came around asking about you?"

I've always known that if I ever get caught for illegal biohacking, it wouldn't be because of Kingsley. The man keeps his own interests in check, but he also keeps his word. Usually, I'd admire the discretion, but not now. Not when his code goes up against my need for answers.

"Kingsley, it's me. I figured you'd make an exception." His vacant stare tells me he's pulled up stuff on his visor screen, probably running facial rec on the image. After a couple seconds, Kingsley's dead stare turns into a scowl.

"Okay, before you say anything, lemme explain," I plead, panicked. "He's a guy I work with and I think he was murdered but the cops are saying . . ."

"We're done here. Fucking reporters." He backs away quickly. "No way you're gonna pin a dead guy on me!"

"C'mon man. I would never! You go down and I go down too, remember?"

It's not enough to stop him, but he's my strongest lead and I won't let him slip away. I grab his arm before he can get any farther. A flash of incredulity streaks across his face.

"You better let go of me." Kingsley glares at me, his muscles tensing under my grasp. I refuse, but he manages to wrest his arm away, showing off the scaffold of steel that encases his torso. He shoots me look of amused condescension, like I'm a bug he needs to squash. "Now walk the fuck away before you hurt yourself."

I could stop, defuse and de-escalate. I do have that choice, but I can't see it. My mind is too muddled by questions and revelations and booze and fatigue and this roiling unease in my gut. No, not unease. Blind, uncontrollable panic.

Why did Simon have an A-Pop vial? And why the fuck do I have one too?

Every second that passes I get closer to only one answer, one that I can't accept.

"If you would just listen to me for one fucking second." I grab him again, more forcefully this time. The distinct whir of Kingsley's XFrame starts to speed up. He makes a point to stare down my hand on his arm. I hold steady.

In one swift and effortless move, he swats me aside. The force lifts my body off the ground, and I fly through the air, slamming onto the concrete wall of Hangar 5.

"Punk ass bitch," he spits without looking back.

A sharp pain stabs at the shoulder joint where the wall hit bone. I crumple down to the pavement, a wave of agony coursing through my body. There's a ringing in my ear, the thumping of blood flow mingling with muffled bass beats. Clubgoers walk past, oblivious, and soon, their shuffling legs and designer sneaks start to blur before my eyes.

My vision darkens.

20.

The pain hasn't subsided. My head is still ringing, and I'd been curled up in a fetal position in the robocab for the trip home. I reassume this pose as I collapse on the couch. I turn on the vidwall and zoom-focus the camera on me. With small, controlled movements, I slip into my VR suit. I don't even bother with the base layer.

The suit runs its imager and soon pulls up a full scan. There are scrapes from hitting the wall and getting up off the sidewalk. The screen zooms in on my reddened face. I lift my hand to it; my left cheekbone feels tender. I ask the program to run Body Analytics. Numbers run on a side panel with grids showing my heart rate and blood pressure. Elevated but not unusually so. Blood alcohol at 0.075. Blunt impact on my shoulder and elbow, a slight concussion on the back-left side of my head.

The AI voice prompts me to seek medical assistance. She doesn't automatically call 911 for me, which I guess is a good sign. She tells me I'm stocked up on pain meds and offers to order more. She populates a list of painkillers sorted by strength and availability without a prescription. I ignore her and hoist myself up toward the bathroom.

I grab the cartridge of oxy and inject a dose. The hiss alone sounds like relief. Wish there was something I could take for the bruise to my ego, though maybe I deserved this. That was supremely idiotic, going after Kingsley. He'd have pummeled me even without the XFrame, and if it weren't for his restraint, I'd need a lot more than a hit of oxy.

Gotta kick myself, too, because I needed Kingsley. I'm betting he had a lot more to say. If I'd only finessed it a bit, stopped my rage and panic from getting the best of me, I might've gotten him to tell me if Simon bought from him.

One thing is clear though: Simon died of an A-Pop overdose.

Back on the couch, I run the visor recording from Simon's office on the vidwall. I then take the empty A-Pop vial out, raise it up side-by-side to the projected image.

The two containers look exactly the same: same size and shape, same pale green cap. I unscrew it and compare the emoji logo stamped underneath. Identical. I close out the video and run a search for "A-Pop." The screen floods me with results, too many to sift through: press releases for a discontinued energy drink from China, a dub-redux band from Austria, countless references to apoplectic strokes. No entry on UrbanDictionary though. This new drug is a branding fail.

Except for Kingsley and Veronica, no one else came into contact with me tonight, and despite what happened, he's right. He had no reason to slip me an empty vial. Neither did Veronica. So where did this come from?

I try to recall the last time I wore this jacket, but come up short. I didn't wear it to brunch with the family, and I didn't go out on Saturday, except that morning coffee with Anders. I might have worn it Friday and the days before? Wardrobe choices aren't the kind of thing I make a record of.

I ask my scheduler to show me the past week. Thursday and Friday were irregular following Simon's death, but the days before were pretty standard. Work, lunch, home, dinner, bar, random hookup, etc. Saturday at C+P, then the usual dicking around the apartment, Sunday down in Cape May with my folks.

Oh, and there was Laszlo on Friday night. I should probably check for unexpected visitors too. They wouldn't be on the scheduler. I scroll through my messages and my apps, but it appears there was only that one. I check my apartment's security log too, pull up the record for the last couple of weeks. No visitors since the start of the month, until Hannah came by on Wednesday, July 8th at 7:05 p.m.

The night Simon died. An hour and change before I supposedly came to see him.

Again, that blind panic overcomes me. I quickly send Hannah a message to call me ASAP.

I ask the vidwall's AI to consolidate all my logs and arrange the items chronologically. Every detail of the last few weeks shows up in an organized, color-coded array. I check that date on my logs again. Wednesday, July 8, 2043. Work, logged as ending at 6 p.m. Hannah's visit. Didn't see anyone else until C+P Thursday morning, when I found Simon dead.

See, I knew I was right. It struck me as odd when Tetro showed me that video. Hannah was here; I was home at seven. But how did I end up on the security cameras at 8:30?

I run a search on all messages and calls from Simon dated July 8th. No calls, no emails or pings before 7 p.m. I scan each word, and there's nothing about us needing to meet at 8:30 or me needing to return to the office.

So why did I see Simon later that night?

At first I thought it was shock following his death, but this failure of my memory is looking like something else entirely. For a few hours on Wednesday night, I don't remember anything. Not how I came to be at C+P, nor why I ended up in that office.

That period of time, from when Hannah left here until the time I showed up on that video, is a complete blank.

And in that time, Simon died.

❀

In the rush of panic, I realize now that there are more things I don't remember. Things from the last few days that I'm only now noticing. Missing items, forgotten conversations. Hannah's passport,

Charlie's breakup. The Black Party with Kingsley. Snippets of time that seem to have happened to others but not to me.

This forgetting also explains this feeling that hasn't left me since I found Simon that morning. It's like this weight around my neck, an inward pull deep in my gut. I felt it with Paolo too, it's something I've been working through for the last two years in therapy. There's guilt, sure, though this new one is different. It's not from a sense of omission, or a sense of having failed, the way I failed Paolo.

This time, with Simon, it's from a sense of having done something.

Drunk, injured, and concussed, my thoughts spiral into paranoiac territory.

I think I did something wrong, I need to figure this out, I don't remember anything, and I might have taken A-Pop, but I'm not sure, but why do I have this vial, and is that why I can't remember, why is all of this happening, is this all my fault, oh god I am scared, I am so fucking scared.

Images of Simon flash in my waking mind. For the first time in years, I beg for sleep. It does not come.

The front door chimes. Veronica come to save me.

"What the fuck happened to you?" she starts, but her manner shifts when she sees my injuries. She runs to my side, then to the bathroom, raiding my first aid kit for supplies. She asks the AI to order a batch of chicken soup from a 24-hour diner. Then, she restates her question, nicer this time.

I tell her about Kingsley, but I choose to omit the finer details of our long history with Levantanil. I trust her fully, but I care for her too much to burden her with keeping my secret. I do tell her everything about A-Pop, and Simon, and why I needed to know what Kingsley knew. I tell her about the strange vial, the confrontation, and the pitiful way I ended up unconscious on the tarmac after a single shove.

She listens intently, nodding every so often in commiseration. She resists the urge to reprimand me about pursuing my theories, which is how I know she's resigned to the fact that I won't let this go. After I've eased her in with all the details, I tell her what I think happened on Wednesday night.

"I'm missing hours, Vee. In those missing hours, Simon died. The cop said I was with him, but I don't remember that. And now there's this vial, and I don't remember how I got it."

"And you're certain they're connected somehow?" she asks.

I nod.

"You have an empty vial and you don't remember part of Wednesday night. That's all we know," she says, reassuringly. "Everything else is the type of thing people forget all the time."

"This has something to do with Simon. I feel it in my gut, especially after tonight," I reply. "I need to know how I got this vial, and I'm sure Kingsley holds the answer."

Veronica sighs. She eases me to lean back onto the couch and then goes to get me a glass of water. I lie on her lap, and she strokes my hair in silence. Her fingers snag through ringlets that she tries in vain to smooth. The motion of her fingers, pressing gently on my scalp, soothes me.

"Thanks for being here," I say. "For putting up with all my craziness."

"Listen, how many times have we had disastrous nights like this? Tonight doesn't even break the top three . . ." she laughs. "Usually I'm the one laid out drunk or strung out of my mind or bawling because of some carajo. You gotta let me take care of you for a change."

Right then, her visor begins to beep. "Speak of the devil."

She screenshares a message. A photo of Kingsley, gray eyes, wide grin—*where u at.* I sit up so quickly the blood rushes from my head and I get woozy.

"Why are you—how is he—what the fuck is going on?"

"He found me at the VR dens," she replies. "Must have been after you'd left. If I'd known what he did, I wouldn't have been so friendly."

"It's 4 a.m. That kind of text is a lot more than friendly."

I shoot up off the couch and start pacing with nervous energy. My shoulder starts to hurt again. Veronica holds my arm and stops me from drifting.

"Calm down, we're just talking," she says. "Besides, didn't you say you needed him? Maybe this is how you can get your answers—"

"No, Vee. You can't," I reply, reading her mind. "Do you see what he did to me with one flick?"

"I'm not like you, okay? I'm not going to get all up in his face," she says. Then, under her breath: "And here I thought you've gotten a handle on your rage issues."

I'm too agitated to let the remark slide. "I do. I have. This, tonight, was not rage," I argue. "He was the one who lost his temper."

"Either way, it's clear your style didn't work, so let me help you," she replies with a glint in her eye. "I have a very light touch."

"You also have a girlfriend."

She draws in a sharp breath and averts her eyes. "Damn it, do you want my help or not?"

21.

An extended meditation session calms my nerves following Veronica's visit. I may be losing my mind, but at least we've got a plan in place. Perhaps the matter with Kingsley is salvageable after all. I'm basking under the glow of the Aurora Borealis in Juneau, when suddenly I'm pulled back into reality. Hannah's calling.

"What's going on, Jamie?" She turns on video and blows up on my vidwall. She's in front of her vanity, putting her face on for work. I check the time. It's too early, even for her.

"I need to ask you something. It's better in person."

"This doesn't sound like an emergency, not one that requires a three a.m. all-caps text with multiple exclamation points." Her sharp tone confirms that this is a bad idea. I should just figure this out myself. I try to conjure up a convenient excuse to get off the call and spare her.

"What happened to your face?" she asks. The welt on my cheekbone is starting to purple.

"It's not as bad as it looks."

"How did you hurt yourself?" she asks, stern but clearly worried.

She knows when I'm downplaying things. I waffle for a response, but the next thing I know, she's on her way to my apartment.

As I wait for her arrival, I make a mental outline of what I'm going to say. She can help me piece together what happened Wednesday night. The problem is, I'll have to tell her about everything else. I can't just ask her, hey, what time did you come by? Have you seen this vial of A-Pop before? No, I have too much to explain. I need to start from the very beginning, and that means starting at the end.

※

Last summer was our last summer. Hannah and I made plans to do a road trip to Toronto over Labor Day weekend, taking all the scenic routes and making day-long stops at the Catskills, the Finger Lakes and Niagara before crossing over. I had asked Simon for a few days off well in advance, which he approved, but as with any other vacation, he reserved the right to rescind it if a story broke.

At the time, *The Simon Parrish Files* was developing a piece about corruption in the city's transit contracts. Purchase prices for new subway parts had been padded, and over that weekend, our whistleblower recanted his statements. Simon wanted to regroup with the whole team present and was adamant that I take the first available flight back down to the city.

It was Friday morning when I got his call. I told Simon I couldn't fly because we were doing a road trip, but I would be in the next day. Quite expectedly, his reply was a loud refusal—delivered in full volume through the vidwall of our hotel room in Seneca Falls. Hannah heard it all, and worse still, she saw how easily I gave in to Simon's demand.

On our drive back to the city, all I did was rant about Simon. In between expletives, I promised Hannah I'd quit soon, or at least ask for a transfer. I'd polish up my résumé and start calling grad school buddies who could connect me to new opportunities. She listened and nodded, weariness painted across her face. After a while, she broke her silence.

"Jamie, stop," she said with a sigh. "You're only telling me what you think I want to hear. And this isn't what I want to hear."

"What do you mean?"

"This is the same-old, same-old. You'll clean up your résumé, call your headhunter friend, take some meetings. Then another assignment will reel you in and you're back where you started: at Simon's beck and call. I'm sick of hearing it."

I told the car to make a sharp turn into a charging station that we happened to be passing. Once it pulled into a parking spot, I took both of her hands into mine, apologized for the weekend, and promised I'd be better.

Tears welled up in her eyes.

"I love you," she says. "But you're not here. You haven't been in a long time. And this—what we have—has not felt like a partnership in a long time."

"That's not fair, I . . ."

"I tried, Jamie. I really did. I was there through Paolo, through all of the nightmares, through your nervous breakdown. I was there when you stepped foot into New Dawn and I was waiting for you the day you were released . . ."

The litany was becoming unbearable. "Well forgive me for grieving, I didn't know my trauma was such an imposition!"

"Fuck you, that's not what I'm saying and you know it," she yells back. "We had such a rough year, and I weathered all of it without feeling a single shred of doubt about us. I was certain we were gonna survive. Then things got worse. *You* got worse. You pulled away. Now you spend barely any time with me, and when you do, your head's elsewhere. It's like you've got this completely different life that's separate from mine."

"That's not true."

"Jamie, I'm not the type of woman who falls apart alone. But there's nothing lonelier than being with someone who's not really there."

"I'm here now. Let me do better." I clutch her hands in mine, like a prayer.

"We're in the middle of the highway because your boss wants you back from our vacation," she replies. "That's the opposite of being present."

We parked at that station for what felt like forever. Trucks whizzed past as we ran out of tears and sighs and deep breaths and soft kisses to the backs of each other's hands. We tired of repeating words that we'd already said, not just that day but many days before. Finally, as the sky began to darken, I told the car to drive us home.

That night, she took the bed and I took the couch. After she closed the bedroom door, I fixed myself a whiskey sour. I polished it off quick and made another, and then another, and then another. I wanted nothing more than to shut out my memories and dull the ache. To not think or feel. I wanted to sleep. Begged for sleep to come, to come back.

I had to settle for passing out drunk.

I moved out the following weekend.

She arrives, and I offer to make her a coffee, which she accepts. I pour her some dark roast in an old mug, a ceramic marigold thing we picked up as a souvenir on a trip to San Miguel de Allende a couple of years ago. We got a matching pair.

"Some weeks before you and I broke up, I met a guy named Kingsley. He sold me this drug called Levantanil. It makes people Sleepless."

I recount to her my journey into unsleeping, from the moment I took the pill, to the changes I went through, to everything thereafter. Each word felt like a thorn being pulled out of me. Did I think it would be easier, doing this now? There is a universe where I didn't do what I did, where I never became Sleepless at all. Where Hannah and I were still together. I sometimes peered into that universe, in random imaginings during the wee hours of my Sleepless nights. Never until this moment, here in front of her, has that universe felt ever more desirable, or more distant.

"It could have killed you, Jamie." Hannah says after a long pause.

"It felt right at the time," I say. "I wanted to be Sleepless. And I couldn't wait for it to randomly happen to me."

"You wanted it that bad?"

"I didn't think there'd be any risks."

"You going to prison was a risk. Not telling me was a risk."

"I . . . I meant health risks."

"I know what you fucking meant," she replies. "That's the problem, Jamie. You only thought about *your* health. *Your* safety. *Yourself.*"

"I'm sorry, Hannah. I should have told you."

What I left out: I didn't think it through. I didn't think of you. How many times had you given me a way in? An opening so that I could tell you. And how painful it must have been seeing me reject it every time, closing a door you'd been trying to hold open.

"What am I supposed to do with this information, Jamie? Is this what I came here for?"

"Something's wrong with me," I say. "I think I did something horrible, and I need your help."

I slide her my tablet. I scroll through my logs as I explain the gaps in my recollection of time. "I saw you Wednesday night when you came by for the passport, and then there's about four hours I can't account for." I remember playing China Shop, venting out my boredom and frustration on VR, but most everything between that and Hannah's visit was a complete blank.

"I think the Levantanil is fucking with my brain."

She takes control of the tablet and swipes back and forth, reviewing the records of my security system, my calendar, my messages. Anticipating her next question, I remind her that my GPS trackers are off, as they've always been.

"I was hoping maybe I said something to you about heading out, or maybe I was dressed to head out? I can't imagine why I'd be back at work after coming home. How much do you remember?"

"Not much. I was in and out, Jamie."

I need to pry more, help her remember something. I search her face for any sign of alarm or concern, but she only has a look that telegraphs, *Are we done here?*

I decide to tell her the rest.

"When I found Simon, I saw an empty pill tube by his wine glass. The cops think it's a suicide, but I've always had my doubts. Then last night, I found this empty pill tube in my jacket pocket. It's exactly like the one in Simon's office."

"All right, and?"

"I was at the club last night. Kingsley was too. Shortly after I talk to him, I found the vial on me. I thought it came from him so I asked him. Things got heated, then this happened." I turn to show my bruised face. "He claims the vial wasn't from him, and I have no idea how I got it."

"And you don't know where you were Wednesday, when Simon died."

"Yes. So you see, I need your help to know what happened that night."

A flash of pity streaks across her face. She sees my pain, recognizes it for what it is. Yet soon enough, that pity disappears, replaced with something harder.

"This all makes sense now," Hannah says.

"What do you mean?"

"I knew you were Sleepless, and that you'd been lying to me all this time."

For a moment I thought she had made sense of Wednesday night, that she remembered a detail that I'd missed. Her reaction— the way she nodded to indulge my train of thought, the blank stare as I talked about vials and pill tubes and A-Pop—was yet another thing that I had missed.

"I wanted to tell you—about being Sleepless," I say. "I thought about coming clean about that part at least, and I figured I would keep the biohacking to myself . . ."

"Because you thought I might tell someone, get you in trouble. Because you couldn't trust me."

"No, because I couldn't force such a huge secret on you," I insist, reaching out to hold her.

"It wouldn't have mattered. You could have told me half the story and it would still be a complete lie." She brushes me aside, her hands cold with sweat. "That's why we had to end, Jamie. All the lies. I did know half the story. I knew you were Sleepless. Never got to confirm it, but I could tell. What's worse than you lying is that I *let you* keep lying."

How could I not know that she knew? Of course she did. I don't know which is the greater sin—that I lied to her all that time, or that I forced her to lie to herself as much as I did.

"If that wasn't bad enough," she continues. "Toward the end, you forgot things. Small things here and there, like when you were supposed to pick me up from work, or when it was your turn to get dinner. All the small pledges that make up a relationship, broken. Soon enough, you forgot about me."

"It wasn't like that at all . . ."

"Yes, it was, and that's what made it clear that I had to walk away. How many times did I tell you how I feel? You'd promised to change, but then you'd always go back to how you were. You were either lying about wanting to be better or you didn't care enough to commit to it. Either way, I knew this was over."

Tears start to stream down my face. She holds hers back, rising from her seat toward the door.

"I tried to understand," she continues. "Told myself you were busy with work, Simon was running you ragged. You were recovering from Paolo's death. The more I tried to convince myself, the more they started to sound like excuses. Like lies. Lies that I told myself to ease the pain of being forgotten."

"I never forgot about you, Hannah. Never."

"Yes, you did, Jamie. And now we know why."

22.

Encrypted video connection from noorJ . . . Gateway open.

"Thought you'd disappeared on me," I tell him. "You got something?"

Noor nods slowly. "This took more time than I thought it would. Traipsing around C+P was tricky, what with all the safeguards they've put up. I did manage to get in, of course, but there was nothing in Cleo Johnson's work files."

"Do you need more time?" I ask, with some impatience.

"Hold your horses. I had to go wide. Very wide. I had begun to think she was spotless, but I'm nothing if not tenacious."

"So you found something? A connection to Dwyer?"

Again, the slow head nod. He pulls up a data vizualization of what he's found, filling up my view. Charts and diagrams with the players' names, highlighted documents, animated arrows—it's so precise and professional, you'd think he was presenting on one of C+P's broadcasts.

"I began to dig into her family background. Found that her parents are heavily invested in a green energy company called Azeofuel.

It's a closely-held corporation headquartered in Delaware, but with holdings all over the country. Her folks own 30 percent of the company."

Huh. I didn't know Cleo came from money. "And is she invested in it too?"

"If I could finish," he says, prompted by the graphics. "Azeofuel does it all: wind, solar, geothermal, but their biggest business is in biofuel, particularly ethanol. Corn fuel, basically. And guess where all their ethanol refineries are?"

"Minnesota." I say.

"Got it in one."

Noor pulls up a map of the Azeofuel's land holdings, a wide swath all along the country's northern border. "Dwyer pretty much runs the state, and in the past two elections, the company made contributions to his campaign at the maximum legal limits. Azeofuel got a lot of subsidies and tax breaks in exchange."

He then shares more campaign finance records, state tax legislation, and a timeline tending to show causation between the two. "It's not a lot, but it's something."

It's more than something. Cleo knows every story that comes out of the newsroom. She should have disclosed this connection. "I'm sure this is not all of it," I tell him. "How much longer do you need?"

He takes a while to reply, and there's hesitation in his voice when he does. "Honestly, I don't know if anything else will turn up. I've gone pretty deep, and this here's the only thing that ties her in any way remotely close to the senator."

"Looks very close to me."

"You sure? To me, it looks like your garden-variety pay-to-play, and Cleo isn't directly in the game." He pulls up more financials, more spreadsheets. "And no ties to the Senate Freedom Fund or any anti-Sleepless groups either, like you asked. No calls, fund transfers, hidden interests."

"Or she could be doing all her dealings through her parents," I say, trying to convince Noor as much as myself.

"Why do you seem so bent on this woman anyway?" he asks, neutrally.

If it's not Cleo, then I have some serious questions that need answering. That's why I'm so bent. I need it to be her in that room that night somehow. It has to be her, because it can't be me.

"No particular reason," I reply instead. "But she's my only lead so far."

"You sure? Because if you have any other intel that you haven't given me yet, now's the time. Might help me do the search better."

"No. I got nothing else. Just give it another look, all right? And get back to me—soon."

Noor sighs. "It's your money."

✺

Tuesday, 07/14/2043, 9:11 AM

I'm barely holding it together at my desk. Watching the feeds is giving me a migraine, and my mind's already full up with theories about the night before Simon's death, especially after that conversation with Hannah. Things are supremely fucked right now. As if to snap me out of it, a company-wide message comes in from Maxwell.

It's an invitation to Simon's funeral. The service is set for Friday afternoon, out in Jersey.

Seems like the medical examiner cleared him quick. Quicker than I'd assumed, anyway. The ME's office is a busy place, handling all deaths in the county. In cases of murder, they'd need to do a full autopsy, which means waiting in queue for over a week. If we're having the funeral so soon, does that mean the coroner has ruled it a suicide?

I walk over to Maxwell's corner office and see that the panes are frosted. Two ghostly figures pace around the room, both gesticulating wildly in silence. Staffers walk past with interest, watching this shadow dance. I lean closer into the wall and hear thumping, Maxwell slamming his fists on the desk? I've never seen him lose his cool; that's more Simon's style.

Just then, his assistant Portia marches out of the office, tears streaming down her face. She looks right through me. I hesitate but Maxwell already sees me standing in the entryway.

"What do you need?"

"Uhm, I saw the memo about the funeral . . ."

"What about it?"

"And it didn't say anything about the coverage." A plausible reason for my follow-ups. "I'd like to be involved, if that's all right."

He shoots down my attempts brusquely. "Look, I have more pressing matters to deal with. Now if you don't mind—?" Maxwell turns to his screen, and I have the sense to hold my tongue, so I decide to leave. I'll have to get my confirmation elsewhere.

"Wait, I apologize," he says when I'm at the door. "I honestly haven't thought about our coverage. Though the family wants privacy, we've been able to convince Rita to allow our news crew into the temple. We also offered to provide a security detail to keep other news outlets away, make sure the service doesn't turn into a circus. Cleo's making all the arrangements, so it would be better for you to ask her."

"Thanks, I will." I clear my throat. "Is everything all right? I saw Portia . . ."

A scowl begins to form on his face. "Like I said, this is not a good time. Go to Cleo." He waves me off, and I slowly retreat. I let out a deep sigh once I'm out in the hallway. *It was suicide.* Maxwell might not have an answer for me now, so I tell that to myself over and over, like a mantra. For the last few days, I'd convinced myself it was foul play, but somehow having that empty vial on me has made it easier for me to disbelieve murder.

That's called denial, and I'm pretty good at it.

Then, from the far end of the hall, I see staffers rise from their cubicles and step out of their offices. The commotion builds, and I find the source. Detective Tetro heading straight at me, alongside two other detectives and a bunch of uniforms.

I break into a cold sweat and find myself immobile. Tetro's eyes meet mine. All sounds become muffled then muted, except for the sound of his oncoming footsteps.

Tetro reaches me and takes a moment, staring me down. He then asks me to step aside. I comply with the command, and suddenly it feels like I'm moving through quicksand, like my bones are made of rubber. The cops then open the door to the corner office I had just left.

What follows is the calmest, most polite arrest I've seen in my entire career.

Despite the look of shock on Maxwell's face, his movements are measured. He asks what the matter is. In response, Tetro only gives him an atonal request to accompany the men to the precinct.

I fumble around for my visors and start recording. All the officers have theirs on, and as I look around me, so do all the onlookers. "What are the charges?" Some staffer bellows from outside the office, followed by another. "Where's your warrant?"

The cops don't hear a thing. Tetro reads Maxwell his rights as the two other detectives begin to flank Maxwell. Tetro makes no mention of the charges, and Maxwell doesn't ask either.

"I'd like to have a moment to summon my lawyer," he requests.

"You can do that at the precinct."

Maxwell presents his wrists and one of the officers tells him there's no need for that. "We'll walk out together, calmly." Tetro still grabs onto a forearm though, as he escorts Maxwell around his desk. "That's it, Mr. Cartwright, easy does it."

The cops act more like orderlies propping up a frail patient than officers making an arrest. They pause outside the office doorway as Maxwell searches for his assistant in the amassed crowd.

"Call the firm. They'll know what to do," he says when he finds her.

The surrealism of what's unfolding before me delays a realization. Though his hand is tight around Maxwell's arm, Tetro's sight is set on me, glaring as he leaves. I hold my breath, sure that my entire body is trembling, and watch as Maxwell Cartwright is taken away for the murder of Simon Parrish.

"Assholes!" Cleo screams as she flings her visor onto the conference room table. The staff jolts back in surprise but quickly resume their assignments, working their tablets and phones to get the latest info on what's going on. "I swear, if our own fucking lawyers hang up on me again . . ."

The atmosphere is thick with tension. Now the ranking officer at C+P News, Cleo has gathered the entire staff in one place and, in a matter of hours, assembled a war room. Staffers that usually work remote have been summoned, and those overseas have their faces up on the vidwall. It's all-hands-on-deck. A roomful of top reporters ready to go into battle, with Cleo at the front line.

"This is fucking ridiculous. Maxwell didn't kill Simon. He wouldn't have," she says. The rest of the staff murmur in agreement. She storms out of the room, yelling at an assistant to get the lawyers back on the line.

Cleo's certitude is too heated, almost authentic, and for a second I forget that she'd have cause to lie. That she'd been lying about her ties to Dwyer. If she were somehow involved in what's now a murder, it would be too obvious for her to be readily pointing at Maxwell. Still, I keep a close eye at her. Who knows when she might slip?

In one corner of the room, Elliott and I have built a makeshift workstation with a couple of moving desks. For the last hour, he and I have been watching the news feeds for any updates on Maxwell's arrest, but nothing new so far. Still no word from the field staff either. We knew sending them to the precinct would be fruitless, but we're still holding out hope. Even my contacts at Central Booking haven't returned my messages. At this point, we're tired of refreshing our inboxes and are now left staring at our screens, waiting for a new ping to arrive.

"I told you suicide didn't make sense," I mumble under my breath, breaking the lull.

"And murder by his best friend and business partner does?" Elliott says, looking unconvinced. "Look, the cops are on top of it. Let's just see where this goes."

That's what I'm afraid of.

Soon, Cleo runs back into the war room and slams her hand down onto the comm projector. "What do you have?" she asks tersely, as soon as the other line shows up on screen.

"He's retained private counsel, Strathairn-Shaw," says Landry, a baby-faced junior associate from C+P's Legal Department. The staffers whistle at the mention of the firm's name. Maxwell's going with the big guns. "Our lawyers are working with them on a joint defense, so it took a while to coordinate and get more info. Anyway, it's as we feared. Top charge is first-degree murder."

Cleo hits the desk again. "Fuck. What else?"

"They've got video of Maxwell going into Simon's office with a bottle of wine, which is how the cause of death was introduced into Simon's system. The NYPD rushed the tox screen and found it was a type of opioid, some new street drug. Stronger than heroin, very lethal even in small quantities."

My temples start throbbing, and I can't bear to hear whatever's coming next.

"They also have witness testimony saying he and Simon have been fighting about the Zephyrus buyout," Landry continues. "Turns out, Maxwell has a long history with the CEO of Zephyrus and stood to gain billions from the deal."

"Yeah, well, so did Simon," Elliott says. "But he didn't want to dance with the devil."

"Anyway, that's what they're looking at as motive," Landry replies. "The Strathairn lawyers aren't too worried about that though. Maxwell insists Simon was on board for the deal, and says he has proof."

"He indulged Maxwell, and their friendship's the only reason the Zephyrus offer got as far as it did," Cleo says with a scoff. "But Simon never would have sold out."

"Even with all the concessions?" I ask. "I heard Simon got Zephyrus to give in to his list of demands."

She pauses to consider this, with a glimmer of mistrust in her eye. "Nothing would have tempted Simon. The only demand he had was for Zephyrus to leave our damn company alone."

I can't get a read on where Cleo's head is at. She doesn't think Maxwell killed Simon, but she also agrees that Maxwell has motive to kill him. This could be a feint, but I don't see her endgame, nor any consistency.

Landry continues. "The ADA said they have statements from various board members saying that Simon has been pressuring them to vote no on the offer. Their theory is that Simon did convince enough of them, which pissed Maxwell off."

"Wait a minute—last I heard, Maxwell had majority yeses. It was as done a deal as it could get," says Gregg Goldin, huddled with his news team at the other end of the room. His tone makes it clear which side he's on. The rest of the staff glare at him. I do, too, but

I'm also watching him intently. Maybe there's something more to his acrimony against Simon than political differences and turf wars.

"No, the folks on the Board say it's been a tie for a while," another staffer counters. Most everyone nods in agreement.

"That's what I heard, too, but in the event of a tie, the board president casts the tiebreak," Mia Stuart replies with her authoritative fact-checker voice. More knowing nods.

Since news of the buyout offer broke, everyone in C+P has become an expert on Robert's Rules of Order, the company's charter, and of course, each board member's potential leanings. Through gossip, most of the staff have tried to deduce how each of the Board's ten members intends to vote on the offer, for good reason. After all, layoffs could be coming if we get acquired. Better to know these things ahead of time, jump ship and try to land elsewhere. Preferably at a news agency that isn't owned by another megacorp like Zephyrus.

"It's 5-5, and as president, Maxwell has the tiebreak vote," I add, casting a sideways glance at Goldin. "So the offer's going to get accepted."

"Right. Which means Maxwell wouldn't have any reason to kill Simon if he was already going to win," says João Oliveira, bringing the room to a hush. I thought he'd already left town, but of course a reporter of his caliber would want to stay for the fireworks.

"Well, according to the ADA, Simon had been wooing one of the Board members, Briana Foley," Landry replies. "She was originally a yes vote; then Simon persuaded her to change her mind. The day before he died, he told his no-vote faction that she'd changed sides. Foley's flipped vote makes it four votes in favor, six against. No deal."

Noises of restrained glee go off around the room. This was apparently news, despite everyone's propensity at chasing down gossip about the Board votes. Cleo looked simultaneously relieved, stunned, and ready to burst into a victory dance. Everybody else did too.

"For real? You mean the deal isn't happening anymore?" one of the video editors asks.

"And I was *so ready* to become a corporate shill," yells someone in the back of the room. The place erupts in laughter.

"Looks like Simon got his way in the end," Goldin says, dejected.

"And even with Simon gone," Elliott adds, with some hint of elation before catching himself, "It would still be five against on a Board of nine."

"Right. So the prosecution's theory is that Maxwell couldn't stomach the defeat, which is why he killed Simon." Landry's words deflate the momentary jubilation.

A revenge killing, made to look like a suicide. I'd think it was far-fetched, but my threshold for the improbable has escalated in the last few days. Simon, Anders, Cleo . . . everyone is capable of anything. Including, and maybe especially, Maxwell Cartwright.

"It's not exactly his style though," Oliveira counters. "Maxwell doesn't act out of rage or spite."

I'd tend to agree. Maxwell is deliberate and reputed to be so, as affirmed by the nods of assent in the room. Though maybe that's it —the more out of character the crime, the easier it is for Maxwell to deny it.

"Yes, it's not his style, but the opportunity was there," Elliott says, to looks of displeasure. "All I'm saying is if anyone were to make a murder appear as a suicide, Simon's recent behavior provided great cover. I mean, look at us. We all thought it was a suicide until now."

The rest of the staff softens, their faces downcast from reproach. I look at the others around me, guiltless, secure in the knowledge that I had always believed otherwise. Yet I'm equally guilt-laden at the idea of murder, given what I found last night.

"And although it's not his style," Cleo adds, "You never know what someone can be driven to do when the stakes are this high."

"I know Maxwell, and he's more methodical than this," Goldin says, waving off the speculation. "And Simon's death doesn't help him at all. Right now, the vote is still four against and five in favor. Maxwell loses either way. Do we really think Maxwell would kill Simon for petty revenge?"

The man's point lands with a thud, and the room falls silent. The lull is broken by Liang Li Fang, the Beijing bureau chief patched in via holopresence.

"Briana Foley. Simon's death would doubtless delay the Board vote, at least for a few days. That would have bought Maxwell time to flip her back to a yes vote. Especially since whatever Simon enticed her with presumably died with him."

"Even if it means throwing the company into turmoil?" Goldin asks rhetorically. "If this is about the buyout, then why would Maxwell do anything to scare Zephyrus away?"

Zephyrus won't scare easy, that much I know from talking with Maxwell himself. And the vote is not going to get delayed either; he's told me that much. He might not have seemed too eager to move forward with the vote, but maybe the turmoil doesn't matter. If Zephyrus is determined enough, then Simon's death wouldn't deter them. And it certainly wouldn't have deterred them if Maxwell was acting on their behalf.

"Oh, Gregg, you know full well that very little would stop Zephyrus from buying us out," Cleo replies with contempt.

"Maybe not a suicide, but a murder might," Oliveira says.

"All that matters to them is whether they have the votes," Liang counters. "And Simon's death at least brings them closer to getting Foley back on the yes side."

"Not to give anyone a reason to fear or cheer," Landry says, interrupting the debate, "but this is exactly what we're banking on. There's clear motive for revenge, and some form of benefit to be gained, but they're not airtight. All these questions you're raising show reasonable doubt, and that is a defendant's best friend."

The lawyer's words bring another hush onto the war room. Everyone wants the buyout offer to get rejected, and with Maxwell's arrest, that appears all but certain. At the same time, no one wants to believe that Maxwell is capable of murder. Some raise doubts about him, but that's what journalists do, explore all angles regardless of what one believes. And despite the questions, it's clear that Maxwell is beloved, flaws and all, as much as Simon was.

Part of me can't believe Maxwell did it either, but there's a pill tube in my pocket, and I shouldn't want the cops suspecting anyone but him.

"So what happens now?" Cleo asks, the conflict evident in her tone.

"Now we wait for arraignment, try to argue for bail while the case proceeds. We don't know when that'll be, as the judges down here are pretty random when it comes to scheduling. But we'll be ready, you folks don't need to worry. We've got a hell of a defense team." Landry tries, but he's talking to a roomful of people trained to be skeptics. We can tell the chances aren't as good as he makes them out to be.

"Son, give it to us straight," says Oliveira. "How's it really looking?"

Landry clears his throat. "They've got the wine bottle, the pill tube, the surveillance video, and at least a couple solid reasons for murder. Do I think they have enough to go to trial on? Absolutely. That's my view of it. But I'm just one of many lawyers, and I'm not the one running the defense."

"But if you did?" Oliveira presses.

"I think we've got ourselves an uphill climb. There's no one else who fits."

"What about the other Board members, or Briana Foley? Did the cops talk to her?" Elliott asks, to the room's assent.

"They already did, and she's not a suspect at all," Landry replies. "She's been in Gstaad for the past two weeks, won't fly back until the funeral on Friday."

"It's looking pretty grim," Cleo says, with a quaver of uncertainty. "But you've got it handled, yes?"

"We're working on it, but there's a good chance of conviction," Landry replies. "Unless we can pin the blame on someone else."

I know how it looks. The timing of it all, the missing hours Wednesday night. Everything points to me. I had the opportunity, and I have the means in my jacket pocket. The only thing I don't have is a motive. And if it isn't Maxwell, I'm in a roomful of people who might have one. Cleo, Goldin . . . hell, even the interns are looking good to me right about now. Anyone is. Anyone but me.

Cleo ends the conference call, then turns to bark her orders to me and Elliott: Work your court contacts, get more info that the DA won't share and that our own lawyers are too slow to share. Assemble a team to cover the arraignment, find out if the judge will hear Maxwell on bail. And of course, run interference on our competitor news outlets.

She keeps going, but all I can think of is how I was right. The state of play keeps changing, but at least the cops have finally seen what I've always known: Simon was murdered. Now I have to prove who did it, and more importantly, how an identical vial ended up on me. Was Maxwell trying to frame me, and it backfired on him?

Or is there someone else? Is there someone trying to frame *me*, but inadvertently put Maxwell in the cops' crosshairs instead?

Questions upon questions rattle around in my head, tuning out Cleo's words. How did I end up in Simon's office? Why don't I remember any of this? And yes, the most important question of all.

Did I do it?

"Jamie, are you getting all of this?" she asks, snapping me out of my daze. "You should be recording this."

I really should. Who knows what else I might forget.

Part

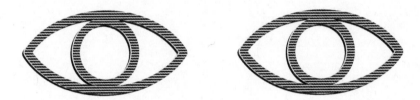

Two

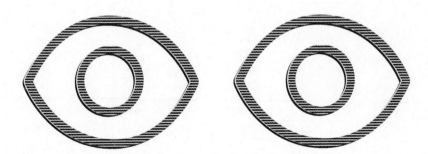

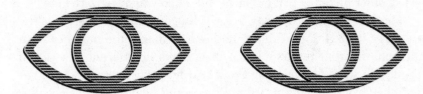

23.

One of my earliest memories was my sixth birthday party. Back then we lived in the old house in Maplewood, the smaller one, and my parents threw a backyard barbecue. I remember a bouncy castle, the scent of sweat-glazed plastic intermingling with grilled pork belly. The part I remember most vividly was my gift—Mom and Dad got me my first tablet. I remember frantically ripping out the wrapping because I recognized it for what it was from the size of the box. There had been some stern conversations between my folks and my grandparents, who thought that Charlie and I were too young to be exposed to electronics. I'd long assumed that Lolo and Lola won that argument, so I was overjoyed when I unwrapped the tablet. I started playing with it right away, and I remember my parents on either side of me, showing me all the apps I could download.

That probably wasn't my earliest memory, and that memory probably wasn't as vivid as I first experienced it. Most of it is my memory of what I saw from the videos of that day. I don't quite remember the scents or the feel of the wrapping paper as I tore it to shreds. I remember the visuals—the tablet and the noises and the expressions on people's faces—because I remember watching the vid file, the one I still have in my hard drive along with copies of every other birthday party Charlie and I had when we were kids.

Memory's funny that way. A recording of a memory becomes the memory itself. I don't think it necessarily makes the memory false (or true, for that matter), but it does make it different. It's sad to think that what I remember about that birthday party is what I remember from viewing it, from a recording made on a device, shot by another.

It's a different point of view. I was there, but isn't mine.

I guess what matters most is remembering what I felt in that moment. I felt surprise, joy, excitement, gratitude and a bit of pride at my parents bucking the elders' wishes. That's not on video and that's not from anyone else's point of view. If I try hard enough, I can reach for those emotions and feel them again in this moment. I can be with my friends again, a boy of six, launching myself into the air, flying inside a blown-up artificial fortress.

Am I to lose this too? What else is slipping away from me? Who else?

✳

Lolo often quoted one of the great heroes of old, some writer or other, who once said something along the lines of, "He who doesn't know how to look back to where he came from will never reach his destination." I'm sure it's pithier in Tagalog. He would then lament, with indignation, the Filipinos' collective amnesia. He believed that all the ills that befell our homeland have their roots in our people's inability to remember. Every dictator, every colonizer, every natural disaster that we failed to anticipate, all sprang from our ease in forgetting.

He never did share his exegesis on why we were how we were. I have my own guesses; the heat, for one, melts your brain. Lolo though, he extrapolated the principle to the level of the individual. In his old age, one could hear my grandfather muttering Santayana: "Those who do not remember the past are condemned to repeat it." He also had the vexatious habit of saying it whenever Dad fell on hard times, or when I suffered any setback, as though the many heartaches of my teenage years could have been avoided by an assiduous record and a propensity for reexamination.

It now appears that I've inherited my people's curse. Another calamity arising from a lapse in remembrance. On the personal level, it wouldn't be such a big deal—everyone forgets, memory doesn't always serve—but I find myself in a very particular circumstance where not remembering means death. Simon's, and if I'm not careful, mine too.

✦

When Elliott told me about his fondest memories of Simon, or when Anders told me about the last time he spoke to him, they were telling the stories to themselves more than to me. I happened to be there as their audience, but eulogies, like the intimate ones I've been hearing all week, are not just a form of remembrance. It's a way of crafting a new memory: a memory of how we prefer to remember someone. The stories we choose to tell, the words we use in the telling.

If I've truly lost some part of Simon, then I might as well try to save the best parts now. I slide on my visor, and stare off into the picture window in my den. That anecdote about my C+P job interview isn't as crucial in the grand scheme of things, so I decide that I won't be talking chronologically. I press record and speak.

I'll always remember Simon for how he saved my life.

The summer of '41, like the others that preceded it, was the hottest on record. Reservoirs all over the country were drying up, and New York was one of the worst-hit regions. Tensions ran high as the governor edged closer to unveiling yet another statewide rationing plan. Everyone had seen how poorly that worked out, only a few short years ago. Around that time, a source came to me directly, not through the usual C+P channels, about a large-scale water hoarding operation up in Otsego County. Apparently, a poultry processing plant had been stealing water out of reservoirs and pumping it into their tanker trucks in the middle of the night. The poultry farm happened to be owned by the governor's brother-in-law.

Simon was hesitant about letting me pursue the story on my own. He didn't think I could handle it; he said I was new and needed to cut my teeth with less high-profile assignments. It took a lot of wheedling, but he eventually gave in. He let me have free rein to work the story from whatever angle I wanted, and he promised that if I got enough material, he'd put it on the schedule for *The Simon Parrish Files*.

For weeks, I drove upstate and down, pounding the pavement, baking in the summer heat. I got interviews, hours of footage, water level numbers, precipitation data, but nothing that directly led to the governor's mansion. I had been engrossed in the work, even more than usual, since I was racing against a clock. The legislative session was set to end soon, and the rationing plan was coming up for a vote. Left with no choice, I sent down a draft of my piece in time for the Sunday online edition, hoping we could run the story before then. The public had to know before the ballots were cast.

I had just arrived at the C+P offices from a long drive upstate when Elliott broke the news to me. Our editorial board decided to hold the story. They claimed it wasn't ripe yet, and that it would cause more problems than it was worth. The connection to the governor was tenuous, and going after the chicken farm wasn't worth it if the story could develop into something bigger, given more time.

"Time is exactly what we don't have!" I yelled at Elliott.

"I'm sorry, Jamie. I know how hard you worked on this."

"I have enough. Three sources. What the fuck else do they want?"

"They said they need more."

"Where's Simon? I need to talk to him now."

Sunburnt and sleep-deprived, my entire body trembled in rage. I stormed my way into Simon's office, but he was still meeting with the ed board. Elliott tried to calm me down, but there was no stopping me. No one was going to care in a fucking month. By then, the legislative fight would be over and soon enough we'd all be lining up in the streets for our daily ration of water while the governor's cronies stole from the rest of us.

Finding no recourse and no outlet to vent my rage, I found myself standing over my desk, gripping my keyboard on each end. My fingers curled tight around it as I raised it over my head. I then slammed it down onto my desk with a loud crash, bringing it down over and over. Plastic cracked on resin, breaking off into sharp pieces. Buttons and keys flew all around me, their letters forming my unspoken expletives in the air.

By the time Elliott got his arms locked around me, I'd destroyed the tabletop, and the keyboard had completely broken into large, jagged splinters. My screens were cracked by shrapnel. I stared down at the wreckage, insensate. I hadn't been hearing or seeing anything else, not really, aside from the immediate destruction that I'd been causing.

As a wider awareness returned to me, I saw Simon standing in the hallway, his eyes filled with regret. He called for security, and they escorted me out of the building.

Elliott took me home, and Hannah took over my care when we got to our apartment. Depleted of all energy, I slept for the greater part of that day. Hannah looked over me and never left my side, worried but unquestioning. I never explained to her what had happened until much later. Until I had to.

In the middle of the night, when I felt that I had gotten my second wind, I crept out of bed to grab my tablet. I re-read my piece and polished it off. Triple-checked my citations, did a quick online fact check on every detail. Added the pictures, and cobbled together the video clips into something halfway presentable.

After an effortless bypass of the posting protocols, I put the story up on the C+P website.

The worst that could happen was that I would get fired, I thought at the time. How wrong I was.

What followed were endless inquisitions of various committees, trying to decide how best to fire me. I was placed on an extended leave, without pay, as HR and Ethics and the editorial board decided my fate.

Wallowing in my apartment, I decided to fill my days watching the live feeds from the legislative sessions in Albany, hoping that my story had made a difference somehow. The piece was up on the C+P site for a few hours before the higher ups saw it and took it down, but by then, a rival media outlet had already picked it up and run it on their own site. It wasn't enough though. Water rationing got passed, effective immediately.

Then the lawsuit came. Perrillo Poultry filed a million-dollar libel suit against me, and against C+P. The lawsuit went into extensive legal discovery. The details of my nervous breakdown came to light, but so did more evidence of Perrillo's water-hoarding operation. The story was also gaining more traction in the media, and the governor's approval ratings were crashing. In the end, the farm agreed to settle the suit for a lot less money than they had hoped to get. They asked only for two things: an iron-clad nondisclosure agreement, and some sort of personal repercussion for me.

Four weeks in an inpatient facility and an indeterminate time in an outpatient treatment program was probably the best thing that I could have hoped for. The longer I stayed at the New Dawn Treatment Center, the more I felt my so-called righteous fury dissipate. I also began to understand that I had issues. The lack of impulse control, the survivor's guilt, the hubris that comes with being a young, ambitious reporter, the despair that comes with feeling like there's so much to do and so little time. On top of how I'd been neglecting my body for months, all of that had made me into a tinderbox ready to ignite.

Though it wasn't entirely voluntary, my stay at the Center got me the tools to cope with those issues. There were a lot of therapy sessions, group and solo, and there were meds. They worked, for the most part. As I maintained my regimen and attended my sessions in earnest, I began to feel better. Still, one of my burdens remained unlifted.

The nightmares still came.

Every night, flashes of that fateful morning still visited me and shook me awake from slumber. The cold tile, the blinding sunrise, the open window. My hand reaching into thin air, Paolo's head splattered on the pavement. The doctors tried all sorts of interventions for me, but after a while, I felt that they'd given up. They claimed that the nightmares would stop once I'd dealt with the underlying causes. I wanted to believe them, but part of me feared that the nightmares would never end, and that I would live with those visions for as long as I slept.

I didn't tell my family about the whole ordeal until after I was discharged. I didn't have the energy to explain the long road that led to my meltdown, didn't want to hear them dissect what they thought had happened. When I finally told them, Mom cried, Dad stewed in stoic misery. They helped my recovery as much as they could, but underneath their support was a silent shame. I knew what they thought. Their son, mental. This just can't be. This doesn't happen, not to us. The subtext of denial was there, in every unasked question, in the awkward pauses.

Aside from Hannah and Elliott, the only other person who came to see me at the treatment center was Simon. He came about a week after I was admitted, bringing with him a stack of books. Hardcover new releases. It's the kind of gift from someone who didn't know what to bring, but knew he wanted to bring anything but flowers. That afternoon, Simon and I roamed the sprawling lawns with quiet unease, both of us uncertain of the contours of this visit. He wasn't here as a friend, that much I knew, but he came, and my apprehension at his arrival was at least tempered by the possibility of his forgiveness.

"Thank you," I said finally, "For the books, and for the company. I don't get much of either in here."

"I got your letter," he said.

"Yes, that. The therapists have been asking us to write to—" I began. He raised a finger, the way he usually did, like a maestro conducting a rest.

"I haven't read it," he said. "And I don't want to."

My heart sank. "I know I've let you down, Simon—"

"When you snapped," he said, struggling on the word, "I saw myself in you. I recognized then that this was my doing. That I made you this way. The least I could do was see you."

"It's more than I deserve."

"You need to stop whipping yourself up," he replied. "That's not what I'm here for."

I said nothing more; Simon had evidently come for a monologue, and it was best not to interrupt until he was done.

"I wasn't the least bit angry when you published the post," he continued. "To some degree, I was proud. It's probably what I would've done myself. But unlike you, I've learned to make better choices. To foresee the outcomes of my actions, and to prepare accordingly. To discern when to keep going and when to give up. Skills I've neglected to teach you."

"I wasn't thinking," I said after a pause. "I was going with my gut."

"No, you were going by your grief," he said. "I've seen you bury yourself in work since your cousin died. If it wasn't the Perrillo story, you would have found another one to distract yourself with."

"This isn't about Paolo," I explained.

"How could it not be? It's only been a few months, and you've told me how close you were to him," he replied. "Look, I've been where you are. The loss of a loved one, professional defeats, the cruelty of an unjust world . . . the despair all becomes unbearable. Overwhelming."

Simon took a moment here, gazing onto the meadow the way one does when they're really looking within themselves. I could tell that Simon was telling me these things for his own benefit as much as mine.

"What I feel isn't despair," I said. "I'm pissed."

"Rage is merely another form that despair can take," he said. "And it's a form I know well. Not every depressive hides under blankets, shielding themselves in the shadows of their sorrow. Some lash out. Like you and me."

Right then, I felt a kindred bond with Simon, one borne out of a common flaw. Sharing a part of himself was more than I could have asked for, and it was also more than he could muster. As though enervated by the least shred of vulnerability, he soon after said goodbye, leaving me to carry the weight of his words.

My month-long sentence felt longer without online access, but Elliott updated me on the outside world. Through him too, I got news about C+P, much to my counselors' dismay. For good reason. He told me about the closed-door meetings deciding my fate, and his detailed accounts did cause some anxiety. Yet it all worked out in the end, and the executive committee decided to keep me on. Full reinstatement, not even probationary status.

"How did that happen?" I asked Elliott, dumbfounded.

"The vote was close, but word is, Simon had to cash in a few favors with the committee members," he replied. "He lost a lot of goodwill in the process, but he really went to bat for you."

Through Elliott too, I learned how Simon protected me during the Perrillo lawsuit. He made sure that the C+P lawyers represented my interests, and that I'd be financially insulated in case of a loss.

Because of him, C+P fought the suit on my behalf as vigorously as it did its own suit.

When my term at New Dawn ended, I walked out of the facility with no outstanding balance. Fully paid by C+P, they said, but I knew who footed the bill. The same person who wired a substantial sum into my bank account the day after my discharge. I never thanked Simon for any of these things; I didn't know how. I sensed that he wouldn't want my thanks anyway. He'd want to carry on like normal. So I did. Although, he did ask me for one thing.

"I want you to see this guy," Simon told me my first day back at work. "He's partners with my therapist. Their practice specializes with cases like ours. I've been getting better because of them. As will you."

"You sound so sure," I said. "How do you know?"

"Because we simply must get better. We can't afford not to."

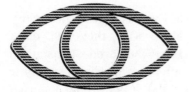 

24.

Pixel by minuscule pixel, the blank room gradually materializes into a replica of my therapist's Upper East Side office, a minimalist study in taupe. It's daytime in this VR milieu, and though the curtains are half-drawn, midmorning light fills the high-ceilinged room. There is little ornamentation, and none that reveals anything about the doctor's personal life. He also doesn't have diplomas up on the walls, or rows upon rows of medical books.

As the room is fully rendered, the system chimes that Federigo Cassis has joined the conference. His voice arrives first, greeting me with a *good evening.* He asks me to take the chaise longue, and as I do, his avatar appears on the wingback right before me.

On Simon's referral, I started seeing Dr. Cassis two years ago, right after New Dawn. Initially, our psychotherapy sessions were frequent and intense, as was the medical regimen he placed me on. In time, I slowly regained my grip on my mental health, save for some lingering issues with my sleep.

He helped me, too, after I took Levantanil to stop the nightmares. I agonized over the decision whether to reveal this deep secret, but I also recognized the risk of going through the transition to Sleeplessness without a trusted medical professional, so I disclosed. When I told him the full story, he was concerned and a bit disappointed, but mostly unfazed. He guided me through my hyperinsomnia transition with no fear, given the robust legal protections afforded doctors and patient confidentiality, and possibly, too, because he had seen the same, or worse.

"How are we doing today?" he asks in his usual upbeat manner, immediately placing me at ease.

"Thanks for meeting on such short notice," I say. "It's a bit of an emergency."

"All right, then let's get started." He taps the arm of his chair, his way of marking the session recording. "What's going on?"

"I've been having trouble remembering things," I start. Over the past few hours, I've been debating how much I should tell him. I trust Dr. Cassis, but I want to set aside Simon's death for now.

"Things like?"

"Conversations I've had. With Hannah, with Charlie, with this other guy . . ." I reply. "Last week I forgot that Hannah was coming over to pick up something. That usually wouldn't have slipped my mind."

"And the other things you've forgotten, were they the types of thing you usually would forget?"

"Honestly? No. But I never noticed it," I say. "I suppose I should have."

"And these are all personal interactions, I assume? Not the sphere of your life that you typically devote most of your attention to."

There's a subtle rebuke there, but he's not wrong. "Well, except for one thing, which is work-related. I lost a few hours on Wednesday night."

"What do you mean 'lost'?"

I measure my words carefully. "I'd gone to my office that night after my usual hours, and I don't remember any of it. I only learned I was there because someone later told me."

"Is this why you've come to me now? Because the memory lapses have affected not just your personal relationships, but your professional life as well?"

"Yes, I suppose I didn't worry about it or even notice that it was happening until . . . the stakes were higher."

"When did you start noticing this?" the doctor asks.

"It's hard to say. How do you remember when you forgot something?" I let out a slight laugh. "I think maybe for a couple of weeks now."

"How have you been resting?" he asks.

"I may have been overdoing it lately, but nothing too crazy. I am taking breaks, I meditate for hours . . ."

"You don't have a history of memory deficiencies . . . have you been having any other issues? Hallucinations, auditory issues, balance problems?"

I shake my head. Dr. Cassis makes notes on his tablet, then stares at the space in front of him. His hand gestures tell me that he's probably reading through my medical file. He taps the chair arms again, then swings a hand into the air. Before me materializes a translucent blowup of an article from a medical journal.

"There have been countless studies about how hyperinsomnia impacts cognition, memory, perception, and many other brain functions," he starts. "Because of the scale and how widespread the population is, it hasn't been easy to learn anything with quite the certainty that scientific rigor would require."

"Yes, Doc, I know all about these 'studies,'" I reply bitterly. I can't believe he'd go down this road. "Links to Alzheimer's, dementia, depression. Name a defect, someone's linked it to Sleeplessness. I've read the forums, and I've seen the social media posts. People have been blaming all kinds of mental issues on being Sleepless, but they're all just bunk."

"Come, Jamie, give me a little credit. I've seen those posts too, but those aren't what I'm talking about."

"Sorry. Please, keep going."

He magnifies the article in front of me. "As I was saying, it's difficult to find any correlations between Sleeplessness and any other condition, given the sheer size of the affected group. It doesn't mean those correlations don't exist, and it doesn't mean documenting them is impossible.

"When it first manifested, the conventional wisdom among neuroscientists was that hyperinsomnia would cause all sorts of problems related to memory. After all, sleep is the time when the brain synthesizes the experiences we have during our waking hours. Yet more than a decade since the pandemic first hit, they still haven't found a case where a Sleepless person developed amnesia with Sleeplessness as the direct cause. There are some who claim that it has happened, but for the most part, the researchers who have studied those cases did not find a link between hyperinsomnia and memory loss.

"I suppose there's enough anecdotal evidence, which fueled not only those rumors and conspiracy theories we see online, but the number of those alleged cases also spurred this new study."

Dr. Cassis zooms in on a journal article. "A Five-Year Prospective Cohort Study of Chronic Anterograde Amnesia in Hyperinsomniacs," *The European Journal of Neuroscience*; Vol. 84, Issue 6 (September 2041); Slimane, Miriam M., et al.

"This study followed a number of hyperinsomniacs who exhibited symptoms of what's called 'encoding failure.' The researchers found a direct causal link between a person developing hyperinsomnia and then losing the ability to "encode" new memories. In some cases, it happened right after the change, and in some, the failure manifested months or even years later."

If he were monitoring my vitals, Dr. Cassis would see the anxiety rising in me. "Is that what's happening to me?"

Dr. Cassis then proceeds with a lecture on "data theory." How memories are encoded, stored and retrieved just like computer files. "Human brains organize our daily experiences—unconnected thoughts, sensations, emotions—while we sleep. Despite not sleeping, hyperinsomniacs don't seem to have a problem retaining and recalling memories. But this new research shows that the Sleepless may not be as good with encoding: the creation of new memories."

"No new memories?" I say in a rush of panic. The implications are staggering: if what he's saying is true, then I may have found the reason why I'm missing a few hours on Wednesday. And why I don't recall how I got a pill tube exactly like the one on Simon's desk. "What—what about changes in personality? Mood swings? Did those studies find that too?"

Dr. Cassis leans in, distressed. "Why, have you experienced that as well?"

"No, I don't think so," I reply. "If I did, I likely wouldn't remember if it happened, and I didn't encode it, right?"

"Yes, but there would be other signs. Indications of what happened afterward. Say, another person remarking about your behavior, or a change in your environment that you ordinarily would not have done," the doctor explains. "Has any of that happened to you lately?"

Yes, way too often for comfort. If Sleeplessness isn't as benign as we thought, then it might affect more than just memory. It might have caused a shift in personality, one that might have driven me to act in a way that I could later forget. It could have brought out the worst side of me, the one that takes things to the extreme. But doctor-patient confidentiality does not extend to ongoing crimes, and right now I'm at a minimum holding onto evidence of a murder, so I lie.

"No, that hasn't happened. I have been a bit on edge though. Tense."

"That's understandable, given all the stress you've going through," he replies. "And it can't be easy having all these difficult personal interactions. Are you sure it's no more than 'tension'?"

"I'm sure." The confidence in my voice seems enough to allay the doctor. "So it's just encoding failure then?"

"Yes, that's what I've found," he replies, much to my relief. "Personality changes, sudden or otherwise, are too broad a category for study, but my review has found nothing to indicate that the Sleepless are prone to them on account of their condition."

"But why memory?"

"Well, not all memories are the same," he replies. "There are skill memories, like knowing how to swim; and factual memories, like knowing what you had for breakfast today. The Slimane study suggests that some hyperinsomniac brains experience a backlog in encoding factual memory because their brains are too busy storing, organizing and retrieving other memories, not to mention running all other brain functions, all day every day, 24/7/365. Think of it like your hard drive getting full. With encoding failure, your brain isn't deleting or losing memories. It's just not making any more."

When I first became Sleepless, I worried about the price that hyperinsomnia would exact. I soon powered through the change with a reckless sense of invincibility, taking after the countless Sleepless people around me. Now the bill is due, and this disease is determined to collect.

"How have we not known about this?"

"It's a developing area of study. Understandably, any researcher worth their salt would be extremely cautious about making any bold pronouncements. I share this with you only as a possible explanation. One possibility among several."

"Please—tell me there are better ones."

"Well, we haven't mentioned the other thing," the doctor replies, with care. "Jamie, the way you became Sleepless isn't exactly typical. It's possible that Levantanil's causing it, if not contributing to it, aside from the other factors I've mentioned. The symptoms of your encoding failure might be a bit accelerated, given the way the drug forced the onset of the condition."

"I know others like me." Well, one other. Elliott. "And they're fine."

"I'm afraid we both know that's not proof of anything," he replies. "But I'm certain that it gives you some comfort to know that. In any case, this is yet another variable, and we haven't covered them all."

"Well, what else is there?"

"Let's talk about your boss, Simon," the doctor says after a long pause. "I heard about him in the news. Is there a reason you haven't mentioned him at all?"

"I didn't think it . . . No, no reason." I spare him the excuse I wanted to say.

"Why don't you tell me what happened."

"How is this relevant?" I ask. Dr. Cassis only gives me a stern look in response, the one that he's fond of giving me when I'm being withholding. I relent and tell him everything, from finding Simon's body to Maxwell's arrest. Everything except finding the A-Pop vial in my jacket.

"You saw him the night he died, *immediately* before he died. Then you found him the next morning," he summarizes. "This all must be difficult."

"Yes. It really is."

"And have you been thinking about Paolo lately?"

I had suspected he would come up as soon as I spoke about Simon. "Honestly, I haven't thought about him in a while. He did come up over brunch with my parents on Sunday."

"Your boss—your mentor, to use your word—died in what appeared to be a suicide. That hasn't caused you to think about Paolo at all?"

"Apparently not as much as you think I should."

"It's not a matter of 'should.' I'm trying to see if you're actively avoiding your emotions about Simon's death. The same way you did when Paolo died."

"I'm not avoiding anything. I'm preoccupied with my missing memories, and Simon's murder."

"But that's precisely it, Jamie. Your missing memories, the inability to encode new ones. It may be connected to how you're dealing with Simon's death."

"How?"

"Let's say Levantanil caused your encoding failure," he explains. "It's possible that it is also compounded by the shock of a traumatic event, such as finding Simon, or even prior trauma. When you saw Simon that night, you likely saw behavior that you've seen before. Behavior quite like what you saw in Paolo when he died."

"You think that's connected?" I ask.

"It's all connected. You don't sleep anymore, you don't dream. Dreaming is how we process trauma. REM sleep lets people relive these negative experiences in a neurochemically calm environment. Take that away, and couple that with an encoding impairment, and the result could be what you're going through."

"Great. Sleeplessness is making my brain full up with memories, and trauma's refusing to register the few memories that my brain can still manage to take in."

"I do want to stress that these are all theories. This research study I showed you is first-wave, and it is not conclusive. We also can't rule out the possibility that whatever you're experiencing might have nothing to do with Levantanil or your being Sleepless at all."

That's reassuring, though it doesn't help me in the here and now. "Well, there must be something I can do about it for the mean time."

"I'll look into this further, and review your health data for the last few months. I want you to see me again this weekend. I will have more news for you then, and I might need to do some scans as well. In the meantime, I want you to take careful notes and records."

"Your solution is homework?"

"It's not a solution, but it may lead to one. It's to help us see if there's a problem in the first instance, and how severe it is," he says. "For now, make sure to keep track of everything. What are you remembering, what are you forgetting, what are you remembering you forgot? We'll also need to know how you feel shortly before and after a lapse of memory, that's if you're able to realize that such a lapse has occurred. The more complete a picture we have, the better."

"And how do you propose I do all of this?" I ask.

"Use your visor. Record everything."

❖

Before I took Levantanil, I buried myself in research. I read everything I could get my hands on about hyperinsomnia. Many of the academic papers went over my head, and I had to consult with experts and doctors, Dr. Cassis included. Of course, I made my inquiries in the guise of professional research, since I couldn't very well disclose that I was planning on biohacking myself.

I'm back at that again, dusting off my old Sci-Hub and Elsevier accounts to access medical journals, searching keywords and following links down a hyperinsomnia rabbit hole. Following Dr. Cassis's lead, I read studies on Sleepless persons' cognition and memory. I scroll through pages and pages of charts and tables and diagrams that, a year ago, would have given me great pause. Studies like "Impact of a Behavioural Intervention on Cognitive Impairment in Persons with Hyperinsomnia," *International Review of Neurobiology*; Vol. 222, No. 5 (April 2041), pp. 160–78 (19 pages). Or "Improving Neurobehavioural Function in Hyperinsomniacs by Enhancing Memory and Learning," *British Medical Journal*; Vol. 455, No. 6447 (June 2037), pp. 1478–91 (14 pages).

For years, the warning signs had been there. And it couldn't have been that I didn't know to look for them. Elliott was right: I wanted this, and I didn't want to dissuade myself by looking too hard for an out.

As I delve into these studies, one name repeatedly comes up: Miriam Slimane. Aside from the article that Dr. Cassis sent my way, she has also authored many others I found. She seems to have the most robust body of work in the field of Sleepless neuroscience. So, I download everything I can find on her, starting from her CV.

Well before anyone knew about hyperinsomnia, she'd been a prominent sleep researcher with Harvard Med and the Division of Sleep Medicine at Brigham Hospital. When the pandemic hit, she started work at the CDC's Epidemiology and Surveillance Branch as its top sleep expert. She'd authored the earliest studies on hyperinsomnia, including "First Hundred Cases of Hyperinsomnia: Case Note Review of Early Psychiatric and Neurological Features," *Journal of Cognitive Neuroscience*; Vol. 51, No. 3 (February 2033), pp. 222–31 (10 pages) and "Working Memory and Information Processing in Adults with Younger-Onset Hyperinsomnia," *Journal of Neurophysiology*; Vol. 191, No. 3 (August 2033), pp. 216–25 (10 pages). Every major research study at that time, and since, has been co-authored by her, supervised by her, or cited to her. In 2038 she received a major grant from the National Science Foundation for her work in "Sedative Hypnotics in People with Hyperinsomnia: An Analysis of Risks and Benefits," *Journal of Sleep Research*; Vol. 45, No. 4 (August 2039), pp. 168–82 (15 pages). Then, in 2041, she won prestigious awards for her study "Hyperinsomnia: A New Understanding of Its Biological Bases and Clinical Implications," *Cellular and Molecular Life Sciences*; Vol. 96, No. 2 (November 2040), pp. 66–84 (19 pages), including the Lurie Prize, the UNESCO Prize, and the Jenner Medal. No scientist has ever won so many prizes in a single year for the same study.

Shortly after that, the research trail ends with the study Dr. Cassis showed me, "A Five-Year Prospective Cohort Study of Chronic Anterograde Amnesia in Hyperinsomniacs." That was her last publication. I dig through the CDC archives, their entire site, for anything about Dr. Slimane after September 2041, but that's it.

I try to look elsewhere—see where she might have landed. I'm guessing it'd be a plum academic post or a private research facility, maybe a major pharmaceutical conglomerate. Slimane doesn't have quite the public profile, but given the international acclaim she's garnered, hiring her would have been a significant coup for any institution. There would have been a major PR push, news clips, public announcements. She's a leading mind in the industry, and wherever she goes, funding and prestige would be sure to follow. Yet I find nothing, not even a pro forma press release.

I do a more general search with her publicly available biographical info. Full name, DOB, parents' names, schools and affiliations. She's not on any of the social media sites, or any site for that matter. Save for her publications and old news releases, there's no trace of her online in the last two years. I'm not even sure she's alive, though my civil records search does not show any deaths with that name. No one's this unsearchable, unless they scrubbed their info off the Internet.

It's starting to look like she simply walked away from it all. The CDC, her research, the entire field of Sleepless neuroscience altogether. Retreated to some sort of private life, never to be heard from for the last two years.

No one does that, especially not someone with her stature. She'd devoted her life to discovering the inner workings of the pandemic, of this condition that's afflicted a quarter of the globe. There must be a reason she turned her back on all that. Did she start a family, or find herself a new purpose in life, one that didn't involve scientific research? Or maybe she's fallen from grace, quietly pushed out of academic circles because of some sordid violation. No one just disappears like that. There's got to be a story here.

I put together all of Dr. Slimane's publications and populate a table of all the researchers that she worked with throughout her career. I run a search on those people, starting with the most recent, and get their latest contact information. Soon enough, I've generated a sizable call list. It'll be a lot of cold calls, but in time, I'll find this doctor. I need to. Because if anyone can figure out what's going on with me, Dr. Slimane is it.

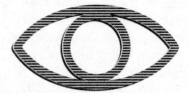

25.

Wednesday, 07/15/2043, 07:25 AM

Strathairn-Shaw's army of lawyers make quick work of the NYPD central booking system and the arraignment part of the supreme court. Citing Maxwell's status in the community and his contributions to journalism, the lawyers get him released on a million-dollar bail, which Maxwell has no trouble ponying up. As quickly as he'd been placed in detention, he just as quickly is back on the streets.

Following his release from custody, rumors soon spread of a press conference, scheduled for some time this morning in front of the C+P Tower. Damage control. Thus, a throng of news crews has congregated about the lobby of the building. They're all huddled a good distance away from the security scanners, but with a direct line of sight onto the elevator banks.

I manage to dodge my fellow reporters, not a few of whom are industry friends. I barely reach the elevator unscratched, but just as I think that I've successfully avoided the chaos, the scene that greets me up in the newsroom is even more frantic. The desk jockeys are all on multi-stack screens, juggling tablets in both hands, still wearing the clothes they had on last night. The war room is brimming with activity, and every office space is occupied. Every sound booth and studio has a lengthy timetable that runs to the next day.

Compliance is all over the place too. The suits stand about the floor, all with their visors on, watching to ensure that no one does anything compromising. C+P is clearly keeping a tight lid on the place, and I don't blame them. I can already see the headlines, more sensationalized than the ones from the past few days. If there's anything sexier than famous people dying by their own hand, it's murder. Better yet, murder staged as a suicide. By the longtime friend and business partner, no less.

Through one of the studio windows, I see Elliott looking over an AP's shoulder, evidently giving notes on the broadcast copy. The chyrons right behind them announce "Breaking New Developments in Cartwright Case." I tap on the glass and beckon.

"What the hell are you doing? You know we can't work on any Simon story."

He gives me an incredulous look. "*Everyone* is on this story."

"The lawyers already said no. We're potential witnesses."

"Wild horses, Jamie."

I wonder where his concern is, the treatment of Maxwell or death of Simon? The circumstances have made it so that it can't be both. Murder cancels out drug-induced suicide. Me, I'm rather preoccupied with something else entirely. I pull him aside and we duck into one of the soundproofed booths.

"Need to talk to you about a couple of things," I say, with an unnecessarily hushed tone. "I went to see Dr. Cassis last night." Elliott nods knowingly. He probably thinks I'm having another "Paolo situation."

I continue. "See, I've been forgetting things. Small things, mostly, but I also don't remember most of Wednesday night."

"Yeah, I thought that was weird when you were asking me about that the other day," he replies. "You still don't remember anything?"

I shake my head. "Doc thinks it may have something to do with being Sleepless."

I tell him about the studies I read, give him a brief primer on encoding failure. He appears to understand but otherwise is unconcerned. He questions the sample sizes of these studies, their preliminary and inconclusive nature. Finally, he points out the obvious.

"You know, we're also not the typical hyperinsomniac."

"Dr. Cassis knows that, but says it might be a contributing factor too," I say. "That's why I need to ask: Have you been forgetting things?"

"No more than anyone else," he says with a shrug. "People forget things all the time."

"This is different."

Since last night, I've been analyzing all the recent instances of my forgetting. As much as I can, I recalled how the gaps came to be, how I felt before and after, just as Dr. Cassis asked. I've categorized these gaps into "normal" and "not normal." Seeing Kingsley at the Black Party, the money I owed Noor from poker, my responses to Tetro's questions: all things I'd normally forget. Hannah saying she'd visit, Charlie sharing his heartbreak: not normal at all. And of course, those three or so hours on Wednesday night.

That latter category, I've decided, might have been caused by encoding failure. They don't feel like memories I retained and then later failed to retrieve. They feel like memories that never existed to me at all, moments that I never experienced.

When I've been subsequently reminded of an episode, as when Hannah told me about a previous agreement to meet or when Tetro showed me the surveillance video, there has been no glimmer of recognition. Not a single detail is shored up from my mind. Despite my bluffs otherwise, there was no feeling of *oh, yes, you are right, that did happen, and I did forget.* There were only blank spaces.

And those blank spaces seem to be multiplying.

"Hell yes, it's different," Elliott replies. "Our boss just died. You found him dead. It's only natural that you'd miss things here and there. You of all people should know how trauma like that can mess with your head."

The tenderness of his tone only drives the cut deeper. He should've known never to invoke Paolo like that.

"How does one even know what they've forgotten, anyway?" Elliott continues. "You forget what you've forgotten, and that's that. Sometimes you might remember that you forgot something, but for the most part, what's forgotten is just . . . gone."

"Well, then forget I said anything," I say, leaving the audio booth. He pulls me back.

"Jamie, hold up—" he says. "What aren't you telling me?"

That a man's getting tried for a murder he maybe didn't commit. That I might be involved in more ways than I realize. That I'm standing here with Simon's cause of death nestled in my breast pocket. I can't tell him any of that, but I do need his help.

"This isn't a suicide anymore. It's a murder investigation. Whatever happened on Wednesday matters more now. And I'm the last one who saw him alive, but I somehow *conveniently* don't remember a thing," I explain, my tone escalating. "You heard Landry. Those lawyers are gonna have to pin this on someone so they can get Maxwell acquitted."

"Yeah, but no one's going to think it's you," he replies with a nervous laugh. "I mean, c'mon, you adored the guy. Maybe a little too much."

"That doesn't matter. They need a patsy. Someone who looks bad, and I'm it. If you can't foresee the shitshow that I'm about—"

Elliott raises a palm in appeasement, then pulls out his tablet. His hand gestures tell me he's syncing it with his visor. He asks it to pull up his GPS trackers, his calls, and everything. Through the translucence of his visor display, I can see him glance at me intermittently as we wait. It's a patient, pitying look, the type usually reserved for wounded animals.

"All right, I got a missed call from you a little before 8 p.m. Wednesday. What was that about?"

That's odd. I pull up my logs again, the one I compiled at home.

Elliott - Wednesday, 07/08/2043, 19:49:57.

Was I maybe too focused on Simon, or incoming stuff, that I completely missed this? Or is this another memory blip?

"You don't remember why you called?" Elliott asks.

I think back to that night, but don't remember anything after seeing Hannah at my door. I shake my head. Another blank space.

"Okay, so I was out grabbing dinner when you called. Sorry about not picking up." He patches in his display into my visor. "Now you told me you received a packet from your source for the Dwyer story . . . what time did that happen?"

"Much, much later."

"And you wouldn't have had to call me about that, right?"

"I'd have no reason to," I reply. He and I were on totally different tracks with that piece.

"I wanna help you, but we need something more to go on," he says pensively. "How about this, why don't we try retracing your steps? It's been exactly a week since. We can rendezvous tonight, go through the motions of what you did last Wednesday, see if that does anything."

It's not a bad idea. At least it's something I haven't tried. "Sounds like a plan. Thanks, man. I really need to make sure of this."

"Whatever will get you off my back." He leads us out of the soundproof booth, and heads back into the studio. "Meanwhile, you should make yourself useful elsewhere. It's all-hands-on-deck."

"I will, but not on any Simon stories." Especially not when I might be more than a mere witness.

"Suit yourself. What about the Dwyer story then? Cleo's still dead set on spiking it, but—"

"We won't let her."

"Worse comes to worst," he says, "We could always go renegade."

I laugh. "Yeah, because the last time I did that worked out great."

"Seriously though, we gotta talk to her. Sort out whatever issue she has with that piece."

Just then, as though our conversation had manifested her, Cleo bellows our names from the other end of the floor, her voice cutting through the din of the newsroom.

✿

The first thing I see is the unmistakable shock of copper hair. There he stands, in a sharp black suit, flanked by a troop of private security. Next to him is Cleo, who waves me and Elliott over to them. She's got her game face on, a warm smile backed by an intense gaze.

"These are Jamie Vega and Elliott Nahm, EPs of *The Simon Parrish Files*." It catches me off-guard; the new title still hasn't sunk in. "Boys, I'm sure you've heard of Mr. Rafe Lochner?"

Everyone has. CEO and board member of Zephyrus, LLC, and three other Fortune 100 companies. Top one percent of the one-per-centers. Son of the sitting Treasury Secretary, husband of the current ambassador to the African Union.

As a point of more pertinent interest, Lochner is one of the foremost hyperinsomniacs in the world. The Lochners bankroll the Open Eyes Federation, the biggest global nonprofit benefiting the hyperinsomnia community. Which makes him Sid Thorpe's boss.

Monday night seems too long ago now, and too much has happened since that night at Hardwick's. I've tussled with Kingsley, found some damning evidence, dealt with Maxwell's arrest, and discovered that my brain has holes in it. Not on account of the encoding failure, I'd almost forgotten that I had this thread I needed to pursue.

Lochner extends a hand. "Pleasure to meet you both." He repeats my name, does the two-hand shake. He's been trained well. His sympathetic head tilt and the beats of his intonation are all straight out of a media handler's playbook.

I couldn't discount the natural charisma either, nor the subliminal effects of his PR machine. When he became Sleepless, he used his prominence and resources to change attitudes about Sleepless people. His celebrity status made him the poster boy of the cause and helped win over the bigots, who soon began to think that someone as dashing and powerful as Rafe Lochner couldn't be all that bad, even if he was Sleepless. Standing before him now, I can't say I'm not equally swayed.

He peers directly into my eyes as he delivers his condolences, and I can see in those emerald pools that he has prototype IRIS contacts on. His eyes flutter subtly, and I know he's received a data packet.

"I saw one of your recent episodes, the one about the faulty carbon recapture towers. What a gripping exposé."

"Thanks. Did you just read that from your IRIS?" I ask without missing a beat.

"You got me," he says, laughing. "These things are brilliant. I can't wait to launch them."

Those contacts are the next big leap in consumer tech. In a few years' time, the visors on everyone's faces are going to be replaced by these smart lenses, and we'll all have supercomputers sitting atop our corneas. All the news, information and entertainment streamed directly into our eyeballs. Full communication and recording capabilities too. The technology is impressive, and I come close to asking Lochner when I can buy one.

"Is that why you bought out the company that makes them?" Elliott asks with thinly veiled antipathy. Cleo beams, and I realize this is why she's summoned us over. She wants to gloat, now that she knows the Zephyrus offer won't be accepted by the Board. Thank you, Simon.

"Absolutely," Lochner replies. "I've always been meaning to dip my toes into wearable tech. IRIS was a natural acquisition."

"You've been dipping your toes in news media too. Is that why you're here today?" Elliott follows up.

"Are you planning on attending Maxwell's press conference?" I ask.

One of his aides intercepts. "Mr. Lochner isn't scheduled to make any public appearances today."

"I'm only here to give my personal regards to Maxwell," he says.

"Well, Mr. Cartwright isn't scheduled to make any public appearances today," Cleo replies, mimicking the assistant with sarcasm. "The press conference has been canceled."

This was news to me and Elliott, but apparently not to Lochner. "Yes, I heard. This last-minute change is very unfortunate. I was hoping to have a word with him. I know how difficult this must be."

"You and Mr. Maxwell are close," I say.

"Yes, we are."

"Do you believe he killed Simon Parrish?"

The assistant jumps in with a canned response, but Lochner raises his hand. Swiftly, he swings his arm around my shoulder. I recoil, startled but unable to resist. I bristle under his arm, but Lochner doesn't seem to notice, or care. He leads me onto the other end of the floor, unaffected by the sea of chaos thrashing all around us. Cleo and Elliott catch up to us, and Lochner's posse follows close behind.

We arrive by Maxwell Cartwright's office, cordoned off with yellow NYPD tape, although crime scene processing hasn't come around yet. The space looks the same as it did yesterday, Maxwell's mementos and artifacts resting peacefully in their glass enclosures. Lochner points to a small cannon mounted on a pedestal, nudged in the far corner of the room. The cast-iron artillery is about a yard long, and its muzzle is pointed up and out toward a view of the skyline.

"They call it a swivel gun, but it's actually a ship's cannon. Anti-personnel. Easy to load, maneuver, and aim. Guess how old it is?"

I don't know how to respond to this. What is this about? His manner is less rehearsed, yet somehow more inscrutable.

"Two hundred and sixty years old," Lochner continues. "It had been with my family for ages. It would've fetched a pretty penny at auction, but I thought it better to gift it to Maxwell for his fiftieth. I told him too, he's free to sell it. But of course, he didn't."

"You two are very close. Message received."

"That cannon was part of the armament of a great frigate, one of the best that ever served on the British Royal Navy," he says. "That ship fought countless naval battles and ferried myriad provisions, not unlike the ships that I own. It was one of the swiftest and fiercest vessels of its era."

"Mr. Lochner," I reply, with gritted teeth. "Is there a reason you're telling me all of this?"

"That frigate was called the HMS Zephyrus. And please, call me Rafe."

✦

Surprisingly, no one from C+P tried to sneak footage of Lochner's short visit. I expected a concealed visor or two, but the most that the staffers did were crane their necks and catch a glimpse of the man before turning back to their calls or screens.

"Way to stick it to him," Elliott teases as we watch the Lochner retinue leave the floor.

"Why's he even here?"

"The C+P Board is having an emergency session today," he replies. "And I'm certain it's not just Maxwell's arrest that's on the docket. Lochner's here to make his final pitch before they all vote on Monday."

Monday already. Where did the time go? "How do you know this?" I ask.

"Yes, Elliott," Cleo says, sneaking up from behind us. Her sights are set on Lochner as he disappears into an elevator. "However did you hear about that?"

"The heightened security, and the fact that quadcopters have been landing at the tower helipad all morning," Elliott says, giving her a probing look. "Tell me I'm wrong."

Cleo remains stoic, a rare feat.

"Rumor is, Lochner's family edited their genetic line to propagate red hair so that the allele doesn't die out," she says to change the subject. "Disgusting what the ultra-rich spend their money on, but he is quite the looker, isn't he?"

"Sure, he's definitely . . . disarming." My choice of adjective visibly repulses the two of them. Given what I've discovered about her, I'm in no mood to banter with Cleo, but I won't pass up a chance to observe her in close quarters. "Anyway, that probably won't be enough for him to flip any votes. Not with five days left to go."

"I agree," Cleo says with a hint of glee.

"You think?" Elliott asks. "Then why does Lochner look so smug?"

"That's just his face," she replies.

"Too bad it took Simon dying for C+P to be saved," I add, hardly needing to muster any sadness. Cleo's smile deflates, and I can't tell if her expression is out of mourning or out of guilt. She tries to respond but decides to hold it in instead.

"But what if he does win someone over last-minute? He doesn't look too worried," Elliott says. "And as we've seen, Briana Foley's very changeable."

"Lochner also has to deal with his own board of directors now," Cleo says. "And maybe João is right. A murder trial might be one scandal too many for Zephyrus to handle."

"The company's a fucking mess, but hey, at least it'll be *our* mess, right?" Elliott says with a sigh.

I keep my thoughts to myself, but Lochner's visit convinces me that C+P isn't in the clear. Any other day, he wouldn't have set foot in the building, especially not when there's a precarious deal about to be closed, knowing that the company is in turmoil and knowing how unpopular he is with the staff. Yet he wanted to be here, and he wanted to be seen to be here. This wasn't about his friendship with Maxwell. This was a show of confidence directed at his own company and its board. This was a show of defiance. And based on my encounter with him, this was, toward C+P, a display of his victory's inevitability.

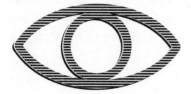

26.

Wednesday, 07/15/2043, 03:38 PM

The newsroom's beginning to feel claustrophobic, both from the number of bodies shuffling around and from the weight of everything that's happening. A dead body, an arrest for murder, board meetings and takeovers—C+P is getting put through the wringer, same as me. I have to get away from here.

I leave the building and head into the west entrance of Bryant Park, my mood lifting as I cross its threshold. The haze over the grass, the humid thickness of the summer air, the sweat seeping into the back of my shirt. Sure, it's right across the street from the C+P Tower, but that's all the distance I need.

I amble down the path along the length of 42nd Street, the one shaded by London plane trees on both sides. Before long, my walk is disrupted by a commotion coming from far ahead of me, by the back steps of the New York Public Data Vault. I follow the sound and soon find myself before a mass of people gathered for a demonstration.

A thin, bespectacled man paces back and forth on a low platform, addressing a crowd of about sixty, all of them rapt and riveted by his every word. Behind the speaker stands a line of young men, barely teenagers, in matching navy shirts and army pants. As the bespectacled man pauses for his applause line, the crowd cheers—no, *roar* is the more appropriate word for it. They raise their fists alongside holo-banners and crude cardboard signs of varying quality, though they all bear the same messages and the same logo emblazoned throughout.

The logo matches the tarp serving as the speaker's backdrop: an upright spearhead piercing a circle. Underneath is a singular name: Exsomnis.

I immediately put my visor on and start recording. I approach the assembly from the side, and find a stone bench to stand on for a good view. I affix an audioscope to my lapel, and then slip the Sensor Band onto my index finger. It syncs with my visor, allowing me more precise control of my camera and sound levels. I amp up image stabilization.

Let's see what we've got here.

". . . to usher in the world that we were meant to inherit. A world that recognizes the primacy of the Sleepless people!"

The speaker's words are followed with grunts and whoops and fierce applause.

My eyes couldn't roll back far enough if I tried.

Many fringe groups cropped up in the early days of the hyperinsomnia panic in the '30s. Most of them were of the mystical and fundamentalist kind, and they preached that the pandemic was God's punishment for humanity, and the Sleepless were the harbingers of death. As we've all seen, the lack of reliable scientific information served as a fertile ground for the spread of disinformation and the rise of hate groups.

Exsomnis was one of those groups, but in those days, it was the outlier. Built on an idea of genetic supremacy (back when many people mistakenly thought that hyperinsomnia was genetic in nature), the group believed in transhumanism and the goal of creating better humans through technology and large-scale directed evolution. To them, hyperinsomnia was a means to achieving their ultimate dream of human immortality, and the Sleepless represented the next step in human evolution toward that dream. Those who weren't Sleepless were deficient, and their inferiority had to be eliminated.

Exsomnis modeled itself after the popular supremacist groups of decades past, complete with the Latinate name and slogan, and the vaguely militaristic iconography. And much like those supremacist groups, Exsomnis used extreme measures to achieve its goals. The group gained infamy in 2033 following the suicide bombing of the Hyperinsomnia Research Institute in Wakefield, Maine. At the time, the institute had begun clinical trials for a cure for Sleepless people, and predictably, this did not sit well with Exsomnis. The bomber turned out to be a dues-paying member of Exsomnis' New England chapter, and though the group denied any involvement in what they called the act of a "lone wolf", the 50,000-member group was placed on international watch lists as a terrorist organization.

The leaders of Exsomnis then laid low, and the group softened its messaging and eased up on its recruitment efforts. It also tried to rebrand itself as a more charitable organization, keeping the name and symbology but focusing its efforts on building partnerships with Sleepless outreach programs. Thanks to an aggressive PR campaign and the legitimacy bestowed by well-regarded nonprofits, it seemed like Exsomnis was finally leaving behind its radical past.

Today's rally dispels any such notion.

"The inferior class says that our days are done," the speaker starts. "That our ranks are dwindling, that the Plateau will extinguish our kind in a matter of decades." He paces around, nodding with exaggeration at each pause, mocking a concession to these claims. "But this simply isn't true! No longer are people afraid to declare, I am Sleepless. No longer are the Sleepless afraid to declare, I am superior. No longer are the believers afraid to declare, I am Exsomnis."

The crowd cheers, raising their signs and chanting "Sleepless and proud! Sleepless and proud!"

The speaker lifts both his hands, and the boys behind him further whip up the frenzy with roaring and chest thumping. "There's more of us now—coming out of the shadows, recognizing the power that being Sleepless has given us, and wielding that power with pride!"

This is precisely why you should be here, I hear Simon whisper in my ear, recalling his admonishments about being jaded. He's not wrong, and it's been surprisingly easy to overlook how hatred breeds in all places, Midtown Manhattan being no exception. Not without some smugness, Simon used to warn everyone against thinking anything can be "old news". *That's how we miss things.*

"Go home!" a panhandler yells at the crowd from her cardboard rug on the pavement, her midday peace disrupted by the racket. The speaker laughs, and his followers join him. I almost agree with the tiny old woman, until she punctuates her sentiment with "You fucking freaks!"

I wasn't sure if she meant that the Sleepless in general or just the supremacists, but I capture the moment on video just the same. I suppose that's something I share with the Exsomnis folks. Despite the science, and despite the strides that Sleepless folks have made, to others, we're still abominations. Turning my focus back on the stage, seeing the furor and bigotry on full public display, my stomach lurches at the idea that I have something in common with Exsomnis.

The rally proceeds to a recitation of the names of the Exsomnis dead, the "heroes" who died for their cause. It's a short list, and a quick fact-check reveals that the deaths had more to do with various personal squabbles than martyrdom for Sleepless supremacy. Worse still, a number of these "heroes" were victims of Sleepless hate crimes from early in the pandemic, whose memory was now being exploited despite them not having been members of the supremacist movement at all. Their mention is what finally drives me to leave. I wrap up the recording, and as I stow my gear away, a tap on the shoulder interrupts me.

"Jamie Vega?" says a raven-haired woman with a Boston accent. Her face crinkles as she smiles, and she reminds me of one of my aunts. "My name is Brenda Xu, and I work for Strathairn-Shaw. I was hoping we could talk for a few minutes."

I inspect her credentials as she flashes me her phone, though I have no reason to doubt her. She looks like the type from one of those centuries-old white-shoe firms, with her sharp pantsuit and tight bun. Plus, it was only a matter of time before I'd be cornered by Maxwell's lawyers.

"I'm not a lawyer," she emphasizes, "Though I do work for the firm as an investigator. Wheels are turning quickly on the case, and the NYPD hasn't been the most cooperative, so I was hoping you could shed a light on a few things."

"What kind of things?"

"How are his relationships with the people at work?" she asks. "I'm particularly interested in Cleo Johnson. I hear she and Simon both opposed the Zephyrus bid?"

That's a surprise. Did she also find what Noor found about Cleo? "You'll have to ask her yourself," I reply.

"Hard to get a hold of her up in that tower of yours. Would you say she and Simon are close?"

"For long-time colleagues," I say with a dismissive smile. I know what she's trying to imply, and I won't indulge it.

"She must have been devastated by his death."

"Listen, if you wanna know about Cleo, you can ask Cleo. So if there's nothing else . . ."

"Actually, there is. I'm trying to build a timeline," Brenda replies. "You came up as the last person in Simon Parrish's office that night. Suppose you can tell me what you saw."

"Not much. I saw Simon and said goodbye to him, that's it."

"How long did that take?" she asks. Either the NYPD haven't shared the surveillance clips with her yet, or she's trying to catch me in a lie.

"Short." I say. Best to be vague. I make a display of having packed my gear away, and then start walking back down the tree-lined path. She follows, of course. It's an interesting reversal, being on the receiving end of this pursuit. Usually I'm the one hounding another for information.

"And I don't suppose you can tell me what you two talked about that night?" she asks.

"It's confidential. I'm not allowed to disclose."

"Journalists enjoy a lot of legal protections here, that's one of the things that makes this country great." She sounds sincere enough, though her goal is obviously frustrated. "I worked a case in Uzbekistan once. I can't tell you how differently they handle things out there."

"Sorry I can't be more helpful." I up my pace, rushing toward the crosswalk before the light turns red.

"I'm sure you could if you tried harder," she says, catching up to me. "It might be better for us to sit down somewhere, have this all taken down. I think if we got together and sat in our offices, say tomorrow or Friday, you'll have more to say."

I'm not stupid enough to give his lawyers a statement, and I'm insulted she thinks I am. "I don't think that'll change things," I reply firmly, the mask of cordiality slipping.

"It'll be a short interview," she says. "I'd rather skip all the court orders and subpoenas."

"Is that a threat?"

"It'll be in your interest too, getting ahead of this now."

"How d'ya figure?"

"The sooner you cooperate, the sooner we can avoid a trial for Maxwell. You wouldn't want that. Our lawyers are cutthroat, and they'll do anything to get the client off." Her intonation becomes deceptively treacly. "They'll know exactly who to string up in front of a jury. Tell me, do you think it'll be hard to persuade a jury to look at the guy who last saw Simon Parrish alive?"

"You sure can try," I scoff.

"We don't try, Mr. Vega. We succeed."

 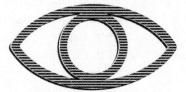

27.

Wednesday, 07/15/2043, 11:27 PM

Despite the hour, the midday sun streams down from a cloudless sky, warming the people of the sundome town as they toil through their endless day. The one down here in DC is called Hyperion Hill, and is one of the biggest in the country. It's the size of a small village, and just as populated. A thousand solar simulators hang from a mesh high above a mile-wide expanse. A metal cave with a firmament of scaffolded lightbulbs.

DC's full of hyperinsomniacs. All the A-types working for the government or for companies with an interest in how things get done. Next to New York and Wakefield, this city's all right for our kind, and Hyperion Hill is where many of the Sleepless are, putting in the hours nonstop. The firms that are here (data crunchers, consulting groups, and tons of lobbyists) require it. They've set up housing for their employees, given them daylight 24/7 and a few amenities for the little downtime that they avail of. Not everything is here, but it's got enough. For the most part, folks in here don't have to leave the dome and walk into a world where day turns to night.

The dome has a lot of green spaces, filled with meticulously cultivated trees and flora engineered to thrive in the artificial environment. I locate the designated alfresco café, the one set up in an alcove garden near the south gate. I don't go in, but instead take a park bench across the street, where my visor can capture a clear view of the intersection: the crossing leading to and from the café, the booth where DumWaiters collect their coffee orders for delivery, the table where we're supposed to meet. From this distance, I'm wondering if Sid Thorpe is somewhere nearby doing the exact same thing: spying from afar, waiting for my arrival. I press record.

After a while, you don't even notice it, I try to convince myself. The eye strain eases, the tiny red dot in the corner fades into the periphery.

Fuck, I'd always made fun of those who wore their visors 24/7. They're almost always pimply-faced fanboys, early adopters who line up and wait overnight in front of physical stores and warehouses every time a new visor model gets released. Once bought, the visor becomes their entire life; everything's transacted and experienced via the thin band over their eyes, social codes be damned. Now I'm forced to become one of them.

As I wait, I pull up a side panel to go over my notes on the OEF. The Open Eyes Federation is a nonprofit "dedicated to the welfare of the hyperinsomnia community and their families." It has a long and robust donor list, almost entirely made of Fortune 100 companies, and though its home base is in the nation's capital, it has a global presence. It spends most of its money building coalitions with grassroots nonprofits serving the Sleepless, funding international programs to improve Sleepless and non-Sleepless relations, with the end goal of justice and equity for all hyperinsomniacs.

As for Sid herself, my background search comes up mostly clean. I look up any connections between her and Simon, but there's nothing aside from her tenure as his former second-in-command. Lots of shared bylines and producing credits, all of which I've seen before. Then there's the three-year gap in her résumé between C+P and ending up as the comms director for the OEF. Quite the long sabbatical, and there's nothing online to indicate what she'd been up to. Most of the media on her are OEF releases, photos and clips from society galas and fundraisers. In most of them, she's right next to Rafe Lochner and his wife.

Then, a figure in a dark overcoat walks briskly down the garden walk. I barely glimpse her face, but the long, dark hair, the four-inch Louboutins and the clutch held in a gloved hands tell me she has arrived. She takes a table in the back corner of the café, nestled against a row of dwarf poplar trees. With no prompting and uncanny prescience, she looks straight at me from across the street, her eyes beckoning.

I make my way past the suits zipping by, those hyperinsomniac hustlers making the most of their hours.

"I must say, this is an honor and a surprise, Ms. Thorpe." I say when I take my seat. "Thanks for agreeing to see me."

"An honor? Come, there's no need for flattery. Courtesy though . . ." She waves away my visor and I hesitantly slide it off my face. I hope I get to remember all of this.

"You go by Isidra now," I say. Likely an effort at rebranding to leave behind her media days.

"Well, that *is* my name. But Sid's fine too. How did you find me?" she asks. A DumWaiter brings her a cup of black coffee.

"You're not exactly in hiding," I say. "That, and Simon got sloppy. Left tracks, ones that led me to you."

"He's never sloppy."

"What were you and Simon working on?"

"Who says we were working on something?" she says.

"You two talked a lot."

"Did we?"

"I'm just pulling on a thread here," I say.

"So you know nothing." She rolls her eyes.

"Whatever you two have going on, it's important enough for you to meet regularly. Was he leaking information to you?"

She laughs. "Now why on earth would he do that?"

Enough of these games. "Ms. Thorpe, I owe Simon a lot. It's pretty fucking heartless for you to laugh in my face knowing that he's dead."

She casts her sight low, slowly teasing the lip of her cup with an index finger. That last word struck a nerve. I continue. "I never believed it was suicide, even before the cops called it a murder, so I've been doing my own digging. I discovered there'd been data breaches within C+P and that Simon had been hiding something. I think it was a story, one that he hid from everyone and fiercely protected. That story might have led to his death, and I won't give up until I find out what it is."

She takes in all that I said, then finally asks, "How do you figure I fit in?"

"He was arguing with you, in the last few days before he died," I reply. "Did it have something to do with our story on Senator Dwyer?"

"Isn't this all moot? Cartwright did it, and he did it because of the buyout. At least that's what the news keeps saying."

"I have reason to believe it's not that simple."

She waits for me to say more, to elaborate on my doubts, but there's nothing I can disclose right now, not until I have a better sense of how she fits in. She grows weary of the silence. "Well, if you won't tell, then I won't either."

For better or worse, being Sleepless feels like having an eternity before you. That's the draw, isn't it? More time. But it only feels that way when you're not racing against something else. At first, it was just my memory and the need to solve Simon's murder before I miss something crucial. The visor helps with that. But now, I'm also racing against Brenda Xu. The sooner I find proof that I didn't kill Simon, the safer I am from taking Maxwell's place as accused murderer.

Sid Thorpe's my strongest lead, and she needs to understand: I have no time for games. If that means I'd have to do to her what's being done to me, so be it.

"The cops don't know about your link to Simon," I tell her. "They don't know about your late-night calls, your arguments. Yelling and screaming, shortly before he's murdered. And, you work for the CEO of Zephyrus. I bet the NYPD would be mighty interested to hear what I have to say."

Her eyes narrow, measuring me. I hold steady and keep up the bluff.

Finally, she folds. "*No one* can know we've been talking."

"Give me some answers, and I swear I won't tell."

She pulls her visor out of a coat pocket and starts scanning me for bugs or wires. Then she pans behind her, around the café, and across the street. "Simon wasn't leaking information to me. It's the other way around. How much do you know about Rafe Lochner?"

"Quite a lot. Your boss is pretty public," I say. "Owns the OEF and several dozen companies, with his sights on more, including C+P."

"I can tell you don't like him," she says. "Simon didn't either. So you can see how incongruous it would be for Simon to be giving Lochner information through me."

"So there is no mole?"

"What does it matter?" she says. "There will always be leaks, everywhere. Look at the business you're in. Look at what I'd been doing with Simon. Some things are simply too big to be kept under wraps."

Was Anders right after all? Was the C+P mole hunt a convoluted plan for Simon to cover his own tracks? It seems excessive to involve the tech security team, and firing Anders is an extreme method of deflection, but I suppose he'd have to, if he was targeting the man who was poised to become C+P Media's new owner.

"This thing about Lochner that you've been feeding Simon—it's big?" I ask.

"Yes. Simon wanted to stop the buyout by any means necessary, and I was providing him the ammo to finish the job," she replies.

"What kind of ammo?"

"The kind that will ruin the Zephyrus empire."

So Simon was developing another story. On top of his plans to flip the board votes, he also had some secret project that could bring down Lochner. Plans upon backup plans. This opens up more possibilities. Another reason to want Simon dead, more than the Dwyer story or the C+P buyout. More importantly—another name on my list of suspects. Someone who had supporters within C+P, and had near-infinite resources to carry out a murder and get away with it. He might not have been in Simon's office that night, but this story moves Rafe Lochner to the top of the list.

"What's the story?" I ask.

"I can't say, but it turned out to be a dead end, even before Simon died."

"Now that he's gone," I say with hesitation, "Maybe I can help you."

"You don't even know what this is."

"Then tell me. Start from the beginning."

Sid tilts her head slightly, and before she could refuse, I continue. "Look, we're on the same side. I'd do anything to stop Lochner from turning C+P into his personal mouthpiece, and clearly you would too, or you wouldn't be risking your job to help Simon. Trust me."

"I want to trust you." She purses her lips and looks me in the eye. "But it's hard to trust a man who only minutes ago threatened to blackmail me by going to the cops."

Without warning, she rises from her seat. She reaches her hand out and smiles, teeth bared.

"Stay seated. Do not look around. Someone's watching."

Her lips hardly move as she whispers. I do as told.

"Now nod slowly. Count a couple of beats, then stand. Do not break eye contact."

I go through the motions, my heart racing. It takes immense willpower for me to keep my head still. I'm pretty sure I know who's watching. Brenda.

"Give me a quick hug," Sid commands. "Nothing too showy."

"Let me help you," I whisper as I lean into her.

"Sit back down. Lose my number."

Sid turns away with her head cast down, and I detect that it's both to avoid being identified and to play-act for the benefit of our observer. I shift my gaze surreptitiously, but my peripheral view only shows faceless bodies walking briskly under the bright sunlight. When enough time has passed, I search my surroundings more closely, but there's no Brenda in sight.

Before I leave the café, I grab the napkin from our table and scribble down the details of our conversation. Lochner, a lead that could ruin his empire. A clear motive for murder. I add in my thoughts too. I can't risk losing anything. I may already be losing them with every passing second. Socrates once said the written word is the enemy of memory. Right now, it's the only friend I've got.

28.

Thursday, 07/16/2043, 09:42 AM

C+P's main editing suite is wall-to-wall with the different faces of Simon Parrish. Simon as a six-year-old, holding on to his nana's hand. Undergrad Simon, in his bomber jacket and skinny jeans, on the lawns of Oxford. Conflict correspondent Simon out in the ruins of Syria, the villages of Kashmir. Family man Simon crouched before a fireplace with his wife and children in matching Christmas sweaters. Then clip after clip after clip of hard-hitting news anchor Simon, bespectacled and besuited, going toe to toe with a rogues' gallery of high-profile miscreants. The editors are hard at work stitching these disparate episodes together, weaving them into a narrative, calling it a retrospective. In memoriam. This isn't real, this is just a highlight reel.

I don't need to see the rest to know that there won't be a section about volatile boss Simon. There won't be anything about any of his flaws and shortcomings, his alleged dalliances, his drug habit. No mention of his professional failures, the failed titles and startups, the many stories that didn't get traction or results. I'm watching the editing crew, all decent and hardworking folks, and I can't help but think how dishonest this piece is. This picking and choosing, intended to elicit an emotional response. Selectively manipulating memories to manipulate the viewer's emotions.

A person's not much more than the sum of their memories, and the same applies to someone when they're gone. After death, Simon becomes not much more than the sum of what everyone else remembers him as. And is this all that Simon is going to be, now? This puff piece?

"It's not as bad as I expected," Elliott says as he walks up next to me, arms crossed in guarded observance. The whole room gives him a side-eye. He lowers his voice. "Tough crowd."

"Careful, or you're not gonna like how you look the next time you're on screen."

"By the way, what was up with ditching me last night?" he asks. "I thought you wanted me to help you retrace your steps?"

"I did, and I still do," I reply. "But something came up with this other thing."

I've debated whether to clue Elliott in on this lead with Sid Thorpe, but what would I say? That Simon was working on this secret story about Lochner? That I couldn't get any more from her because some private dick has been following me? Honestly, it sounds too tinfoil hat conspiracy theory, even for me.

"It's this Doctor Slimane," I lie instead. "I'd tell you more but it's too boring and up in the air."

"Still couldn't track her down, huh?"

"Yeah. I made a ton of calls since yesterday, mostly old colleagues. Everyone says she's the best in the field, but no one seems to know where she is, why she's gone, or how to reach her."

"Hmm. So what's your next move?" Elliott asks, eyes still on the screens.

"Might need to pay a visit to a sister down in Baltimore," I reply, sighing. "It's weird how she was super prominent, then poof."

"You really think this is worth your time?" he asks, charitably. "It's not like I haven't been listening to you, but I've had this on 24/7, just in case." Elliott taps the edge of his visor. "And I haven't noticed any memory issues."

"Maybe it hasn't happened yet." He could also be in denial, but I don't say that. "Best way to be sure is to ask the expert. If only I could find her."

"Well, as much as I support you, I'd also rather you focus on other things. Look around. We're in the middle of this catastrophic shakeup. Aren't you worried about how we're all going to survive?"

"My immediate concerns are a little more particular," I say, lowering my voice further. "Someone from Strathairn-Shaw paid me a visit yesterday. A private investigator. Seems keen on getting me tangled up in Maxwell's murder case."

"Chinese-American lady with the funny Boston accent? Yeah, she caught me on the way in," he replies with some irritation. "What do you mean tangled?"

"She's saying I gotta answer her questions or else the lawyers are gonna start pointing fingers. At me."

"What, because you were there last night?" he asks. "So what? You had no beef with Simon."

"Still. These lawyers can conjure up a scapegoat from thin air. So before they get to me, I need to prove that I didn't do it."

"All right, sure. This is why I said we should retrace your steps," he replies. "You want to try tonight?"

"Thanks, but I think I have a better idea."

Elliott narrows his eyes in amused interest, but doesn't pursue it. "You're a man of many secrets, Vega."

He's right. A good memory jog might help me remember, but I have to do it under conditions as close to how they actually were. I need to recreate Wednesday night as it happened, and for that, he's not the one I need.

"Can you believe this?" I say after a while, turning back to the screens of the editing suite. "Simon's so full of life, and his puff piece feels so devoid of it."

"No disrespect to the *Rise and Shine* team, but he would barf if he saw this," Elliott replies, miming the act. "There's no texture, no mess. It's all gloss."

"You can't even tell what happened. How he died."

"Well, that's not what this retrospective is for," he replies.

"Frankly, I don't know what this is for."

"It's for us to lose the Dwyer story, that's what." Elliott turns to me. "Which reminds me—please tell me you have a plan on how to get Cleo on board."

"I have some ideas."

I proceed to tell Elliott what Noor found on Cleo. Her parents' holdings in Dwyer's home state, how their company made large contributions to his senate campaign. Elliott's response is as measured Noor's.

"It doesn't sound like much, Jamie."

"It's more than enough."

"You think if you brought a lead like this to Simon, he'd let you run with it?" he asks, disbelieving. "All due respect, I think he'd yell you out of his office if you came to him with something this thin. Why are you so sure about this anyway?"

Sure, no. Desperate, more like. In the last couple of days, Simon's changed from suicide to murder victim, and I've changed from reporter with a perfectly functioning brain to an amnesiac and potential murderer, or at the very least, the fall guy. The only way to clear myself is to do exactly what Maxwell's defense team is doing: find someone else.

"I just need Cleo to talk," I reply. "And showing her what I found might do the trick." Either that, or coming on too strong blows up in my face, same way it did with Sid.

"She does respond to chutzpah," Elliott muses, bolstering my resolve. "It's a fine line, but if we show her how far we're willing to go for this, she might respect it enough to give in. Besides, what's the worst she can do, fire us?"

We chuckle but soon fall silent. He's the first to speak. "You need me to back you up?"

"Oh, so now it's 'you' and not 'we.' Fucking wuss," I say, tapping his chest with the back of my palm.

❂

I hardly recognize my own office anymore. For the last couple of weeks I've been running around town and working out of the C+P war room, and so coming in here now doesn't give me a familiar comfort. There's a half-full tumbler of coffee from who knows when, and a thin layer of dust has settled on my keyboard. I could tidy up, sort the stack of mail that's collected in my inbox, put away the books I'd checked out for research on arcane campaign finance laws. Maybe straighten the framed diplomas and the commemorative photos from stories past, all slightly askew.

And here I thought setting up this meeting in my own space would give me a sense of control.

"What's this about, Jamie?" Cleo asks as she enters. She takes a hold of the seat before my desk, bracing herself like a prizefighter.

"We need to talk about the Dwyer story," I reply, calmly. "It needs to air, and fast, before he gets a chance at a coverup."

"Not this again," she says, exasperated. "Just leave it, Jamie. *Rise and Shine* is almost done with the retrospective."

"Do you really want to mark the end of Simon's era on the show with a puff piece? It'd be like spitting on his grave."

"The episode's *about* him but it's not *for* him," she replies firmly. "It's for all of us. The ones left behind. We're the ones who need to remember, and to heal."

"And what about the work Simon put into the piece? The work the rest of the team did?"

"A month or two is all I'm saying, just until the dust settles and we figure out how to move forward with *The Simon Parrish Files* without Simon Parrish. I promise you I won't let the story go to waste."

I don't want to be right, but I can't afford to ignore any detail. Despite what Noor says, the way Cleo's been acting toward the exposé makes me think her connection to Dwyer isn't loose at all. And if her business interests give her cause to kill the Dwyer story, what else might she be capable of?

"That's not good enough," I reply. She doesn't seem moved, so I go for it. "You know, if you're trying to kill the story, the least you could do is be upfront about it."

"What the fuck are you talking about?"

"I know about Azeofuel, your family's holdings in Minnesota . . . what is it, Dwyer grants the company some subsidies, and in return you spike a story or two?"

Cleo's eyes widen. "You think I would trade my reputation for goddamn corn subsidies? I don't own that company, my parents do.

And not that it's any of your business, but I haven't seen or talked to them in over a decade."

"That doesn't prove anything."

"You're the one with something to prove, and I gotta say, this is fucking weak. I thought Simon trained you better than that." She tsks, shakes her head condescendingly. She's right, it's no smoking gun. I may have let my zeal carry me away on this one, but I know no other way to be.

"I still haven't heard any reasons," I reply firmly. "Why are you trying to spike the story? And don't give me another goddamn excuse."

"It's Simon, all right? He was the one who wanted to delay it."

Her stance, her words, the fire in her eyes, everything about her tells me she's being truthful. Yet it didn't make a lick of sense. Simon had driven everyone hard on this piece, as hard as he always did on stories that could bring down a corrupt politico. There was no reason he'd compromise our own work.

"I don't get it," I say when I recover from my disbelief. "Why would he risk Dwyer getting off the hook?"

"I wish I knew why. Hand to God, I wanna get Dwyer as much as you do," Cleo replies. "But that's what Simon wanted. He said the story can wait. When you know someone as well as I knew him, you trust them and do as they say. Even when they don't make sense."

"Like you are now."

"Then let me enlighten you," she replies, challenged. "About three weeks ago, he told me he wanted to delay the Dwyer story. He didn't tell me much, but I didn't question him, and I would never tell the man how to run his own damn show. So I let it go. Looking back, maybe I let go of one thing too many."

"What do you mean?"

"He'd been acting odd. More secretive and withdrawn than usual. Paranoid. Not unlike how you are now."

"It's not paranoia if someone's holding out on you."

"I don't know if you've noticed, but besides a dead CEO and another one indicted, the company's also had threats of corporate espionage," she snaps back. "I didn't think my conversation with Simon about this tiny little news story was need-to-know. Especially since, need I remind you, I don't answer to you."

Her hackles are raised, but whatever line I shouldn't have crossed is now miles behind me, so I keep pressing. "You said it yourself—you know him well. You must have some idea why he'd do that. He must've given you something."

"He said that he was paving the way for something else," she replies. "Wouldn't tell me what, but he swore to clue me in when it's ready. All he said was that it's big. Bigger than a dirty, flipflopping senator."

That certainly verifies what Sid Thorpe told me, the little of it that she did. Simon had Lochner in his sights, and that kind of story, well, that's something he needed to keep close to the vest.

After a pause, Cleo continues. "That asshole Dwyer is probably gonna be the next Republican nominee, but can you blame me for doing the one thing Simon asked? I didn't agree with him, and he sure as hell didn't make any sense, but I couldn't fail him again."

"You've never failed him."

"He was in trouble, and I dismissed all the signs. Whatever this thing ends up being, suicide or murder or whatever, I knew something was wrong. I knew and I didn't do anything about it."

Her words land hard, reminding me of my own failures. How surely I'd known something was wrong with Paolo. How I missed it again with Simon. Guilt fucks you up, makes you do irrational things. My own recent history bears this out. Would I have done different in her place? I wouldn't bet on it.

"This other story Simon was working on . . . I think I know what it is."

"What do you mean?" Cleo asks.

"I think he was going after Lochner." I can give her a little bit, try to draw something out of her without revealing what I learned from Sid. "When I found him that morning, I saw a note on his desk. He was meeting a contact."

"What does it say?"

"Zephyrus, a phone number and a time," I lie.

"That could mean anything."

"I know, but I have a feeling about this. Simon didn't tell you anything about it?"

Cleo shakes her head. "The buyout's not happening anyway. Lochner's no longer a threat now that he doesn't have the votes."

"For a man who's lost, he seemed quite confident yesterday," I reply. "Besides, Simon had something on him. I'm gonna get to the bottom of it, if that's the last thing I do for him."

"You might be chasing shadows," she replies. "But you won't find me stopping you from gunning after Lochner."

"Thanks. And sorry about, you know, the whole looking into your parents thing."

"Meh, they deserve it. And if you find something juicier on them, I'd love to see it."

Cleo stands and surveys my small space, taking a moment to give me the once over. "We're all trying to do right by Simon. My way— which of course is the correct way—is buckling down and making sure C+P survives this mess. It's a turbulent time, and I'm the only one left steering the ship."

"For what it's worth, I think you're doing a tremendous job."

"I'm one day in, so let's hold the reviews." Despite her words, it's obvious she's pleased to receive the compliment. "And you—you'll have your own way of honoring him. If you think that means winding up Simon's unfinished business, then godspeed."

29.

The steel table feels frigid beneath my folded arms. I should have picked up that coffee on the way. Not to drink—the jitters won't look good—but just to keep me warm. Cops in old movies used to say "sweat" as a shorthand for turning up the heat on someone. The guys at Three Police Plaza don't talk that way anymore.

Soon enough, Detective Nathan Tetro is going to walk into this cramped interview room, put on his standard-issue visors, the one with the NYPD seal on the top right edge of the band. Then, he'll start recording. He'll a few ask questions, I'm sure, but there was something about his tone when he called me in. He was too self-satisfied. So I'm not here to answer questions either. I'm here to react when he tells me three things I already know.

First, he'll tell me it's a murder, as if I don't already know, and that Maxwell is the prime suspect. Second, he'll tell me what he found on the scene: the pill tube, the wine, maybe even Simon's chicken-scrawl notes. He'll ask questions about them, details, but it'll be my reaction that he's really after. Finally, he'll ask me about the Zephyrus acquisition. That's where it'll all get dicey.

"Sorry to keep you waiting," Tetro says as he arrives, visor on as expected. He's got his tablet too, and a glass of water which he slides over to me. He's wearing the same suit he wore when he arrested Maxwell, same gray tie too. For a detective, he still sticks to a uniform.

He gives me the preliminaries: thanks for coming in, just a few follow ups, completely standard. He hands me the tablet and makes me sign a waiver for the recording, confirming that I'm aware of my rights and that I'm giving them up.

"As you know, Maxwell Cartwright's been charged with the murder of Simon Parrish." He stares me down, and I return the favor. "We've built a timeline of what happened the night of, but we have some gaps that need filling in."

He doesn't follow this with a question right away. I remain impassive. In my mind this is just another round of poker, and I have to control every muscle. The cameras catch everything, and what I say isn't the only thing that can be used against me. Blinking a bit too fast, breathing a bit too rough, my body temperature slightly running hotter—any physiological anomaly is going to be picked up and analyzed by the NYPD's AI.

"Did you see Maxwell Cartwright that night, when you came into the office at around 8 p.m.?"

"No." The more accurate answer is that I don't remember, but that kind of talk complicates things.

"Why'd you go to the office at that hour? I don't think we covered that last time we spoke."

"Had to file something away for a news story that was gonna get picked up by the wires the next morning. I forgot to do it before I left the office, so I went back for it." I'd anticipated this question, and though I still don't know why, I had to give him something that didn't entail seeing Simon. Something that was also plausible, jargony and arguably confidential. The answer works, and he doesn't pursue it anymore. Yet his breath slows, and I can tell he's ramping up to something.

"Was Simon the only person you saw that night?"

"Yes." Likely true, so I chance it.

"He was drinking? When you went into his office?"

"I think so, yes."

Another camera angle could corroborate this or prove it wrong, but it was a safe bet that around that time he'd been drinking the wine that caused his death.

"You remember what you two talked about?"

"I've been thinking about it all week, and I don't. Must have been something minor."

"Last time we talked, I thought maybe you were just in shock. It's traumatic, I get it," he says in faux sympathy. "But last time, we also weren't looking at a murder. Now . . . you still don't recall what happened?"

"No, I don't."

"See, if you'd just tell me, then I could rule you out easy," he replies. "But this? This whole amnesia thing you've got going on, this only makes me think you've got something to hide."

I can see how he'd think that. Tables turned, I'd think the same thing too. Now that he's grilling me about a murder case, I wonder if I should have lied to him all along. I could end this by lying, telling him some specific but innocuous detail about a work assignment that Simon and I would have talked about. Should I chance it, with the cameras turned on me and their algorithm assessing every tic and blink of my eye?

"Honestly, I don't remember. And believe me, I want to figure this out just as much as you do."

"Not that much left to figure out, at least as far as Cartwright's part in it. He was in Simon Parrish's office about half an hour before you got to the building. He brought the wine, which contained an illegal narcotic," he continues. "Which caused what at first appeared to be a suicidal overdose."

He expects me to fill the silence, and trying to read in the lines on my face. I put on the most neutral face I can muster.

"You don't seem surprised," he says.

"This was all in the indictment. What was the substance?"

"Some new street drug they're calling A-Pop. Narcotics says it's big with the club kids. Caused an instant cardiac arrest, since Simon had all these heart complications."

I steel myself and wait for him to ask me about the vial. Either the one in Simon's office or the one I found in my pocket.

"Simon wasn't wild on the Zephyrus acquisition, was he?" Tetro asks instead.

"He didn't talk to me about that, but I heard he wasn't."

"Cartwright was in favor of it?"

"Yes."

"And he led the Board members who wanted to approve the offer?"

"Yes."

"And Simon won?"

"No one has won yet. The Board vote isn't until four days from now," I say. "But yes, that's what it's looking like."

"That's must have pissed Maxwell off real bad."

Like I said, this is where it gets dicey. The detective's right, there isn't much left to figure out. The wine, the buyout bid, his appearance on surveillance. I'm still unconvinced that Maxwell would murder in the heat of revenge, but there are other things at play. A delayed Board vote, a chance at salvaging the buyout, boardroom machinations . . . things that I don't expect this cop to understand, but as it is, he's already got what he needs.

Means, motive, and opportunity. Everything points to Maxwell.

"I can see that the gears are turning," Tetro says. "Tell me what you're thinking."

"It's too easy."

"Exactly." The detective slams his palm on the table. "That pill tube we recovered from the scene—When we tested it, do you know what we found? Nothing. No fingerprints, no trace amounts, not drop of wine, not even a single speck of dust. Nada."

For once I say exactly what I'm thinking: "That doesn't make sense."

"No trace amount of A-Pop in the wine bottle either, which still had some wine left over," he continues. "But there was a trace amount in Simon's wine glass. So we know that's how he ingested the drug. Here's what I'm thinking: Cartwright brings the wine over, slips the A-Pop into Simon's wine glass. Simon dies, then Cartwright plants the pill tube. What do you think?"

"Murder made to look like a suicide. Sure, that tracks."

"But . . . ?" Tetro says, leading me on.

"But for one, Maxwell must've known he'd show up on camera with the wine."

"That's right."

"And he'd know that a tox screen will show the cause of death was some new street drug. Not the kind Simon would take, since he's not a known user."

"Correct again. Simon's not exactly a club kid."

I should stop talking, but I can't help myself. "And as far as planting the pill tube, it doesn't make sense for Maxwell to leave it completely spotless. It raises red flags."

"So you see where I'm at?" he says. "Cartwright's a smart guy. He runs a goddamn media conglomerate. He'd do a much better job covering his tracks."

"Presumably."

"And so this is where you come in."

"What? How?"

"Cartwright couldn't have known you were coming by after he left Simon's office, right?"

"Right . . ."

"And Simon was still alive when you got there. After Maxwell left Simon's office," he says. "An overdose of this kind kicks in quick. Less than thirty minutes, the M.E. tells me. If Simon had collapsed when you were in his office, you would have had the chance to call 911."

I nod slowly, trying to follow his line of thought. I know he's not trying to make me feel worse by posing these what-ifs. Yes, I might have been able to save Simon from an overdose, but Tetro's got another angle.

"Yes. I'm the last to see him alive. I'm the first to see him dead. And yes, maybe I could have somehow saved his life," I reply, testily. "I must be damn lucky."

"I believe in luck. Years on this job, I've been lucky tons of times," the detective replies, punctuating it with a world-weary sigh. "What I don't believe in is coincidence."

"What are you trying to say, Detective? Am I a suspect?"

"It's like you said: you're the last to see him alive. You found the body. You don't remember anything from that night. What do you think?"

"Why the hell would I want Simon dead?" I ask.

"You tell me."

My jaw clenches, and I can feel my teeth grinding down hard. He rises steadily from his seat, casting a shadow over me. I need to keep my cool, or I might not walk out of here.

"Should I be asking for my lawyer?"

"Do you feel like telling me something that might require you to have a lawyer present?" he asks with a shit-eating grin.

"I've told you everything I know."

"See, lemme tell you what I think, then you tell me if you've really given me everything," Tetro says. "Cartwright goes in there with the wine, then leaves. Then you get on the scene. You go in there, spend twenty minutes talking to Simon right after Cartwright laces the wine, and we still don't know what that's about."

"I already told you—"

"Yeah, you forgot, whatever. Doesn't matter. What matters is no jury's gonna convict you. Not without motive or access to the murder weapon. Cartwright's got a clear reason to kill and a penchant for wine." He steeples his fingers, joints cracking. "But now we're finding out all these holes in the evidence. Things seem too perfect. Almost like Cartwright's being set up. You and I worked through it just now. It's too neat. A halfway decent defense attorney can make hay out of that and get a jury to acquit Cartwright."

"Sounds very much like a *you* problem."

"Here's what I think." Tetro's grin turns into a scowl. "I think you two were working together."

"How do you figure?"

"I think you two set it up so that either of you looks plausible. Which means there's enough reasonable doubt for a jury to be uncertain which one did it. One had the motive and the means, but the other had the opportunity. Not a single person to pin the whole thing on, which means Maxwell gets off, and so do you."

"That's real damn creative," I say, actually impressed. This one's not as dense as I thought. "I'd like to see you prove it though."

"You just hang tight. As soon as I find you a motive," he replies with bared teeth, "or find a connection between you and A-Pop, this murder case is gonna be a *you* problem."

 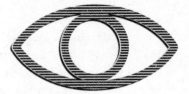

30.

My former home, a Chelsea one-bedroom loft, looks to have doubled in size after the vestiges of my life had been excised out of it. The walls are barer, the floors are cleaner, shelves have more space for the books and objets d'art to breathe. Hannah has redecorated, and our old furniture looks different set against the new items she's picked to make the place her own. There's a reason I don't come by here, and it's that ineffable grief from locational déjà vu.

"Let's get this over with," she says.

What to me is a matter of life and death was to her just another inconvenience, just Jamie being Jamie. If she only knew how the walls are closing in on me. Every new day places me in greater jeopardy, and since the last time Hannah and I spoke, more and more people seem convinced that I might have killed Simon. Brenda Xu, Detective Tetro . . . who's next?

"I knew all those desperate messages would work," I say, trying to be cute. Downplaying my worries might put her more at ease.

"I know you, Jamie. This will be another one of your fixations. The sooner you flush it out of your system, the better."

"Seriously though, I can't tell you how much I appreciate this."

"Look, I've thought a lot about our last conversation," she replies. "You taking that pill, all your excuses. I knew it was about Paolo and the nightmares. And now with Simon . . . I know I've said it's over between us, but I don't want that to happen to you all over again."

"Thanks. I promise it won't," I reply. "But my only way out is through."

Hannah hesitates at first, but eventually recounts her recollection of Wednesday night. To aid her, she scrolls through her tracking data on her tablet. "I went to your place Wednesday night at 7:05." She then repeats our conversation, describing how dejected I looked when I realized I'd forgotten the passport.

"Again, I'm sorry about that," I offer.

"Yeah, well, this all started because of me. It shouldn't have taken me this long to realize that I didn't have it somewhere in the apartment like I thought."

"Well, I'm kind of thankful you haven't had the need for it before now," I say, to her puzzlement. "If you weren't leaving on this trip, you wouldn't have come that night, and I wouldn't have your help piecing together what happened."

"You're welcome," she replies with sarcasm. "Anyway, you were wearing that wrap jacket, the black one." The same jacket that had the empty A-Pop vial. "You told me you didn't have the passport, so I told you to get it and that I'd come back for it the next day. Then you said you'd leave to go get it right away. So where would you have gone next?"

She asks the question slowly, waiting for me to arrive at the answer she already knew. "The last time we crossed the border was the road trip to Toronto, and . . . ?"

I remember now. It was in that red duffel, together with all the other empty luggage.

"I went to the storage unit," I exclaim, pleased at the discovery.

"That's the next stop then."

❂

We reach Pods on Demand close to seven, around the same time that I would have been here Wednesday night, if I went straight here after Hannah dropped by. The vertical warehouse has five fully automated loading bays for container pods and a dozen smaller bays for room-size pods. As Hannah and I walk up to the building, I wear my visor and start recording.

"Doctor's orders. In case my brain goes on the fritz again," I explain. She steps away to avoid my line of sight.

We enter one of the smaller bays, an empty steel room with a massive door taking up the entire far wall. I key in my code and place my handprint. The system confirms my identity, and a voice prompt warns us to mind the gap. A low humming reverberates as the far wall opens and the building's guts slowly spew out my pod, a 15 x 15 x 10-foot box. I key in another code on the pod's front panel, and its sliding doors open with a whoosh.

Temperature control supposedly prevents mustiness, but the air is still thick with the smell of old fabric and yellowing paper. Furniture, boxes, and outsize items of interest line the edges of the room in a disarray. The speed bike I haven't used since college, a couple of flat panels, a plastic Christmas tree, a phlegm-green ottoman that once belonged to Hannah, a trash bag filled with tattered linens, a vintage Noguchi coffee table, nested suitcases of various sizes, all unzipped and splayed open.

"Can't believe this thing is still so packed. And I already took all my stuff out," she says, surveying the mess.

"I accumulated more things this past year. Since I moved out."

To wit—the surfboard, the dragon boat paddle, the frame violin, the bags of soil for the garden, the tap shoes, the apiary suit. The pulp paperbacks that never got digitized, the obscure movie DVDs that never went to streaming. The LEGO Death Star that exploded into a million pieces when it tipped and fell off my work bench. The ill-conceived and thankfully abandoned attempts at metalworking. The welding helmet that came with them. The helmets that came with the Krav Maga and the rock climbing and the snowboarding, a line of disembodied plastic heads hanging down a coat rack. The costumes and uniforms that got used once or twice before being left behind in the wake of my next new Thing.

Hannah disappears behind a slim bookcase. "You should really label these boxes."

She tiptoes around the bookcase holding up a framed painting with both hands. "The Scream." A ghastly face in gray, contrasting with the dark blue water from under a bridge, ribbons of orange and yellow lining the top edge, evoking a sunset. We'd made it together, copying the old Norwegian classic. I couldn't bear to put it up in the new apartment.

"Is this jogging your memory at all?" she asks.

"Kind of." I squeeze in between a clothes rack and try to circle the space. I approach the matryoshka of suitcases and pull out the duffel, a timeworn brick red bag that still had airport tracker tags from prior trips. I run my hands inside it, fake-searching its empty shell. Nothing comes to mind.

I start putting the duffel and the rest of the bags inside each other. I try to recall if I stacked them neatly the last time, the way I usually do. I'm not in the habit of leaving things open. Was I rushing to leave? Did I just not care to close them back up?

"Okay, well, let's walk this through," I say, more to myself than her. "I go in, load up the pod, open the doors, open the duffel, get the passport. Then I put back all the bags, close the doors, send the pod back."

"Have you checked the log?"

I go over to the control panel and look up the access data. Last opened Wednesday, 07/08/2043, 19:41:22. At least the timeline checks out so far.

"I didn't know you fenced," she says, running her hand through the steel mesh of the fencing helmets. Another one of the disembodied heads on display.

"Yeah, a few months back."

I shuffle over to where she is, over by my sporting accoutrement. I notice that the fencing bag isn't where I put it last. The jacket and breeches are here, but the epees are nowhere to be found.

"I think I know what happened next."

❂

Steam rises from the sidewalk grates and adds to the oppressive heat of the summer night. Robocabs speed past delivery persons on their VeloTracks, and parcel drones whiz past overhead. I find myself gazing at Hannah as we walk toward the train. I wonder if she realizes how she's saved me tonight. She glows under the warmth of the streetlights.

"Where's your conference again? Berlin?" I ask. She averts her eyes. I knew something was up, and her manner gives it away. She's not a bad liar, like I was before I trained it out of me through poker. It's that she can't lie at all.

"It's not a conference," she replies finally. "I'm going on vacation. Maldives."

A kick of jealousy hits me at the mere mention of the place. She doesn't say any more. She's trying to protect me, and that comforts me somewhat.

"Are you going with anyone?" I pry anyway, fearing the worst.

"No, just myself. I want to see it before it disappears."

"You and I always talked about Maldives," I say. "For after."

At first, it was for after she finished grad school. Then it was for after I landed the job at C+P. Then, a respectable amount of time after Paolo's death. Then, after we got married. A series of afters that never came.

"Would have been nice," she says.

"Thanks again for all the help." I say after a long silence. "You didn't have to. I definitely didn't expect you to, given how things ended Tuesday night."

"That was just . . . overdue venting. Things that I should have screamed at you a year ago, if I hadn't been more tired than angry." She slows her pace to a full stop. "Paolo's death broke you, but that's not what broke us."

"I was scared."

"I knew that, and I know now that your fear was bigger. That it was about the drug, the biohacking."

"Would it have changed anything, if I told you all of it?"

"Maybe. I saw how horrible the nightmares were and how useless the therapy was," she replies. "I'd still have disagreed with your choices, but I might have understood better. You did what you felt was right for you. Too bad it required breaking my heart."

"If I could do it all over again—"

"I know. I wish you could."

We reach the subway stop too soon. The entrance chyron announces that her train is arriving in three minutes. What I want to say won't even fit in three hours. I want to tell her I'm sorry, over and over. I want to tell her all about the past year, what she's missed, what I wish I had shared with her. She looks into my eyes, and I desperately want to believe that she intuits all of it. I know she does not.

"I don't know if indulging you tonight has been healthy," she says. "But I want you to find the answers you're looking for. And I want you to take care of yourself, Jamie. Promise me you will."

"I will." For the little that my promises are worth, this time I mean it. She leans in for a hug, but my arms are frozen to my side. I take a deep breath, trying to etch her scent into my memory. She lets go and walks through the gate, turning for one last look before heading down the steps. I wave at her and then, knowing that it would be the last time that I do, I quietly say goodbye.

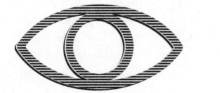 

31.

Thursday, 07/16/2043, 10:12 PM

Waves lap up on the edges of the limestone outcropping, slowly filling in a cluster of rock pools as the tide comes in. Dusk descends, and the beach cave behind me is empty, growing darker by the second. I shift into a crevasse in this pool, and warm water rises around my shoulders. My swimsuit snags on the rock. In the clear water, a school of small fish join me, coming in through unseen tunnels in the corals around my feet. One of them nibbles at my big toe. The lot swims away when I twitch.

I've spent most of the night here, and the exhaustion of the last couple of days has yet to dissipate. Everything has overlapped, reassembling into a blur. Kingsley and the vial, Veronica. Maxwell's arrest, my trips to the doctor and Three Police Plaza. Hannah. As if those weren't enough, two new threats have emerged: Tetro, who'd always posed a danger but more so now with his ideas of conspiracy; and Brenda Xu, who might be stalking me, or worse. On top of that, two of my best leads have turned out to be dead-ends. Cleo, and her connections to Dwyer; and Sid Thorpe, who scares off easier than I thought.

Learning why I returned to C+P Wednesday night was a much-needed win, though not enough to balance the account.

I shoot a message to Veronica. *Been a while. Everything alright with you and K?*

She replies instantly. *Yes. I got some good stuff from him.*

I sit up, fingers trembling in anticipation. *Like what?* If Veronica pulls through with Kingsley, then I'd have another lead to pursue, instead of considering the possibility that I have no other suspect but myself.

Stuff. I think he's about ready to talk. More later.

I can't be restful, not after that promise of another win, so I get to working again and pull up my log. The schedule appears across the bright, ReVRie-generated sky. I dismiss the Tropical Tidal Pool milieu, and my surroundings turn into an empty room of white, save for holographs of my timetable, my copious notes, and a list of visor files.

Here's what I've learned after meeting Hannah: at around 6 p.m. on the night Simon died, I left the C+P offices to go home. At 7 p.m., she came by my apartment, and by 7:41, I was at the storage unit.

This is around the time the encoding failure starts. Hard as I try, with all the records and conversations I've had about this period, I remember no details at all. A totally blank space in my mind.

At 7:49, while at the storage unit, I picked up the passport and then saw my fencing gear. Elliott had been meaning to borrow my swords, and I'd been putting off the hassle, but since I was there, I decided to grab them. I then placed a call to Elliott, presumably to talk to him about the epees. When Elliott didn't pick up, I probably took the strip bag and all the epees and brought the gear to the office, since it was en route to my apartment. Better than lugging them all the way home only to bring them to work the next day for the hand-off.

That's why I was at C+P after 8 p.m.

If things went as I think, then I must have dropped the bag off at Elliott's desk, then saw Simon in his office on my way out toward the elevators. As the surveillance video showed, I then entered Simon's office at about 8:30. Why I stopped by his office is still unknown, though from how it looked, my manner was casual. I probably wanted to check in on him for being there so late, maybe I'd wanted to say a quick goodbye. I then left at 8:48.

That's more probablys than I'm comfortable with, so I hit up Elliott on vidcall. He picks up on the first ring.

"Hey there. Quick question. You got my fencing gear?"

"Yeah, I did. You left the bag on my desk a few days ago. Didn't I thank you yet?"

"Nope. That's why I called Wednesday. That missed call on your phone? It was because I wanted to talk to you about the epees," I say, exasperated. "Ell, I've been wracking my brain over this, why didn't you tell me?"

He looks confused, worried. "Sorry, I thought I did. I guess I might've forgotten."

"This is what I was telling you about," I reply. "Have you been forgetting anything else?"

"Nah, I don't think this is anything." He's acting cool, but I'm not convinced. "I just forgot. It's been a wild couple of days."

"I don't know, man. What if Dr. Cassis is right, and Levantanil might have something to do with it? Maybe you should go see your doctor."

"Maybe," Elliott replies. "Did you find anything else about that researcher? The one that's gone missing."

I can't tell if he's now worried and interested, or if he's just deflecting. Either way, the answer's the same. "No. Still have no leads on why Dr. Slimane disappeared or where to. It's starting to feel like a dead end."

"Well, lemme know if there's a way I can help," he replies. "You know what this means, though? The reason you were at C+P that night had nothing to do with Simon at all. That's gotta be a relief to know, right?"

"Definitely."

No nefarious schemes, no secret meeting, no manipulation brought me to C+P that night. I wasn't there for Simon or because of Simon. I hadn't planned to be there at all. I was merely an accidental, incidental passerby to the man's final moments.

That leaves two open questions: what happened in that room for close to twenty minutes, and how I ended up with an identical empty vial of A-Pop. I still don't know where I'd get those answers, but after tonight, I know I'm getting closer.

Once I hang up on Elliott, I zoom in the list of my recordings, sorting them chronologically to do a full review. Another pass might reveal something. A missing detail, some new tidbit that I hadn't contextualized in the moment. As I browse the list of video files—every interaction I've had, every waking moment—dread overcomes me.

Is this the kind of life I have to look forward to? Will I have to get every experience on video?

I shudder at the thought of having to wear a visor at all times, of having my memory replaced by cloud storage, the act of remembering and reminiscing reduced to an upload/download process. And even then, even with perfect recall aided by recordings, I have to live with the loss of autonomy. The parts of my life I commit to the cloud will have to exist outside of me, in a chip within a server on a server farm out on a rig in the middle of the Pacific.

And what of the others who might end up like me? Will we all have to pay some tech giant for external storage space? I guess I shouldn't be surprised. We've already outsourced most of our brain functions either to other people or to devices. There was a time when people had to memorize nine-digit phone numbers, or write them out on paper at least. There was a time before online profiles, before video, before pictures, where all anybody had were stories. Words shared and transmitted to form a collective memory.

With each technological advance, we've chipped away at the need to remember. Levantanil is just the latest one, trading memory for time. I only wish I'd known the price before I had to pay it.

There's a lot of unanswered questions, and with them come branching possibilities. None of them seems to end well for me and the state of my memory. And Dr. Slimane, the only one who can answer them and possibly give me a bit of hope, is nowhere to be found.

Just before I press play on the first of the video files, a chime issues from my front door. My VR milieu pulls up the vid feed from the front door peep hole, but no one is there.

I exit the program and walk to the door. Lying on the floor right by the threshold is a folded note. I open the door but the hallway is empty. I unfold the slip of paper, which bears in black marker: *Roof, 30*.

The air is still, muggy. High above me, nearby towers seem to sparkle, their office windows still lit up in activity despite the hour. I move stealthily along the edge of the rooftop, finding my way past utility booths, elevator bulkheads, ventilation exhausts, around the makeshift greenhouse that the residents set up. I see through the glass that my own box of greenery has wilted in the neglect of the past week. My eyes take time to adjust, but when I see the figure in the overcoat, I instantly know.

"You told me to lose your number."

Sid Thorpe steps out of the shadows. She beckons for me to follow, leading me into a service shaft way. She seems tense, which heightens my unease, but also my interest. "We can't trust phones. Lochner owns three telecoms and half the internet."

"That explains the subterfuge, but why are you here?" I ask.

"Our last conversation was only getting good, until we were so rudely interrupted by your tail."

"You sure it wasn't yours?"

"If you're going to be in on this," she says, each word as taut as piano wire, "You'll have to learn how to sense whether you're being followed."

"If?" I ask pointedly, sensing her bravado.

"Well, you're no Simon."

The comment stings. "Look, if we're going to work together, we could at least start with some candor," I reply sharply. "I might not be as good as him, but as far as I can tell, you need me. That's why you're here. You can't take Lochner down while you're working covertly, and the best way to fuck him over is through C+P, the company he's been trying to acquire for a while."

She smiles. She's either impressed at my deduction or pleased at the delicious irony inherent in her plans. Maybe both. I continue. "And I can tell from last time that you'd want to do things Simon's way. Going to another news outlet won't do, not if you want to save his legacy."

"I was in C+P way before you ever stepped foot in that building, so I can see how you might forget," she replies, though not with any force, "but I worked there for years. I have other options."

"Oh, yeah?"

"Cleo Johnson, Sorensen, Oliveira . . . they're all still there, and they still pick up my calls."

"Yet *I'm* the one you called. So let's cut the crap and get to the meat of it."

"Fine," she relents. "I needed Simon, his cachet, and the backing of C+P. If what I have ever goes public, it needs to be from a trusted source. Otherwise, it gets buried, dismissed, debunked with lies upon lies."

"But now he's gone."

"And you're no substitute, but you'll do. More than enough." This last part she stresses, and I take it as an apology. "Like I said, I have contacts within C+P, so I'm familiar with your work, both on the record and off."

"What do you mean?" I ask.

"That Perrillo story from two years ago. Very ballsy. It's not every day that a reporter takes down his target and his company all in one shot."

"C+P got out of it alright," I reply, still chastised by the incident.

"You did what you had to do, consequences be damned. That's what I need. Simon might be gone, but you're as close to him as anyone can get."

Reminding me of one of my biggest mistakes and complimenting me with a comparison to Simon in the same breath? This woman's good at pushing buttons.

"Why don't you tell me what you need me for."

Sid clears her throat then inhales, as a diver prepares to take a plunge. "I work with the Lexell Collective. You've no doubt heard of them?"

"The think tank that runs those pricey leadership summits?" I ask, grasping at my recollection. The group made a splash a while back with its ten-grand-a-pop conferences for "global visionaries," whatever that meant. "What's that got to do with anything?"

"Lexell's an international network of thinkers," she says. "Researchers, academics, leaders in their own fields. Luminaries, but not the flashy ones that the public gets to see."

"And here I thought it was yet another money-laundering outfit for Eastern European kleptocrats."

"You're thinking of the Factor Ten Forum," Sid replies, not missing a beat.

"And how are you different exactly?"

"Our Collective does a lot more. Monumental, seismic change, the kind that operates better in the background, untainted by politics or public sentiment," she explains. "It's by design that the rest of the world thinks all we do are annual conferences and grant funding, if they've heard of us at all. It lets us hide in plain sight."

"So how are they connected to Simon?" I ask, my cynicism overcome by my intrigue.

"For the last couple of years, I've been trying to learn everything I can about Lochner and the Open Eyes Federation."

"You've been working undercover?"

"Yes. I do believe in the OEF and the help it gives to the Sleepless," she explains. "But let's be frank. It's also a brazen PR tool and a widely-accepted scam to avoid paying taxes, like every other billionaire-owned philanthropy. Which makes it a lot easier to do what I'm doing."

"Which is what exactly?"

"As you know, Sleepless supremacist groups have grown exponentially all over the world. They're not all the same, some are worse than others, like Exsomnis," Sid says. "One of my goals is to get solid proof of Lochner's connections to extremist groups. In the course of working for OEF, I discovered that he's been secretly funding Exsomnis through a slush fund he set up for offshore charitable donations."

Most everyone has discounted Exsomnis as loud but ineffectual troublemakers, provocateurs with no bite and no numbers. After all, their membership has been dwindling the last few years. If I hadn't paid close enough attention, I just as easily might have discounted them too. As it turns out, all their bluster about Sleepless ascendancy had something more behind it—the backing of a multibillionaire.

"You have proof of this?" I ask.

"Yes, but that's not the end of it," she replies. "It's not just Lochner. Exsomnis is everywhere in the Zephyrus group of companies. The top brass at OEF, all his holdings, they're all members. They can't afford to be 'out and proud' about it," she says mocking one of the group's battle cries, "but they all believe in their supremacy over non-Sleepless people."

"Is that when you went to Simon?"

"Not right away. Taking Lochner down was not my mission, not entirely. But when I found out that he was buying out C+P, I had to let Simon know. I couldn't let Lochner buy the company. Not when I know who he truly is."

"You've known that for a while, but you only told him a couple months ago?" I ask. Sid nods, chastened. Must be the look I'm giving her. We're four days away from the Board vote. "And why didn't he blow this wide open right when you told him?"

"He wanted to, but then I told him more."

"More than Lochner's ties to extremist hate groups?"

She cinches her coat more tightly around herself. "I'd also found out that Lochner, using money laundered through the OEF, had begun producing a pill. Artificial hyperinsomnia."

Surprise is hard to feign, and Sid stares at me, cocking her head. "Oh. So there are some things you know."

"I've suspected," I say, slowly planning my next words. "I didn't know about Lochner, but the rumors about illegal hyperinsomnia development have been going on for years. Biotech, military contractors, everyone's trying their hand at replicating it. Of course, no one's been able to. Yet."

"Are you Sleepless, Jamie?"

"Yes."

"Ah." She pauses to consider a question, but I bring her back on topic.

"So what did you find exactly?" I ask.

"I got a hold of someone from Lochner's R&D department. Someone I've put in touch with Simon."

"And this R&D guy—"

"—is telling me that it's done. They've cracked it. Perfect replication. What is it the Exsomnis call it? 'The Great Unsleeping.' In pill form."

"How good is this source?"

"Very. They made the pill themselves. They're calling it Levantanil."

Sid lets me digest the information, and all I feel is nausea. Who I'd become, who I'd made myself to be, is because of those people. Those hatemongers who viewed themselves as superior, and who had no trouble using violence to drive their point across. I'd gone to bed with those people, and I didn't even know it.

"Simon knew all of this?"

"Yes. He's even met my source himself. About a month ago, remotely through encrypted networks. Simon vetted them, and at the end of it, he was convinced that what they had was legit. He started to put the pieces together. The ties to Exsomnis, the international treaty violations . . . Lochner wouldn't survive the scandal, not to mention the criminal consequences. Simon was so excited, but then a few days later, the source went dark. I've been unable to contact them since."

"Fuck. Do you think they're dead?"

"No. This one's too valuable to kill off," Sid replies. "And Lochner's not done with them yet."

"How so?"

"The source developed Levantanil, but it hasn't been perfected. Yet. They didn't tell me any more than that, but they should be safe as long as Lochner and Exsomnis still need them."

Hell yeah it's not perfect. I've got holes in my memory proving that. I contain myself from sharing what I know; it won't help to have Sid doubt my abilities so soon after agreeing to work with me.

"If they're alive, where would they be?" I ask instead.

"Lochner's more likely to have them under close guard as a hostage-slash-indentured servant." Sid shakes her head. "I'm working on locating them, but it's taking some time."

"Meanwhile, we're four days away from the C+P buyout vote."

"Like I said, I'm working on it," she replies with evident frustration. "But the source is not the only piece of the puzzle. I need Simon's files. The source gave him data files when they met, so that Simon can verify their story. He's got the only copy, plus he'd have extensive notes, records of his conversation with the source."

"That's a no-go," I reply. "C+P's legal team pretty much seized everything Simon had at work. And even if I can get them, Simon heavily encrypted everything. By the time a halfway decent hacker breaks into his files, Lochner's probably done renaming C+P to Zephyrus News Network."

"Are you saying you can't help me?"

"Well, I might be able to give you something else." It might have been my eagerness to prove my worth, or my fear that she'd drop me before we've begun, but in that moment, I had to tell her. She's already trusted me with much, and now's the time to return the favor.

"I took Levantanil. A year ago."

"What are you talking about?" A hint of concern registers in her voice. "How?"

"It's out there," I reply. "Been so for a while. It's pricey, but it's moving. I can tell you what I know, and find out how Lochner's distributing it. His whole operation, at least here in New York. Might even be able to piece together how he's doing it in other places. I hear it's spread to Japan and South Africa."

It's her turn to be stunned, and it's gratifying to see the cracks in her composure. "We've been trying to find out their distribution networks here, but they know how to cover their tracks. How much do you know?"

"Enough. I know who to buy from, for starters. From there, it's only a matter of following a trail."

"Good. You need to get a clean line," she says. She gets a pen and a slip of paper from her coat pocket. "Here's how you can reach me, and *only* through a first-gen encrypted burner, all right? Find out what you can, and get back to me ASAP. You think you can do that?"

"Absolutely."

"Meanwhile, I'll keep looking for my missing source." She turns to leave. "Wait a half hour, then take the service stairwell down. Not the elevator."

"Hold on," I call out after her. "You haven't told me your mission with this collective. Why did they need you to follow Exsomnis?"

"The Lexell Collective isn't interested in that," she replies. "Not in itself. Exsomnis and the OEF . . . those are just leads."

"Toward what?"

"The Collective aims to avoid global catastrophes. Extreme weather patterns, economic and ecological collapse, political uprisings, worldwide pandemics, threats to the human race. Sleeplessness is not at the same level as these, at least not yet," she explains. "But it will be, if someone forces an abrupt and seismic change."

"Which is what Lochner's doing with Levantanil," I reply.

"And without any understanding of the wider consequences. We've learned much about Sleeplessness in the last ten years, but there is so much more that we still don't know," she says. "We need more science, more infrastructure, more resources to ensure that humanity can continue to cope with our new reality. Most of all, we can't allow Lochner to dictate the terms of how we live in a Sleepless world."

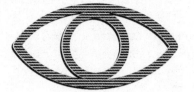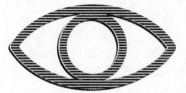

32.

The funeral for Simon Parrish is at a Hindu temple out in Secaucus, New Jersey, in a ceremony closed to the general public. The guests, all in white, gleamed in the afternoon sun streaming in through narrow vertical windows. Most of the guests are from C+P Media. Some are celebrities within their own circles: media magnates, bestselling authors, fashion editors. Simon would have been surprised at the number of people in attendance. On some level he might have been insulted: it's apparent a lot of them came to network.

After going through a rigorous security check (eye scans at a funeral, really?), I pass through a pavilion lined with ornate stone pillars. At the end of the long central aisle, Simon is lain in an open casket. In his white linen tunic, garlanded with yellow and orange mums, he has never looked more at peace.

I scan the crowd as I take my seat in one of the back pews. It's a full house, and the overwhelming show of sympathy might coax a tear from one's eye. Me, all I'm thinking is that somewhere in this temple is the person who killed Simon. Friends, family, enemies. Everyone who had access to Simon, and everyone who could have gotten close enough to me to plant the vial. They are all here. I should get to work. I put on my visor, slide my earcuff in place, and start recording.

Simon's wife Rita and their two teenagers are hard to miss in the front row. I make a mental note to quickly talk to her at the end of the service. The cremation follows right after, and Rita will likely not receive anyone afterward.

I spot Maxwell Cartwright in the second row, shoulders hunched, next to his wife and daughter. I expected him not to show his face in public, but C+P security has done a good job of driving other press away. If he's been invited here, then the family must have made the almost impossible choice of viewing Simon's death as a suicide. We're all going to have to pretend that Maxwell isn't a suspect, that there is no murder case being built against him.

Simon killed himself. That's what we're telling ourselves today.

Beside Maxwell are the remaining members of the C+P Board of Directors, in a rare appearance outside the boardroom as a complete set. In the row behind them is the entire C+P news staff: Cleo, Elliott, our army of news anchors. The *Rise and Shine* team, the *Goldin Hour* team, the post-production and editing staff, assistants, fact checkers, and interns. The lawyers too, a few of whom are outside counsel from Strathairn-Shaw. To my relief, Brenda Xu is nowhere in sight.

Unsurprisingly, the higher-ups from Zephyrus are here as well. Rafe Lochner and his team have taken an entire row for themselves.

The program begins. Prayers are uttered and eulogies delivered. Recurring themes emerge from the speeches, a parade of platitudes: Simon Parrish was a great man. Too great, that his reasons might seem unfathomable, but that it's not for us who are left behind to make sense of it. That sometimes it's those we least expect. That everyone tries to seem strong on the surface, but we don't know what demons lie beneath. That we don't need to know, or even understand. All we need to do is honor his life through our own. I've heard it all before.

Thankfully the service is quick, and soon enough the casket is escorted out a side exit. As the mourners are ushered through the temple's front doors, I keep my eye on Rita, who has stayed behind to talk to some people. Extended family, judging from their features and their garb. I slowly make my way closer, toward the front of the temple. Before I can muster enough courage for the approach, someone taps me on my shoulder.

I spin around and find Simon's son Rocky towering over me.

"My condolences," I say, caught completely off-guard. "I . . . have been meaning to find a moment with your mother. You know, to extend my sympathies."

He has his head cocked to one side, a posture reminiscent of his father. One can already see that, even at thirteen, he would grow up to look exactly like his father. He too had that thick mop of hair, the bushy brows, the incisive gray eyes. He doesn't say anything, and I notice his eyes are teary and bloodshot. He could hardly hold himself upright.

"I worked for your dad, and he taught me a lot," I continue. "He was a great man. I'm so sorry for your loss."

"Great? Yeah, whatever," Rocky replies, drawling. "He was a shit father who never cared about us. All he cared about was his fucking job and his fucking awards and his fucking face being all over the fucking news." He stammers through the rant, and that's when I realize how high he is. He stumbles as he takes a step to walk past me. I look around for help and see Rita pacing toward us.

"Thank you for coming, Jamie," she says, taking her son by the shoulders. "Rakesh, could you ride with your sister and aunties, please? I'll follow shortly."

"The service was beautiful," I tell her. I feel compelled to say more, maybe offer some encouragement or ask how she's doing, but our rapport had always been contained within the bounds of niceties. We've only had a handful of conversations at C+P events, and always with Simon around.

"It was a lovely service, wasn't it?" she says. "And I thought it would never happen. It took a lot to convince the pujari to hold a public ceremony, given how he . . . died."

"Simon would have liked how it turned out." As soon as I say it, I know it to be a misstep. I feel like everything I could say to a grieving person would be the wrong thing.

"I seriously doubt that. He isn't very observant," she says. "He'd appreciate everyone coming though, especially his team. He spoke highly of all of you."

"C+P won't be the same without him."

"For better or worse."

She is beckoned away by one of the Indian aunties, who says their car is ready to leave for the crematorium. I repeat my condolences, and we say our goodbyes. As she leaves, I am struck by how Rita doesn't seem to be in deep mourning. She doesn't spout off the usual pablum that one in her position typically says, and her words definitely have a tinge of bitterness, not unlike her son's. Grieving looks different for everyone, I know, but the way they spoke of Simon is at least a sobering reminder of how his passion for work ruined his personal life. Something that I acutely, unfortunately, understand.

As I walk out of the temple, small groups are still huddled about in the lobby. I program a robocab pickup and wait on the front steps. In the distance, across the street and past the carports, a looming figure eyes the crowd. The sharkskin suit, the dark visor, the stone-cold visage. Detective Nathan Tetro is here, and he is watching me.

❁

I march toward the detective with a mix of thrill and trepidation. He remains motionless, looking past me. His attention is fixed at the thinning crowd of guests.

"Are you following me?" I ask, surprising myself with a directness that I didn't think I could have used with him.

Tetro inhales as though readying himself for a denial. Instead he turns back to the crowd. I can see through the corner of his NYPD visor that his scanners and layers are on. "I wanted to go in and pay my respects, but I'm wearing the wrong thing."

True, his all-black outfit would have made him stand out. I myself might have worn black if a C+P memo hadn't announced the culturally appropriate dress code. In any case, Tetro wouldn't have been admitted by the security detail anyway.

He's eyeing the crowd keenly as they exit the temple, not observing any one person in particular. The exodus of mourners finally slows to a few stragglers, temple ushers and elderly members of the Parrish clan. Then, the detective turns to face me.

"Can I help you, Mr. Vega?"

"Have you been following me?" I ask again. "This is starting to feel like harassment, you know."

"No idea what you're talking about," he says, scoffing. "And besides, you're the one who came over here. I'm standing here minding my own business."

Truth is, I'd been raring to have a chance to talk to Tetro since last night. Now that I've smoothed out the timeline of Wednesday night, things are falling into place. I just need one last detail, one that will finally answer the question of who killed Simon, and Tetro's my best chance at getting it.

"Your business happens to involve me," I say. "Or am I no longer a suspect?"

"That depends," he replies. "You gonna tell me what you and Simon talked about that night?"

"I've already told you, I don't remember. But I do know something else now."

This grabs his attention. "Keep talking."

"I'd forgotten why I went back to the C+P offices Wednesday night, but I've figured it out," I begin to explain. "I went back to drop off some fencing gear for my coworker, Elliott. He wanted to borrow them, and I swung by the office after I picked them up from my storage unit. Anyway, I went in, left the bag on Elliott's desk, then headed out. As I was leaving, I noticed Simon in his office, so I popped in to say hey."

Tetro absorbs this pensively, like he doesn't know what to think, but he's not satisfied. "Elliott will back me up. You can ask him," I add.

"I don't have to. You managed to miss the C+P cameras but the street-level ones saw you come into the building with a bag, and then saw you leave without one. Been wondering what that was, actually." Tetro chuckles.

"That ought to buy me some of your trust," I say. "If not a couple of answers. Off the record." That last part doesn't usually work, but at least it might mask my intentions.

"I don't think you understand your position here. You're in no place to be demanding trades."

"How about if I tell you what Simon was working on before he died?"

I'd been weighing this since last night, trying to find what I can give Tetro so that he'll get off my back, or at least give me some information. Explaining my presence in the building wouldn't have been enough. I knew that. I had to give more to get more.

Tetro crosses his arms, appearing uninterested. He stifles a yawn. He's performing too much, so I know I have him hooked.

"But first, you have to give me something," I say. "What did Maxwell Cartwright say? About that night."

"Denies doing anything," Tetro replies. "He said Simon was in good spirits when he left, and admitted to bringing the wine to Simon's office. Also said he never saw you. Now if what I'm thinking is right, then of course Maxwell would say he didn't see you. That's what partners do. Protect each other."

So he does think I'm a suspect, and that Maxwell and I have teamed up somehow. This disappoints me, but not as much as his answer does. "C'mon, Detective. You already told me about the wine when you brought me into headquarters. You've given me nothing."

Tetro takes a breath and smiles in submission. "Cartwright says he didn't kill Simon, claims he had no reason to, because he was certain he had the votes for the Zephyrus deal. According to him, that was actually why he came over to Simon's office. Simon asked him to come, so that he could concede gracefully and congratulate Cartwright. They had a couple of drinks, then Cartwright left."

He recounts all of this with the sharp edge of a skeptic. As for me, my mind is racing to process all this information, and fatigue is beginning to set in. Processing Simon's death and tying every thread together is taking up a lot of energy. One thing is clear though: Maxwell has been consistent with every other prior statement he's given.

"None of this explains your part in all of it," the detective continues. "You wanna tell me more about that?"

"What part? I saw Simon at work that night, found him the next morning," I say defensively. "That's it."

"So you keep saying," he replies. Neither of us has given up anything that the other didn't already know, but at least that dance is out of the way. He's primed to talk. He steps closer, looms over me with a rapacious look on his face.

"Your turn—what was Simon working on before he died?"

Pursuing the Dwyer story was a major setback. I'm lucky Cleo didn't throw me out of the building, but I wasted a lot of time spinning my wheels with nothing to show for it, not to mention the piles of money I paid Noor to infiltrate C+P and do a deep dive on Cleo. It's not a total loss though. It's given me a way to get Tetro off my back, and get more intel in exchange.

I point at the corner of my eye and Tetro willingly stows away his visor.

"Simon was investigating a US senator who took secret donations from homegrown extremist hate groups. Mason Dwyer, Minnesota Republican. You might have seen him in the news?"

There. A shiny thing to distract the detective from looking at me. That should give him new questions, new leads, new suspects to interrogate and tail. I name more names and spill the details of the Dwyer story, give him a rough timeline and possible starting points for his new quest.

Because I'm not a complete monster, bile begins to rise from my gut. I begin to feel sick. Dirty. Not dirty enough to stop me from violating journalistic ethics, but at least enough to recognize that I've crossed a pretty big line. But the detective's listening intently, and I can tell from his too-practiced poker face that my payoff's coming. That makes it all worth it.

When I finish, Tetro doesn't say a word. Already his mind is elsewhere, planning his next moves. I let him sit with it. He can go down this rabbit hole; I know he won't find anything at the end of it. Does he think I'm leading him down the wrong path? Maybe. But specificity makes the lie, and I've given him too many details that would be impossible to ignore.

"So what do you think?" I ask, after a long pause.

"You did good."

"I say I did more than good. So how about giving me a little bit more?"

He chuckles wryly, amused at my gumption. "Fine. You get one more question."

"A question and a followup," I counter. He shrugs in agreement. He already got what he wanted. Now it's time for me to get the final piece of this puzzle.

"What exactly did Briana Foley tell you about the Board vote?""

✺

The walk back to the carport feels shorter with the thoughts racing through my mind. Tetro has brought me closer to unraveling what happened that night, and I am buzzing with anxiety. As I wait for the robocab I ordered, someone appears before me from behind an elm tree. The person takes on a military stance, legs apart and hands back, imposing yet somehow solicitous. Their slicked-back hair draws a sharp contrast with their white linen suit, cut in epicene proportions.

"Mr. Vega," they say. "I work for Rafe Lochner. He would like to have a word."

They're too rigid compared to the rest of Lochner's publicity staff, and too lithe to be part of his security detail. Their build is more like a dancer, and every line of their suit draws the eye up and down the length of their tall frame. There is a delicate edge to them, like a rough uncut diamond. Before I could ask for their name, their hand weighs on my shoulder, steering me with a strength that defies my expectation.

They escort me toward the now-deserted parking lot behind the temple, where a platinum Maybach is idling. The rear passenger door slides open, and the hand guides me inside with a firm shove.

"Hello, Jamie."

Lochner's hair forms a flaming halo as sunlight streams in through frosted windows. He has eschewed his suit jacket and is down to a pinstripe vest and shirt, crisp and creamy white. I become aware of how disheveled my clothes must appear, how sweat has permeated my jacket from standing unshaded on the sidewalk.

"Decha was gentle, I'm sure?" he says. "I hope you don't mind the subterfuge."

"What is this about?" The back of the car is roomy, but I can't help but inch toward the door.

"I wanted a do-over of our first meeting," he starts. "You must admit, it was under less-than-ideal circumstances. I wanted an opportunity to talk to you without so many other people around."

"You have an odd way of going about this," I reply. He leans forward and crosses his legs, brushing against mine. "What is it you'd like to talk about?"

"The NYPD hasn't been forthcoming about their investigation into Maxwell, and seeing the detective talking to you just now, well . . . this interests me. The C+P Board is voting on the acquisition in three days. We're at a very critical juncture."

"Last we talked, you seemed sure the offer was going to be accepted," I reply.

"I still am. I've dealt with setbacks like this before. Nothing quite as salacious, of course, but I'm confident we'll prevail."

"Doesn't the murder investigation complicate the Zephyrus side of things?" I ask. "One of our founders is dead, killed by the other, right at C+P headquarters. Your Board must be ready to pull out of the deal."

"Acquiring a company in such a state of upheaval might not sit well with the more risk-averse of my Board," he says. "But they will submit to me. They always do."

"The public isn't going wild over the deal either," I say, "With you ramming it through during a murder investigation. It's a bit mercenary."

"True, but soon enough, I hope never to worry about the public's perception again."

If there ever was any doubt that Lochner aims to convert C+P into his personal PR firm, he's certainly dispelled it. "Your portfolio's massive enough as it is. You have a couple of media conglomerates already. Why do you need C+P?" I ask.

"As with most things about me, this has never been a matter of *need.*"

He averts his gaze from me, onto the temple grounds outside the window. I fidget in my seat, wrestling with the impulse to leave and the itch to get more out of him.

"When I started out, the family owned all the major shipping lanes," he continues. "The English Channel, Malacca, all of the new Arctic Circle lanes. Seventy percent of international trade passed through our routes. Aviation was the next natural offshoot. When energy became a big problem for us, I took us into solar and renewables. Now our fleets are fully carbon-neutral, and so are the vessels passing through our lanes."

Lochner draws a deep breath, satisfied. "We've become the engine of the world. Fuel and roads. We make things run."

"But that wasn't enough."

"Of course not, especially not after I became Sleepless." He pauses and gives me that knowing look shared by people like us. "The world was upended by the pandemic. When people started getting hurt and killed, I knew I had to do something. That's why I set up the Open Eyes Federation. I wanted to help the Sleepless on a global scale."

"You wanted the fame, the good PR. The tax breaks."

He doesn't issue a denial. "I harnessed that influence and those resources to improve our plight. Through the OEF's efforts, we've largely eliminated sleep-status discrimination all over the world. We're also the major funder of hyperinsomnia-related medical research."

I guess that's one way of describing what he's done with Levantanil. I'm hardly able to contain my resentment.

"This is all well and good, Rafe," I say. "But what does this have to do with C+P?"

"You asked me about my interest in your company, and in telling you about all the good that I've done, I'm hoping you might see that I've more left to do. Maybe then you'll clearly see what's coming ahead."

"And what's that? Digital media domination? Big data?"

"What's ahead is infinity."

He edges closer to me, eager, charging the air with his excitement. "You see, Jamie, one desire leads to the next. And then the next, and the next. Fulfilling one only spawns the desire for more. Desire is exponential. Desire is a hydra."

The man's craving is insatiable, eager to consume everything in its path. It looms, and the back of this car, formerly cavernous, now feels oppressive with its presence.

"Now tell me, Jamie. What was it that the good detective spoke to you about?"

If there's one thing I know about desire, it's that it reveals a weakness. Him wanting to know what the detective seeks, that's a weakness. Him openly asking me for it, is a larger one. He's not as confident as he wants to appear. He fears that there are vulnerabilities in his plans. For once, when it comes to Lochner, I feel that I have the upper hand.

I tell him the basics of Maxwell's statement to the police. Lochner is not as smooth as he thinks he is, but I see no harm in giving him a taste. Most of the details are ones he already knows, or could easily learn through his lawyers and associates. Still, he is riveted by my every word.

"For what it's worth, I don't think Maxwell killed Simon," Lochner says when I finish.

"It's not worth a lot, seeing as you're his friend."

"That doesn't mean I'm wrong. Murdering Simon imperils the acquisition, and Maxwell would never have done anything to prevent it from happening."

"Put another way, Maxwell would do anything to make sure it does."

"Then that's the question, isn't it?" Lochner smirks as though we were merely discussing office gossip. "Is Simon's death more or less likely to prevent the deal?"

"You said it yourself—nothing is going to stop Zephyrus," I reply. "Your board will submit to you and that deal will be inked. Simon's murder isn't going to affect the vote either way. For all your apparent concern with Maxwell, I don't think his arrest or conviction matters either. All that matters is your greed."

The man doesn't tolerate the faintest hint of aggression, and his expression sours. He leans back, but not as a retreat. More of an open-armed challenge. Daring me to come at him.

"Thank you, Jamie. I appreciate your candor. Now, in the interest of fairness, maybe you'd like to ask me something in exchange?"

I've gotten all I needed from this man. His plans for our company, his willingness to go all the way, his confidence in the board

276 | VICTOR MANIBO

votes, and his qualms about the murder investigation. The only
thing left is to leave.

"I got nothing."

"Are you sure?" he asks. "Come now, I'd prefer you ask me directly, rather than having to go through my underlings."

A crooked smile slices through his face. He knows about Sid
Thorpe. He's the one who's been watching me. He's onto us, and
he's not afraid to let me know it. I'll have to deal with this quick, but
for now I decide to ignore the bait.

"No idea what you mean," I reply. "But if I ever do need something from you, it's good to know I have access."

"Certainly," Lochner says. "Especially now that you're about to
become a part of my staff."

"Let's see what the C+P Board has to say about that."

With that, I slide the door open without ceremony, somewhat
surprised that he hasn't locked me in. Surprised too that his guard
dog is nowhere in sight. The Maybach thrums behind me then drives away, leaving me standing in the sweltering hot afternoon.

As soon as the car's made its turn, I take my earcuff out from my
shirt pocket. With a bit of prestidigitation, I got to start recording
before Decha got me into the car. I only hope it picked up some audio through my clothing.

I press play and . . . nothing. Not even static. The cuff's totally
dead, no power at all. I reconnect it with my visor, but it's also been
bricked. Damn it. Targeted EMP field, if I had to guess. Of course
Lochner took precautions. I kick the pavement in frustration, and
do it again when I realize I'm stuck in the middle of Jersey with no
ride. How am I gonna get back to the city now?

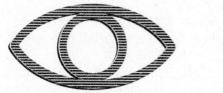 

33.

"That took forever." Legs propped up on my coffee table, Veronica flips through a movie menu on my vid screen. I'm at once relieved that she's still here, and embarrassed that I'd kept her waiting. "Is there a reason you're not picking up my calls?"

I shake my head wearily and plop down on the couch beside her. "I'd rather spare you the details. Short answer—I got hit with an EMP and my devices are bricked. Had to walk a half mile to find a phone to pick up a robocab." I fling my visor and earcuff on the table.

"Yikes. You have a guy for that?" she asks, pointing to the devices.

I nod.

"Good."

"Speaking of forever . . ."

"Yeah, I know, I've been busy, all right?" she replies, half-apologetic, half-*I'm the one doing you a favor here.* She slides her visor onto my face, and gets ready to sync it up with my vid screen for herself. "It's not exactly easy getting a guy like Kingsley to open up."

"Tell me again how you did this?" I ask as my eyes adjust to the view.

"I can get away with a lot of things when someone's distracted." She winks at me through the visor. "Turn your brightness down; this starts outdoors."

I nod my assent, and she starts playing. Slowly the view around me illuminates. It's high noon, and I am sitting on a park bench, staring into the slate gray eyes of Kingsley Smith. He is wiping his brow, sweat slicking up his buzzed head. As usual, he is overdressed in his coat.

"We could move somewhere cooler," says Veronica's voice in my ear. The immersion is so total that I feel the words coming out of my own mouth.

Kingsley shakes his head. "I'll acclimate. Just that I don't go out in the day much."

"Are you Sleepless?" Veronica asks casually. He shakes his head again. "I am, though I'm also not a day person. Not usually. But a girl's gotta hustle."

"Tell me more, hustler." Kingsley gives me a sly smile.

"How much clumsy flirting do I have to endure?" I ask Veronica, pausing playback.

"Oh, shut up. He's hot, okay?" She pipes in, and for a second she overlaps with her own voice. She has started telling Kingsley about her two jobs and various side gigs, freelance work, that sort of stuff. She shares this in her usual breezy way, and I can tell from her voice that she isn't feigning interest. Neither is Kingsley. His eyes are locked on hers, on mine, and it unsettles me.

I flick my hands and scrub the recording forward. Veronica protests, but lets me do it anyway. She tells me to stop at a certain point, and I resume normal playback.

"That was nothing," Kingsley scoffs. "I've dealt with a lot worse in my line of work."

"Jamie said you were really pissed," she replies.

"In the moment, yeah. The guy was being annoying, so I took care of it. I'm past it now though. I hope he wasn't too hurt," he says. Veronica chuckles in real-time and I feel a sharp kick of shame.

"All right, can we fast forward?" I ask.

"As you wish," she says, wresting playback control from me. My field goes dark for a few seconds before illuminating back on. I'm again looking at Kingsley's sweaty pate, but this time it is a wide-angle shot. Steady too, from a stationary probe. He is half-naked, lying on his side on Veronica's bed. His XFrame rig outlines his arms and shoulders, and forms a tight scaffold around his chest. A thin blanket covers him from the waist down, but just barely.

"Aw, come on," I complain. "Do I really need to see this?"

"Nice view, yes?" she replies. "Don't worry, I skipped over the good parts."

"Vee, seriously though. What about Torian? Is she cool with this?"

"No. But I'll handle it," she says, then shushes me. "Just keep watching."

Veronica's hand is running over Kingsley's XFrame, tracing the curves of the lightweight metal, avoiding contact with his skin. Kingsley has a melancholy smile on his face.

"The exo-suit was supposed to be some sort of employee reward," he says as he stares up at the ceiling. "From Avalon. I was there for five years, working my way up from product runner to head warehouser. Online retailers get a bad rap, but Avalon's not as shitty as the rest of them. I got a generous benefits package, and the pay was all right. The work was still backbreaking though, and there were entire shifts when I had to work through the pain because I needed to meet my shipment quotas.

"Avalon noticed that too many of the warehousers either quit or go on forced leave for 'medical reasons,' which the company had to pay for. Worse, some of them sued the company for their injuries and whatnot. They crunched the numbers, and even with all those expenses, it was still cheaper to hire humans than to fully automate their warehouses all over the world. So Avalon bought out the company that makes XFrames and then developed their own exosuits specifically for the upper-level warehouse folk. Some of us were skeptical, but Avalon said that we'd get to keep the exosuits even if we end up leaving the company. That made us sign on to be their test subjects. They also agreed to pay for installation, maintenance and upgrades—for life. Sounds like a good deal, right?"

Veronica shifts in place and withdraws her hand. She rests her head on her arm, rapt in attention.

"Back then I wasn't even doing a lot of heavy lifting anymore. The job was mostly up to the drones and assembler bots. But the machines still needed wrangling, and there were a lot of accidents. Drones dropping crates, autocarts colliding with one another. It was like herding animals. Lightning-fast, solid steel beasts that could crush you to death.

"I was one of the first to get the suit. After Avalon got the all-clear from the FCC, the CSPC, and whatever agency they needed to get permits from, their doctors examined me. They made sure the installation and linkup would be seamless. And it was, for a time.

"When I first got control of the XFrame, I felt like a superhero. Do you know I can flip a car over? I did it once, too. Story for another time. Anyway, about six months in, my body started rejecting the suit. The pain penetrated my muscles, went right to the bone. Eventually I got paralyzed. Went into a coma for about a week. By that time, the entire East Coast warehouse crew had been outfitted with the exo-suits. I found out later that all of them went through rejection too."

"How horrible," Veronica replies, resting her head on his chest.

"Avalon footed the hospital bill and gave us all a new upgrade. But their health plan didn't cover gene therapy, which was really what we needed to stop the pain completely. They offered to cover the extraction surgery instead, but since they were automating all their crews, extraction meant termination. Can't work in an Avalon warehouse if you don't have an XFrame.

"I couldn't lose the job, and I couldn't afford the meds. Not the ones Avalon's doctors scripped. So I found alternative meds. Worked like a charm, and a lot cheaper too. Soon enough, I started sharing it with the rest of the crew."

"And that's how you started dealing?"

"Not at first. I wasn't charging them. I couldn't bear the guilt, you know? These folks wouldn't be in this situation if I hadn't given them my word. Soon enough, my suppliers took notice of me. They saw the XFrame, needed some muscle. That's how I got my start."

"The man likes to talk," I say as I pause playback.

"I have a way of making him talk," she corrects me.

"Please tell me there's more."

"I did you one better—I set up a meet. You're welcome."

Friday, 07/17/2043, 08:04 PM

We had to take the subway all the way out to Brownsville, because a robocab would have been too conspicuous. Where we're headed, folks walk. Don't even take the bus. I thought Veronica was kidding when she showed me on the map, but I understand when we get there. The block we're on is particularly rough. Condemned brownstones one right after the other. At the end of the block stands a dilapidated four-story motel. The neon light out front is dead, and the lobby is pitch black.

Kingsley meets us by the doorway and wordlessly leads us up a narrow staircase, stained and sticky with various human fluids. The air smells of sweat and piss. When we reach the top floor, he ushers us into a room that contain only a ratty mattress and two wireframe chairs.

"The things I do for you," Veronica whispers in my ear.

"Sorry, babe. We needed to be out of the way for this," Kingsley says, overhearing her. He draws the curtain but leaves a gap open to look down onto the sidewalk with his visor. I do the same. A couple of runners are chilling under the corner streetlight. "Plus, I got some business here."

"And here I thought this was a purely social call," I reply.

"I don't do 'social calls.' Don't expect you'd want one anyhow seeing how the last one went down."

"All right, boys, take it easy." Veronica places a hand on his shoulder, and he unclenches.

"Look, I do appreciate you meeting with me," I tell Kingsley in appeasement. "I just have a few questions. It's about Levantanil."

He doesn't react, and I can see the gears turning in his head. "I thought this was about A-Pop?" Veronica asks me.

"Yes, A-Pop is Simon's cause of death, but that's not important right now," I explain. A look passes between Kingsley and me, and he instantly gets it. Veronica doesn't know about me and Levantanil. I only hope that despite our scuffle, he's still willing to adhere to his code of secrecy.

"At this point, I know all I need to know about A-Pop," I continue. "However it ended up in his system is not on you, Kingsley, so you don't have to worry about that."

"A nosy reporter asks me about an OD, and you better believe I'll walk the other way," he replies. "Everything always gets pinned to the dealer. A tainted batch, a deal gone bad, whatever. And if you're a Black man, it doesn't take a whole lot more than a connection, especially if the dead guy is rich and famous."

"I totally get that, and I'm sorry for hassling you the way I did. I should have used a lighter touch," I say, giving Veronica a knowing look. "Anyway, what I really need to know about is Levantanil. Before my boss died, he was working on a huge story about it. I think it's related to why he was murdered."

"What's it got to do with you?" he asks.

"Simon wasn't just my boss. He was like a father to me. He taught me everything I know." Including lying through my teeth, and knowing how to play a source. My eyes begin to well up, and Kingsley looks affected.

"Fine. What do you wanna know?" he asks.

"Everything. Start from the beginning."

Kingsley glances at Veronica. She nods, assuring him on my behalf. He glances at the window instinctively. I turn to where he's looking, and my visor's giving me the all-clear.

"Got my start when one of the Genomage guys approached me," he says. "Those nerds were wild about the XFrame technology. They wanted to see what they could do with it, make one of their own. So this guy came to me saying he knows I was going through rejection. He said his group can hook me up with narcotics to help with the pain. In exchange, I had to let them tinker with me and the suit. Seemed like a fair trade."

"I thought they were just a bunch of biopunk weirdos," Veronica says. "I didn't know they dealt."

"They do all sorts of shit. Biohacking, of course, but also gene editing, brain implants, hybrid organs, life extension . . . most of all, mind-altering drugs. And they're not just doing it for kicks either. They got a network, they got money, they got an entire operation. Party drugs are big business. And of course, now they have Lev."

"Is Zephyrus behind all this?" I ask. "Or Exsomnis?"

"I don't know what Zephyr—is," he replies, after the initial surprise. "But they're all part of Exsomnis."

"Holy fuck," Veronica says. "You know Exsomnis is a terrorist group, right?"

"Terrorists, psh. They're bigoted assholes, for sure," Kingsley replies. "I don't like them, but that won't stop me from taking their money. They're protective of their business though. They don't play around."

"You don't seem too worried."

"That's 'cause I ain't told you shit. Nothing that a bunch of other folk don't already know anyway. That's the problem with y'all in your high-end jobs in your shiny skyscrapers," he says, drawing out his words in mockery. "You're so busy, you miss out on shit that's been going on on the street level."

"They're playing with very dangerous science," I say. "They're replicating the most effective pathogen since the Black Death. That never bothered you?"

"Sleeplessness ain't killed anyone. As far as I can tell, they're seizing an opportunity," Kingsley replies. "Everyone wants to be Sleepless, but you can't just catch it, so they created, what do you call it . . . a workaround."

As much as my frustration wants me to, I have to set this debate aside. Kingsley is getting antsy, keeps eyeing the corner of his visor, or out the windows.

"How does the whole operation work?" I ask. "How do they make and distribute Levantanil?"

"Exsomnis is the top of the chain. They run all the other parts," he explains, gesticulating to drive his point across. "Below them is the Genomage crew. That's their mad scientist group. Half-science lab, half-drug ring. Also below them is the OEF. That's the bank, how they get money and how they launder money. They got the same structure and same M.O. in every major city they're at."

"Which cities?"

Kingsley lists off every major metro area up and down the coasts.

"Simon was talking to someone on the inside," I continue. "Someone who works directly in making Lev. Do you have any idea who that might be?"

"Nah, like I said, I'm low on the food chain. My contacts are all local. Distribution. Whoever you're looking for is out there in their head lab, overseas."

"Johannesburg," I say, to Kingsley's surprise.

"Not anymore. They moved," he replies. "And it slowed down the whole damn supply chain. Do you know how much I've lost this month?"

"Moved when? And where?"

"About a month ago."

Around the time Sid and Simon lost contact with their source. "Do you know where?"

"Morocco."

Sid needs to know all this. That's where the missing source is going to be, and if she and her Swedish collective are gonna take the whole operation down, they need to know where the labs are.

"You know, you could've saved yourself a lot of trouble," Kingsley adds. "You could've just asked your friend all about this Lev business."

"My friend?"

"Elliott. He's the one who recruited me."

My blood runs cold at the mention of his name. Veronica looks at me, alarmed. Before I could ask any more, Kingsley shoots up from his seat and dashes to the door.

"Shit. Someone's watching."

He bounds down the hall onto the rickety fire exit ladder, and I run after him, Veronica right behind me. My visor picks up a figure from the sidewalk, wearing dark pants and a dark hoodie. Full visor gleaming in the faint streetlight. Kingsley chases after them, the ladder rattling and clanging from his weight.

I make my way down, tracking the figure as it runs down the street. I try and catch up to them, but I'm well behind Kingsley. He's still in hot pursuit, but his quarry's got a large lead, and he can't gain on them. I can't gain on either of them.

The figure makes a right at the corner, and as it does I catch a glimpse of her face. I've only met her once, but that chin, those high cheekbones are unmistakable. She turns and runs down another street, disappearing into a row of derelict flophouses. From afar I see Kingsley slow down, defeated.

"Fuck! I hate when that happens."

"Don't worry, you're not in trouble," I reply, panting as I run up to him. "Her name's Brenda. She was here for me."

34.

A line slowly builds by the security entrance to the US Naval Observatory. Out-of-towners and astronomy nerds wait as each of them are eye-scanned, wand-waved and turnstiled through to the lobby. Most of them make a beeline toward the deep-sky telescope building, eager to skip the tours of the horological gizmos.

"Who's ready to go to see an eclipse?" an educator type excitedly asks a cohort of teenagers. I stalk right by the coat check with my visor pointed toward the glass entry gates.

A green outline alerts me to her arrival. Sid Thorpe breezes past security right on schedule. She spots me right away, undistracted by the mass of people milling about. She catches my eye as she hangs left toward a corridor that leads to a small exhibit room full of antique astronomical equipment.

"I'm not particularly fond of gears and cogs and such," she says evenly, standing before a medieval telescope. "Still, you picked the right place. Security scans, lots of interference, a crowd to get lost in. Extra credit for picking a military installation. They have the best blockers around." She slinks across the room toward an atomic clock, a relic of the first space age.

"I only hope it's enough," I reply, looking as casual as I can. "Lochner's been following us. One of us at least. He told me at the funeral, in not so many words."

I have another tail following me too, but it's best not to worry Sid right now. And if I'm being honest, it's also better for me not to worry about Brenda either. There are more pressing matters, such as Exsomnis and Elliott.

"How was the service?" she asks. "I'm sure it was quite tasteful, knowing how Rita is."

"That doesn't matter. What do we do about Lochner?"

She gives me the once-over. "He's just covering his bases. No harm will come to you."

"And you? Aren't you worried that your cover's blown?"

"If it were, then I wouldn't be standing here in front of you." She continues her circuit of the gallery, stringing me along the route. "I've been at this for a while, and Lochner isn't the first industrialist we've had to contain. I've managed to work at the OEF for years without him knowing."

"How sure are you?"

"He's got his ways of doing things, but so do I. Lexell's capabilities may be opaque to you given our low profile, but it's run by the most brilliant minds in the world, with nearly unlimited resources at its disposal. My disposal. Which allows me to do some counterintelligence and protect myself."

"It's only a matter of time."

"Then it's a good thing we're so close to the end," she replies. "Now, what is it you found out?"

"Your source. They're in Tangier," I start. "The OEF is operating from out of there now. There's a good chance your source is still alive and still on the inside."

"And you know this how?"

I tell her all that I learned from Kingsley, leaving his name out of it, of course. I still have to protect my sources. She listens intently, and I can tell I'm filling in a lot of her knowledge gaps. I tell her too about the shakeup in the supply chain, when the source lost contact with her and Simon.

"Two weeks ago, Lochner moved his labs to Morocco. It's a big country, but if I had to guess, they're in Tangier. Zephyrus bankrolled the land reclamation that kept it above water. Since then, Lochner has pretty much owned the city. Not to mention all the intercontinental and trans-Atlantic lanes that rely on it. Add a corrupt prime minister and lax biotech regulations, and you have a prime port for an illicit drug lab."

She tilts her head slightly, and I catch a thin smile cut across her profile. "Well done. This is all very useful. What do you propose we do now?"

"Whatever it takes to get this source out in the open, and fast. The C+P Board is voting on the buyout in two days. I'm sure Lexell has resources for this kind of rescue operation."

She leans on a doorway, eyeing the security bot making the rounds. The crowd thins out in the exhibit hall as the time of the eclipse approaches.

"When I started out, I had one mission: secure the source," Sid says. "That mission now includes stopping Lochner from acquiring C+P and building his news media monopoly. There's a lot at stake here. You get that, right?"

"I do. And if you and I work together, we'll get to do both."

The security bot reaches our corner. A hazy cone of blue light sweeps past us and we are prompted to walk toward the refractor building. The eclipse isn't starting for another half-hour, but they need to get everyone inside soon.

"This source is the key to all of this. She's a top hyperinsomnia researcher, worked for a nonprofit and the CDC before being pirated by Lochner," Sid continues. My heart begins to race as she tells me more about this source's credentials. "He hired her specifically look into the causes of the pandemic, but as you know, he'd gone too far in what he's done with their research efforts. When he had his fringe scientists make Levantanil, she turned."

Her. Her background matches, and the timeline fits.

"Who is she?" I ask Sid, hoping she says the right name.

"Miriam Slimane."

"I've been trying to find her," I reply, stunned. "Not for you. On my own."

Sid's taken aback, a rare display of emotion. "What? Why?"

"When I told you I took Levantanil, that wasn't the whole story," I whisper, pulling her away from the crowd and down an empty corridor. "I've been having trouble with my memory. Some sort of amnesia called encoding failure. I'm not creating new memories, or at least not consistently. I looked into it, and every major study told me that it might have some link to Sleeplessness. And each of those studies was conducted by her."

"How bad is it?" she asks gravely.

"Bad enough that a memory lapse hit me on the night that Simon died."

"This is why Lochner wants Dr. Slimane," she explains. "To force her to fix this side effect."

"So what do we do?"

"We need to secure her," she replies. "She has everything on Lochner's operations. Lab reports, financials, emails, audio recordings . . . a mountain of proof that definitively ties Lochner to an illegal hyperinsomnia drug ring *and* to a Sleeple ss supremacist terror group. If that's not enough to stop them, I don't know what will."

"We only need to get to Tangier," I say.

"We don't have to. She's being brought here." Sid lowers her voice. "Tomorrow night, there's a research summit at the Hyperinsomnia Research Institute up in Wakefield. All the world's top experts in the field will be there. My intel says Lochner's arranged for Dr. Slimane to make an appearance. I'm going to extract her then."

She's going to be here, in the country. The one person I've been looking for, the one on whom everything hinges. The mind I'm losing, the company I've devoted my life to—she can save them both. I resist the urge to head up to Maine right this second.

"I'll help you."

Sid stands impassive, gauging my resolve. She then walks back toward the crowd as it enters a packed vestibule. I follow, eager for her answer. The observation platform hardly has any space for us to squeeze into, but a small gap presents itself near a railing.

"We get one shot at this," she warns. "If we fail, we're probably never going to find her again. Worse, we could get caught. Are you sure you want to do this?"

"Look, I've got skin in the game," I tell her. "Slimane's the only one with the answers I seek, and she's going to help stop C+P from being bought out by a Sleepless supremacist. Not to mention I get to finish what Simon started."

"You're forgetting the most important thing," she replies. "This is more than a treaty violation by a global conglomerate. Lochner and Exsomnis have one goal: a Sleepless world order. Now they're close to perfectly replicating hyperinsomnia." Sid looks around at the people gathered near us, fumbling around with the sky map that we'd been handed at the entrance. "Think about any crisis we have today. Food, energy, water. Discrimination, wealth inequality, labor exploitation. All the ills that we suffer under. Without the right planning and the right information, a more Sleepless world would magnify those exponentially. And all because of Lochner's greed and desire for supremacy."

"Exactly. So what makes you think my answer's gonna be anything but yes?"

An announcement plays over the speaker system, reminding everyone to don their visors or any other pre-approved eye protection. A massive telescope is slowly lowered, and the viewing platform rises in concert. The domed roof of the observatory opens up. Humidity descends on the crowd, whose necks are craned up to a clear, cloudless view of the morning sky.

"No doubt you've looked into Lexell. Did I ever tell you how it got its name?" Sid asks as she slides her visor on. "It's the name of a comet. The closest one to ever pass Earth, more than any other comet in recorded history."

"Yes, I know," I reply with a grin. "How do you think I got the idea to meet here?"

"We're on the precipice of another close call, Jamie. A potentially cataclysmic one. I hope you're ready."

A chorus of oohs and aahs swells through the chamber. The sky begins to darken as the moon edges along the sun, casting a shadow over everyone. Sid's eyes are up toward the sky, but mine are still on her.

"Ready as I'll ever be."

35.

Saturday, 07/18/2043, 03:11 PM

Conviction was easy to feign in front of Sid. With her, and with the thrilling spycraft of what we'd been planning, I couldn't help but say yes. Especially since it meant a chance at getting answers about encoding failure. I got swept up in the possibilities, and I may have been swayed by desperation too.

That conviction feels shakier now that I'm back in the city. Focusing on the mission might shore up my resolve again, help me forget the more immediate mess here. Simon's death, Brenda's pursuit, Elliott's betrayal. As I head into my apartment complex, I start up my visor and assemble a list of things to pack for Maine.

A call comes in when I get into the elevator. Detective Tetro. I pick up, voice only.

"Mr. Vega, I'm afraid I'll have to ask you to come downtown again."

"That's the third day in a row, Detective. What is it that you want now?"

"It's better to discuss it in person. We have something you might want to see."

"It's the weekend. Why don't you get some rest?" I say, sarcastically, but he blows past it.

"Tried your place, but you weren't in," he says. "You didn't cross state lines, did you?"

Almost by instinct, my hand swiftly presses the button for Floor 8. One below my apartment floor.

"Of course not," I say after a slight pause. "Where would I go?"

The doors open on eighth, and the elevator rings out two short chimes. Tetro takes a beat too long to reply. "Where are you?"

"I'm afraid that's none of your business, Detective." As light-footed as I can, I get off and summon another elevator to head down.

"Remember how I told you I only needed one of two things to take you in?" Tetro asks. I listen intently at the other end of the line, and get nothing but his voice. "Well, I got one of them."

"What's that?" I ask, knowing the answer. Brenda's gone to the cops, and evidently she's drawn them a connection between me and A-Pop via Kingsley. Whatever she may have seen at the motel wouldn't count as hard evidence, but she's savvy enough to spin Tetro a story that'll have him coming after me.

"Wouldn't you want to see it in person, get a chance to explain yourself?"

"Detective, I'm sure it's not important enough that I'd have to show up in person." The elevator chimes again, and I get in, hit the lobby button. "If whatever you got is any good, you'd be coming at me with a warrant."

"Where did you say you were again?"

"I didn't. I know my rights."

"Yeah, yeah—what makes you think I'm not standing in the middle of your apartment right now holding a shiny new warrant?"

Fuck. I hang up, turn my visor off completely, and shoot out of the elevator soon as the doors open. I keep my eyes peeled for any cops, backup teams that might have been eyeing the lobby. No one's there, and I rush out of the building, running toward the closest subway stop.

I'm not going down for Simon's murder, not when I'm this close to solving it. There's only one place left I need to go, and I jump onto the next downtown train heading toward Murray Hill.

Saturday, 07/18/2043, 03:48 PM

The row of apartments feels unsafe, sinister, as I walk past them toward the door at the end of the hall. Like I haven't been here before. What once felt to me like a refuge is now a lie unmasked.

I knock, and Elliott opens the door without a word. His expression is welcoming, but a tad unsure. He beams a smile anyway, and the curl of his lip reminds me of how he's deceived me with his glibness so many times before.

It sends me over the edge.

I grab a wrist and twist his arm to his back. His face slams on the door as I push him onto it. "You work for Lochner, don't you?"

"What the fuck?"

"I know you're part of Lochner's Levantanil operation." I spin him around and clutch his collar. "Try and deny it."

"Jamie, you don't know what you're talking about!"

"Don't I? Simon was looking into the operation right before he was killed. You were working with Lochner to spread Levantanil, and you're also his inside man at C+P. Tell me I'm fucking wrong!"

Elliott avoids my gaze but chooses not to feed me another lie. He shrugs me off, and I unhand him.

"I've had bugs in the C+P offices for a while. Simon's, Maxwell's, the boardroom too. All the highly-sensitive locations in the building." He paces to the bar, pours himself a shot of whiskey. He offers me one, and I only give him a glare.

"That's how you know everything going on. Well before anyone else does."

"Lochner needed to know how the C+P Board was going to vote on the offer," he continues. "I was well-placed, being so close to Simon. That was the only reason I did it. Until I heard Simon talking to Sid Thorpe."

"About Levantanil."

He nods, a bit surprised. "Yes. The two of them have managed to link Lochner to Exsomnis and to the Levantanil operation. They had evidence, a whistleblower. We had to do something."

"You told Lochner about Dr. Slimane, and he made her disappear," I say, trembling in rage. "That was you."

"We had to secure her. She's critical to our production process, and to our greater aims. We couldn't let her defect. Simon would have exposed us otherwise. That's also why I tried to steer you away from finding Slimane."

"The one person who could help me, and you made sure I wouldn't get to her," I reply, stunned by the many ways he'd lied and manipulated me, how he'd cost me my memories.

"Why would you do this? How could you?"

"All we want is Sleeplessness for everyone," Elliott replies in an assured tone. "People say we are supremacists, but in truth, we're egalitarian. The same way the pandemic was. It promised its gifts with no regard to race or sex or station. But it didn't spread to everyone. There's still an imbalance between those who need to sleep and those who don't. We aim to erase that imbalance. Like Prometheus bringing fire to all of humanity."

He speaks with the zeal of the convert, and despite my ire, I recognize that he's not a mindless puppet. It wasn't brainwashing that made him join forces with his hypercapitalist overlord and an extremist group—it was a sincerely held belief in equality. This is who Elliott has always been, who I've always known him to be. Only difference now: he's decided to take extreme measures to achieve it.

"Lochner doesn't care about egalitarianism. All he cares about is power," I say. "Same as Exsomnis. Their whole purpose is about asserting a hierarchy. Whatever line they've sold you, they don't really want everyone to become Sleepless. They just want the Sleepless to be the dominant class."

"You don't know what you're talking about," Elliott replies, and though he waves me off, I see a hint of hesitation in him.

"And what do you think happens when everyone's Sleepless?" I ask. "Have you thought about the larger consequences? How it will fundamentally change how the world works, and not necessarily for the better?"

"The invention of the lightbulb reshaped the world by freeing us from the celestial schedule," he explains. "It gave us more time to think, to work, to do. A world without sleep will do the same. How is that not better?"

"All it'll give us is more time to fuck things up. More than we already have."

"That's not true at all," Elliott says. "Look at how Levantanil has improved your own life. Haven't you yourself enjoyed the benefits of taking that pill? Didn't it make you a happier, more successful person? At the very least, it made the nightmares stop, now didn't it?"

"None of that is worth the price," I reply. "If I had known that Lev came from Exsomnis, I never would have taken it."

"That's a lie, and you know it." He sets his empty snifter down on to the bar. "You've always wanted to be Sleepless, more than you ever liked to admit. You would've taken any risk to become one. And now? You *love* it."

I would have protested against his presumptuousness, but right now the truth is a moving target. There's a part of me that would risk anything to have my mind working normally once again. Yet deep down there's also the part of me who doesn't know how to be anything but Sleepless. Who doesn't *want* to be anything but.

Sensing that he's swayed me, Elliott asks, gently, "Do you really not remember anything about the night Simon died?"

I shake my head.

"I've been wanting to tell you something since the other day," he says.

"What, that you killed Simon? And then tried to frame me for it?"

"Frame you? Don't you mean Maxwell?" The confused look on his face is either a fine piece of acting or a sign he doesn't know about the empty vial.

"Did you?" I yell.

"I was nowhere near you or that office on Wednesday night," he replies. "And I had no idea Simon was going to die. His murder was as much a shock to me as it was to you. You saw me the next morning."

"Yeah, trying to retrieve your bugs from his office before the cops came."

Elliott stalks around the living room, weighing his next words. "They're well-hidden, but they would've turned up in a police sweep. Good thing you'd called me before you called 911 Thursday morning. Gave me a chance to get there and get my bug out," he admits. "But those tears were real, Jamie. What I felt that morning, what is still feel, is true anguish."

"Fuck your tears and fuck your anguish."

"Simon's death was never part of my mission, or Lochner's plans. We had already secured the doctor before Simon could get his hands on her, and we were already poised to win the buyout vote. So you see," here he pauses to smile, "We didn't want Simon dead. We didn't *need* him dead." *We*, he says. My rage roils at this casual display of betrayal. "Even if we did need him dead, I never would have agreed to such a plan."

"I don't believe you."

"I wouldn't lie about this. Not about Simon. Which is what I've been trying to tell you, if you'd only let me." He turns away from me to look out his window. "I can show you the truth."

"What truth?"

"About what happened in Simon's office Wednesday night."

That fucking night. My life has been upended since that night. I lost my mentor, and I've become involved in his death some nefarious way. I've feared that I may have killed him. I've gotten beaten and stalked and harassed and surveilled. I've chased missing doctors and whistleblowers all while dealing with the fact that I've been losing memories and that I stand to lose more.

I've risked life and liberty and sanity, all because of that night. The only thing I've truly wanted to uncover its mysteries, and now the only thing standing in my way is Elliott.

"I had the place bugged, Jamie. I have the recording."

"What does it say?" I ask, trying to hide the tremble in my voice.

"After the cops said it was a suicide, I didn't bother listening to the audio file," he replies, deflecting. "It wasn't until Maxwell was arrested that I played it back."

"The cops are after me, Elliott. I need to know what's in that audio file," I insist, lunging at him. "Tell me what it says."

He dodges, palms raised defensively. "I'm sorry, Jamie, but I can't let you stand in the way of our plans. We need control of C+P, and our Levantanil operation needs to remain unfettered," he says. "And as long as you're against us, the audio file is my insurance."

The layers of his betrayal have no end. Being part of Exsomnis, manipulating me into taking Levantanil. The corporate espionage. Keeping me from getting help for encoding failure. Betraying Simon, me, the entirety of C+P and the very principle of journalistic integrity. All while pretending to be my friend.

"This is not how I wanted this to happen," he says, scowling in disappointment. "I had hoped to enlighten you, in my own time and on my own terms. To bring you to our side. But now I see that's impossible."

"I'd sooner die than be on your side."

"You've made your choice," he replies. "I hope it's worth never knowing the truth about that night."

Heat swells in my chest, a flame threatening to consume me. I come at him, trying to get hold of his arms, but he parries. He says something snide—I can tell by the way his lips pull sideways—but I can't hear the words. All I can hear is my fury drowning him out, drowning out all sense of control.

I lunge at him again, and this time I catch his arms. I pull him closer, raise my leg for a kick. He struggles free, and I lose my hold, stumbling back. He charges at me, tackling me onto the floor. We wrestle, and I manage to get on top of him. When I have him pinned down, I punch his chest, his face. He tries to speak, and blood spews from his mouth.

He writhes under me, trying to kick free. His foot lands on the coffee table and its glass top crashes down behind me. He hits my side with a hook, and I counter with a stronger one across his face, and then another, until he is knocked out, face turned lifelessly aside.

As I get off him, I see a bloody shard of glass in his grasp. It takes a while for me to notice that the side of my shirt is soaking red. I put both hands over the wound, and for the first time feel its existence.

I stagger onto the couch, my side dripping with blood. A wave of pain courses through my body. Energy drains from me as I breathe, and with what little strength I have, I slide on my earcuff.

"V. Need your help. I hurt myself."

"What? How?"

"I'm at Elliott's. You still have his address?"

"What happened?

"I . . . I don't remember."

Part

Three

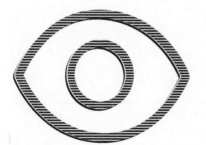 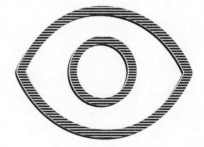

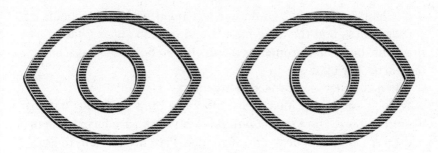

36.

Sunday, 07/19/2043, 6:15 a.m.

The maglev train pulls out of Penn Station with a smooth, even glide. The automated whistle, meant to evoke a bygone era, startles the bedraggled drifter across the aisle. He pulls down his baseball cap to shield his eyes from the glare of the fluorescent light. Sleep debt hasn't been a problem of mine in a long time, but I've got other issues. I lean back on my seat and, after the conductor drone hovers past me, I gently lift my shirt and inspect the skinseal on my side. Some blood has already seeped through, and the brown patch has turned into something redder, puce.

Seeing it magnifies the dull ache coming from underneath. I take shallower breaths. Kingsley said that would help, though I could tell he was bullshitting me. Still, the stitch job was clean. He had nimble digits, for someone whose joints were constrained by an XFrame.

What I need is more oxy, though maybe not so soon since the last dose. He only gave me so much. Veronica's orders. She thinks it might have adverse interactions, though with what, she doesn't know. Really, what could be worse than whatever's already happening to me?

"It happened again," I told her last night, in between bouts of consciousness and the drug haze. I told her too about Elliott's admissions, his grand pronouncements, his audio recording. The key to clearing my name.

Then, another blank space in my mind.

I don't remember much else after charging at Elliott, but my wound is there. More than a reminder, it is a precise form of memory. A record of pain dealt and sustained. Veronica filled in the rest, though there wasn't very much else to figure out.

A message from her comes in through my visor now.

We got him to the hospital in time, but he looks really bad, Jamie.

I feel a ripple of pleasure at the news, and I immediately hate myself for it. And then I recall all of Elliott's lies, and it eases the momentary guilt.

All that talk about Exsomnis, the fire of Prometheus, about evolving the human race, that was not the Elliott I knew. It didn't sound like him, except for that one time at Nighthawks, during one of those early morning diner sessions that I now recognize to be his method of indoctrination. There was this specific moment that now gains new meaning. Elliott talked about the teachings of Buddha, whose name literally means "one who is awake." He wasn't even religious, but he rambled about Buddhism and transhumanism and some drivel about opening one's eye and enlightenment. At the time, I chalked it up to fatigue. I should've known that it was something more sinister. Another one in the series of *should've knowns* that I missed.

The train leaves the underground tunnel, and the cabin illuminates with the mauve of the early sunrise. I look out at the Bronx neighborhoods coming to life. In a few moments, I'd be crossing the Connecticut border, officially making me a fugitive. I suppose I'd been so since Tetro's call yesterday, but doubly so now that I've left Elliott in the state he's in.

It might be the weak light of dawn, or the fog-laden parks of Pelham, but a solemnity comes over me. One that is in sharp contrast to how I was last night. In this state of calm, I'm able to judge what I've done. How utterly stupid it was, how reckless. I promised myself I'd never get to that point again. The last time I lost my shit like that, I got institutionalized. Now I risk the same, only this time, it'll be a penal institution.

The drifter, awakened by the sunrise, looks at me with narrowed eyes. I turn away toward the window, close my eyes, and pretend to sleep.

❀

The valley opens up before me as the train winds its way through the outskirts of Wakefield. The sloping hills shine verdant in the sun, a hydroponic miracle unrecognizable from only a few years ago, when it was nothing more than a gulch along the Appalachian Trail. From the distance I can already see the staggered terrace farms, the spires of the arcology towers, the curves of the sundomes that dot the city. I shield my eyes as we pass through the sparkling fields of solar panels, a radiant beacon that blinds me as I enter the city limits.

For decades, this whole area had been barren. The creeks dried up in the late '20s, and soon the land became unsuitable for farming. A handful of hamlets remained, their livelihoods tied to the state college campus nearby. Everything changed when hyperinsomnia broke out. Soon after the first cases were reported in the area, the CDC set up shop, then established the Hyperinsomnia Research Institute. The valley attracted the brightest minds in the fields of epidemiology and genetics. It also attracted hyperinsomniacs of all stripes. A few came on a religious pilgrimage of sorts, but most wanted to live where everyone was just like them.

As the number of Sleepless grew, the hamlets grew too. More shops and housing, longer business hours, expanded public services, infrastructure projects, and general policies of openness and accommodation. It seemed like a correction from the horrors of quarantine that initially beset the community after the outbreak. The Sleepless moved in, and those who didn't like them moved out. Then the Sleepless transformed the valley into a world of their own making. The hamlets soon incorporated into one mega-city, which they christened with the uncreative name that it now bears.

Everywhere, I see signs of newness. This is a city built without the restraint of the past. Wakefield never needed to contend with the architectural bones of ancestors from which their modern structures could rise. And because of the tireless labor force, major corporations built satellite offices in Wakefield. Others, mostly data science firms, even moved their HQs. Their logos now sit atop their skyscrapers, high above the holo-boards and the twisting lines of maglev tubes, above the designated pocket of drone airspace, above the multi-level promenades.

As my train slows to a crawl toward the terminus, I slide on my visor. I pull up a grid map, but the screen also greets me with enhanced holo-ads, assaulting my senses with pithy slogans from Wakefield's tourism board.

Where every day lasts forever
Risen from the ashes
The TRUE city that never sleeps

I disembark onto an atrium bustling with the orderly chaos of the midmorning rush. Traffic signs point the way to the robocab lot and the livery drone ports. An overhead display shows a map of the city, and I am jostled more than once as I try to get my bearings.

Everyone breezes past me, intent on reaching their destinations, visions glued to their visors. Earcuffs, too, are lodged uniformly in place around every left lobe. Exosuits are as common as wristpanels, and most of the latter are implants. Seamless tech integration might be the only other common running thread among the locals here. Other than that, the Wakefielders are a diverse community. Not surprising when the city is founded by Sleepless people from all over the world. All races, all genders, all ages, all identities are here, all sharing one common trait.

I step onto the sidewalk and wait for my ride. A cold current courses through the air. Outdoor climate control, in the dead of summer. It feels good, having come from a hundred-degree morning in the city, but it's not enough for Wakefield to win me over.

My New York pride predisposes me to hate this other "city that never sleeps," and I'm even more averse to it because of the sheer number of Sleepless people all in one place. Each of them is a walking reminder of who I forced myself to become. In their eyes I see myself reflected, the fool deceived into taking a great, miscalculated risk. Worse, in them I see how things could have been. Maybe I would have become Sleepless the natural way. Maybe not. Either way, I would still be making memories. Instead, all I have is more hours. No bad dreams, sure, but in exchange I get no dreams at all and vanishingly few memories.

And what is one's life if not the sum of their memories?

A cipher, that's what I'm about to be. I recall my grandfather and his Santayana mantra: those who forget the past are condemned to repeat it. Forgetting my present, what have I condemned myself to?

I settle into the robocab, and my visor automatically links up with the dash screen. I open the sole unread message from an unknown sender. Sid, with encrypted instructions for the meeting. After I've written it down on a scrap of paper, I delete the message, then redirect the robocab GPS manually.

Then, another message comes in. I hit play.

"Mr. Vega. Detective Tetro again. You already know what this is about. You need to come in downtown. The sooner you do, the better it's gonna end up for you. Don't force us to put an APB out for you."

When I committed to Sid's plans, I knew I'd risk putting myself in Tetro's crosshairs. Skipping town ain't exactly the kind of behavior that'll get him off my back. Quite the opposite. Yet I willingly took that risk because I had to see the plan through. For Simon. Little did I know the detective was already on to me, armed with a warrant too. And then I had to go fuck up even more by beating Elliott senseless.

I hit delete on the message. I turn up the cab's window shade and envelop myself in darkness. I recline my seat flat, and close my eyes. My stab wound still throbs despite the change in position. I dose myself with another shot of oxy. The day's barely begun and already it's another long one.

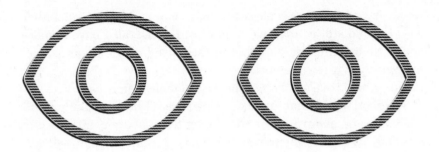

37.

We're calling it a safe house, though in reality it's a cramped studio in a low-rent megacomplex at the edge of the city. I redress my wound while Sid paces around the room. We have some time until we have to go, but it looks like she's planning on avoiding me until then. She doesn't like close contact, but this apartment has no corners to retreat to. Just a desk, a kitchen counter, and a coffee table. An outdated flatscreen hung over the wall in front of a lumpy convertible couch, one that's probably never been used as a bed. Not to sleep on, anyway.

"What's it like, this encoding failure?" Sid asks when she finally tires of the silence. "Is it like normal forgetting?"

"It is, and it isn't," I reply. "It feels the same, but slightly worse. With forgetting, there's usually a sign, a subconscious reminder, something that triggers recollection. With encoding failure, there's none of that. It's a blank space. You know how when you have a word on the tip of your tongue, but you can't quite pin it down? That's what forgetting feels like. What I have is more like not knowing the word at all."

"That sounds horrible."

"Feels even worse," I reply, sighing. "Not making memories, going through life and having it all pass through me like a sieve. I could take pictures, I could have my visor be on autorecord 24/7, and it still wouldn't be the same. I could play the day back over and over, and it still wouldn't be a memory."

"When did it start?"

"I don't know. It's a bit perverse in that way. You don't know what you've forgotten, and when. But I do know I forgot seeing Simon the night he died. That's when I noticed a real problem, and I started thinking back to my interactions, and my relationships. Then I realized that it started months before that. That I'd been suffering from this and didn't have a single clue."

"And all because you took Levantanil," she says, with regret on my behalf. It's a strange moment of empathy; I have no doubt she's capable, but she strikes me as a woman who might view its display as a weakness. In response, I only nod somberly, hoping to prompt her into conversation. It works.

"My father was Sleepless," she begins. "He was one of the first cases down in Atlanta. The CDC was only a couple miles down the road from where we lived, but that didn't help us any. He got rounded up early. He spent five months in quarantine, another six in mandatory outpatient 'observation.' They really messed him up. He was never the same after.

"He eventually got better, or so I thought. He started working again, picking up extra shifts at the warehouses. He worked four jobs total. We didn't need the money; C+P paid me well, and I helped my folks out a lot. But he wanted to work. Met his quotas, covered extra shifts, impressed his bosses. He found his self-worth in the job.

"Then he died with no warning. The doctors called it cardiomyopathy, but we all knew what it truly was," she says bitterly.

"What was it?" I ask.

"Hard work is a virtue, we're all told. Keep your head down. Be a good employee. There's nothing more fulfilling than a good day's work. Bullshit. My father worked himself to death. And being Sleepless drove him to an early grave."

Another one driven to death by the hustle. All too well, I recognize the mélange of anger and resentment in Sid's voice. I feel it now too, hearing her father's story.

"I'm so sorry," I manage to say.

She gives me a faint smile. "When I myself became Sleepless, I didn't take it well. At all. I was a mess, and that simply wasn't acceptable for an executive editor of a major news company. I quit C+P to find my bearings, reassess my sense of self. That's when Lexell found me.

"Their recruiters made a strong pitch. Told me they're a group of thinkers that seek to avert global disaster. It sounded absurdly unrealistic, but it turned out to be true. From top to bottom, everyone in Lexell had sterling credentials in their fields, the best at what they do. In some shape or form, they've forecasted, prevented or fixed every major catastrophe since the turn of the century."

"How do they do it?"

"The more public-facing operations involve a lot of consulting with governments and international institutions. Through research, data analytics, and collaboration within the group, they develop means to combat whatever they come up against. They have close to unlimited funds, too, thanks to a hefty private donation."

"From who?"

"You know Harold de Vries, that Wall Streeter turned socialist?" she asks. I nod, the name ringing a faint bell. "When he died in the '90s, he gave his billions to all his children. One of them set up unrestricted funds specifically to form Lexell. Like a cooperative, the money's run by the organization members themselves, which they grow through futures investments. As you can imagine, this group can be quite savvy at that."

"So it's got no ties to big business?"

"No. Not like Lochner and his OEF." Sid's expression gains a cold edge. "Lexell is engaged in many other projects, but most of the money now goes to hyperinsomnia. It's been their main focus for the past ten years since the outbreak. Trying to understand every aspect of it so, they can equip the world with the right resources to prevent another pandemic."

"That's how they got to you."

"They found me at the right time," she says, nodding. "I needed to do something about my new condition, and I needed something to direct my energies at. They knew I had the skills to be an operative, convinced me this was the ideal use of my talents. Most of all, they made me see how Sleeplessness is not this black-and-white thing that other factions have made it out to be."

"How do you mean?"

"Sleeplessness is not the next step in evolution, like Exsomnis believes. And it's not this blight on humanity either, no matter what the religious wingnuts or the anti-Sleepless leagues say."

"You think everyone on this spectrum has a point?"

"The truth always lies in the interstices," she argues. "Lexell doesn't take any absolutist views, especially with so much left unknown, and I don't either. We also acknowledge when certain factions might have a point. Take the radical environmentalists, for example."

The mention reminds me of Hannah's mothers, and though I would not call them radical, I don't know if the same is true of those they choose to associate with. Sid senses some pique on my part and gives me a quizzical look.

"They're not completely off-base," I say hesitantly.

"Their fears are rooted in concerns that Lexell is itself invested in," she replies. "But their view of the Sleepless is rigidly pessimistic to the point of hostile, and their methods are reactionary. They want regulation, even if it means oppression. On some level, I know where they're coming from. Climate change remains an urgent problem, and here comes Sleeplessness making it worse."

"And you're different how?"

"We have a more holistic view," Sid replies. "We have sustainability experts in our staff, but we also have experts from other fields, including the social sciences. This has allowed us to be open to the idea that Sleeplessness might not be a complete obstacle to sustainability. It may well turn out to be, but until we know more, we don't pursue a course that treats the Sleepless as a bane to the environment."

"But Levantanil is."

"For better or worse, if the world has any chance of accommodating more Sleepless people, it's not going to be with this haphazard, money-driven way that Lochner wants to do it. Any population increase must be met with careful planning, social and technological advances, and a lot more research, all of which we don't yet have."

"That's why you need Dr. Slimane," I say.

She nods. "Now more than ever. She's made startling discoveries during her work in Lochner's labs, and her talents need to be directed toward answering the most pressing questions about Sleeplessness."

And toward helping me regain my ability to remember. "Lexell sanctioned you going public about Dr. Slimane's work?"

"Yes, and so I went to the one person I trusted," she replies. "Simon was on board the moment I told him. He wanted to bring down Zephyrus, Exsomnis, Lochner—which to him were all one and the same. I only wish he'd been able to see it through."

"You're doing this for him too," I say.

"I guess you could say that this is for Simon. Maybe my father too. Most of all though, I'm doing it because I don't want a world of exploitable worker bees. A world straining under the weight of all the Sleepless and our unceasing needs and wants, beholden to people like Lochner and the rest of the one percent."

She turns away and starts unpacking her luggage, which tells me she's done talking. It's more than I could have asked for, and I choose not to pursue any more.

Instead I decide to meditate until it's time for us to go. I need to dull my senses, especially as the oxy begins to wear off. I try to silence my thoughts, but worry builds within me. The two episodes I've had—at least the two whose consequences I remembered—have led me down disastrous paths. Simon dead, Elliott in the hospital. Now I need to be guarded against my own self. What else have I done that I don't remember? What else could I do that I wouldn't?

I swipe on my visor and block out all sound with my earcuff. I'll need all the calm I can get.

"Do you regret it, taking the pill?" Sid asks once I rise from my lotus pose. I check the time, and it's been about an hour.

"Yes and no," I say with a lifeless shrug. "If I knew then what I know now, I probably wouldn't have done it. But that's the hindsight talking. All I know is that I don't want encoding failure. Hopefully the doctor can help with that."

"She might not have the answers you want."

"A chance is all I'm asking for," I say. "The possibility of having the best of both worlds—the Sleeplessness without the side effect."

"And if that's not possible?" Sid asks with sympathy.

"Gun to my head? I want my memory back, even if it means not being Sleepless."

❖

Tall, well-tended evergreens line the walkway beside the auxiliary building of the Hyperinsomnia Research Institute, and a low, grassy hillock separates the squat structure from a dense wood that borders the facility's grounds. The rows of spruces, together with the untended hedge of greenery running alongside it, provide the perfect amount of cover. In the broad daylight, I can hardly peek through to the other side, where a two-story carport is partially obscured.

Dr. Slimane, no doubt under watch by Lochner's men, is scheduled to appear at the HRI for an international summit on the state of hyperinsomnia research. High-level stakeholders in the field will be there. Researchers and their institutional funders, academics, and of course, representatives from major pharma corps. After her presentation, she'll be whisked away to Tangier, back into Lochner's underground production facilities. Tonight's her best chance for a safe escape, and Sid and I are her only hope.

The plan is straightforward enough. That doesn't mean it's simple, but it's doable: extract the doctor, swoop her into transport, and get ourselves out of Wakefield before anyone's the wiser.

A small group of women exits the building from a side door. The paper bags and branded merchandise tell me they are tourists come from the HRI museum. I should stop by sometime, learn the history of my kind, recent as it is. The back door, directly in front of me some hundred yards away, has not opened in the hour since I got here. The path from that door leads to where my bench is. The solar lamps on this sidewalk are far enough, but security cameras are posted on every corner of the building. Though, I suppose it doesn't matter if we're seen.

I stand and walk toward the grass line. I press down with my foot. The soil still has a little give, damp from last night's rain. My visor tells me it's about 82 yards from the door to the tree line, accounting for the slope. That'll take about a minute to sprint; with the muddy grass, and if the doctor's wearing heels, it'll be a lot longer.

"There will be enough time," Sid says through my earcuff. "As long as you do your part and secure her."

"You're the boss."

"And don't you forget it."

I decide to do another walk-through to get a better handle on the lay of the land. I amble down the paved path toward the back door of the main building. As I make my way, Sid talks me through the timetable again and pulls up schematics of the HRI facilities on my visor.

Dr. Miriam Slimane will be at a virtual roundtable in the HRI auditorium starting at 5 p.m. After that is a cocktail reception, then dinner at the museum's lobby. First course starts at 6:30. She'll mingle, act like everything is normal, and then slip away shortly before 8:00. She'll wait for me at the back door. Then we cut through the knoll, through the tiny wood, then to the carport where the drone transport will wait.

"I'll be your eyes and ears on the inside," Sid says. "Lochner's people will be watching both me and her, but I'll make sure she gets a chance to ditch whoever's watching us."

"And how will you manage that?"

"Feminine wiles," she says. "You let me worry what happens until that point, but once she's at the rear exit, it all hinges on you."

"I know."

"If all goes according to plan, she should be out of there by 8:15 at the latest. Once she's at the door, you go and take her to the rendezvous point." Sid then pulls up a top view map of the area, tracing the escape path.

"Then we'll wait for you at the rendezvous point," I say. "8:45 at the latest."

"Exactly. And absolutely no comms until then."

"You know, I'm a little envious," I reply. "I'm gonna be out here on the sidewalk all alone, and I might have to tussle with armed security, get shot at, maybe . . . meanwhile, you'll be in there all dressed up at your fancy party nibbling on shrimp cocktail."

She chuckles. "I'd swap places if we could. I hate these summits. And I hate being under close watch."

I pull down my baseball cap instinctively. Sweat drips from my brow in this midday heat. I slowly make a heel turn, scoping out the sidewalk and the view across the street. "And what if it goes south? What if you or the doctor get in trouble?"

"I know how to protect myself, and her. You just worry about not getting caught."

I grunt, both to sound tough to her and to reassure myself. My wound isn't bugging me as much after my morning dose of oxy, but I can't be on any more painkillers tonight.

At the end of the long block, I reach the wooded area that the Sid's map leads me to. The ground is uneven and soggy; I shouldn't have worn sneakers. I search around me but see no clearing or path that cuts through to the other compound's parking lot. Sunset is at 8:15 tonight. The doctor and I won't lose our way in the dark, but we could easily stumble or trip on some rock or tangled roots.

About a quarter mile in, past the trees on the other side, is the public carport and helipad. The quadcopter controls are synced up with my visor, and I find that our transport's parked and ready at our designated spot. From here, it should be a quick flight back to the safe house.

If all goes according to plan, we should have Dr. Slimane secure by 9 p.m. It doesn't leave me with much time to get a video packet ready for the morning broadcasts, but good thing I don't need sleep. This time tomorrow, the world will know about Levantanil, and the C+P Board will have no choice but to reject the buyout.

"Quadcopter's clear," I tell Sid as I do my final inspection of our ride. "Should be good to go."

"You sound nervous, Jamie."

"What can I say? You get a sense of the stakes when you're walking the path."

"Another reason why we needed to do a run through," she replies. "These things get risky, and it's better to burn off all that anxiety now rather than deal with them tonight."

"Speaking of risks—if we succeed, Dr. Slimane will be on the run from Lochner for the rest of her life," I say. "I know you won't be a failure point. I'm gonna do my damnedest not to be either. But her . . . are we sure she's on board?"

"She's my agent, I'm her handler. With that kind of relationship, trust can never be absolute," she replies. "But I know what makes her tick. That's assurance enough for me."

"And what's that?"

"She'd spent a decade of her life trying to uncover the mysteries of hyperinsomnia. Lochner promised her the world, seduced her with the best opportunity to fulfill that dream. Then he turned around and used her life's work for his own ends," Sid explains. "Even if I didn't trust her completely, I trust the human impulse to fuck someone over who's betrayed you."

I think back to Elliott, the rage I felt and the way it quelled when I took that rage out on him. Much as I knew how I'd come to regret it later, how giving in meant endangering myself even more, that impulse was undeniable.

"Besides," Sid adds. "She's the one who came to me. She wants out."

"And if she blinks? I don't want any hitches."

"She'll come through. She's got more at stake than either of us."

"That's exactly what I'm afraid of."

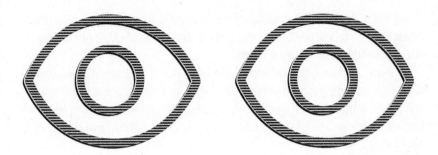

38.

Sunday, 07/19/2043, 05:13 PM

The Old Shillelagh is not my kind of place, but it has the benefit of being the only bar right across the street from the safe house. Sid hated the idea of me venturing out, but we had a couple hours to kill, and being stuck in a tiny room, waiting for go time, was making me anxious. I told her as much, and so she let me go, but only after I promised to stay close.

The bar has an elongated sunken layout, lined with uncomfortable wooden benches and table blocks. People congregate in the center of this pit, save for a few diners who occupy tables at the far end. Most people are casually dressed, befitting the laid-back vibe of the faux Irish pub, though some are in their corporate drone uniforms. Nearly everyone has their visors on, so I guess it's that kind of place.

The folks here don't seem like tourists. Some look old, some young; men, women, and every point in the spectrum is represented. The ones who are dressed professionally seemed like the typical daily-grind commuter, going to or from work, or from one job to another. Here and there, I pick up conversations in different languages, between different kinds of people, and it almost feels like

New York. It was the middle of the day and in any other city (even back home), a bar packed to the gills is an unusual sight at this hour. But Wakefield has its own rules.

I sidle up the bar and eye their selections, trying to find something satisfying yet non-alcoholic. Right as I reach for a tap for a local cider, a blond twenty-something bumps into me, spilling his blue cocktail on my boot. He stumbles to apologize, calling me mate, as if that would help.

"You from around here?" he asks. His eyes are bugged out and not from fatigue.

"No, just visiting."

"Me too. Got in last night. This place is pretty trippy, isn't it?" he says. "Are you Sleepless?"

"That's a pretty private thing to ask," I say.

"Look at where you are, mate. We're in the Sleepless mecca!"

The kid is definitely on something, but he does have a point. If hyperinsomnia were a religion, and were it to have a physical nexus, the ever-rising, glittering city of Wakefield would be it.

I wonder if Elliott's been here.

"I'm from Manchester," the kid rambles on. "It's nothing like this. Still quite behind on a lot of things. And not a lot of our type, makes things a bit harder." The way he says "our type" is intended to build some rapport, but I can't stand tourists back home, and I don't intend to start liking them now. Before I can deploy a withering response, he is rescued by a friend, also drunk. They disappear into the crowd, a critical mass of "our type" huddled in a pool of inebriated conversation.

A holoscreen above the bar begins to flash a C+P news clip, heralded by the familiar chime of a breaking news alert. One of our lead anchors, Corinne St. Charles, speaks with an anxious lilt that I can barely hear through the noise. I frantically make my way closer to the screen and I slip on my earcuff to help. She states the usual disclaimer about journalistic independence that precedes any C+P story about Simon's death, and dispenses with the assurances of unbiased reporting, before the clip cuts to a quote.

"We're heartened to learned about this development, and we're certain more details will surface in the following days," says a besuited, silver-haired man as he walks down the marble steps of the downtown Manhattan courthouse. The caption reads *Randall Strathairn IV*.

"This only vindicates the position that we've long maintained," he continues. "That Maxwell Cartwright is innocent. We urge the DA's office to drop all charges against my client immediately, and to devote its resources in pursuing the true perpetrator of his heinous crime."

"The NYPD has also pursued this new lead," Corinne's voiceover says, before the clip cuts to a menacing closeup of Detective Nathan Tetro.

"Owing to recent events, we have classified Jamie Vega as a person of interest in the murder of Simon Parrish."

Time stops, the rest of the pub ceases to exist. All that remains is the sound of my ragged breath and the detective's words piped into my ear.

"We have reason to believe that Mr. Vega was responsible for illegal surveillance activities at C+P News, activities that Mr. Parrish discovered shortly before his murder. He may have been acting in concert with Maxwell Cartwright, but we are not ruling out the possibility that Vega was acting on his own."

The chyron reads *New Suspect in Parrish Murder* as Corinne reappears on screen. "These developments arose following Vega's vicious assault of his coworker, Elliott Nahm." The clip then shows a wide sweeping shot of Elliott's living room, all wrecked and bloody. "Early last night, Vega allegedly attacked Nahm in his Murray Hill apartment after Nahm discovered Vega's surveillance equipment and promised to report Vega to the authorities."

"It was such a shock," Elliott says, captured on camera as he sits upright in a hospital bed. His cheeks and mouth are all bruised, but his words are crisp. "I never knew that he was capable of killing someone."

That motherfucker.

"We believe the C+P data breaches and Mr. Parrish's murders are connected, and Vega is right in the middle of both, in addition to the brutal assault of Mr. Nahm," Tetro says as the clip returns to him. "His whereabouts are currently unknown, and he is believed to have fled the state. The NYPD is coordinating with local and federal law enforcement, and any information as to his whereabouts can be sent to . . ."

The screen is then populated with my headshots, cribbed from the C+P website and my social media profiles, along with my name in big, block letters and a link to the NYPD tip line.

A patron cranes her neck from the end of the bar, gaze bouncing between the holoscreen and my face. Faintly I hear her yell as I shove my way out of the pub and make a mad dash across the street, oncoming traffic be damned.

❂

Back at the safe house, Sid gawps at the flatscreen, stunned by the reports featuring yours truly. Other news outlets have picked it up, and not without a bit of gleeful sensationalizing about the unfolding drama within the ranks of their top competitor. The less reputable sites have labeled me a murderer.

"I didn't do any of it," I stress. "Not the spying, and most definitely not the murder. Elliott flat-out admitted to me that he was Lochner's inside man."

Sid waved her hand to shush me, completely absorbed in the reportage, as though parsing every word out of the news reader's lips. I myself couldn't stand to look at the screen, and hearing Elliott's voice grated in my ear.

"You believe me, don't you?" I yell at her, tired of being ignored.

"Of course I believe you," she yells back. "You wouldn't be in this room if I didn't. But this changes things, Jamie. This compromises the whole plan."

"It doesn't have to. No one knows where I am—where we are," I say. "All my devices are on scramblers and, other than my own stuff, I haven't used any electronics or logged on to any sites with my account in the past 24 hours. Only used cash too, coming up here."

"That's not enough," she says, agitated. "You're a target now, and all it takes is one witness. One camera linked to a powerful-enough face ID algorithm. This city's airspace has dozens of surveillance drones. Did anyone recognize you before you got back here?"

"No," I say, aware of the lie but fully committing to it. "Look, this isn't a one-person job, not the way we've already set it up, and we're only a couple of hours away from show time. It's too late to change things now."

She backs down. I must have said that with enough bravado to convince her, or at least forestall any more resistance. The mission is precarious as it is; nerves and last-minute adjustments will only doom us.

"Even if we succeed in rescuing the doctor, exposing Lochner is not gonna be as effective because of you," Sid says, not uncharitably. "Anything that the doctor says on the record will be tainted by the fact that you're a suspect—for corporate espionage at best, and for murder at worst."

She's got a point. Elliott's maneuver puts me in the cops' crosshairs, and at the same time neutralizes any damage I might do to him and Lochner. Any credibility I have is shot to hell, and the only proof that will clear my name is in Elliott's possession.

"The doctor has an entire cache of data," I say. "If they're as solid as you say they are, that should be enough to connect Lochner to Exsomnis and the Levantanil operation."

"And once it's out, everyone will still pick it apart, coming from you."

"Let's take it one crisis at a time," I say. "Right now, we need to get the doctor out."

Sid retreats to the far side of the room, venting her frustration by rummaging through her suitcase. She's got a right to be. I'm more of a liability to her now than I've ever been.

I slip on my visor and check for messages. Blinking red icons tell me all of them are urgent, and I'm too anxious to let my fear stop me, so I press play.

Two messages from Tetro, escalating in tone and intimidation from the one he sent me only a few hours ago. Then messages from Cleo and a couple of junior C+P staffers, which I don't bother to open.

My eye glides over to a video message from Veronica, which I open in haste: "The cops came by asking questions. They knew that I was at Elliott's apartment and that I helped you. They're saying they'll arrest me next time if I don't tell them where you are. What have you gotten yourself into, Jamie?"

Instantly, a series of frantic text messages comes in from Dad.

Pls call ASAP.

WRU? R U OK?

Pls call. We are v worried. WE LOVE YOU.

COPS CALLING, WHAT SHOULD WE SAY?

It takes all my strength not to call him back right away, to reassure him and Mom that I'm all right, that I will make things right. If they get in trouble, I'll never forgive myself. But I have to resist calling them now; the ID scrambler on my visor can only do so much, and I'm sure my entire family, Veronica, everyone I know and love are being monitored without their knowledge.

Finally, a voice message from Brenda Xu. "Good afternoon, Mr. Vega. No doubt you've seen the news. I did warn you about our capabilities here at Strathairn-Shaw. We'll do anything for our clients, especially VIPs like Mr. Cartwright." Her greeting sounds colder, more distant, unlike her cheery, unassuming air in person. "We've talked to Elliott Nahm, and he's provided us with some interesting information. He's been quite cooperative. Call me and let's talk about how we can help each other."

It's a bluff, a trap to draw me out of hiding. I still don't know what's in the recording, but I've had some time to think about it. I have a sense of what it's going to say. The audio file is going to track with what I now think actually happened that night, and if I'm right, it shouldn't hurt me at all.

Of course, the larger part of me is deathly frightened. Afraid that my theories are wrong, that Elliott was lying. Most of all, I'm afraid of what these lawyers and Elliott and Lochner are capable of, and how they've now all targeted their combined efforts against me.

"How bad is it?" Sid asks, slipping the visor off my face.

"As bad as it could get when you're a wanted man."

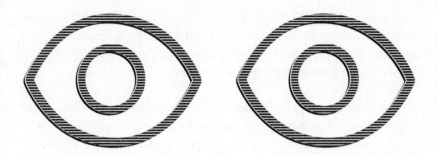

39.

The walk to my standby spot takes me past the front of the HRI compound. From across the street, I see fancy robocabs pulling up at the expansive porte-cochère. The front lawn has an understated brushed-steel sign announcing the facility. The HRI emblem, one that I haven't paid close enough attention to before, features a lick of fire.

The main building's side door opens to a clearing that ends on a bench-lined sidewalk. Streetlamps are judiciously placed, lighting up the median of a wide avenue. No one else is walking by. The road is empty.

When I reach the corner bus stop with a clear view of the side and back doors, I text Sid that I'm in position. Instantly, a beep comes in through my visor. My view is filled with an amphitheater view of panelists on a stage, four men and a sole woman. Dr. Slimane is in a sapphire blue suit jacket, and her hair pulled back in a tight ponytail. The time stamps are from a half-hour ago.

Another image appears, a shot of the doctor, walking down a hallway, flanked by her co-panelists. Zooming in on the far distance, I see two security types in their navies.

Another image, the entrance to the museum reception. Beyond the body scanners is a thick crowd of well-heeled academics, philanthropists, and socialites with cocktails in hand. A message accompanies the picture: *Going offline. See you soon.*

That's my cue.

I leave my post and walk past one of the building's side doors. An exosuited sentry is posted outside, so I keep my head down, even though that meant being unable to train my visor on him. He doesn't move as I pass him, and I walk toward the back exit that leads to the tree-lined hillock.

Another sentry is posted at this door. As with the other, he has the same imposing look, and the same XFrame built for heavy lifting and similar applications. Visors and earcuffs on too.

Waiting by an empty sidewalk bench would be too exposed. There are cameras everywhere, and if I had to guess, HRI has a security system sharp enough to face ID me and send that to the authorities instantly. I keep walking, angling my head aside to avoid the cameras, never looking back until I reach the woods. I crouch behind one of the thicker trees. The streetlights don't reach me, and there's enough cloud cover for the moon.

I turn on audio scope and night vision, which gives me full view of the door and the guard. The man is armed, a stunner hangs prominently on one side and a handgun on the other.

"Guards out. They're not supposed to be here," I voice-text Sid through my visor. She doesn't reply.

Ten minutes doesn't leave me much time for a new plan. I decide to walk back where I came from. The sentry by the back door definitely spots me. I keep my head down. I scope out the side door from a distance. The one posted there is just as armed. He doesn't see me this time.

I start up the path toward the extraction point. The sentry is about my height and slightly more built. Taking him might be doable, but keeping it quiet will definitely be a problem. Here goes nothing.

As I make my turn toward the guard, the side door opens.

Dr. Slimane, breathless and alone, is unmistakable in her bright blue ensemble. The sentry stops her. She turns to face me and then points squarely in my direction. Through my scope I hear her whisper something to the guard.

"That's him. That's the guy."

The sentry turns to me and I head back down the path, quickening my steps. He doesn't address me, but he radios for backup. I pick up the pace, hounded by the sound of his boots thudding on the pavement. Don't run, it'll only get worse.

I get close to the front of the building, and the guard is still trailing me. He still does not yell at me to stop, likely deterred by the summit delegates coming in and out of HRI. I scan the queue of robocabs, hoping to find one I could jump into. All of them are occupied. I keep walking and reach the other side of the street.

As I turn a corner, two guards come my way. I pull up a neighborhood map on my visor and find a row of bars and restaurants located on the next block. That street is sure to be busy; I could lose my tail there. I get to the next block with its sidewalks lined with patio tables filled with al fresco diners enjoying their meals under expansive striped umbrellas. I weave through the ambling crowds, the waiters and busboys tending to their customers, and then turn another corner. When I'm out of the guards' sight, I start running. With every step and every breath, I feel the wound on my side gaping.

The foot traffic is denser in this part of town, and I'm able to sneak a look behind me. They're still following me. With no side streets to turn into, I zigzag through the crowds to shake them off.

I get to a sidewalk outside a sports bar, where a bay of robocabs stands ready to escort drunks home. Groans and howls erupt as I cut the queue and jump on the first car in line. I tell it to cruise at max speed, and it starts blazing down the avenue.

I check my skinseal, and it is soaked through. I ask the cab to take me to the carport using a roundabout way.

I vidcall Sid. No pickup. I send her another message.

Do NOT trust Slimane. Get out of there. I'm heading to the drone.

The carport is devoid of people, and the only motion is from robocabs going to and from their charging docks. The sight of the glossy white quadcopter eases the pain in my side as I get out of my own cab. It slips into a parking spot and leaves me to walk the rest of the unpaved way to the helipad. The gravel path is a slog, and my feet drag, blood seeping out of my side.

Behind me come crunching footfalls on the gravel. Two voices approach from a distance, fast. I dive behind the hedge that lines the path, hoping that I haven't been heard. Through the greenery I spy two guards, outfitted like the others who were chasing me.

One of them stops a few paces away from me, gun drawn. The other checks his visor.

"Eighty feet radius," he says. "We've got her."

Fuck. Sid. She's here, and they've tracked her.

The guards bound away from the path, toward the carport. When they're far enough away, I sneak toward the helipad next to the hedges, following the line of bushes in a low crouch. Twigs and acorns crack with each labored step, but the guards' focus is on the beeline of robocabs exiting the parking structure.

You've got a tail. They're near the drone. I text Sid. Still no answer.

The blades of the quadcopter start whirling, and the noise grabs the guards' attention. I continue on my way, gaining speed as the guards move farther away. If I can reach the drone, I could wait for Sid in there to make our escape. She's got to be nearby.

The engine starts rumbling and the wind whips around the drone, I decide to abandon stealth. I run through the woods, jumping out onto the gravel path and make a mad dash for it.

"Sid!" I shout, hoping she hears me. High-pitched gunshots ring above the noise, as bullets fly past me and ping against the rotor blades. I duck and run and yell for her again.

The blades spin faster and the drone levitates from the tarmac. By the time I reach the helipad, the quadcopter has flown above the pines and into the night.

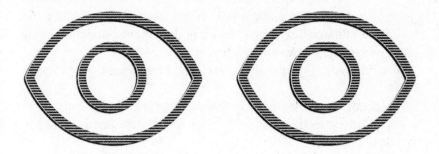

40.

The two sentries stand by the door, staring me down with simmering rage. Both are massive bodybuilder types in full tactical gear, and their looming presence makes the already small room even more claustrophobic. The left one has a shiner on his cheekbone. I don't think I hit him, but the scuffle at the carport happened too quickly for me to recall the details.

From what I can gather of the desk in the corner, the video monitors, and the lack of windows, I've been taken to some sort of security office. We're back at the HRI, that much is certain. My mind races to recall the schematics that Sid sent over my visor earlier. If I have any chance of escape, it'll help to get my bearings.

There's a knock on the door, and Decha enters, again in their crisp white suit, not a hair out of place. They wrest me up from my seat, and the zip ties dig into my wrists. Decha lifts my arm to do a security scan through their visor, and then unhands me once they're done.

"Is someone gonna tell me why I'm here?" I ask.

"Jamie Vega. This is a pleasant surprise," Rafe Lochner says as he joins my captors. His auburn hair has a sheen that matches the gloss of his silk tuxedo. "It must be more than mere coincidence that you've come to HRI the same night I'm here."

"I'm in town for bit of sightseeing. How about you? Fancy party?"

"It appears that I've misplaced a valuable member of my staff," he says, cutting to the chase. "You wouldn't know anything about that, would you?"

"How is that my problem?" I say. They haven't taken Sid, thank god. The doctor may have set me up and fucked us over, but we might yet walk away from this unscathed.

"Sooner or later, I'll find Dr. Slimane. It'll be easier for you if you cooperate." Lochner punctuates the threat by stepping aside, letting Decha loom over me. Yet all I am is confused. I thought he was asking about Sid. Why is he looking for Dr. Slimane? She sent those sentries after me, and Lochner wouldn't have captured me if not for her.

"Am I supposed to know who that is?" I ask.

He smiles as though he'd caught me in a lie. "Yes, you are. The same way you know Isidra Thorpe, your little partner-in-crime."

"Thorpe? What does she have to do with me? Doesn't she work for you?" I ask with an amused smirk. Years at my job have taught me never to answer any questions. Ever. Plus, all the pulp detective novels and cop shows have trained me for this.

"You know," he says, rising from his seat. "I could easily hand you over to the authorities. Put you on the quickest quadcopter back to New York. You're highly sought after."

Sure, I'm afraid of what might happen if Lochner carries out his threat, just as I'm afraid of Decha and their sidearm. But it's too early in the game for me to let fear get the better of me. Cards have been dealt and we're just on the flop; already, Lochner's tipped me off to his hand. He needs me to find Slimane.

"Anyway, why would Thorpe and I be working together? And on what? We have no business in common," I reply defiantly, deflecting from the threat. Giving him the performance expected of a captive.

"Oh, but I think you do," he says. He lifts an open palm and Decha takes that as a cue to clear out. They exit along with the two sentries. My gaze is on Lochner, but my attention is all over the room, the desk, the door and windows. How can I get out of here?

Once we're alone, he continues in a hushed tone. "I know you two are working against me. I know you know about Levantanil. And I know you took it."

Here I keep mum, just shake my head in limp denial. He fills the silence. "I know how Elliott led you to it, and everything that's happened since. So you see, Jamie, all this resistance is useless."

"So you also know what I did to him," I reply, my words laced with a warning.

"I assume you discovered his secrets and had some sort of falling out."

"That's an understatement," I scoff. "The guy wanted to destroy the world. Just like you and your hate group. Yeah, I know about Levantanil. I know you're making it illegally and I know you want everyone to be Sleepless."

"And would that be so bad?" Lochner replies. "For someone who's taken the damn thing, you sound hypocritically disgusted by the idea."

"I'm one person. If everyone becomes Sleepless, the world will break."

If I were to guess, the two sentries are right outside the door behind Lochner, and so is Decha. Even if they aren't standing guard, escape's going to be dicey. The window is no bigger than an air vent, and I still have the zip ties to contend with. There is no fight here, and neither is there flight. Freeze is not an option either, so I must fawn. Lucky for me, that's the option that works best with Lochner's type. I only need to make sure I execute it with a deft hand.

Lochner pauses, weighing the cost and benefit of further discussion. Just as I thought, the balance tips in favor of grandstanding, and he takes the bait.

"The world won't break. It will be better," he starts. "Being Sleepless is a gift. A fairer world is one where everyone has this gift. There will be new challenges, sure, but we will overcome them, the same way we as a species have overcome many others before. Don't you see? All that creative, productive potential, just waiting to be harnessed."

"And that's all that matters to you?"

"Human history has never seen anything like this since the widespread use of electricity," he continues. "When we gained the ability to turn night into day, we also gained the ability to do more. We gained time with family and friends, time to engage in our interests. We got to work more too. The resulting increase in economic activity and prosperity was unparalleled."

His patter speeds up in excitement. "The only limit was our own bodies. Our need for sleep. Now Sleeplessness has done away with that, and Levantanil will grant everyone that gift. Imagine the increase in economic activity, Jamie. The ability to work whenever, wherever, for as long as you want. And then the time to enjoy all the offerings life affords. It'll be the end of poverty, of want."

"It'll cause more want, more poverty. The world won't be better if everyone's Sleepless," I reply, ramping up. "It'll only magnify the problems we already have. No matter how egalitarian you say you are, making everyone Sleepless will still uphold the status quo where the likes of you are in power. Everybody equally gets more time, but the value placed on each person's time, the worth of each person's efforts, will remain unequal. No, Sleeplessness isn't the end of want. Not under the capitalist system that we have. The only thing a Sleepless world will give us is more of the same."

Lochner is unmoved, but persuasion was never the goal. There's no arguing with a megalomaniac, but I can keep giving him opportunities to feel self-satisfied.

"This is where we differ, Jamie," he replies with a disquieting smile. "Given this gift, I believe that people will use it to make the world a fairer place. To solve the problems we face now, and the problems that are yet to come," he explains. "Meanwhile, you seem to think everyone will squander that gift away. Use it for their own ends. Don't get me wrong, I bear no illusions that the road ahead will be easy. But on the whole, I believe in the best of humanity. And you—you expect from it the worst."

"No, you believe in a labor surplus and expanding your empire."

"People can decide for themselves if they want to be Sleepless," he counters. "I'm merely offering them the choice."

"It's a false choice!" I yell. "People want to be Sleepless so they can live. So they can work the second, third, fourth job. So they get hired, so they get promoted. So they can buy the shit you make, the goods you sell, the services you provide. Everyone will choose to be Sleepless, because they can't afford not to be."

My voice grows hoarse, and I hope it achieves the intended effect. Bitterness, resentment, but ultimately, resignation. Rightly or not, Elliott believed that I would be so easily recruited into their ranks. No doubt Lochner thinks the same. The pull by the side of his lip, a tell I've learned from our conversations, is a sign that he thinks he's achieved a measure of victory. Time to ratchet things up.

"I've got it all figured out, Lochner. Your entire operation. How you have a group of biopunks running offshore drug labs, how you're using your shipping business to move product, and how you're using the OEF to fund the operations and launder the drug proceeds . . . and how you and the rest of Exsomnis run the whole show."

"I wouldn't go so far," he says dismissively. "I am not Exsomnis."

"There's no use denying it. I already know."

"Jamie, Exsomnis is nothing more than a social club of discontents and the maladapteds. They're merely a means to an end." He circles my seat and walks behind me, placing his hands on my shoulders. "I'm not going to deny that we share some of the same goals. For one, they have been extremely useful in evangelizing the benefits of Sleeplessness. But I don't believe in their grandiose theories about evolutionary destiny and Sleepless supremacy. I've said so countless times in my advocacy work: I'm for equality, and I condemn any suggestion of Sleepless superiority."

Hollow words, given how he's in bed with them. Whatever he might say, Exsomnis is more than his renegade PR outfit for Sleeplessness. Their members are all over his corporate empire, and they run his drug ring. He can tell himself whatever he wants, but he can't distance himself from this.

"Exsomnis is not just your tool, they're who you are."

"You can say what you want, but I know who I am," he continues. "I'm not a supremacist, I'm just a capitalist fulfilling a need."

"And what about all the secrecy, the deception? Why did Elliott have to lie to get to me?" I ask, adamant. "What need did that fill for me?"

A subtle glimmer surfaces in his eyes. "In hindsight, it may have been unnecessary. Indeed, this conversation tells me it was ill-advised. Despite your protestations, your quarrel is not with Exsomnis ideals, nor with a more Sleepless world. I can tell you agree with me. You understand why I do what I do. You wouldn't have taken the pill otherwise."

When a man is so convinced of his rightness to the point of delusion, his imagination narrows, as I am witnessing right now. To Lochner, it's beyond the realm of possibility that my resistance is real, for how could it be when he is clearly in the right?

"I suppose you'll tell me about my own quarrels then?" I ask. I wear my disgust on my face, but keep my emotions in check. It won't do to antagonize him any more than I have.

"You're mad that you were betrayed. That Elliott managed to do all these things under your nose. As an investigative reporter, you're humiliated, and as a friend, you are hurt. This is not about the rest of the world. This is personal."

All true, but not the entire truth. I hang my head low.

"And in the heat of your anger, you got swept up in this collaboration with Isidra Thorpe and Dr. Slimane," he continues. "It's quite understandable. But now I've told you the whole truth, and now, I trust that you'll reconsider your view of the situation."

Empathy, honesty (or the appearance of it), and bringing the matter down from lofty ideals to baser personal urges—the man may not be studied at interrogation, but he is adept at the techniques of persuasion. A lesser man would have broken by now. I consider it for a moment, but instead I try one last play to push him over the edge.

I straighten my back and stare him in the eye. He remains still, his mien expectant yet also somehow steadfast. The kind of look that someone has when he's certain he has an ace in the hole. Finally, I ask.

"Did you know? That the pill causes amnesia? That I have it?"

"Oh, Jamie. I'm so sorry. When did it start?" he asks, worried. A crack emerges in his veneer of confidence. He leans in to meet my face, close enough to feel his breath on my skin. His eyes peer into in mine, and I see the flickering of his IRIS contacts as it makes its scans.

"So you did know about that side effect," I say.

"I did, but not before we started distribution. I'm sorry, truly I am." He stares off into the distance, waiting for an info packet to get beamed into his eyeballs.

"That thing causes brain damage. I can't remember things anymore. Why the hell would you go into production?" I ask, sounding disappointed more than anything.

"I never lost sight of that problem, Jamie. That's why we're working on it 24/7. With enough time and ingenuity, this too will be solved," he replies. "My labs will perfect Levantanil, and we'll find a way to help those affected."

Lochner falters as he says this, lacking the conviction he's shown thus far. His voice softens, as though distracted, and I notice how he's blinking a tad too fast. The IRIS contacts illuminate his gaze, and then, the pieces click in my mind.

All those new acquisitions and investments made by Lochner —the IRIS contacts, the server farms, visor manufacturing, video content development. All those tech and media companies. Millions of people, years' worth of recordings, the collective experience of every person who ever wore a visor. Lochner isn't gobbling up companies for sheer greed. He isn't buying C+P just to gain his own propaganda machine. It's all part of a grander, more lucrative plan. One that dovetails perfectly with his goal of making everyone Sleepless.

He doesn't want to get rid of encoding failure or perfect Levantanil.

He's trying to own our memories.

I can see it now: video manipulation, targeted advertising. Lochner's content replacing everyone's thoughts and experiences. That was the end game. It's not enough to have the means to make everyone a 24/7 slave to capitalism; he wants to have control over our minds too.

"I promise you," Lochner replies. "We're doing everything we can to disjoin encoding failure from Levantanil."

"And how close are you to doing that?" I ask, adding a note of entreaty in my voice.

"Very close."

Even if he did believe it to be possible, let alone close, fixing en-coding failure isn't his priority. He poured all that money and the full weight of his influence into acquiring all those tech and media companies. His actions tell me he's already decided which course of action will make him more money, and it doesn't involve perfecting Levantanil.

"I sorely want to fix it, Jamie. And I want to fix you." Lochner clasps his hand together, asserting an appearance of control.

"But none of that is possible without the doctor," I say, helping him to his point.

"Yes. We need Dr. Slimane safe and secure, back in my labs, so that she can continue her work." He pauses to look me in the eye again. "And if you tell me where Dr. Slimane is, I promise you, I will do everything in my power to ensure you regain your ability to remember."

There it is.

The journey has been touch and go, but now the give-and-take can finally commence, with just enough doubt for Lochner not to elim-inate me completely. He'd been puffed up and primed, led to believe he'd led me along. He's thinking he's won over my respect, if begrudging, or at the very least he's convinced we share mutual interests. Now I can fawn.

"They're in a safehouse, on the city outskirts."

When Sid devised this plan, she selected four different locations as base of operations. Backups upon backups. I give Lochner a dummy address, complete with descriptions that would lend verisimilitude to the lie. He calls out to Decha, and they reenter the room. They stand behind Lochner, cross-armed and barring the exit. I repeat the information as Lochner stands to leave.

"Where are you going?" I ask, struggling against my restraints.

"We can't release you yet, I'm afraid. We can't risk you changing your mind at the last minute and alerting them. Besides, we have to verify what you've told us," he says.

"I'll lead you to them," I offer desperately. This part isn't an act. There's a greater chance for me to escape once I'm outside this box, and a greater risk of death once they realize I've lied. "As a show of good faith."

Lochner stays silent, only taking the silk sash that hangs around his neck. He clutches both ends and pulls the sash taut, turning the delicate fabric into a fine length of rope. He moves behind me, running the cord of silk against my neck, arresting it from motion. He twists the scarf a couple more times.

I struggle against my restraints, but the zip ties do not loosen. The plastic burns against my wrists. Lochner must think it's pointless to resist, but I make a show of it, for myself as much as for my captors. I'll be damned if this is where it ends.

He moves the scarf away from my neck, and relief rushes through me. He ties it around my eyes instead, and the ball of a knot presses on the back of my head. I yell my protestations, but hear nothing from either Lochner or Decha. All there is is darkness, and the pain of hard plastic digging into my skin.

"If what you've told me is true, then you shall be released. Once I've secured the doctor, I'll do as I promised and give you your reward." Lochner says. "For now, I must leave. But remember this, if you can: no matter how this goes, I will find you again."

The door clicks, and the sound of Lochner's footsteps disappear.

An arm slithers around my neck, cool to the touch. Decha pulls, trapping my neck in their forearm, as their other hand presses down on the back of my head. I try to wrestle free, but their hold is strong and so are the ties on my limbs. Decha tightens their grip, pulling and pushing, crushing my airway.

I can't scream for help or plead for my life. All I manage are desperate gasps, my breaths coming in quick, short bursts. My consciousness starts to dim, catching up to the darkness of the blindfold. Decha's words are the last thing I hear before my senses leave me.

"Good night. Sleep tight."

"Sixty-first floor."

The announcement has a distant quality, like an echo. A chime reminds me to alight, the doors already open. Another passenger enters the elevator, bumping into me. He glances at me apprehensively, and I catch my reflection on the sheen of the elevator's glass sidings. My face looks as bad as it feels. I exit without a word.

My feet know where I'm going, and I walk down the hall with purpose, but I struggle to recall what that is.

Why am I here? Where is here?

I pat down my pockets. I don't have my visor or my earcuff. Lochner's words start returning to me, in faint snatches of sound, out of sequence and out of context.

How long was I out?

This is the fourth time it's happened in the last two weeks, twice in the last couple of days. It may have happened as frequently in the past, but now knowing about the encoding failure makes me more keenly aware of when it happens. Recovering from an episode feels quicker too. Piecing together what happened in the gap—well, that still proves impossible.

The disorientation dissipates, and I hasten toward my destination.

I've been here before, I'm here now, and I know why.

I survey the long hallway, make sure I'm not being followed. When I reach it, I plant my ear against the door of the safe house. I hear Sid's voice talking to someone. I knock and announce myself in a low whisper. The door opens and I find myself face-to-face with the woman in the sapphire pantsuit with the tight ponytail. Dr. Miriam Slimane.

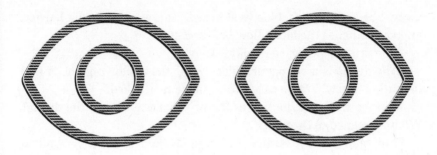

41.

"Took you long enough," Dr. Slimane says, arms folded. Sid shoves her aside and pulls me into the studio, closing the door silently.

"I got your messages. I'm glad you made it," Sid says. "What happened to you?"

"What is she doing here?" I demand. Dr. Slimane comes closer to me and I step back, holding my hand out in futile defense.

"I'm sorry. I needed a quick distraction," she says, with a faint hint of remorse in her voice.

"You could have fucking told me," I tell Sid.

"I was being watched. It took me ages to slip away once they realized Dr. Slimane was missing," she replies. "How did you manage?"

I crash on the couch, and the pain on my side intensifies as I become reacquainted with its existence. I lift my shirt and show them my wound.

"Pre-existing condition. Long story." I turn to Sid: "I didn't want to worry you."

Dr. Slimane rushes to the bathroom and returns with a towel. I direct her to the oxy in my backpack and I inject a double dose right away. She rolls up the bloody skinseal. The wound throbs harder, and she stanches the blood flow before it starts.

"The drone will have a medkit," I say.

"The drone is a couple of miles away," the doctor replies. "I had to dump it elsewhere, in case I was still being tracked."

My eyes widen at the two of them. "That was you in the drone? What happened to the plan?"

"I'm really sorry, Jamie," Sid says. "Like she said, we had to improvise."

"I was calling out to you. At the helipad. Didn't you hear?"

"What? No, I didn't." Dr. Slimane says.

"They were fucking shooting at me."

"Well, I'm glad you got away," Sid says. She pours me a glass of water, a ploy to avoid my gaze. She hands it to me and I snatch it from her, both out of thirst and indignation.

"I didn't get away," I say. "Lochner got me."

I proceed to tell them about the admissions he'd made, how he never showed any shame or compunction about what he and his ilk have been doing. I told them, too, about the depth of his plans, how he was never going to stop at Levantanil.

"He's going to fuck everyone over on both ends: Levantanil for those who want it, and then memory recording and storage tech to cope with the encoding failure," I say. "Making a buck off of both the disease and the workaround to the side effects."

Sid and Dr. Slimane look at each other, astonished and searching for confirmation. This bit of Lochner's grand scheme was news to them. "Why do you think he's been buying all these tech companies and content providers?" I continue. "He's gearing up to invade, and the world's already primed to buy what he's selling: more time and total connectedness."

"That motherfucker," Sid replies, breathless.

"That's only the beginning with Lochner," I say. "Once he has ownership of our memories, he'll also have the power to manipulate them. He can deep-fake everything to his advantage. Business partners, world leaders, anyone within his reach won't be able to trust their recordings. Not when Lochner has total access and the technology to alter them for his own ends."

"We've been watching Levantanil all this time; I should have known he would exploit encoding failure as well," Dr. Slimane replies.

"What else did he say?" Sid asks.

"Not much else," I reply. "I think I properly pissed him off at that point, then I . . . guess I escaped."

"Escaped how?" the doctor asks.

"I—I actually don't remember."

Dread begins to overwhelm me as the sequence of tonight's events become clearer. All the details are now merging with the somnambulic trip that I'm now waking up from. My conversation with Lochner slowly becomes vivid in my mind, like opening one's eyes into sunlight. The blindfold, Decha's headlock, and then nothing. The elevator ride up here.

Another blank space. Another memory lost.

"What do you mean?" Slimane asks with increasing alarm.

"He has it. Encoding failure." Sid answers for me, firm but slow. Judging by the horrified look on Dr. Slimane's face, breaking it gently was necessary. "He took Levantanil a year ago."

"Yes, and I've been blanking on some of my experiences. Including just now. Lochner had his goon knock me out, and the next thing I know I was in the building."

"How much time did you lose?" the doctor asks.

"An hour, maybe more," I say.

"Fuck me. You were walking around Wakefield for an hour, getting from HRI to here," Sid replies, breathless. "Do you know how many cameras could have caught your face that entire time?"

"I may have forgotten the last hour, but I didn't forget that the cops are looking for me," I say firmly. "I'm sure I had the sense to be careful, even if I can't exactly remember doing so."

"Excuse me if I don't bank on your sense of certainty right now," Sid says. "Let's get this over with quick and get out of here."

The two of them stare at each other, exchanging an unspoken message. Sid starts packing up all our things, and Dr. Slimane helps me to my feet. "No one escapes from Lochner. Believe me, I've tried. The only way you'd be here is if he let you go."

"Take your shirt off," Sid barks. I follow, and the doctor turns me around, helping me undress.

"They usually put it in around T-6," Dr. Slimane says as she palpates a spot on my upper back. She sets me back down on the couch and turns me to my side. "A tracker. I had one on me too. Until tonight."

The doctor's fingers move around my back, centering on a small spot between my shoulder blades. "They might have implanted it while you were unconscious," Dr. Slimane says. "It only takes a quick jab of a pneumatic injector."

Sid hands Dr. Slimane another towel, and, after digging deep into her purse, a Swiss army knife.

A searing pain slices through my back.

"A warning would be nice!" I yell.

"You're lucky the implantation was a rush job. It'll be easier to take out," Dr. Slimane says, without a hint of remorse. "Now stop moving, I'm going in."

"Lochner's men are probably en route." Sid says, listening by the door. "How much longer?"

"Let's not rush the doctor while she's got a penknife pointed at my fucking spine," I say.

"Okay, this time it's really going to hurt," Dr. Slimane says.

I scream in agony as the steel probes beneath my skin and scrapes bone.

✿

The coast is clear as we run toward the elevator. Sid explains that we'll have to get off on the third floor and then walk down the rest of the way through an emergency exit. Leaving through the lobby is too risky; Lochner's men are likely all over this building by now.

The elevator hurtles down, giving me a sense of weightlessness, and my entire body throbs like a raw nerve. The longer I press down on the skinseal at my side, the worse it gets.

When we get to the service stairway, I stop to brace myself. The two dash down and I try maintain the same pace, though I know I'm holding them back.

"You two should go. I'll catch up with you," I say. "It'll be a while until they sweep the building."

"We're not leaving you, not in your condition," Dr. Slimane says.

"What else are they going to do to me?" I smirk. "Besides, I'm not the one they're after."

"We can all make it," Sid says. "Once we get to the copter, we'll get you patched up right."

I relent and continue on the way down. A door-slam from below us stops us in our tracks. I peek down the stairwell.

Decha's heading up, gun drawn.

I grab Sid's hand and we run back the way we came. Dr. Slimane follows, and the clatter of our footsteps tells Decha our location. We wind our way back up, making each turn with an eye at the pursuer steadily gaining on us.

We'll have to take a risk with the elevators. We rush out of the emergency stairwell, head down a residential hallway, then run toward the closest elevator bank. Sid mashes the buttons when we reach it, with Decha close behind, making their turn down the hall. They raise their gun and slow their sprint into a saunter, seeing that our only means of escape is still making its way down to us from about twenty flights up.

"Please come with me, Doctor," they yell from the other end of the hall. I put myself in front of the two women.

Decha's lips thin into a mocking smile. "Ready for a real fight?" They hold out an open hand, beckoning me to come closer. "I won't hold back this time."

A kick of shame dampens my resolve, but I've got no choice. I can buy the two of them enough time to get out of here if I hold off Decha for long enough. No assurances that I'll walk away alive, though. I tell the women to stand back, and I raise my arms in surrender.

"I'm in no condition to fight you," I say, moving my hand over the bloody spot on the side of my shirt. I slowly make my way toward Decha. "No one needs to get hurt, so why don't you put the gun down."

"I only came for the doctor."

"Fine," I reply, inching closer. "But you have to let me and Sid go, and promise that the doctor won't get hurt."

"Sure thing," Decha says, staring me down as I stare down the end of their gun. Every muscle on their body is taut, unflinching and undistracted. This ploy isn't working. I'll have to act now.

I charge low at Decha and try to tackle them. They don't shoot, but instead they sidestep, dropping to a knee. They then hit the wound on my side with the butt of their gun. I double over in agony and stagger onto the carpet. Gun aimed at my head, Decha stands over me and starts kicking my side. They only stop when the elevator bell dings.

They turn around and dash toward the doctor, but they're instantly stopped by two shots, right on the chest. Decha lands on the floor with a loud thud.

I find Sid standing in the middle of the hallway, her gun in front of her. She approaches me, keeping it pointed at Decha, whose body lay next to me. Their chest rises and falls in slow, labored breathing, until finally it stops.

"You good?" Sid asks.

I nod, dazed and in pain.

I take her outstretched hand, and she lifts me off the ground. At the end of the hallway, Dr. Slimane holds the elevator door for us in stunned silence.

The doctor and I settle into the back seat of the robocab as Sid jumps in front to take charge of the controls. She directs our car to the north end of Wakefield, where our ride sits waiting in a pay-per-hour drone hangar. After refueling, the copter should be able to take us on a short hop to Portland. From there, we can catch an all-night maglev to wherever, get the doctor's story on record, then the two off them can jet off and begin their long journey to Stockholm.

"You're losing blood," Dr. Slimane tells me. She wipes the sweat off my brow with her sleeve. "How's the pain?"

"I'll be fine."

"Sorry, Jamie, but I'll have it take the long way, just in case," Sid says, checking on me from the front seat. "Hang in there."

"I'm trying. How about you? You okay?" I ask. She's been mostly silent since killing Decha.

"I never like doing it," Sid replies. "But it had to be done."

"Your encoding failure," Dr. Slimane says after a long silence. "Tell me what happened tonight."

"It felt like no time had passed. I didn't even know what happened until I started remembering where I was last."

"And it's happened before?"

"Yes, three times. That I can tell." I summarize my previous episodes to her.

"When we were in the initial test phase for Levantanil, we found a minor impairment in the subjects' ability to encode episodic memories," she says after a long pause. "Yours seems more severe. You were unable to form a memory for what sounds like several hours. That's unlike anything I've seen."

"My doctor thinks it might also be trauma-related?"

"If anything, trauma affects retrieval, not encoding," she replies.

"If it's not related to my past trauma, then it's probably because of something in Levantanil."

"No, it's not that either." The doctor pauses, and her reluctance is so obvious that Sid turns to pay attention. "Prior to working for Lochner, I've done studies that showed a minor incidence of memory problems with natural hyperinsomniacs. Those earlier studies were never quite conclusive. Working for Lochner, I found that the correlation does exist, and it is not minor at all. Our Levantanil control group—the people who did not take pill and became Sleepless via the pandemic—they had serious encoding failure too."

"Miriam, what are you trying to say?" Sid asks, breaking her silence.

"I'm afraid encoding failure is caused by hyperinsomnia, artificial or otherwise."

"No. It can't be."

"Sleeplessness causes the memory loss, not Levantanil."

Sid and I turn to each other, searching for assurance that the other is unable to give. The gravity of Dr. Slimane's revelation is too immense to grasp. The doctor continues. "Your memory lapse might have manifested more quickly than normal, for various reasons: stress, trauma, and most likely the chemical effects of Levantanil. But let me be clear: hyperinsomnia and encoding failure are inextricably linked. Everything I've discovered leads me to such a conclusion."

"Who else knows about this?" Sid asks. "Does Lochner?"

"No. This is something I'd been meaning to tell you, Sid. But I couldn't," she says, turning to Sid and me in turn, helpless and exposed. "Never in my life have I feared where the science led, until now."

"So what does this mean?" I ask.

"We can account for individual variability, but intermittent memory loss like yours might well be the best-case scenario. Worst case scenario, at some point, all Sleepless persons will have impaired ability to encode episodic memories."

"You don't mean . . ."

"Eventually the Sleepless will stop making new memories. Permanently."

All those millions of people, at risk of losing their memories. Not even having them in the first place. Here I am, believing that stopping Levantanil distribution might forestall a catastrophe. It had already arrived, with the first human who woke for the last time. Hyperinsomnia has given humanity more time, and the unseen price that it exacts is oblivion.

The robocab drives down a quiet stretch of highway, past a solar farm, then into a compound of squat buildings. Each structure is a scaffold of metal frames with just enough space to receive and eject quadcopters into one of a row of helipads. This late into the night, there are hardly any drones heading out; most are flying home into their steel nests.

Our robocab slows as it reaches its destination. Drone hangars line both sides of the compound, and the cab pulls up to park right next to one of them, announcing that we have arrived.

Before we get out of the cab, I spot three figures in black outfits, all of them equipped with visors and XFrames, and with guns at the ready. I point them out to Sid.

"Fuck. They've tracked down our ride."

Sid kills the engine and the three of us keep our heads low. Lochner's men survey the hangar that held our quadcopter. Convinced that it's empty, they then make a circuit of the building. When they turn into another section of the hangar, we slowly roll out of our parking spot, and speed back down the highway.

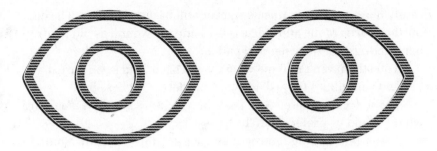

42.

Monday, 07/20/2043, 01:51 AM

In the entirety of the Sleepless city of Wakefield, at this godforsaken hour, there is only one motel with a vacancy, the robocab tells us. It brings us to an older cluster of town around which the new metropolis has metastasized. The homes here are humbler, the shops farther apart, the occasional lightbulb or welcome sign is turned off. A vestige of old Wakefield, it's the part of town where people still sleep, and we just booked its last remaining bed.

The only 24/7 store is the one that matters, and Sid returns from the pharmacy with a stitcher, skinseals, and disinfectant. She also gets me a cheap set of earcuffs and disposable visors, to replace the ones Lochner took from me. The brushed steel feels too light, the glass panel too brittle. I don't put it on.

"It's a burner. We'll need it for coordination," she says. "But remember not to use any of your credentials on it. That way your location data can't get tracked."

I notice she says *you* and not *we*. We might all be on the run, but only one of us has the undivided attention of law enforcement.

She checks on Dr. Slimane's back, making sure the site of her recently liberated subcutaneous tracker still has its dressing. The doctor then turns to me and starts redressing my wound as Sid tends to hers, acting as both healer and patient.

"You still haven't told me where you'd been," Sid says, miffed.

"Did you think I flipped on you?" the doctor replies slyly.

"For a second there, yes. That, or you were dead. Wasn't sure what I would've preferred, to be honest."

"I was put in vans and jets and barges for a month. Shuffled around and hauled from one end of Africa to another, like a prisoner. Sorry I couldn't get a hold of a secure sat phone."

"Someone's got a flair for the dramatic," Sid stage-whispers to me. Though suffused with some rancor, their repartee is familiar, if not friendly. Makes me forget the wild night we've had so far.

"I suppose now we can do formal introductions," the doctor says, ignoring the last remark. She inspects my incision, then uses the stitcher to close it up. She then applies a new skinseal. "Nice to meet you, Jamie Vega, ace reporter."

"Likewise," I reply. "Thanks for not paralyzing me with a Swiss army knife."

"I hope you're not still sore about the guards. I needed to shake them off."

"I am, but I'll get over it." No promises though on how long it'll take. The doctor basically sacrificed me, knowing there'd be a decent chance I'd be captured, and she made that decision without consulting me or Sid. The only reason I'm alive is luck.

"You know, your ex-boss could have killed me," I say with some levity, but the remark still lands like dead weight.

The doctor replies contritely. "Yes, it was a risk, and I am terribly sorry. I hope you'll let me make it up to you somehow."

The sincerity is such a profound shift from her otherwise hard demeanor that I find myself at a loss. I've also been fucked over so many times in the last couple weeks, and this is the first time someone's actually apologized. In reply, I nod and change the subject, seeking to avoid my own show of vulnerability.

"You know, I looked you up," I say. "You had a stellar career, you could have done anything you wanted. Why did you go work for Lochner?"

Sid rises from her seat and gives Dr. Slimane a firm look. One that says, *You can trust him.* To me, Sid says, "Try not to judge too harshly, huh?"

Dr. Slimane brushes her off. "Well before Lochner, I've always had deep objections to the international treaties against caffeine synthetics. Regulations like that stifle discovery, and I felt it most acutely when I was at the CDC. There was only so much I could do without the right materials and equipment. I'm surprised we even have a body of research about hyperinsomnia, given those limits.

"When I gained a bit of prominence, Lochner found me. He enticed me with a generous salary and an unlimited research budget. Most of all, he promised access. He had a way to skirt the rules, he said. He'd get me contraband materials and provide me with cover. I'd have unfettered leeway to pursue the work that I've always wanted to do: find the cause of hyperinsomnia, and a way to prevent it."

"And did you? Find the cause, I mean."

"No. Not yet, anyway." Her regret is palpable, "That was what I was trying to do when I developed the formula that eventually became Levantanil. Using compounds and synthetics I never had before, I succeeded in inducing hyperinsomnia in lab rats. That development made me feel like I was inching closer to finding the cause, or a treatment, which I thought was Lochner's end game."

"But he never wanted to stop hyperinsomnia," Sid interjects.

"I know that now," the doctor replies. "But when he brought me on board, I thought that he had good intentions."

Her jaw clenches, neck muscles taut. I can tell she doesn't fully believe that herself. The more I learn about her, the more I understand that Dr. Slimane is more slippery than I first thought. She knew Lochner would have some way of capitalizing from her work, and she was fine with it. She was fine with breaking the law to pursue her research. She was no saint. But in this whole mess, I suppose no one is.

"What made you turn on him?" I ask.

"When we began human test subjects, we found symptoms of encoding failure. I'd already known from my previous work that this was a possibility, but now I saw it in front of me. Just like you did," she says to me, "At first I thought that the compound caused it. But with more research, it became more evident that it was hyperinsomnia itself.

"I wanted to reach out to other labs, former colleagues, to see if any of them had similar findings," she continues. "But Lochner kept me under lock and key so I couldn't confer with anyone. I redid all my tests, meticulously replicating each step. The conclusion remained the same. Eventually, I told Lochner what I had discovered.

"He didn't care about the encoding failure at all. Instead, he kept me on a tighter leash, told me to keep refining the Levantanil formula, ostensibly so that we could run more tests and finally learn how hyperinsomnia occurs naturally and how it is transmitted. His nonchalance at my discovery aroused my suspicions, and that's when I started snooping around. I then discovered that Lochner had another team working to mass-produce Levantanil. That's when I went to Sid and Simon."

Of course it was all about money for Lochner. Levantanil, the buyout of C+P and all those media and tech firms, the hunt for Dr. Slimane—those have never been about the science or pushing the limits of human potential. A Sleepless world was never about equality, or the optimal way to live. As with everything, it was always about maximizing shareholder fucking wealth.

"When the three of us came together, we pieced together the full scope of Lochner's plans," Sid explains. "The doctor came to us about the development of Levantanil, and I had already previously discovered a strong underground Exsomnis presence within the OEF. Simon was supposed to get us more dirt on Lochner too, and then when I got Miriam to a safe-enough place away from Lochner, Simon would expose all of this to the world."

"I suppose that's your job now," Dr. Slimane tells me. Her words make me feel like I'm being both anointed and indicted. Without a word, I leave the women mid-conversation and head toward the closet. I unzip my luggage and unpack my recording equipment.

"How much time do you need to get ready?" I ask the doctor.

"Hold on," Sid says. "We can get going first thing tomorrow. None of us has any fuel left in the tank tonight."

"No, we need to get started. Now." The two of them straighten, startled by my forcefulness. I boot up my laptop, articulate the legs of my camera tripods. "I don't know when I'm going to glitch again. We don't even know if I'm encoding this moment right now. I'm not taking any chances."

"You know, some of us still need sleep," the doctor replies, yawning.

"The C+P Board is going to vote on the Lochner's buyout offer tomorrow afternoon," I say. "I want this story to be the first thing the world sees when they wake up. I'll upload the report from here, together with the document cache. C+P's probably revoked my credentials, so I'll use a private uplink channel and make sure it's accessible to all the news outlets before sunrise."

"The world will be in a panic once they hear about encoding failure," Sid says.

"Sooner's better than later. Every passing day is a risk. Look at me. Who knows what Sleepless people aren't remembering already?"

"You sound just like Simon," she replies, equal parts wistful and wary.

"This is what he would want."

Sid turns to Dr. Slimane, passing the decision on to her.

"Fine. I want to get this story out as much as you do," the doctor says. "So we'll do the interview now. I'll transfer over all the documents too. But after this, I'm going straight to bed."

I set up my gear quickly—the mics, the lighting, the accoutrements I use for production. A heady thrill overcomes me, one I haven't felt in a long time. Not since two summers ago, when I blew that water-hoarding story wide open. Here I am again, striking it out on my own, no support from Simon or anyone at C+P. The consequences are greater now, but I've grown too. What was it that Simon told me after that disaster? That I needed discernment. I needed to better judge when to forge ahead and when to quit. Well, this is certainly not the time for the latter.

Dr. Slimane doesn't ask for much prep time, and is ready to roll well before my setup is ready. Sid hovers behind the lights, hands crossed, tense in anticipation. I take my seat behind the camera and then nod toward the doctor. She sees the red light, acknowledges my cue, and then with fire in her eyes, she tells the world her story.

❁

Stillness reigns in the early morning hour. Dr. Slimane is stretched like a rod across the length of the couch, unmoving. I don't recall the last time I watched a person sleep, and doing so now lulls me into an easy reverie, only to be pulled back into consciousness by the things she said during the interview.

Every hyperinsomniac, artificial or otherwise.

No new memories.

The words reverberate in my head, imprinting themselves sylla-ble by syllable. Maybe this is my way of avoiding their meaning. Or maybe this is my new way of remembering.

Sid sits stoic across the table from me. Her attention is trans-fixed on the wine glass in front of her, from which she has not taken a single sip. The light overhead casts a golden shadow against her dark face. She's tired, and we still have a long way to go.

She is worried about the morning after. Once the world learns of encoding failure, how will the Sleepless be treated? Are we going back to the days where we're viewed with suspicion and horror? We won't just be sleepless, we'll be sleepwalking too. Moving around the world, barely knowing and not remembering. Experiencing every-thing and retaining nothing. If a person's life is the sum of his experi-ences, what does a Sleepless person have when he remembers none?

"You sure you'll be safe in Stockholm?" I say, breaking the weighty silence. Aside from a vague plan to get out of the country, Sid and the doctor have been avoiding specifics.

"Yes. Though that's not our destination yet," she replies. "We have labs elsewhere in Scandinavia. We'll have to disappear there for a while. She can continue her research, hopefully without the need to break international laws."

"Not your style?"

Sid shakes her head. "As you can probably tell, Lexell toes the line, but we try not to cross it."

"When this is all done, when everyone's safe and sound," I ask, hesitant. "Do you think she can undo Levantanil?"

"With our team's combined expertise and backing, I think Miriam can do it, yes."

On mention of her name, the doctor rises from the couch lazily. Sid and I both make a display of apologizing, but she waves us off. "I wasn't asleep anyway." She walks over to us, taking the chair next to me.

"So is there any chance that I . . . ?"

"A chance that your hyperinsomnia could be reversed?" Dr. Slimane says. "Yes, but not yet."

"You said my encoding failure is the most advanced you've seen. I'm sure I could be helpful."

"Certainly. Live human subjects are always the most helpful," she replies. "But if we do this, you'll have to give up your life, be in hiding."

"If it means finding a cure . . ." I say.

"You've been through enough. Today alone. I couldn't ask any more of you," Dr. Slimane says. "This is my mess. I have to make it right."

"Then maybe you can make it right through me."

Sid reaches out to hold my hand, and her touch gives me a jolt. She gazes into my eyes tenderly. "Jamie, you know we can't take you. Not while the cops are after you."

The three of us sit in silence, our faces cast in light and shadow. Even before I asked, I knew that the need to restore my ability to remember did not outweigh the risk that I pose. I'm accused of murder and corporate espionage. I'm the subject of an interstate manhunt, and my face is still plastered all over the news feeds. I'll only be a liability to them. How could I cross any borders? Sid's gaze stays with me and tells me what I already know, but her sympathy is a comfort.

"Part of me wishes I'd never involved you, gotten you tangled up in this," she says. "This fucking mess."

"I wanted to do this," I reply. "And we've almost won."

"People got hurt. People died," she continues despite my assurance. "That's all on me."

My interview with the doctor mentioned Simon extensively, revealing his conversations and correspondences with her, the scope of his involvement in investigating Lochner's designs for distributing Levantanil. Sid had stayed impassive during the doctor's most damning revelations, but she was visibly affected whenever the doctor spoke of Simon. Her mind is still on him.

"His death is not your fault," I tell Sid.

"I brought him in," Sid says, her voice growing firmer. "I asked him to help me do it. If I hadn't, maybe Maxwell wouldn't have murdered him."

"That's not what happened," I assure her, realizing that she's been laboring under the same misconceptions as everyone else.

"What do you mean?"

"I still don't remember much from that night, but I know how Simon died."

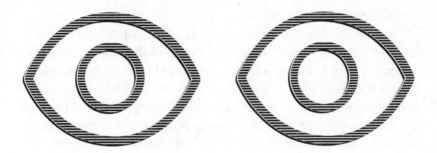

43.

"From the very beginning I never thought this was a straightforward case of suicide. When I saw Simon that morning, dead in his office, my gut told me something else had happened. This was a case of murder."

Sid picks up the drink before her, the one she'd been staring at all night, then takes a swig. She waves the glass in the air and signals me to proceed.

"At first I thought it had something to do with a story that Simon and the team were pursuing. We'd been investigating shady campaign contributions made to US Senator Mason Dwyer. But the more I looked into it, the more it became evident that someone closer to Simon did it."

"Like who?" Dr. Slimane asks.

"I thought it may have been his assistant Anders, whom Simon fired hours before his death. I also thought it may have been Cleo," I say, turning to Sid, who startles at my mention of the name. "She was determined to bury our Dwyer story right after Simon died. But it wasn't either of them."

352 | VICTOR MANIBO

"How do you know?" Sid asks.

"Anders was the one who led me to you, actually. As for Cleo, she'd been acting under Simon's orders to shelve the Dwyer piece because he was lining up another story—the story he was working on with the two of you. Simon's final assignment. He kept that story under wraps, given Lochner's impending buyout of C+P. This was also around the time that he began to suspect that someone from the staff was watching him, leaking confidential information. He became more secretive, paranoid."

"But he wasn't paranoid," Sid says. "He had reason to be suspicious."

"Right. Elliott had been spying on him on behalf of Lochner. Through Elliott's surveillance, Lochner learned that the two of you were working with Simon to expose his illegal Levantanil operation. And that's when he moved his labs and production to a completely different part of the world," I turned to the doctor. "Which was also how he kept you away from Simon."

"Of course. Lochner couldn't risk getting caught," Sid replies.

"The Board vote was a couple weeks away, and it was looking like the buyout offer would be accepted," I continue. "So you can imagine the kind of pressure Simon was under. His plan to stop the C+P acquisition required exposing Lochner's criminal enterprise and his connections to Exsomnis. If that news got out, Lochner would go to prison, which would ruin his reputation and bring down his empire. All that relied on getting you, Dr. Slimane."

Sid starts to tear up and abruptly wipes her hand across her face. "The last time I spoke to him was the day you went dark," she says to the doctor. "Simon flew into a rage. We both thought you'd been caught. He was certain you were dead. I tried to convince him otherwise, but he felt that all was lost."

"That's when Simon decided to set everything in motion," I said, turning to the doctor. "When you disappeared, Simon's erratic behavior escalated. By the time he died, everyone saw how paranoid he had become, which made it easy for them to accept the theory that he took his own life."

"Are you saying that's not what happened?" Sid asks. Dr. Slimane similarly looks confused.

"A couple of nights after he died," I continue, "I found in my jacket pocket an empty vial of A-Pop. It's a new street drug, lethal in the wrong hands. I didn't know where the vial came from, so I retraced my steps, but I couldn't remember all of them. I was missing a few hours on Wednesday night. That's when I first realized that I had some sort of memory glitch."

"The first time that you remember, at least," the doctor says soberly.

"Then the detective investigating Simon's death told me I was the last person who saw him alive, which I don't remember. He also told me that Simon died from an A-Pop overdose. That scared me shitless. I didn't know what I'd done, but I thought maybe I killed Simon."

Dr. Slimane gives me a sympathetic look, the kind usually reserved for terminal patients. She had cause. The worst time for someone to lose their memory is in the middle of an ongoing murder investigation.

Sid leans in from her seat. "But then Maxwell got arrested."

"Which to me only raised more questions. The vial meant I was involved somehow, so I decided to find proof that I didn't kill Simon.

"The timeline was my first stumbling block," I continue. "I left work at 6 p.m. and I was home at seven when my ex came by. That's around the time my memory blanked out, but I did piece everything together eventually. I went back to C+P after 8 p.m. to drop something off for Elliott. That's when I saw Simon in his office."

"Well, that should clear you then," Sid says with more authority that I'd ever felt during this entire ordeal. "You obviously didn't plan on being there that night, let alone plan on committing a murder."

"Right. My return to C+P that night was absolutely unplanned. As far as Simon thought, the only ones who were supposed to be on our floor were him and Maxwell. No one else. This is key."

The women give me a cryptic look.

"You see, shortly before I arrived, Simon had asked Maxwell to come to his office, under the pretext of celebrating the impending Zephyrus acquisition. Simon told him to bring the wine, and that wine is how the A-Pop entered Simon's system."

"He arranged for the pieces to be there," Sid says, realization slowly dawning on her. "And believed there was no one else to witness it."

"So . . . is it that Simon tried to kill Maxwell?" Dr. Slimane asks, turning to both Sid and me. "But then he botched it and drank from the wrong glass?"

"No." Sid replies for me, finally understanding. I expect her to be more shocked, but she merely looks ponderous. She's not rejecting the idea at all. I give her a grave nod in confirmation.

"Simon killed himself and tried to frame Maxwell for it."

I've been agonizing over this idea for three days now, letting the pieces accrete in my mind like sediments settling to form stone. Now that I've spoken it, it assumes a form, a weighty reality, one that in my speaking both burdens and unburdens me.

"Maxwell is shown on surveillance, going into Simon's office, bottle in hand," I explain. "Then, when he left a few minutes later, Simon took the A-Pop. He placed an empty pill tube by the wine glass to make it look like an overdose. But he made sure that the pill tube was pristine, unmarked, so that it looked like it had been planted."

"Why?"

"In order to frame Maxwell for murder, Simon needed to stage the suicide in such a way that would prompt the cops to look more deeply. A smart man like Maxwell would know to cover his tracks, so the scene had to look like it was staged just enough. It needed to look obvious, but not too obvious.

"The planted pill tube was Simon's first clue for the cops," I say. "When forensics found no fingerprints and no trace materials, that led them to the possibility of foul play. Then surveillance showed Maxwell with the wine, and the tox screen came back positive with A-Pop. Then the cops found motive; it wasn't a secret that Simon and Maxwell were on opposite ends of the C+P Board vote. Put those together, and well . . . game over, Cartwright."

"But what about those pill tubes?" Sid asks. "Why did you have an identical one?"

"The one the cops recovered from the scene was planted evidence to frame Maxwell. The one that ended up in my jacket, well, that's a bit more complicated."

"How so?"

"That was the vial of A-Pop that Simon actually used to kill himself."

This is the part that pains me the most. I've turned it over and over in my head, and of all the tiny betrayals that have happened in the past two weeks, this is the one that pains me the worst.

"After overdosing himself with A-Pop, he couldn't leave the actual vial in his office. Not the one with all his fingerprints and trace material. His plan was to dispose of the evidence by throwing it out his office window after Maxwell leaves. The problem was, the window wouldn't open," I explain. "This detail puzzled me when I snooped around the scene, and I then remembered that there'd been maintenance work done on the C+P building exterior only two days prior, and Simon probably didn't know that the window had been jammed shut.

"He had to get rid of the vial some other way, but he couldn't leave his office because then he'd get caught on surveillance after Maxwell had purportedly poisoned him. He also couldn't hide it somewhere in his office, because the room would be swept by the cops after his body was found. So the vial had to leave that room without him stepping out of the room himself. That's where I came in.

"When I popped into Simon's office that night, Maxwell had just left. Simon didn't foresee my arrival at all, hadn't planned on anyone else being there at that hour. With my arrival, he had an expedient solution to his problem. I became his method of disposal. Simon planted the vial on me, and when I left his office, I took the proof of his cause of death with me."

The words leave me, and with them I feel I've lost all of my strength.

When I went into his office that night, Simon might as well have been a dead man, with a lethal dose of narcotics swirling in his blood. He was minutes away from cardiac arrest, from the cessation of his heartbeat, his breathing, his consciousness and existence. Yet when I came to see him, inadvertently and unexpectedly, he did not see a way to escape death. He did not see a loyal friend, a devoted follower, a person who could save him if he changed his mind. His survival instinct never kicked in. He did not have the final flicker of regret, no urge to undo what he'd done. All he had was a plan, and all he saw was a means to an end.

"But he couldn't have known that you'd forget about seeing him, that you weren't encoding it," Sid says, after leaving me some time to catch my breath.

"You're right, he couldn't have. Either Simon counted on me not finding the vial, or he thought I wouldn't say anything if I found it and figured out what had happened." He also couldn't have anticipated that I'd be the first one there the next day, or that I would ask questions and dig deeper into his death.

In the end, Simon didn't think much of me or how I'd end up.

"How did you figure all of this out?" Dr. Slimane asks.

"I'm the only one who knows about the empty vial of A-Pop," I reply. "And without that piece of evidence, the cops had no way of putting it all together. I worked out the timeline too. But most of all, I looked into everyone who could have done it."

"And it wasn't Elliott? He'd been working for Lochner," she asks. "As much as Maxwell was, it seems."

"Elliott's done a lot of horrible things, but this wasn't one of them. His only concerns were helping Lochner and not being found out as the mole. For what it's worth, he loved Simon. Most of all, he had no reason to kill him, and neither did Lochner or Maxwell."

"What do you mean?" Sid asks. "Simon was gunning for Lochner."

"That didn't mean Lochner wanted Simon dead," I reply. "He didn't need him dead."

"How so?" the doctor asks.

"Lochner had Elliott in place, his eyes and ears in C+P, which allowed Lochner to respond to any threat Simon posed. So when he started looking into Levantanil, Lochner was able to pull up stakes and secure Dr. Slimane, thus ensuring Simon couldn't carry on with his exposé. That's all he needed to do. Lochner didn't need to resort to murder, and even if he wanted to, there would have been cleaner and easier ways kill Simon outside of C+P premises."

"What about revenge?" Sid says. "Isn't that what the cops have on Maxwell? Simon got C+P Board members to flip their votes, and so Maxwell killed him, either on his own accord or at Lochner's behest."

"No, because Simon never flipped the vote," I say, to their surprise. "On Wednesday night, Simon invited Maxwell into his office to concede and to celebrate the buyout. Presumably that meant that Simon did not have enough votes. At the time, the rumor was that the Board was tied, and in such an event, Maxwell had the tiebreak vote, as the Board chair.

"But all of that is inconsistent with what Simon told his anti-buy-out faction," I continue. "The day before he died, Simon talked to the other Board members who were 'no' votes. He told them that he successfully flipped one of the 'yes' votes, Briana Foley."

"Which meant that the buyout would not happen," Sid replies.

"Yes. The intricacies of Robert's Rules of Order are probably lost on the fine detectives over at the NYPD, but this inconsistency is more critical than it appears. A flipped vote is motive, or lack of one in this case."

"What do you mean?" Sid asks.

"Briana Foley had been overseas the week Simon died, and only returned in time for Simon's funeral. The NYPD interviewed her, and through one of the detectives, I found out that she never flipped. Briana Foley was always going to vote yes. Which means Simon had lied to his faction."

"Why would he do that?"

"If it appeared to the world that Simon had succeeded, or at least that the vote was tighter that initially believed, that provided a reason for Maxwell to kill him," I explain. "In truth, Maxwell didn't need to get rid of Simon. He knew Briana Foley was always going to be a yes vote, which meant the tie was always going to hold, which meant that Maxwell was always going to get the chance to break the tie in his favor."

"But in order for Simon's ploy to work, the cops needed Maxwell to have an apparent motive for murder," Sid adds. "So Simon made it look like he did."

"In a 5-5 split, the buyout offer would be accepted, and Lochner wins. Simon knew that this was what was going to happen. He failed to flip the 'yes' votes and you, Dr. Slimane, were likely dead. Simon had no other moves left. He had lost."

"And that's why he did it," the doctor replies, dejected.

I only sigh in response. Ever since Paolo, I've tried to avoid the whys of someone killing themselves. I've learned that the whys are more important to those who were left behind than to those who left. With Simon, I felt that at least knowing how it happened would give me some measure of peace.

Because the how is the easy part. The how is bound in fact. The why is not as fixed.

"The Board vote was probably part of it," I reply after a pause. "Simon saw the looming takeover of his company, his life's work bought out by a man he despised. He also knew about Lochner's ties to Exsomnis, and he feared what C+P would turn into once those people took control. And to have his best friend and business partner orchestrate the deal . . . Simon was losing everything he'd built."

"Not to mention he'd failed to stop Lochner's plans with Levantanil," Sid says. "Simon had a vicious side, and he did want to ruin Lochner for more personal reasons, but he also wanted to keep everyone from becoming Sleepless. I saw how devastated he was when he thought we'd lost you, Miriam. He felt responsible for that. For you, and for the rest of the world."

"So he decided to sacrifice himself," the doctor replies.

"And take Maxwell down in the process," Sid adds. "Make sure the architect of the buyout is ruined, throw the entire company into chaos. Even if the C+P Board still voted yes, the Zephyrus Board likely wouldn't want to move ahead with the acquisition anymore."

"Lochner wouldn't have allowed that to happen, but that doesn't matter now," I reply. "Point is, he and Maxwell and Elliott didn't need Simon dead. They'd already won."

"Not anymore," the doctor says. "Not after today."

The way she said it was meant to inspire, to reassure. Yet the only thing I feel is a smoldering rage. Recounting all of this makes the betrayal real. Two people so close to me, Simon and Elliott, both used me as a means to an end, risking my life in the process.

Yes, my efforts here might help save C+P and the thousands of people who would take Levantanil. I might eventually finish what Simon set out to do. At the very least, the doctor's revelations will lead to a deeper understanding of Sleeplessness and how memory works. All that may be true, and yet I also know this to be true: our victories today won't ease the pain of their treachery.

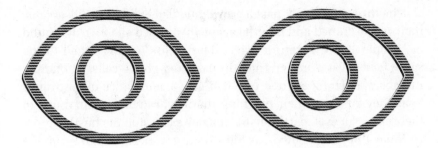

44.

Monday, 07/20/2043, 08:33 AM

A tense disquiet envelops the city. The Wakefield Central Transport Hub is as busy at this hour as any other, but the mania of the commuter rush is compounded with agitation. All around the hub, the vid screens are turned to C+P Breaking News, playing my interview of Dr. Slimane. The feed's been picked up by other outlets too, with differing angles and varying degrees of accuracy and spin:

Sleepless 'Amnesia' Feared
Illegal Artificial Hyperinsomnia Trade Revealed
Zephyrus CEO's Shocking Ties to Supremacist Group
read the chyrons under the clips of the doctor's revelations.

Sid leads our way through the concourse, stealthily eyeing any surveillance cameras that might detect us despite our efforts. The doctor's large, dark-rimmed glasses and a face-rec camo headscarf should confuse any detection algorithms. As for me, I've got on a baseball cap with a similar geometric camo print, and my visor is turned completely dark, a black band across my face. We barely blend in with the average Wakefielder, but the relative mayhem has made it easy for Dr. Slimane and me to slip by unnoticed.

The three of us walk past a crowd huddled before the vidscreens, their necks craned and mouths agape in stunned silence. All around us, people stand frozen in place, their visors on and tuned to the same feeds. A few are engaged in panicked phone calls—to family members, doctors, anyone who can give a semblance of assurance —as they go about their morning routines, catching their trains to their jobs. Not even earth-shattering news can stop the hustle.

Since I'm still "tainted," as Sid says, we were careful to scrub me from the video. Usually it's the other way around, and so the voice scrambler is an odd choice to use on the interviewer rather than the whistleblower, but no one seems to be questioning it. The producer of the clip might be anonymous, but Dr. Slimane is real, with verifiable credentials, and so are the documents in her data dump.

The news feeds are full of nervous commentators and their speculations, asking the questions that have wracked me all night. Some of the talking heads are research and academic types struggling to explain the science in Dr. Slimane's reports. Depending on how a news outlet leans, the analysis is overlaid with either sober skepticism or raving denialism. In any case, none of the pundits seem able to accept the implications, even as they claim to believe the data.

The more worrying footage comes from "man on the street" type interviews, impromptu reactions from a public caught unaware. Their comments range from disbelief to panic, and the sentiments are echoed by the snatches of conversations we overhear as we walk toward our maglev platforms.

"We warned you about those people!" a decrepit church lady tells a reporter, wagging her finger for emphasis. The video clip is met with jeers from the Wakefielders.

"Yeah, I'm Sleepless but it's not like, a sure thing, right?" a college kid tells another reporter. "And if it happens, it happens. It's not the worst thing in the world."

Easier said than lived, kiddo. Wait until you forget your first time.

A local news crew has stationed itself in the middle of the Wakefield hub's busy atrium, gathering crowd reactions to the news. People have mostly avoided the fresh-faced reporter and his cameraman, not with the typical harried annoyance but with fear and anxiety. This city, with all its Sleepless folks, is clearly unraveling with the news of encoding failure. I worry for Wakefield, a place I don't even like, as it comes to the precipice of mass panic.

I turn on my own visor. The first clip is NY1 outside Bellevue, where the hospital staff have been turning panicked people away from the emergency room. "None of this qualifies as a medical emergency!" A burly ER nurse shouts over the crowd. "Please, clear the way, go make an appointment with your primary care providers!"

Instinctively, I direct my visor to check messages, forgetting that it's a burner. No files, contact info, location data, that can be traced to one Jamie Vega. I recall Dad's final messages. *WRU? R U OK? Pls call. We are v worried. COPS CALLING, WHAT SHOULD WE SAY?* I imagine the torment that he and Mom are going through, the sleepless night they've had, the hours wasted at incessant attempts to reach their troubled, wayward son.

The worry and remorse halts me in my tracks, compelling me to abandon the plan, or at least call my Dad back, security be damned. Just then, I'm saved by news bulletins that pop up on the side of my screen.

The Secretary of Health and Human Services is giving a press conference from the Rose Garden at 9 a.m. EST, to address the revelations about hyperinsomnia and encoding failure. Then another: outside the gates of the Zephyrus corporate headquarters in Chicago, environmental groups have gathered in a mass protest, decrying the evils of Levantanil and a larger Sleepless population. And another: a statement from Dalton Hughes, Grand Torchbearer of Exsomnis, denying any ties to Zephyrus or the Levantanil trade, and in the same breath extolling the benefits of hyperinsomnia, regardless of its genesis.

I scroll further and I find no mentions of C+P in any of the early morning broadcasts, nor anything about the manhunt for the prime suspect in Simon's murder. By my own hand, I've managed to bump myself off the news coverage, and but I am nowhere near relieved.

Yes, we did the right thing, and we had to do it quickly, before Lochner has a chance to catch us or buy out C+P. Yet the firmness of my beliefs disintegrates the more I witness what we have wrought.

Maybe we should have planned this better. There may have been a better way to roll this out, instead of springing it onto the world in one massive news story. The chaos in this transport hub is but a microcosm of what awaits us once we've left Wakefield, and today is only the beginning.

Lochner's voice surfaces in my fickle memory. *I believe in the best of humanity. You expect from it the worst.*

We arrive at our platform, the doctor and I keeping our heads down as Sid keeps watch. We position ourselves behind a Hudson News stand, near the crowds but not close enough to be spotted. Dr. Slimane's face is still prominently shown throughout the station and surely on everyone's visor feeds, and the sound of her voice from the interview overlaps with my own thoughts.

"I still can't see why you can't come with us," she tells me, and for a moment I'm uncertain whether the words came from her lips. Sid looks at her, then at me, sympathetic but noncommittal. They both know the reasons, but she's more accepting of them than the doctor.

"The more I'm with you, the more you're likely to be found. And the longer you stay here, the closer Lochner is to finding you." I smile ruefully. "Sid is right. I am a liability. This is where we should part ways."

"We can all disappear together," Dr. Slimane replies. "She's very capable, and Lexell can make things happen. We could lie low for a while, get you identity documents before crossing borders."

"It's not just that," I say. "I have family, friends. This manhunt is affecting them too. Disappearing is not an option, especially not with the mess I've left behind."

"Why not?" the doctor insists. "They'll understand. You've been wrongfully accused."

It's not about understanding, though I doubt my family would understand the choices I've made, the ones that would have to be revealed in order for me to set things right. It's about the anguish I'd caused, and more that I risk causing still. Being on the lam means having no contact with them. They'd be losing a son, not knowing if he's alive or dead. All they'd be left with are questions and the knowledge that their son was a fugitive, and possibly a murderer.

"All the more reason for me to stay. Simon's death won't be resolved unless I go back to New York," I reply. "I need to clear my name, for my own sake as much as theirs."

"What about reversing Levantanil? What about your capacity to remember?" Dr. Slimane says. The desperation in her voice is meant to convey that she needs me just as much as I need her. It's true, but at this point, irrelevant.

"I'm happy to get my answers and get you out of Lochner's clutches. That'll do for now," I reply. "You two need to focus on getting to Stockholm safe. Just promise me one thing . . ."

"What's that?" she asks.

"When all this is over, come get me. Come get me and fix me."

The only morning train to Montreal is the 9:20 express shuttle. The plan is to cross the border, go deeper into Canadian territory, then take a chartered flight out from there, privately owned and operated by Lexell, of course. That should give the women enough lead time to make it off the continent even if Lochner were to locate them somehow. As for me, once I see them off on their train, I'm taking the first shuttle back down to New York and walking into Three Police Plaza.

It's the top of the hour, but already the platform is packed. Passengers are anxious to board, eager to head out of the Sleepless mecca. As we stand waiting for the shuttle, I clutch the doctor's hand. She runs her thumb across my palm like a talisman.

A tall, haggard man jostles his way through the mass, and his elbow bumps into my side. I jump back in pain. My shirt doesn't seem to leak any blood, but I can feel my skinseal coming loose. The man apologizes when he sees me wincing. We share a glance, and a moment is all it takes for a spark of recognition to come to him.

Quickly, I excuse myself and head to the nearest bathroom, and before the man can verbalize where he's seen me from, I've disappeared into the thick crowd. I promptly take a stall, both to hide and to tend to my injury.

I clean the wound, readjust the skinseal and wipe off the trail of blood. It's not as bad as I thought it would be, and I head back out to the platform with more than enough time to spare. Listening for incoming footsteps and hearing none, I leave the stall. I pull my hat down lower and make my way back to the platform.

As I exit the bathroom, someone grabs my arm.

"Where is she?" Elliott snarls. I brush him off instinctively, not entirely sure that it truly is him. His eyes are bloodshot, and half his face still bears the bruises that I made, but the voice and the fervor in his eyes are unmistakable.

"What the fuck? How did you get here?"

"I know how to find you." He pulls me closer with a strength that he doesn't look like he should possess. "Face ID got you all over this city. Whose tech do you think runs all those algorithms? Now where is the doctor?"

"I don't know what the fuck you're talking about." I push him away, and he loses his grip. He recovers, but as he comes for me, I can tell he's favoring one leg over the other.

"A scene wouldn't do either of us any good," Elliott says. He spreads his arms to gesture at the passersby, whose gazes I only now notice are turned toward us. He lowers his voice. "So let's talk like gentlemen."

"Or else what? You'll call the cops on me?"

"No. I have a better idea." He takes his visor out of his shirt pocket. "Hand over Dr. Slimane, and I'll send over the recording from Simon's office. I've saved it all in here."

My eyes widen, jolted and tantalized by the offer. Elliott smiles as he limps closer to me. He leans in for a whisper, his breath bearing the metallic tang of blood.

"He killed himself."

"I know. And I know how."

He looks at me, confounded but not disbelieving. "Well, the audio proves it. It answers all your questions, clears your name. Isn't that what you want?"

I struggle for a response. The recording will show what truly happened that night. It proves that I had nothing to do with Simon's death. It also proves that I wasn't the mole, and that Elliott was behind all of this. And yet.

"What about spying on C+P? Are you going to cop to that too?" I ask.

"It doesn't matter to me. After I get the doctor, I'll be off-grid for a while. Lochner has plans for me."

"He's only using you and your hate group to make money," I say. "You're property to him, just like the rest of us."

"He needs me, and he needs Exsomnis," he says. "We're not his puppets. If anything, it's the other way around."

"Tell yourself that if it makes you feel better," I spit. "Did he tell you his plans to monetize everyone's memories?"

"I didn't know in the beginning, when we took the pill," he replies. "But yes, I've known the plan for a while."

"Then you know he won't stop there. He'll make the visors, all the playback and recording tech, all the storage solutions, and he'll charges as much as he wants," I say. "Each person's entire lived experience will be on a subscription plan."

"Oh, Jamie. You're so naïve," he replies. "This is how we already live."

An announcement heralds the arrival of the Montreal shuttle, and I make quick calculations in my mind. How far are Sid and the doctor, how fast would I have to run to make the train, how much time I can buy them if Elliott gives chase. My eyes shift around, wary of the passengers, of Elliott's stare, of the large clock hanging behind him.

"All I need to do is press send." He waves his visor in front of me. "So what will it be, Jamie?"

"You mean would I give up the only person who can fix every Sleepless person's brain, in exchange for saving my own ass?"

"Again, so naïve. This has always been your downfall," he replies. The pride in his voice reopens the wound of his betrayal. "Human memory is inherently unreliable. Having everything recorded actually makes things better. This is the beauty of Lochner's plan."

Elliott comes closer, taunting me with his visor. I step back, one eye turned to the tracks and the people waiting on standby. He suddenly cocks his head aside and looks behind me. I turn and see Sid and Dr. Slimane pacing about, searching for me at the far end of the platform.

Elliott shoves me aside and runs toward them at full speed, the sheer force of adrenaline powering him through his pain. I chase after him.

"Sid!" I yell over the clamor of the station, the steady roar of the approaching train.

She turns, as does the doctor, and they both run into the crowd. I lose sight of them, but hopefully so does Elliott. I train my visor on him, and see his figure blur as he weaves quickly between passengers. I pick up my pace, pushing my way through the gathering mass.

The shrill shrieking of the maglev shuttle rises above the cacophony of people edging toward the track. I keep reaching for Elliott, but he always seems to be a hair's breadth away from my grasp, one passenger after another blocking me. As I reach the end of the platform, the crowd thins. The view opens up, and I see Sid and Dr. Slimane, anxious to board the shuttle as soon as it stops.

In front of them is Elliott, ready to pounce.

I make a run for it, matching the train's speed. I see him reach Dr. Slimane and wrest her away. Sid places herself in between them. Elliott shoves her aside and regains his grip on the doctor. I finally reach them and lunge, pulling him away from her. He loses his footing, and we both spin toward the edge of the platform.

"Run!" I yell at the women. Away from the shuttle, or onto it when the doors open, run anywhere but here.

I hold Elliott's arms back, and he tries to grapple away from me. He spits out some choice expletives, then drives his elbows into my stomach. He hits my side, but the pain only makes me grip him more tightly. He flails about and then with all his might pushes back, bringing the full weight of his body against me.

I resist, and he pushes back harder, driving me to the edge. The rumble of maglev's engines grows closer and louder. He makes one final push, and I lose my footing, pulling him in with me. The two of us stagger, and we slam into the side of the oncoming train.

Everything blurs into streaks of steel. My head hits metal, then my arms, my back. My entire body is pummeled and my grip on Elliott loosens. Both of us are flung into the air by the impact, and I land on the cold, hard marble floor.

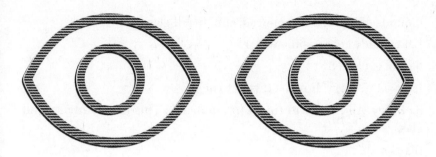

45.

People of the State of New York
v.
Maxwell Cartwright, Sr.
Docket No. 43-CR-21227-MH
Excerpt from Defense Exhibit H
Transcript of Recording

Wednesday, 07/08/2043

(Three short knocks at the door)

S. Parrish: What the hell are you doing here?

J. Vega: I just wanted to pop in and say good night. Is everything all right?

S.: (Unintelligible)

(Pause)

S.: Everything's perfect! Simply perfect!

J.: Are you sure? You don't look so good.

S.: You should go, Jamie.

(Sounds of liquid being poured, clinking of glass)

J.: I should get you some water.

S.: No, get away!

J.: I . . . I'm sorry. I'm just trying to help.

S.: Sorry. All right. I'm fine. I'm not drunk. This is only my second glass, see.

(Pause)

Tell me, Jamie, how long have you been Sleepless? Don't give me that look. How long?

J.: How . . . ?

S.: It's my job to know. The eyedrops, all those late nights. It doesn't take a sleuth.

J.: About a year.

S.: Look, I don't care, I'm not prejudiced. Okay, well, I do care, in a big picture way. (Unintelligible) Oh god, are we ever so fucked.

J.: Boss, what's going on?

S.: How many of you are out there, Jamie?

J.: In the US? About ninety-five . . .

S.: In the world, man, in the world.

J.: A couple billion?

S.: And five years ago?

J.: Not much more than that, especially since the Plateau.

S.: How do you know how many? Did they all come up to you one by one and declare themselves Sleepless, did you take a poll? Count each head? How do you goddamn know?

J.: I don't know!

S.: What if the Plateau didn't happen, Jamie? What if everyone becomes Sleepless?

(Pause)

S.: How many times do you eat a day, Jamie? In the past year, how many times have you had to buy new shoes, replace your lightbulbs, get new games? How many hours do you work now, on a normal day? We grappled with with (sic) these thought experiments years ago, but what about the future?

J: New cases are getting rarer. And some say the Sleepless population will taper out if the trend holds.

S.: No, it won't. Not when so many people stand to gain from it continuing.

J.: What do you mean?

S: (Unintelligible) find out soon enough. (Unintelligible) You should be leaving, Jamie.

J.: Boss, you don't look too good. How about I sit with you for a while?

S.: No! No wine for you!

(Glass clinking)

S.: I've always admired you, Jamie. I may not have always shown it, but that's how I've always felt. You're going places. And you've got a good heart.

J.: How about we get you on your way home? I could call you a cab?

S.: My, you're pushy. Never lose that persistence. It's your best trait. But you really, really must leave. I need to be alone now.

(Pause)

Give me a hug before you go.

J: This (unintelligible) okay?

S: Yes, yes. Thank you, Jamie. You've helped me quite a lot. I'll never forget it.

(Pause)

Goodbye, Jamie. Be safe.

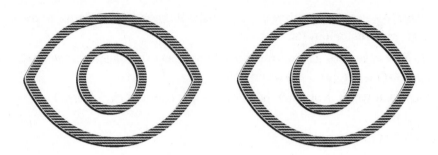

46.

They say that if you're Sleepless, you can think of the future in one of two ways: tomorrow never comes, or, tomorrow's always today.

Either way, there are no tomorrows. Especially if you can't tell the passage of time. Being Sleepless and being in solitary confinement are the same in this respect. Imagine dealing with both.

Officially, my new address is Arthur Kill Correctional Facility. The prison complex juts right up against the edge of the strait, and if you're standing in the yard, you can see New Jersey from across the water. Mostly, I try not to look out.

Here in the Special Housing Unit, I can't even if I wanted to. There are no windows. All I can do is imagine what the other side is like. From the river edge, it's only a quick ferry ride and a ten-mile drive to Maplewood. To my childhood home.

Being cut off from the world is not the worst of it. Solitary confinement takes on a more particular perversity if you're Sleepless. Sleep is an escape. And the agony of being alone with one's thoughts without relief, devoid of that means of escape, kills one's sanity quicker than anything can.

I'm on day three, I think, based on meal pacing and my bowel movements. They're supposed to let me out of the SHU after seventy-two hours, but that lands squarely on Veterans Day, and everybody moves slower on holidays, especially prison guards.

So far today, I've done my jumping jacks, my pushups, my crunches. A hundred each. That's an hour, if I'm counting slowly. I meditated, and I think that was another hour. Played with my food, counted the ceiling tiles, measured the room's dimensions with my handspan. Made a mental list of all the inmates in my cell row, all the corrections officers in my building, all the books I've read in the prison library since I've started serving my sentence. Then sorted each of those mental lists alphabetically. Then came up with new lists. Spielberg's films, in chronological order. People I've slept with, in reverse. The streets in my hometown, starting on our street toward the Garden State Parkway. As expected, the diversions in here are hardly diverting. Especially not when the air is thick with the stink of your own shit fermenting in a bucket.

At one point—I think it was last night?—I started punching the walls. Lightly at first, then progressively harder. I needed some sort of release. Without any sense that time was passing, I also needed an outward sign that reality was changing, was changeable—and nothing feels as real as broken bones.

"Think about what you did," the guard spat as he flung me in here. Like I was a toddler getting a time out, and not a detainee about to be mentally tortured.

And for what? A stupid riot in the mess hall. Someone "slipped" and hit his head on the cafeteria counter, then chaos broke out. Simple as that. Me, I didn't do anything. I just happened to be at the wrong place at the wrong time. This place is full of coincidences. That the riot ended with some kid lying dead in the mess hall is just another one of them.

Do I want to figure out how everything went down, who did what to who and why? Not really.

I'm not that guy anymore, trying to answer questions better left alone.

Blood drips down my left temple, and I wipe it off with a wrist. My knuckles still feel tender from all the wall punching, though the cuts have dried since this morning. At least I think that was this morning. Where did this blood come from?

Above my brow, I feel a deep split in the skin. It stings as my finger grazes over it. A wound is a record, and this one tells me my head made contact with the wall, or the floor. Yet I have no idea how it happened. I search the masonry for fresh tracks of red, and find a smear right by the door at eye-level. A split on my head, a split in time. There it was again. An unrecorded moment, a blank space.

I have no way to verify. I have no visor to consult, no one to ask for an account of objective reality. All I have is once-unbroken skin, and a throbbing pain that reminds me of my defect. It makes me want to bang my head on the wall, and maybe this time I'll remember it.

Solitary is unmitigated torture, one that most people would rather forget. Yet as much as I want to speed this along, to fast-forward through this sleepless, solitary stint, I don't want to forget. I don't want oblivion. This life is mine, this memory is mine, all three crappy days of it. Not remembering it would be the greater torture.

The guards eventually get around to releasing me from my windowless eight-by-ten cell, but before I even orient myself to what day it is, I find myself placed in yet another box. This one is infinitely more pleasant, though. I take my seat in front of the screen, four cameras trained on me from all angles. My palms grow sweaty in anticipation, and when I see Veronica's face, her tangle of hair arrested in a messy bun, the agony of the last three days melts away.

"Sorry you had to wait so long. They took me out a while ago."

Spurred by a longing for human conversation, I carelessly tell her all about my short stint in solitary. The worry on her face escalates into horror the longer I go on. Realizing my error, I try to downplay the experience, try to make psychological torture sound as pleasant as I can.

When she recovers, she catches me up on the latest in the saga of Torian and Veronica. True to form, they're back on again. The cycle continues, and I'm only too glad some things never change.

"Elliott's been calling me," she says after a pause. "He wants to know how you're doing, keeps asking me to tell you he's sorry."

Veronica and Elliott aren't friends, not really, especially not after what happened. I hate that she's once again placed in the middle of things because of me. She's already put herself at risk helping me with Kingsley, and though that didn't end in complete disaster, aiding me in my flight to Wakefield did bring the cops to her door. I thought she'd be spared further headaches now—I'm in prison, aren't I?—but no. Goes to show how big of a mess I've made.

"Fuck his sorry," I reply.

"I've blocked him twice already, but he's using burners and the numbers keep changing," she complains. "I'm not afraid, just annoyed."

"You should report him, add a few months to his sentence," I say. Veronica purses her lips, actually considering my suggestion. I gotta hand it to Elliott though, he's always been resourceful. I'm guessing Exsomnis has some sort of presence in every prison.

After Wakefield, Elliott and I were in the hospital for weeks. We even ended up in the same ward at Eastern Maine Medical. As soon as I was well enough to take a piss without assistance, the state police extradited me to New York to answer for pummeling Elliott and leaving him half-dead in his apartment.

The prosecutor was surprisingly sympathetic to my guerrilla reporting, and offered a plea to a reduced charge. Eight months was the best deal I was likely to get, or so my lawyer said. I'd be crazy to turn it down, she explained. Elliott and I fought, and I pulped him so bad he ended up in the hospital. Those are the facts.

Also facts: Elliott stabbed me in turn; the recording I liberated from him closed Simon's murder case; he was an integral part of a supremacist terror cell engaged in an international illegal biohacking enterprise. Those facts don't matter as much, apparently. As far as the law's concerned, I still almost killed a man, and that's still attempted murder. I was looking at a maximum penalty of ten years, my lawyer warned, unless I took the deal. The injustice was staggering, but at that point I didn't have the will to resist. So I took it.

The only balm was that Elliott got it worse. A prison sentence isn't enough for all his sins, especially when I think about how most of Exsomnis walked away unscathed from this whole ordeal. Their members have gone underground again, the way they did after the HRI bombing ten years ago, but I know they're only biding their time until they can come out again in greater numbers. At least one of them's behind bars, and that's one fewer asshole walking free.

Knowing that Elliott's rotting somewhere upstate does help me not-sleep at night. Seventeen years, all told, in a maximum-security penitentiary. Less, if he's paroled on good behavior, but Veronica reporting him to the Department of Corrections might foreclose that. The prospect puts a grin on my face, but I do no more than that.

"Won't be long now," I say, changing the subject.

"Sprung by spring. It'll be here before you know it." She sighs. "How are your folks holding up?"

The mention both lifts my spirit and brings a heaviness to my heart. "They're all right. Can't wait until I'm home again."

"Do you know what you're going to do once you're out?"

I give her my usual response, a shake of the head and no further details. I've evaded this question before, and though it hasn't stopped her from asking, she at least knows not to press. She can tell that my reticence is probably for her protection. The less she knows, the better.

Such as they are, my current circumstances are a refuge. From the mess of the outside world, the uncertainty of what lies next. Outside these walls are consequences bigger than that of my prison sentence, and I don't know that I can bear what my actions have brought about—or what they've failed to bring about. Arthur Kill ain't paradise, but it's a pretty good purgatory.

I do have an answer to Veronica's question though. When I get out of here, the first thing on my list—right after a well-deserved whiskey sour—will be finding Sid and Miriam.

Prison has numbed me to most emotions, especially longing, but this one holds strong. Some days I still hear that maglev to Montreal pulling in, still see the desperate looks on their faces as they reach for me. That's what I dream of now, if you could call it that. Paolo and Simon still come to me sometimes, their death masks imprinted in the back of my eyelids, but lately it's those two women. It's Sid and Miriam, and that moment on the train platform, that haunt me the most.

Thursday, 11/12/2043, 04:14 PM

The midafternoon breeze brings with it the chemical stench of Arthur Kill, wafting together with the earthiness of dead autumn leaves. As it turns out, being recently released from solitary doesn't spare me from yard duty, and I soon find myself crouched by the fence line picking leaves by hand.

A pair of work boots blocks my path, and I look up at the hulking figure of Morrie the Maori. He stretches out a hand the size of a saucer, and when I take it, he pulls me up and gives me a shove into the chain link fence. The antagonism is for show, I know. Just in case someone's watching. It wouldn't make sense for him to fraternize with the likes of me.

"When did they let you out of the hole?" he asks.

"Few hours ago," I say. "Same as everyone else, I guess." They sent dozens of us to solitary after the guards broke up the riot, Morrie included. I didn't even know this prison had that many SHUs. He looks me down from head to toe, his eyes bloodshot. He flicks the dead leaves from my hand and then gives me a low handshake. Through my work gloves I feel a thin pill tube pressed against my palm.

Same order as before. I've been craving it for days, well before I got sent to solitary.

I kneel to pick the dead leaves back up, slipping the tube into my shoe as I do. My eyes surreptitiously scan our surroundings. All clear. We should be done here, but Morrie lingers.

"New stuff came in. Just as good as the real thing."

"Heard that one before," I say, walking away.

"Nah, for real. Lev-C, they call it."

"Why you telling me? You know I got no use for that."

"Just thought you'd wanna know, is all." Morrie smiles in knowing condescension as he leaves me to my work.

That's the second iteration since our story broke. Lev-C. They didn't even bother coming up with a new name. Despite everything, new hyperinsomnia pills and biohacked treatments are running rampant in the streets. Some of them probably developed by the same Exsomnis outfits, all of them reminders of what I tried to do and how little it accomplished.

It kills me, knowing that nothing we did mattered.

After we broke the news about encoding failure, the world didn't descend into the chaos of the early pandemic days. The quarantines didn't come back up; the Sleepless weren't rounded up. Fear was the predominant emotion, but I'd like to think that science guarded against paranoia and hatred. That, given Miriam's research, people had something concrete to anchor them, unlike the complete unknown of those early days. It also helped that communities and governments had resources and support in place, built up from the decade since the initial outbreak. The memory loss was a new and daunting challenge, but the world didn't feel as lost or as ill-equipped as it had been before.

The synthetic materials embargo is still in effect, and the treaties against illicit hyperinsomnia research got beefed up, with more sanctions and more spending for enforcement units. The same was true of local laws against biohacking. For a while, as my broken bones healed in that hospital, I thought maybe we succeeded. I watched my interview with Miriam on every news feed, our hours-long interview running on a constant loop. I saw how world leaders pledged to stop the spread of extremism and artificial hyperinsomnia. So, I began to believe.

It didn't take long for reality to catch up. By the time I was on my feet again, the news had moved on to something else. The world settled into a new normal.

The Plateau is over. For the first time in four years, worldwide Sleepless numbers have surged. State investigations and academic inquiries notwithstanding, no one's truly questioning how these new cases came about. It's an open secret at this point. It's Levantanil, and the genie isn't going back in the bottle.

Never mind the consequences on a mass scale, the agricultural strains, the water shortages, the energy crises. Never mind the memory loss. People don't want to get left behind; they want to get ahead. Levantanil ensures that they do. Billions of people, all in want. Willing supplicants on the altar of production, essential grist for the mill of consumption. Nothing was going to stop it. Nothing ever did.

✻

It's lights out and my bunkmate's snoring muffles the rattling of his cot as he tosses and turns. It's only when I'm certain that he's dead to the world that I sit on the edge of my cot and gently take my shoes off, adding sharpness to the already pungent air. The pill tube rests inside my sock, right against my ankle. I take it out and place it under my pillow.

I rifle through the mail sitting at the foot of my cot. From the faint fluorescent glow coming off the guard station, I can read, barely, the email printouts from the last few days while I was in the SHU. A message from Anders, another from my brother, a couple of news summaries, the usual. And then, an anomaly.

In the bottom of the pile is a post card. Unmarked, with a wintry landscape in the background and two reindeer on the fore. It's too early for Christmas—we haven't even gotten to Thanksgiving yet—but I guess this didn't raise any red flags. My name and address in neat cursive and a sole message. *Happy Holidays!* No signature, no return address. EU postmark.

I flip the postcard over, turn it aside. A small line of print borders the bottom edge of the front image. It's just the copyright and photo credit.

Since I came in here, I've found myself jonesing for mail drops like a junkie in bad need of a fix. There's been no news about Sid or Miriam since Wakefield. Zero reports about a former OEF exec or a renowned sleep scientist, both of whom have disappeared following the Levantanil scandal. Does that speak to their success at escape, or to our adversaries' success at finding them? For months I feared the worst. But now I know.

They're alive. In hiding, but alive. That's enough hope to live on for the next few months.

In the meantime, I stretch out on my cot and reach for the tube. In the darkness I turn it this way and that, and under the faint light from the cell block hallway, the familiar chartreuse capsules gleam like jewels.

A-Pop. The closest thing to real sleep.

I can rest a little easier tonight, knowing that the two of them made it. I gaze at the postcard again, shift it between my fingers, feel the weight of the paper on my fingertips. The sensation eases my overworked mind and relieves my bone-weary body. I feel so revived, I might not even need the extra assist from the A-Pop.

Ah, who am I kidding? It's been a long day.

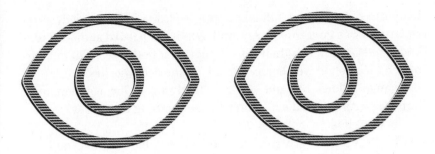

47.

The rec rooms have their vid screens turned to C+P all day, and though I avoid going in there for that exact reason, the guys here don't make it easy. They give me a rundown each chance they get. In the mess hall, in line for the showers, at yard duty or the basketball court. The Levantanil story gave me a peculiar stripe of notoriety, one I don't particularly relish.

In the library, a fellow inmate interrupts my reading to deliver the latest: Maxwell Cartwright's been reinstated as the chairman and CEO of C+P Global News Media. "Looks like your old boss is back on top," he says. "Santa came through for him!" Django's one of the kinder ones, and I can tell he's not ribbing me, so I give him a well-meaning smile. Still, I walk away from him, book in hand.

In truth, the news turns my stomach, threatening to eject my lunch. (Today's Christmas special: an emaciated roast chicken thigh and unsalted mashed potatoes.) I don't like it one bit, but Maxwell being back on the helm of C+P makes sense. He's a founder and, given his acquittal, he's also not a murderer. It also doesn't hurt that he's very close with the owners of C+P's parent company, Zephyrus,

LLC. After the buyout offer got approved, Maxwell's speedy reinstatement was guaranteed. After all, Zephyrus needed someone they know and trust to run their new corporate mouthpiece. I'm not surprised Cleo bolted well before the ink on the deal was dry.

Django follows me and sneers. Clearly my prior assessment of him was wrong. "That's it? Don't you got nothing else to say?"

"Is what it is."

"It don't make you mad they're all out there while you're in here?" he asks. "Especially that Lochner dude. A civil fucking fine, tsk."

He'd also been ousted from all his positions and forced to divest all his holdings, but that means nothing in the world of the 0.1 percent. It's all the same money moving around between the same people in the same families. His wife's still on the Board, and so are his closest associates. Rafe Lochner is still in control. Aside from millions in damages that he can easily recoup in a single fiscal quarter, the only thing he's lost is visibility.

"If you ask me, they should've thrown *his* fucking ass in prison," Django continues. "Taken his entire company too."

It sounds nice, but no. That would have been too fair. We don't get fair. We get the system we buy into. The system where the Lochners of the world get away with everything, and we're only too happy to help them.

Especially now that we're beholden to their devices. I hear there are deep discounts to be had on dedicated server space for memory recordings. Their new IRIS contacts are also scheduled for release in a few months, just in time for the holiday shopping rush. People can't wait to stick them into their eyeballs. Visor sales are way up too; everyone has their hands on the latest visor technology, now with improved file-sharing and instant projection features. Upload, download, share, and show your memories for a nominal per-linkup fee. It's almost as cheap as borrowing a book from a library. Memories on loan.

Ads continue to be a bane of online existence, so Zephyrus's memory services offer an ad-free option. No ads before or during memory playback for a low monthly fee, or for opting in to their new "Real People" program, where customers let Zephyrus use splices of their memories and parts of their likeness to create targeted ads for people in their contact list. Nothing encourages a wife to buy her husband the hot new robocab quite like seeing him drive said car in a slick 15-second commercial.

The Zephyrus suite of memory security solutions has also launched a ton of new upgrades. The latest one locks your recordings from editing. Friends and family who are granted access can still go into the recordings and add in superficial edits (such as playback filters and reaction emojis), but outside parties can't manipulate the file. Deep-faked memories still happen, but not as frequently, especially not after Zephyrus also launched its official verification badge, stamping each recording with its logo and adding an authentication code to ensure memory viewers that the recordings are completely unaltered.

As more people take Levantanil and develop encoding failure, more customers buy into the Zephyrus line of memory substitutes. The technology becomes better the more these customers upload and store their memories. The recordings provide a rich and bountiful mine of data. Every second of a memory recorded gives incomparable insight to the Zephyrus development teams to find and identify ways that their services can be improved.

Does it matter to these customers that their thoughts are invaded and scrutinized to sell them more products? Or that they've become totally dependent on Zephyrus to provide them a sense of the past? Of course not. What matters is they have a full twenty-four hours to live and work and earn and spend.

Experience everything, keep nothing. It's the new way of the world.

"Hey, you think he might give you your job back when you get outta here?" Django says, stifling a laugh. I fling the book I'm reading into the return chute and slam the lid shut.

"Psh. I don't want it anyway."

The truth hurts, and this one exquisitely so. C+P had been the dream since I decided to become a newsman, and I'd been lucky enough to live the dream when I got hired. I then poured my life into that newsroom, losing almost everything else in the process, including my liberty. I tried to save it, to preserve its soul, but in the end it turned out to be just another corporation. And as with any other corporation, I've learned that C+P, too, has no soul worth saving.

◈

Friday, 12/25/2043, 02:06 PM

Green and gold tinsel garlands hang limply from the ceiling of the visitation area. On the walls, cardboard snowman cutouts border awkwardly shaped letters that spell *Happy Holidays* and *'Tis the Season*. Inmates' craft projects. It's not too pathetic, I suppose. Besides, no one's paying attention to the décor in this place. All that matters is that someone shows up.

They've been waiting in the car for an hour, Dad tells me. They know what my scheduled time is, but they didn't want to hit traffic. There's no traffic, that much I know. They just wanted to be here as early as they can, try and see if the guards will give me extra time, which of course they don't. Dad could've said that, shown a bit more vulnerability, but that's not his style. I do get the tightest hugs from him though, after we all exchange our greetings.

They come every Sunday. It's our new weekly brunch plan, except without the food or drink, and alongside other families and their overlapping conversations. Today's different, of course. It's a Friday, for one. And louder in here than usual. There are more children, and everyone's more spirited. My folks are too. Their smiles are wider, their eyes only barely well up at the sight of my thinning frame.

"So what have you been reading lately?" Charlie asks. He's running interference again, making things feel normal before one of us notices that we're all in a penitentiary on Christmas Day. I indulge him, telling him about the latest thriller I'm reading, a caper featuring a troupe of carnival performers pulling off a heist in the Forbidden City. He's heard of it, and promises to pick it up as his next read.

The conversation flows more easily from there, and in this respect, I'm grateful that I started my sentence a few months back. By now, Mom and Dad have exhausted all their sorrows, and we don't have to spend Christmas in heavy silences and unprompted bursts of tears. Dad has also gotten over that phase where he couldn't stop updating me about C+P and Lochner, his commentary laced with bitter indignation. Mom, for her part, has stopped asking after my nutrition and my living conditions. She also hasn't been asking whether the other men are treating me nice, like we were all kindergartners here on a playdate. Now the conversation is books, media, things that bring each of us joy. Sometimes that happens to include neighborhood gossip; I listen with no judgment, because who am I to deny my parents the simple pleasures of suburban life?

"How was Noche Buena?" I hazard to ask. The three of them fall silent, all waiting for someone else to reply. The pause is unbearable, so I assure them. "It's fine. I wanna hear how it went. At least make me feel like I was there."

I meant to make that sound more jovial, but perhaps the sentiment can't be taken as anything but pitiful. Dad's eyes begin to water, but Mom soon wraps her arm around him, reminding him, "No tears. It's Christmas, and we have each other. That's all that matters."

"Well, since you asked . . ." Charlie starts, a mischievous grin plastered on his face, "Mom overcooked the morcon again, so you didn't really miss much."

"Well . . . someone didn't tie the twine tight enough!"

"That's your excuse? Every year, really?" Dad says, and we all laugh. Mom slaps his arm playfully. They then regale me with the rest of the menu, telling me about all the gifts they exchanged. They promise that mine are waiting for me when I come home.

Today's a far cry from our tear-filled visits only four months ago, and farther still from my greatest fears. After Wakefield, stupefied in turn by the morphine drip and the pain in my bones, I thought I'd die alone in that hospital. Surely I'd brought my family enough shame and heartache. It was hard enough for them when I was just mental, but then the news said I was also a potential murderer on a furious rampage, the subject of a cross-border manhunt. The only thing that gave me a measure of peace was the cold handcuffs securing me to my gurney. The cops, Cartwright's lawyers, Lochner's minions—at least now they'd leave my family alone.

Yet despite everything, my family did not abandon me as I'd feared. They drove up to Maine the second they heard what happened. For weeks, they pretty much lived in that hospital, only decamping to the Hilton across the street the second visiting hours ended. Afterward, they stood by me during the trial, and haven't left my side since.

If it hadn't been clear to me before, it's sure as hell clear to me here and now, in this visitation room: I made the right choice. Stockholm would have been the key to me regaining my memory, but I never would have forgiven myself if I'd fled without setting things right and saying goodbye.

❂

It was well after the trial when I got a hold of the recordings that Elliott made. I had to beg my lawyer for them, and she had to pull some strings to get me access, but I needed to hear Simon for myself.

Those last words, muffled through a concealed microphone, are now my only memory of those final seconds with him. A memory of a recorded thing. Is it more accurate? Maybe. Factually at least. The words will always be exact, unlike conversations remembered in one's mind. But the feeling of being there, that's not on tape. The sense of gratitude that Simon conveyed. The same gratitude I must have felt in that moment. The pride that he expressed. The distress that I ignored. Those emotions are irretrievably lost, relegated to a second-order memory of what I can hear from an audio file.

Long ago, Simon told me that people like us needed to be better, because we couldn't afford not to be. I once understood it as the self-inflicted lack of choice typical of determined people like him. The relentless pursuit of self-improvement. There is only one way, and the only way is better. After I got out of New Dawn, Simon began giving me the toughest assignments. They all seemed handpicked for me, designed to stoke the fires of my persistence. Every story was about something I held strong opinions on: Sleepless rights, systemic discrimination, labor exploitation. Until the very end with the Dwyer story, I felt that Simon was pushing me to be better.

I know now that his admonition wasn't about a lack of choice, but a warning. I must be better, because the stakes are too high.

Failure is not an option. The night he died, it felt like those stakes were too high even for him, and it tells me I made the right call. Joining Sid's mission against Lochner is exactly what Simon wanted to prepare me for.

After listening to the recording, I wondered if Simon was trying to tell me something, in not so many words. Maybe he was trying to allude to the real story he was working on, hoping I would take over once he's gone. Maybe he knew my secret, and was giving me an opening to tell him about Levantanil. Of course, maybe he was just rambling. Drunk and desperate, a poison coursing through his body, knowing that his time on earth was coming to an end.

Whenever I think of him now, I ask myself: What was the point? Despite his efforts, the lies and manipulations, despite his ultimate sacrifice, the world still ended up the way it is. Was it all worth it? Simon probably thought so, but I'm here, alive, and I know damn better.

✸

Thursday, 02/11/2044, 06:21 PM

Another week, another postcard. The card stock dispatches grow in frequency the closer my release date approaches. This latest one has a picture of a babbling brook coursing down a bloom-filled meadow. No return address or identifiers, as usual. Just a short message in the same cursive handwriting that I've grown fond of.

A new dawn waits.

It's a promise of hope. Time was, such a promise would have motivated me to set goals and make plans. To keep the fight, to do it all over, but better. Things I wanted to do, before I knew better. I wanted to do right by Simon, I wanted to save C+P, I wanted to stop the rise of extremism, I wanted to stem the unrelenting tide of capitalism. All these wants. Maybe Lochner was right. Desire is a hydra.

The lesson exacted a steep price, but I've since learned how to lop off the necks of my wants, how to scorch their bloody stumps closed. Now I only hope for modest things. To see my family happy, to know my friends are safe. To regain my memory too, if it's possible.

In my half-conscious daydreams I envision Sid and Miriam's life in isolation. The doctor's hard at work in some darkened lab alongside other scientists, concocting a cure for hyperinsomnia, a way to reverse Levantanil. Doing her penance as she promised. Sid keeps them all safe, beyond Lochner's grasp. These imaginings tether me to them the same way each postcard does. They assure me that I haven't been forgotten. That there is a plan for me. This is enough.

Judging by my last conversation with Miriam, it won't be easy. The words "live human subject" inspire nothing but dread. I may have to take another pill, biohack myself again. Maybe they'll have to cut me apart, splay my insides open. Dread won't deter me though, not when I have a chance I become what I once was. No longer Sleepless.

✦

Saturday, 04/16/2044, 01:17 PM

Artificial springtime air is pumped through the vents of the columbarium: fresh-cut grass and notes of lilac, intermingling with the smell of window cleaner drying on the shadow-box panes. Rows of tight niches hold urns of all shapes and colors, resting untouched behind shiny glass. The walls form a honeycomb of stone and steel, in each cell an encasement of ash. I carefully survey my surroundings with suspicion, an anxious tic I acquired during my stint at Arthur Kill, and find that I am alone.

The viewing salons have no wait time, and in short order a mech sets its delivery down on the pedestal. The lights around me dim, save for the one aimed at its center.

Paolo never would have picked a brass urn, I whisper to myself. He probably wouldn't have an urn at all. He wanted to return to the earth, he once said, when his time came. Never truly understood what he meant by that. He had a way with words such that whenever he spoke, I always believed what he said to be true, or right, or wise, even when I didn't fully fathom it. Then he died, and I seized on every word he ever said, trying to find meaning as though I were making up for lost time.

I did that for so long that being comfortable in the ambiguity of

Paolo's death feels like a betrayal. I have to convince myself that it's not, and that I need to abandon the search for neat answers. That being at peace with unanswered questions will allow me to grow. To slough off that part of me that recklessly craves the diversion of a mystery, the part that I've nurtured through countless hours in wakeful nights.

I have to convince myself that that part of me is better off dead.

This is only the second time I've been to see Paolo. Tears fall as I realize I might never see him again. He would understand, I know. I'll always have the memories.

I walk out into the courtyard, where Veronica waits. She gives me an eager wave. Beyond iron gates, a robocab sits idling, its trunk filled with the few belongings I've chosen to take with me.

"Ready when you are," she says. She senses my mood and tempers her chipper disposition. "Sorry I'm late. I thought you might want more alone time."

"You would have liked him," I say.

"I like everyone. It's the reverse that's usually the problem."

"He would have liked you too," I say. "You're both nuts, so there's that."

She laughs and jabs my shoulder.

"There was this one time Paolo came home from a business trip in Rio, shitfaced and reeking of gin."

"Well, booze is my favorite way to deal with long flights," she says.

"He had just closed a deal down there, a big stock sale of some kind. He barged into the apartment, passport in one hand, jacket in another. I asked him where his luggage was, then bam! Knocked out on the floor. Sounds a lot like you."

Veronica chuckles, a reaction more muted than I'd expected. "You miss him."

"Every day."

She takes my arm and escorts me through the gates. The scent of lilac grows fainter with every step.

We settle into the robocab, and I program the destination. Thirty minutes to the airport, the cab announces. Thirty last minutes until I leave my life behind. Then an hourlong jet ride to Berlin, a couple of maglev transfers through Poland, a quick ferry trip from Gdansk. Then more trains, a robocab switch or two, my identity information spoofed every step of the way.

Stockholm by midnight local time. Then tests and procedures for the foreseeable future.

I'm ready.

Veronica reclines her seat flat, and I follow suit. I ask the cab to play some music, and it picks a folk station. I open the sunroof and the midday light washes over me through the trees, their leaves just unfurled in the thaw. The brightness makes me flinch and close my eyes. I rest both hands on my chest, feeling each breath as it pushes upward and comes back down again. A slow guitar intro starts playing, its rhythm lulling me into restfulness, and with its languid strums, I float away on daydreams of sleep.

Acknowledgments

My deepest thanks go to my agent, Eddie Schneider, whose industry and expertise guided the journey of bringing THE SLEEPLESS to life. Many thanks too to all of Team Erewhon, most especially to my talented and hardworking editor Sarah Guan, who elevated this story to greater heights than I ever believed possible, and to publicist extraordinaire Marty Cahill, an inexhaustible font of determination and passion for this book.

I am also grateful to Rob Hart, the first writer who saw the potential in this story of mine, and to Lara Donnelly—we've gone a long way from the Catapult workshops. Thanks also to the people behind NaNoWriMo, the program from which the initial draft of this manuscript grew, and PitchWars, the program through which that draft was distilled and improved.

I'm very lucky to have been welcomed into several writing communities, whose members gave me so much advice, emotional support, laughter, and love. Many thanks especially to my no-drama crew, and to the folks at the pub. This journey would have been a whole lot lonelier without all of you.

Thanks to my family, the Manibo and Boco clans, especially my grandmother Josephine and my uncle Nouel. To the two most important women in my life, who inspire me every day with their strength and their capacity to love: my mother Ramona, who always believed in my dreams, and my sister Anika, my first and fiercest cheerleader. I could never have done this without the two of you.

Finally and most of all, to Sean—my immensely kind, brilliant, and patient first reader. Mahal kita.

Credits

Erewhon Books

Editor: Sarah Guan

Editorial Assistant: Viengsamai Fetters

Cover Design: Dana Li

Production: Cassandra Farrin

Copyeditor: Cassandra Farrin

Proofreader: Kasie Griffitts

Marketing and Publicity: Martin Cahill

Sales: Kasie Griffitts

Legal: Jennifer Uram

Founder: Liz Gorinsky

JABberwocky Literary Agency

Agent: Eddie Schneider

Subsidiary Rights: Susan Velasquez-Colmant

Agency Assistant: Valentina Sainato

President: Joshua Bilmes